TEEN TITANS

BEAST BOY

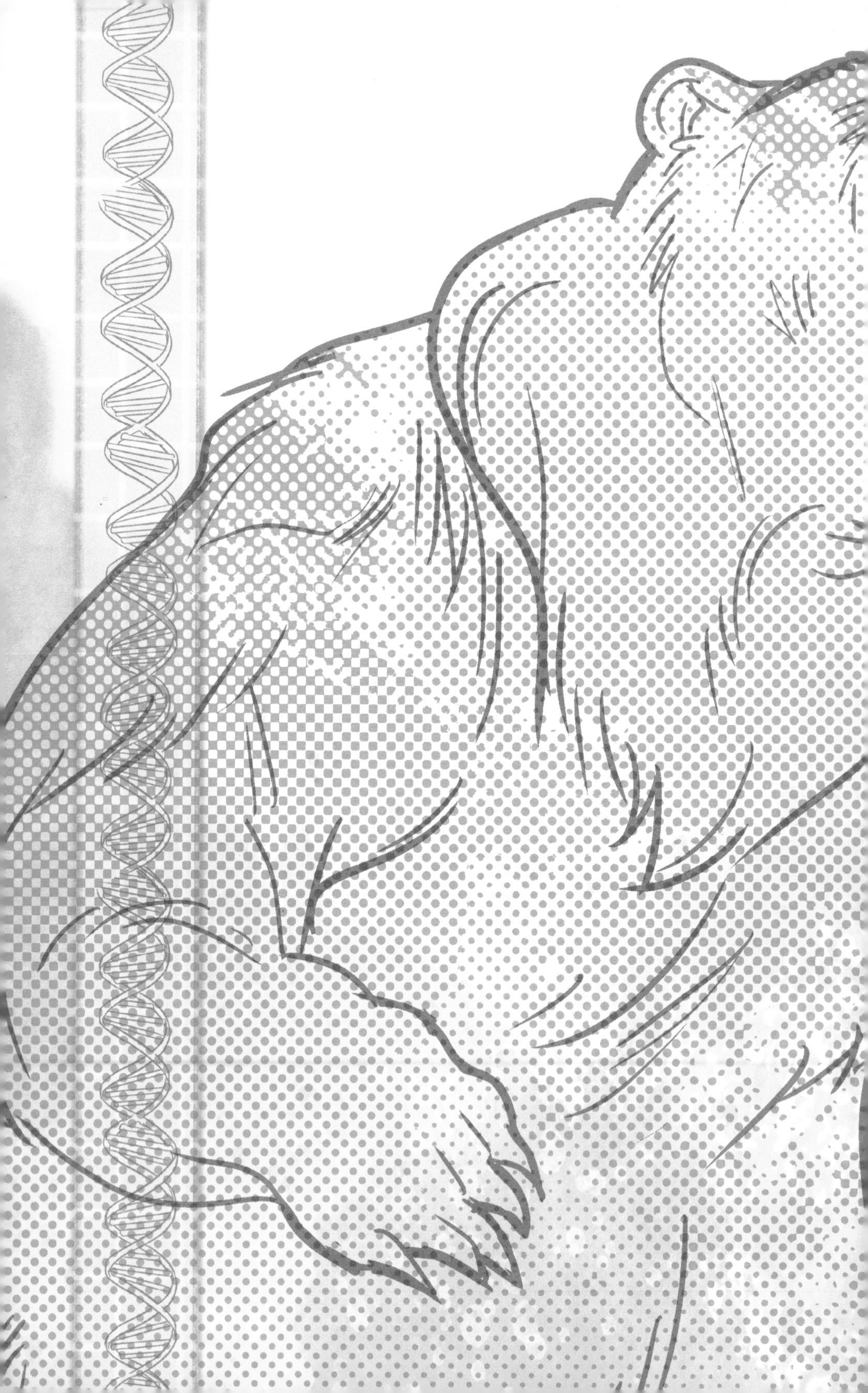

TEEN TITANS BEAST BOY

WRITER
kami garcia

ARTIST
gabriel picolo

WITH
rob haynes

COLORIST
david calderon

LETTERER
gabriela downie

Beast Boy created by
Arnold Drake

MICHELE R. WELLS VP & Executive Editor, Young Reader
COURTNEY JORDAN, JUSTINE FUENTES Assistant Editors
STEVE COOK Design Director - Books
AMIE BROCKWAY-METCALF Publication Design

BOB HARRAS Senior VP - Editor-in-Chief, DC Comics

JIM LEE Publisher & Chief Creative Officer
BOBBIE CHASE VP - Global Publishing Initiatives & Digital Strategy
DON FALLETTI VP - Manufacturing Operations & Workflow Management
LAWRENCE GANEM VP - Talent Services
ALISON GILL Senior VP - Manufacturing & Operations
HANK KANALZ Senior VP - Publishing Strategy & Support Services
DAN MIRON VP - Publishing Operations
NICK J. NAPOLITANO VP - Manufacturing Administration & Design
NANCY SPEARS VP - Sales
JONAH WEILAND VP - Marketing & Creative Services

TEEN TITANS: BEAST BOY

DC Comics, 2900 West Alameda Ave.,
Burbank, CA 91505

Printed by LSC Communications,
Willard, OH, USA. 7/24/20.
First Printing.
ISBN: 978-1-4012-8719-1

PEFC Certified

This product is from
sustainably managed
forests and controlled
sources

PEFC/29-31-337   www.pefc.org

Library of Congress Cataloging-in-Publication Data

Names: Garcia, Kami, writer. | Picolo, Gabriel, artist. | Haynes, Rob,
  artist. | Downie, Gabriela, letterer.
Title: Teen Titans : Beast boy / writer, Kami Garcia ; artist, Gabriel
  Picolo with Rob Haynes ; letterer, Gabriela Downie.
Other titles: Beast boy
Description: Burbank, CA : DC Ink, [2020] | Audience: Ages 13-17. |
  Summary: Seventeen-year-old Garfield Logan finally impresses the social
  elite at his high school, but popularity comes at a price when he
  undergoes sudden physical changes as the dares from his new friends
  escalate.
Identifiers: LCCN 2020015549 | ISBN 9781401287191 (trade paperback)
Subjects: LCSH: Graphic novels. | CYAC: Graphic novels. |
  Popularity--Fiction. | High schools--Fiction. | Schools--Fiction. | Best
  friends--Fiction. | Friendship--Fiction.
Classification: LCC PZ7.7.G366 Tb 2020 | DDC 741.5/973--dc23
LC record available at https://lccn.loc.gov/2020015549

kami:

I was a little nervous when we started working on *Beast Boy*. I've always loved Raven, and Gabriel and I had so much fun bringing her story to life in *Teen Titans: Raven*. I couldn't imagine having as much fun writing Gar. But Beast Boy is Gabriel's favorite Titan (notice the similarities in their hairstyles), and his excitement is contagious. The first time I saw Gabriel's version of Gar for this novel, I instantly knew this story would be special.

gabriel:

Everyone who follows me on social media knows how much I love Beast Boy. He's always been my favorite Teen Titan. He's a character with so much heart. Sure...he's funny and he spends a lot of time fooling around and cracking jokes, but in this book I wanted to show there was more to him than that. I started drawing Gar as part of my "Casual Teen Titans" series online, where I show the characters wearing regular clothes and doing normal, everyday teen things, like hanging out together, doing homework, and going on dates. I really wanted Gar to be relatable. I'm a sneakerhead, so he wears old-school high-tops...and his hair does look a little like mine.

Thank you for making it possible for us to bring our favorite characters to life. We hope you love reading Gar's story as much as we have loved writing and drawing it!

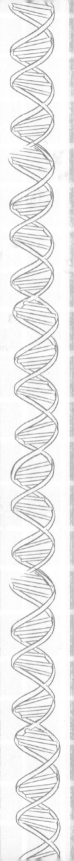

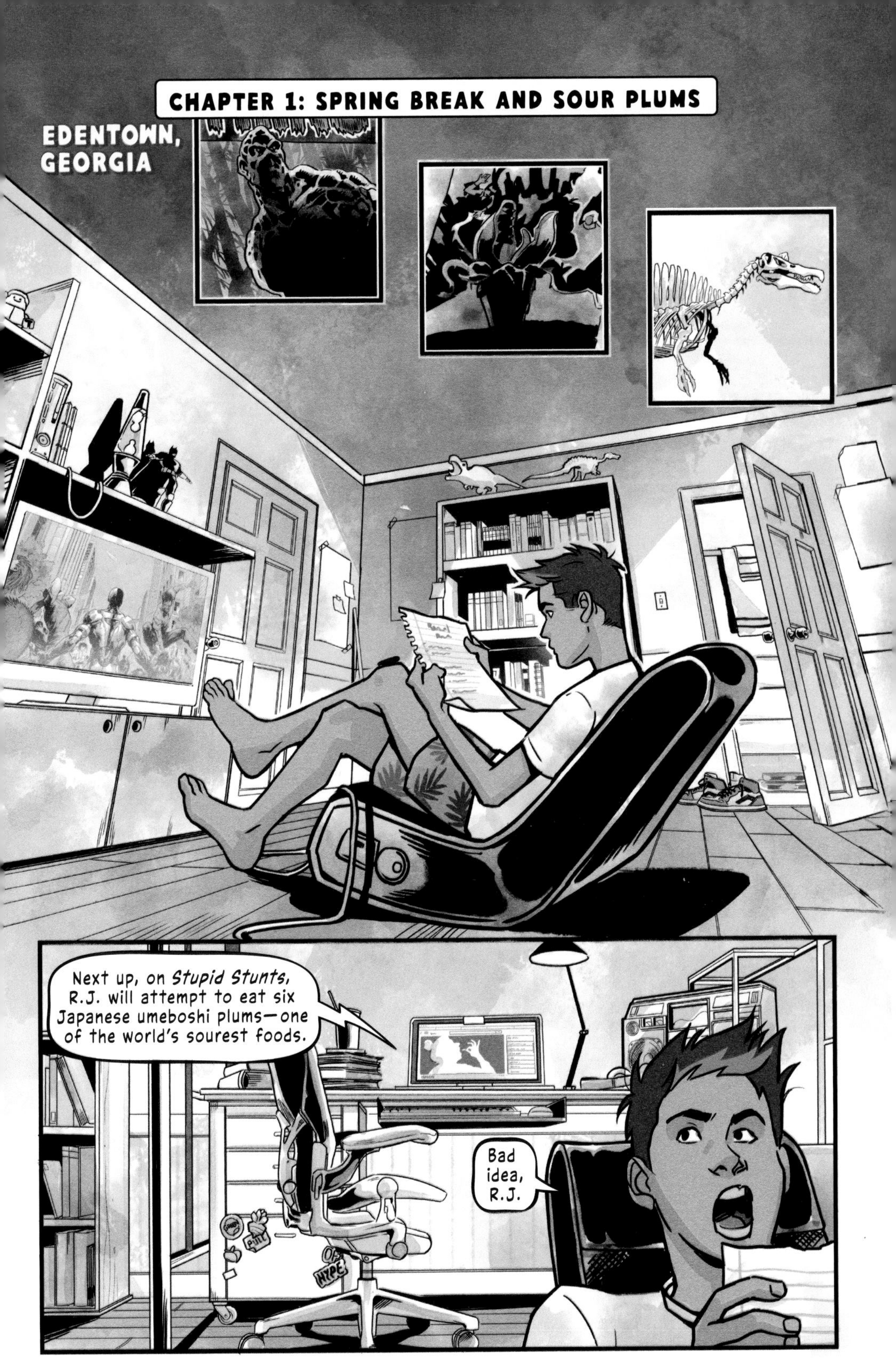
CHAPTER 1: SPRING BREAK AND SOUR PLUMS
EDENTOWN, GEORGIA
Next up, on *Stupid Stunts*, R.J. will attempt to eat six Japanese umeboshi plums—one of the world's sourest foods.
Bad idea, R.J.

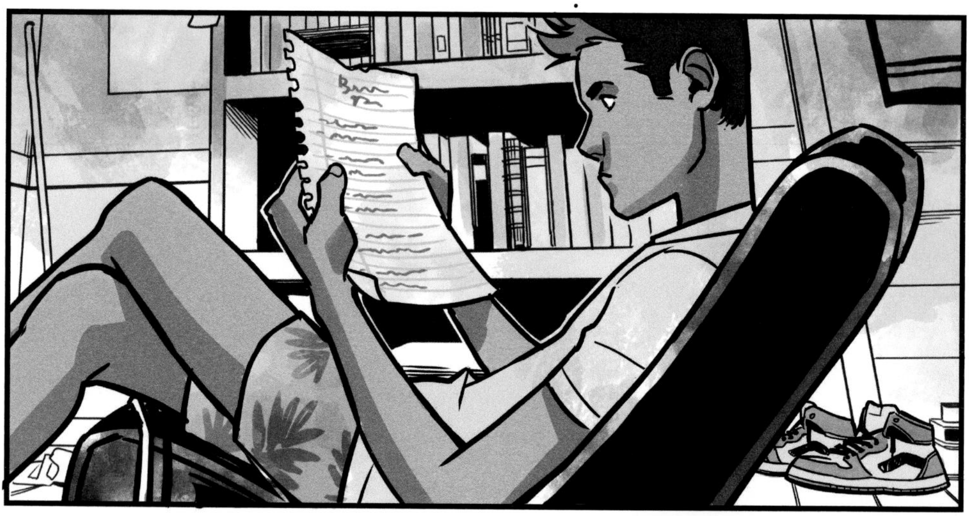

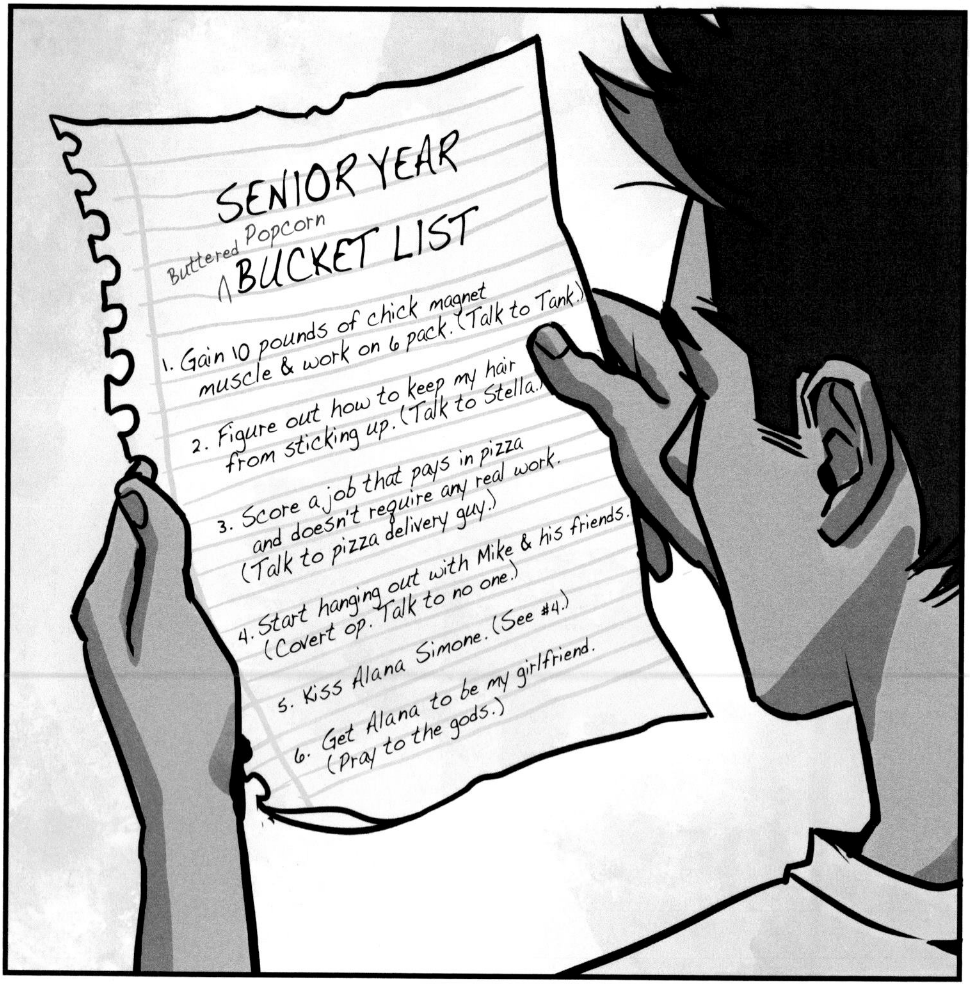

SENIOR YEAR
Buttered Popcorn
BUCKET LIST
1. Gain 10 pounds of chick magnet muscle & work on 6 pack. (Talk to Tank.)
2. Figure out how to keep my hair from sticking up. (Talk to Stella.)
3. Score a job that pays in pizza and doesn't require any real work. (Talk to pizza delivery guy.)
4. Start hanging out with Mike & his friends. (Covert op. Talk to no one.)
5. Kiss Alana Simone. (See #4.)
6. Get Alana to be my girlfriend. (Pray to the gods.)

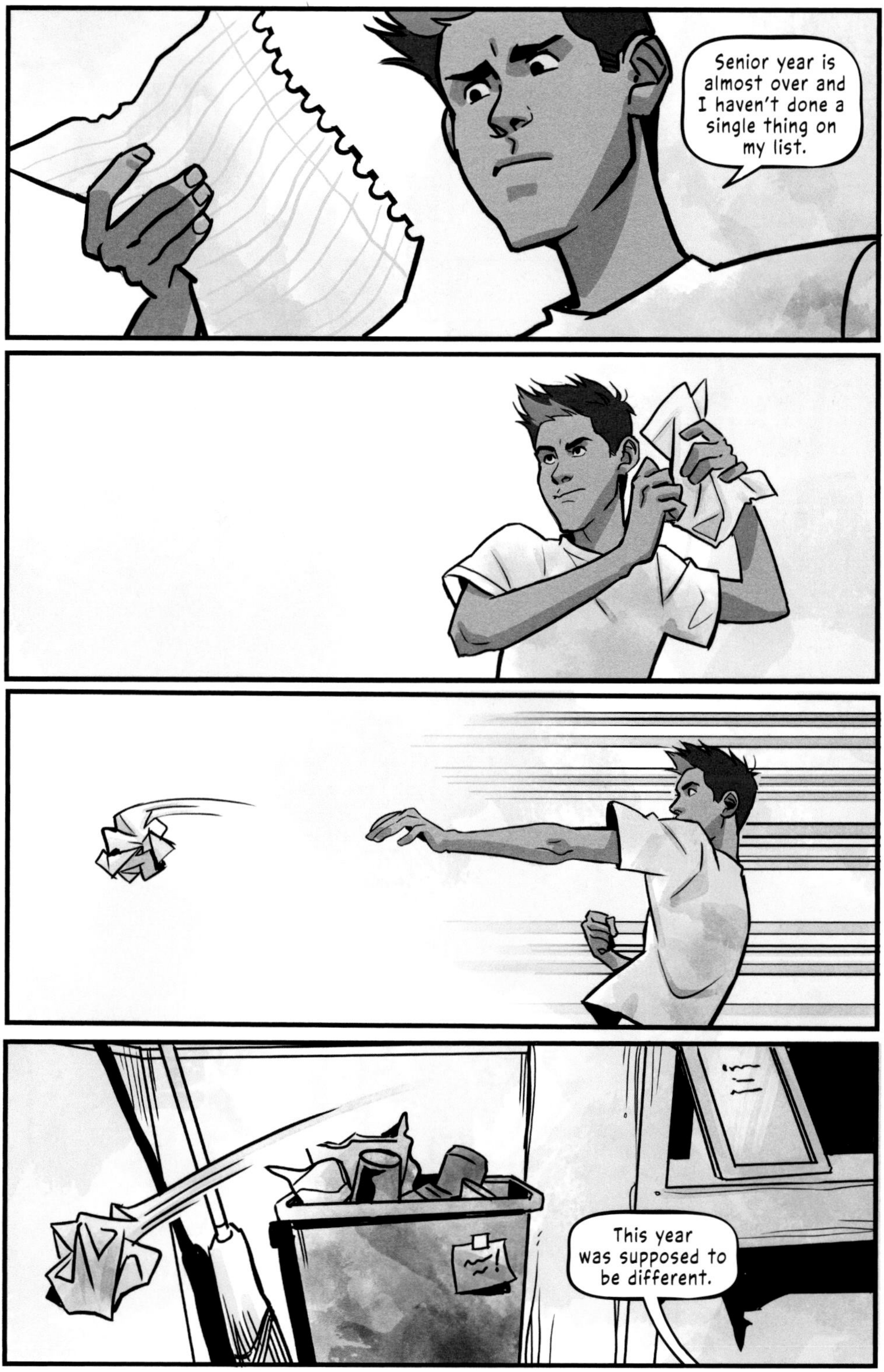
Senior year is almost over and I haven't done a single thing on my list.
This year was supposed to be different.

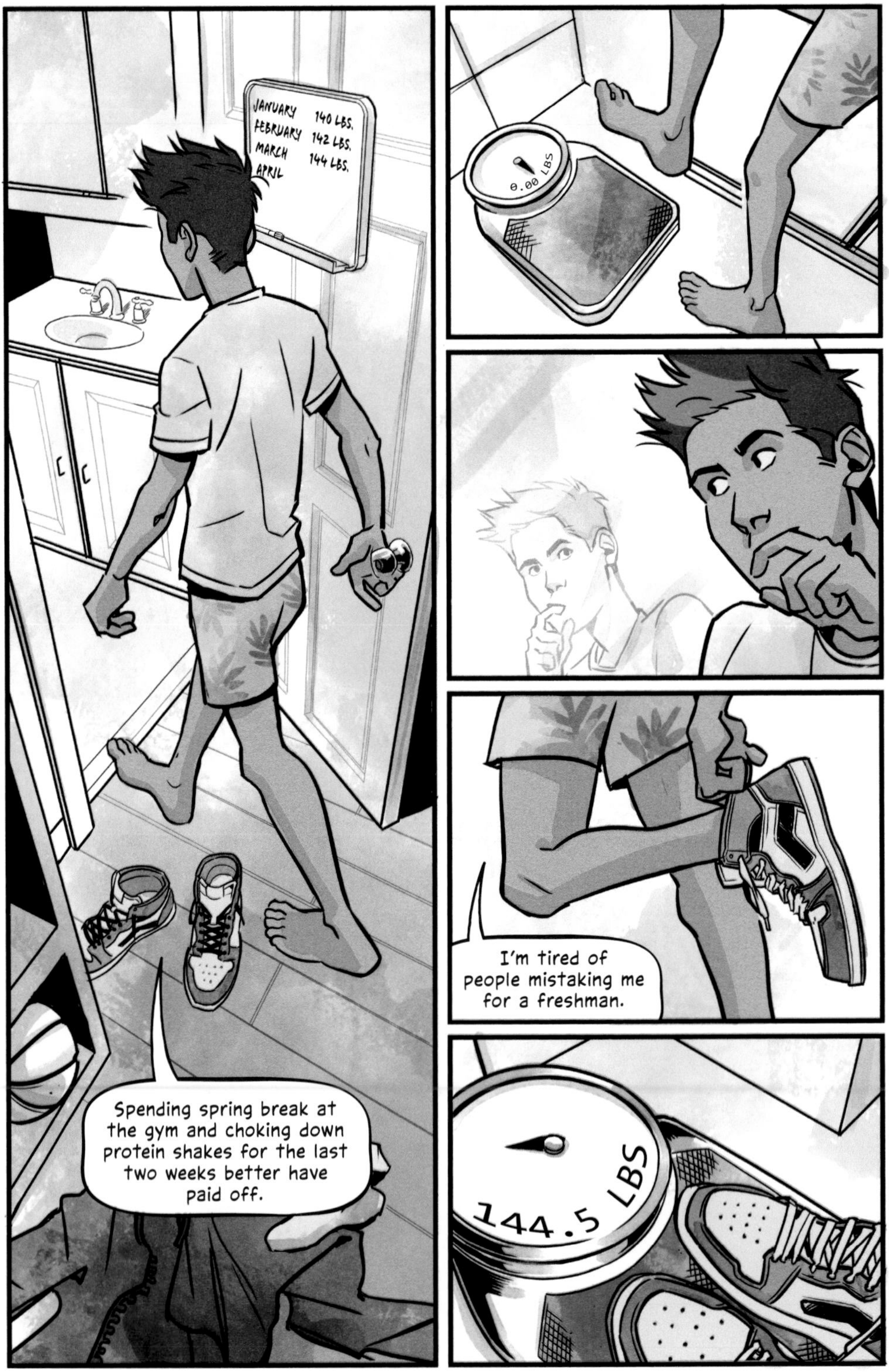
JANUARY 140 LBS.
FEBRUARY 142 LBS.
MARCH 144 LBS.
APRIL
Spending spring break at the gym and choking down protein shakes for the last two weeks better have paid off.
0.00 LBS
I'm tired of people mistaking me for a freshman.
144.5 LBS

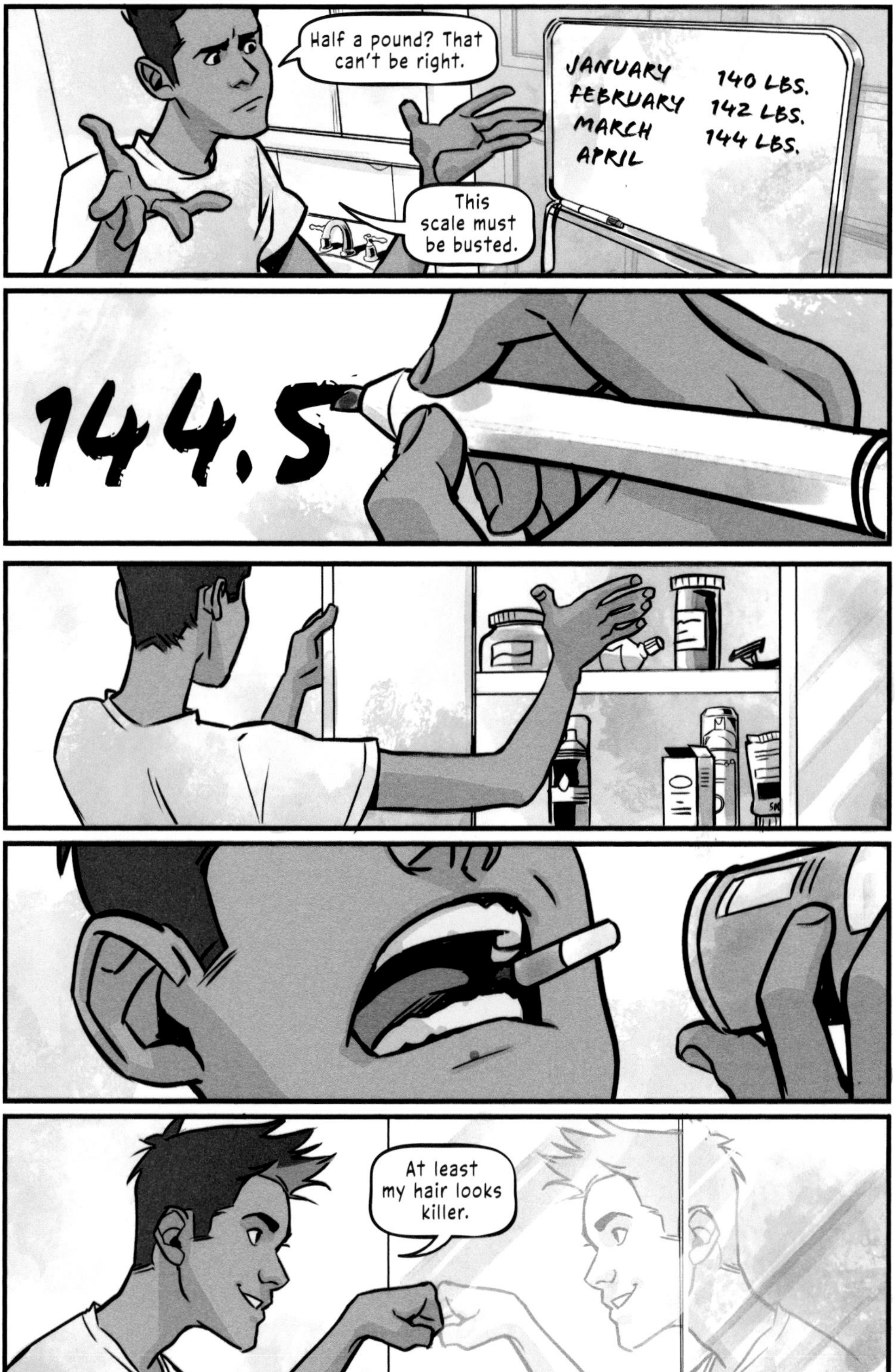
Half a pound? That can't be right.
JANUARY 140 LBS.
FEBRUARY 142 LBS.
MARCH 144 LBS.
APRIL
This scale must be busted.
144.5
At least my hair looks killer.

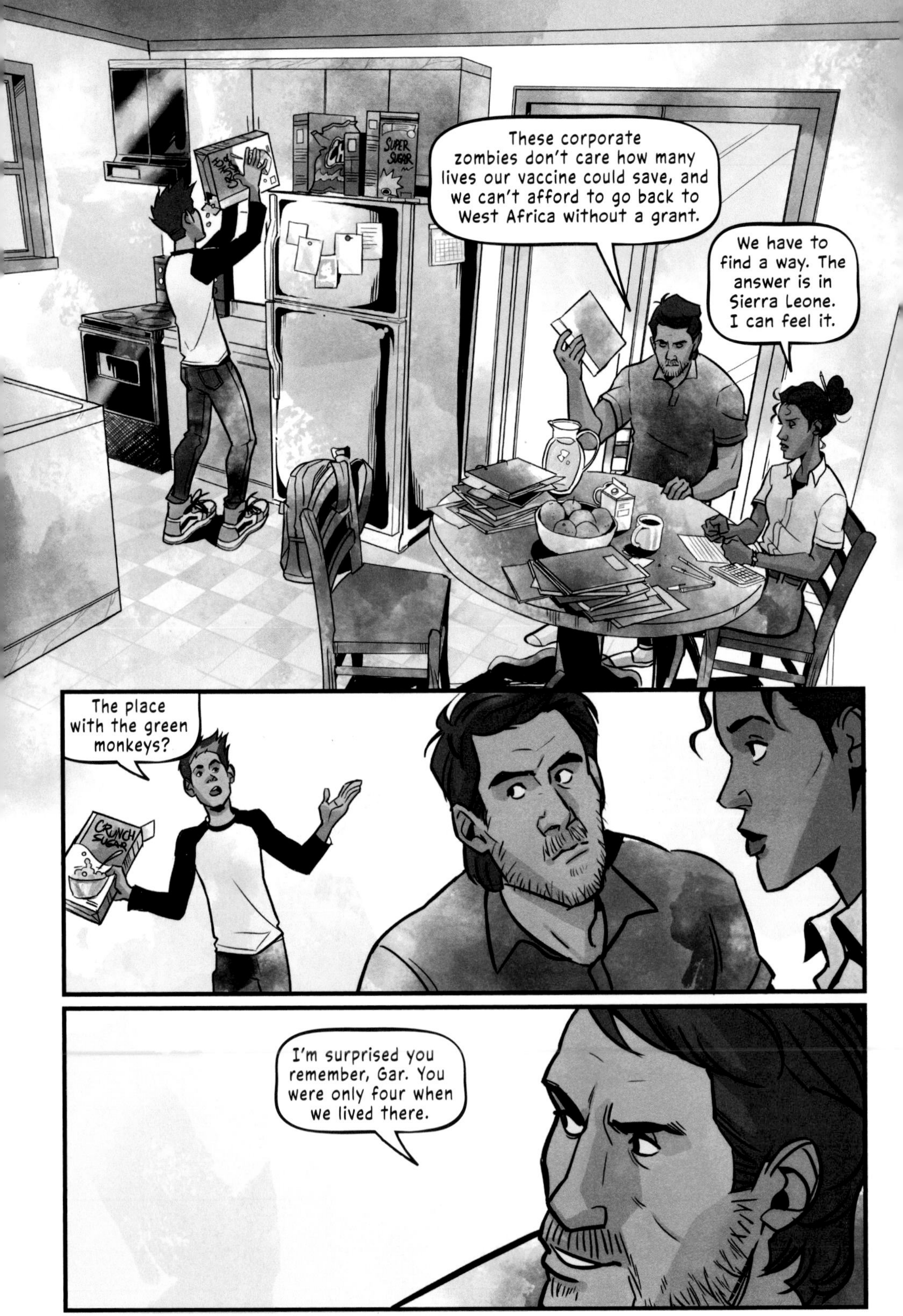
These corporate zombies don't care how many lives our vaccine could save, and we can't afford to go back to West Africa without a grant.
We have to find a way. The answer is in Sierra Leone. I can feel it.
SUPER SUGAR
The place with the green monkeys?
CRUNCH SUGAR
I'm surprised you remember, Gar. You were only four when we lived there.

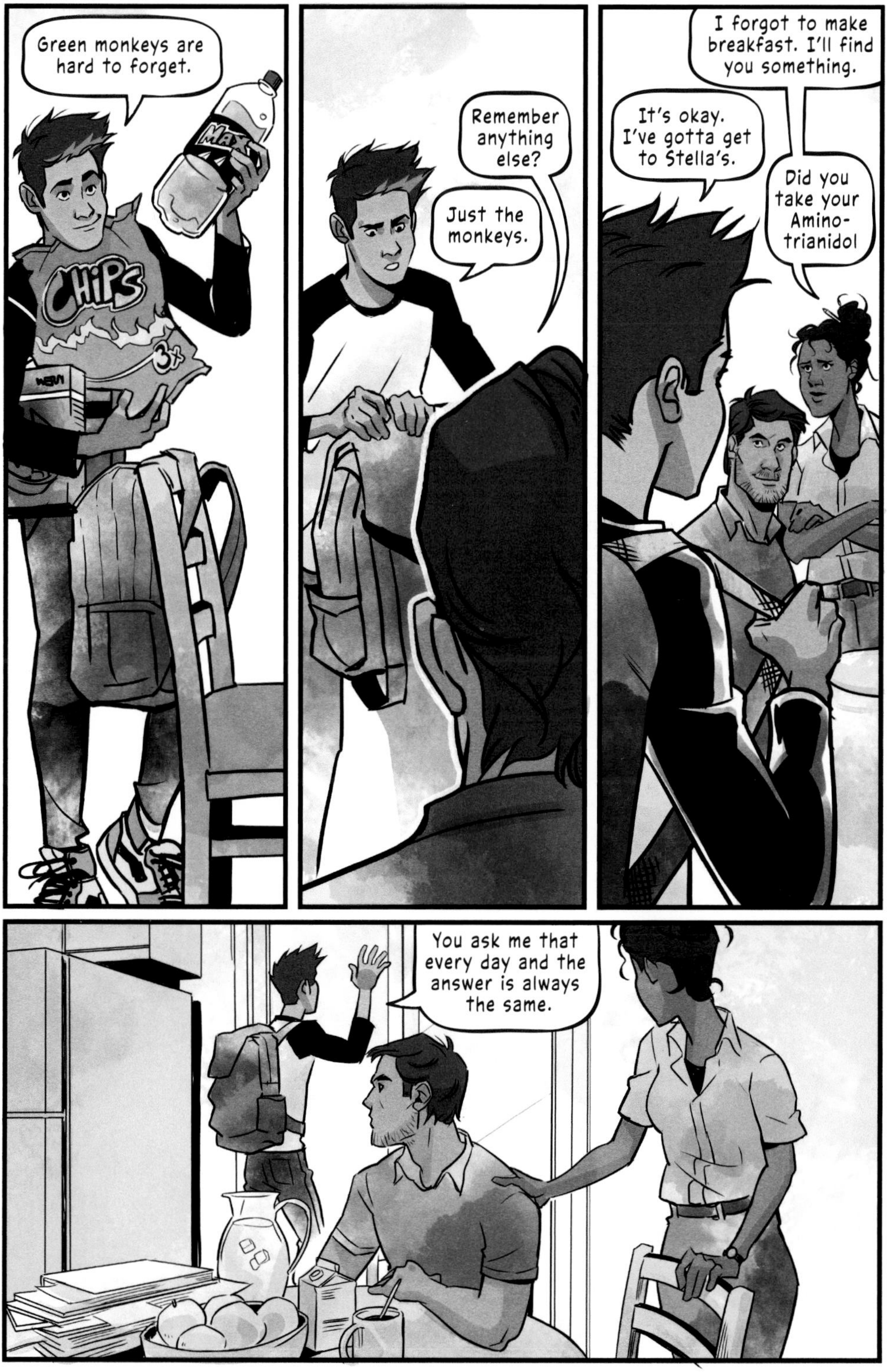
Green monkeys are hard to forget.
CHiPS
MAX
Remember anything else?
Just the monkeys.
I forgot to make breakfast. I'll find you something.
It's okay. I've gotta get to Stella's.
Did you take your Amino-trianidol
You ask me that every day and the answer is always the same.

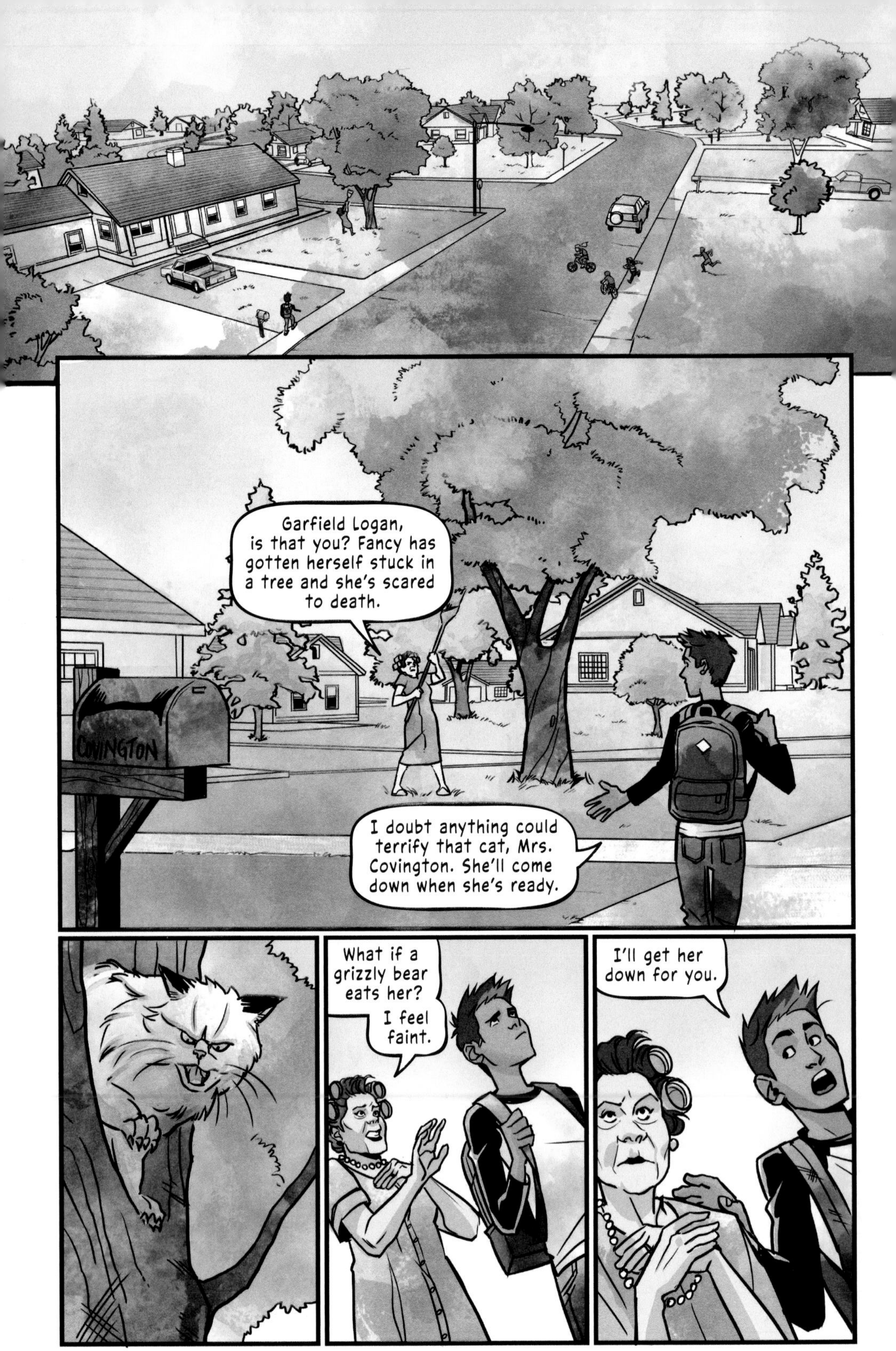
Garfield Logan, is that you? Fancy has gotten herself stuck in a tree and she's scared to death.
COVINGTON
I doubt anything could terrify that cat, Mrs. Covington. She'll come down when she's ready.
What if a grizzly bear eats her?
I feel faint.
I'll get her down for you.

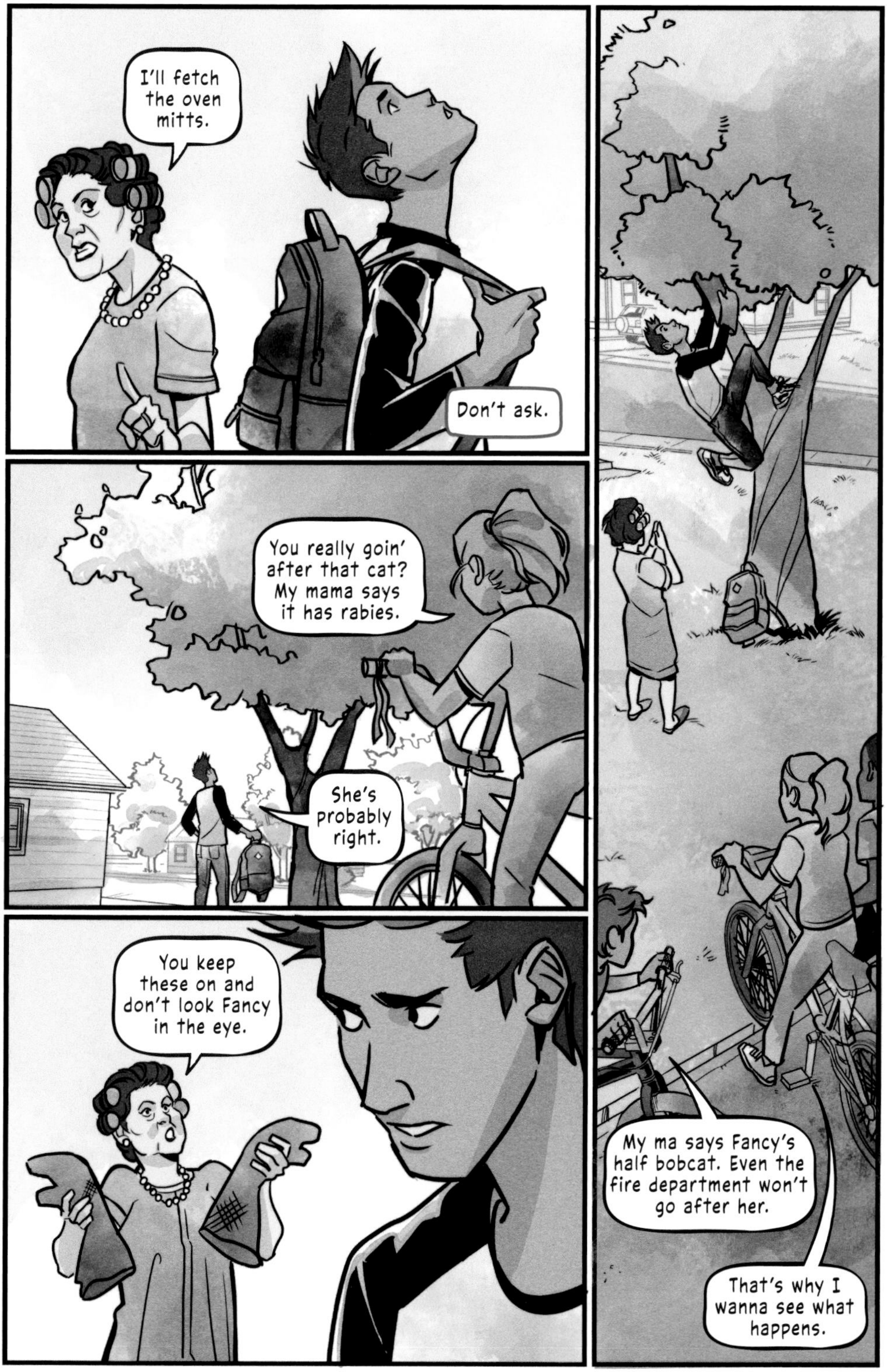
I'll fetch the oven mitts.
Don't ask.
You really goin' after that cat? My mama says it has rabies.
She's probably right.
You keep these on and don't look Fancy in the eye.
My ma says Fancy's half bobcat. Even the fire department won't go after her.
That's why I wanna see what happens.

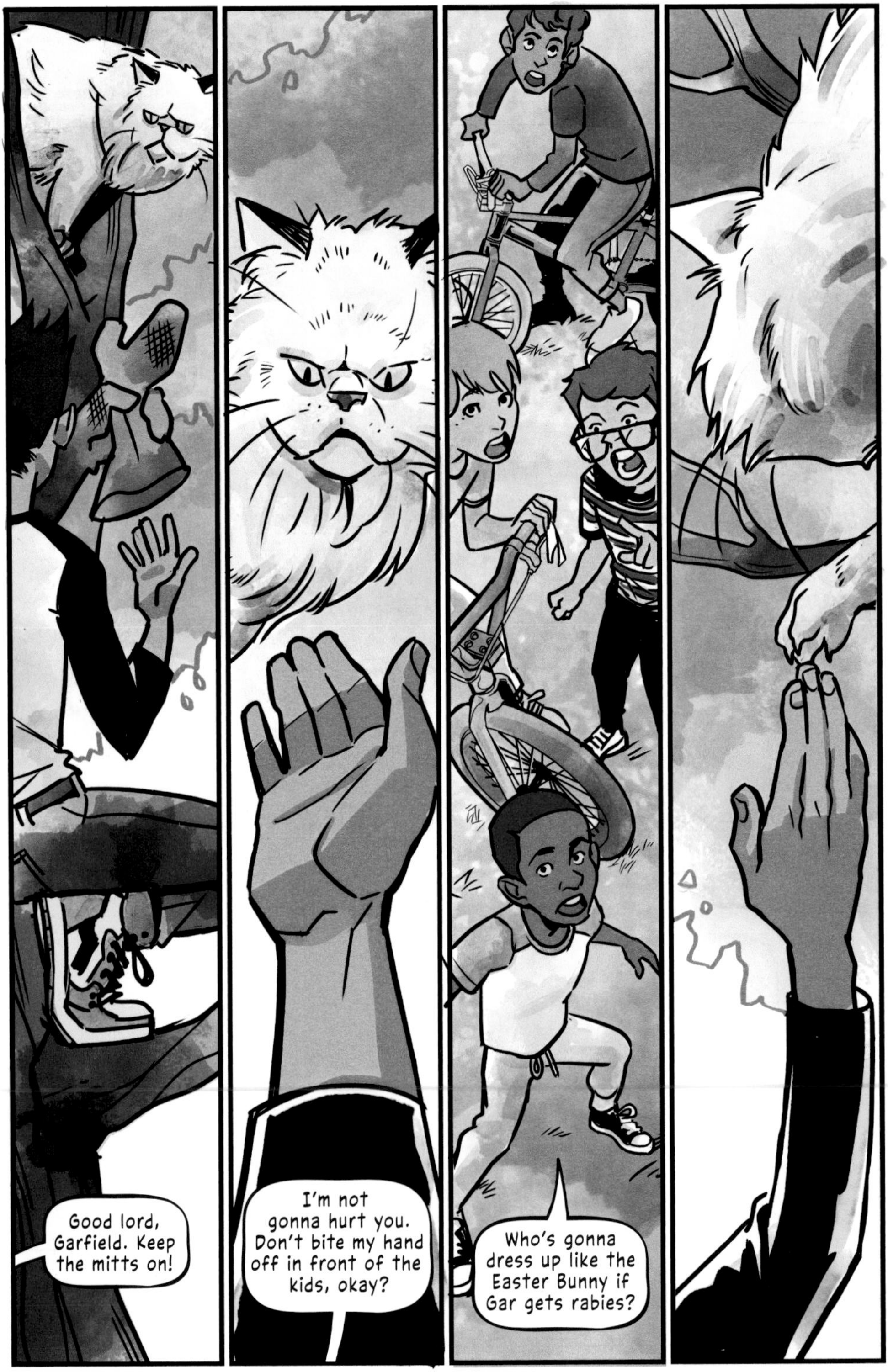
Good lord, Garfield. Keep the mitts on!
I'm not gonna hurt you. Don't bite my hand off in front of the kids, okay?
Who's gonna dress up like the Easter Bunny if Gar gets rabies?

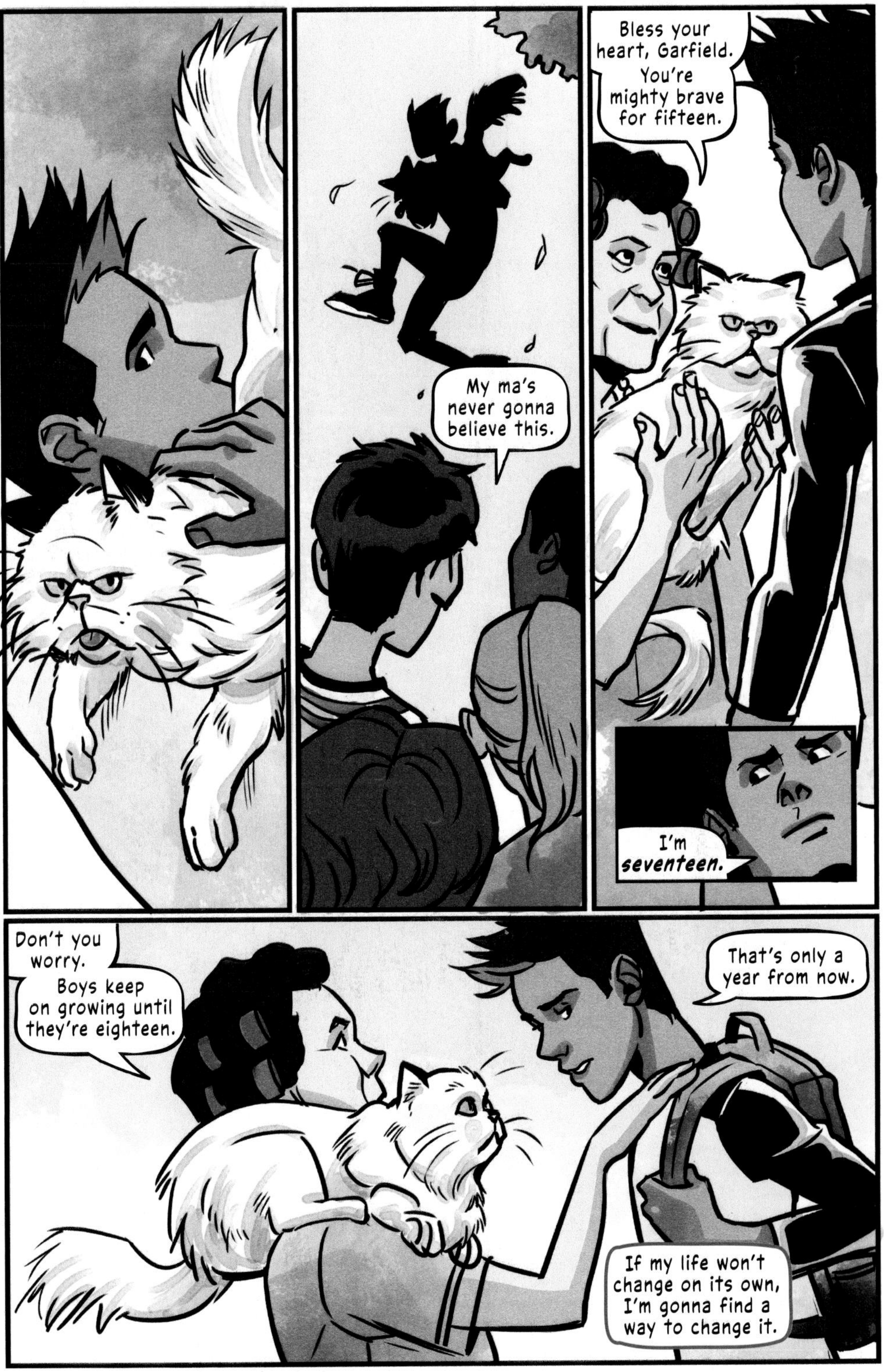
My ma's never gonna believe this.
Bless your heart, Garfield. You're mighty brave for fifteen.
I'm *seventeen.*
Don't you worry. Boys keep on growing until they're eighteen.
That's only a year from now.
If my life won't change on its own, I'm gonna find a way to change it.

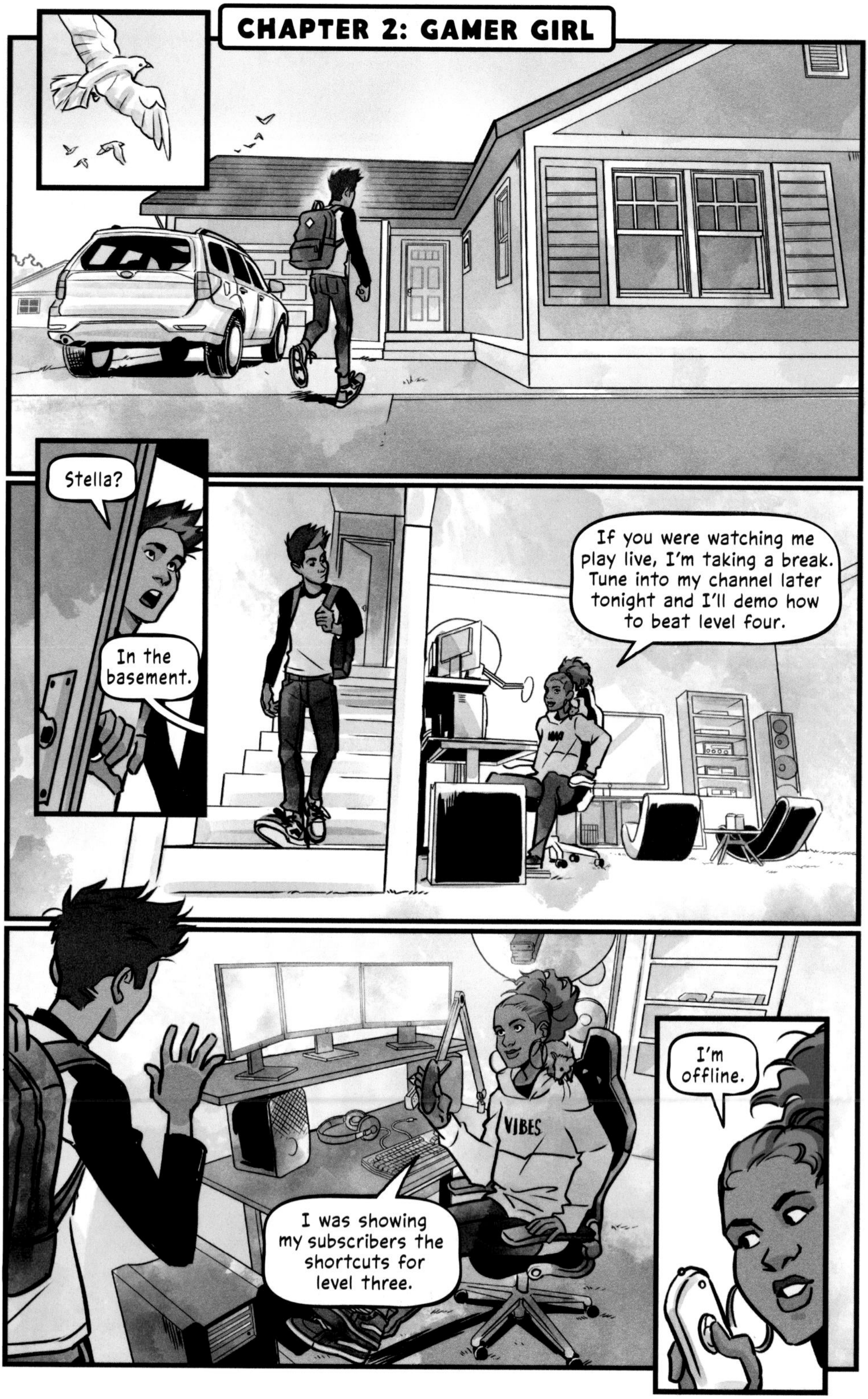
CHAPTER 2: GAMER GIRL
Stella?
In the basement.
If you were watching me play live, I'm taking a break. Tune into my channel later tonight and I'll demo how to beat level four.
VIBES
I was showing my subscribers the shortcuts for level three.
I'm offline.

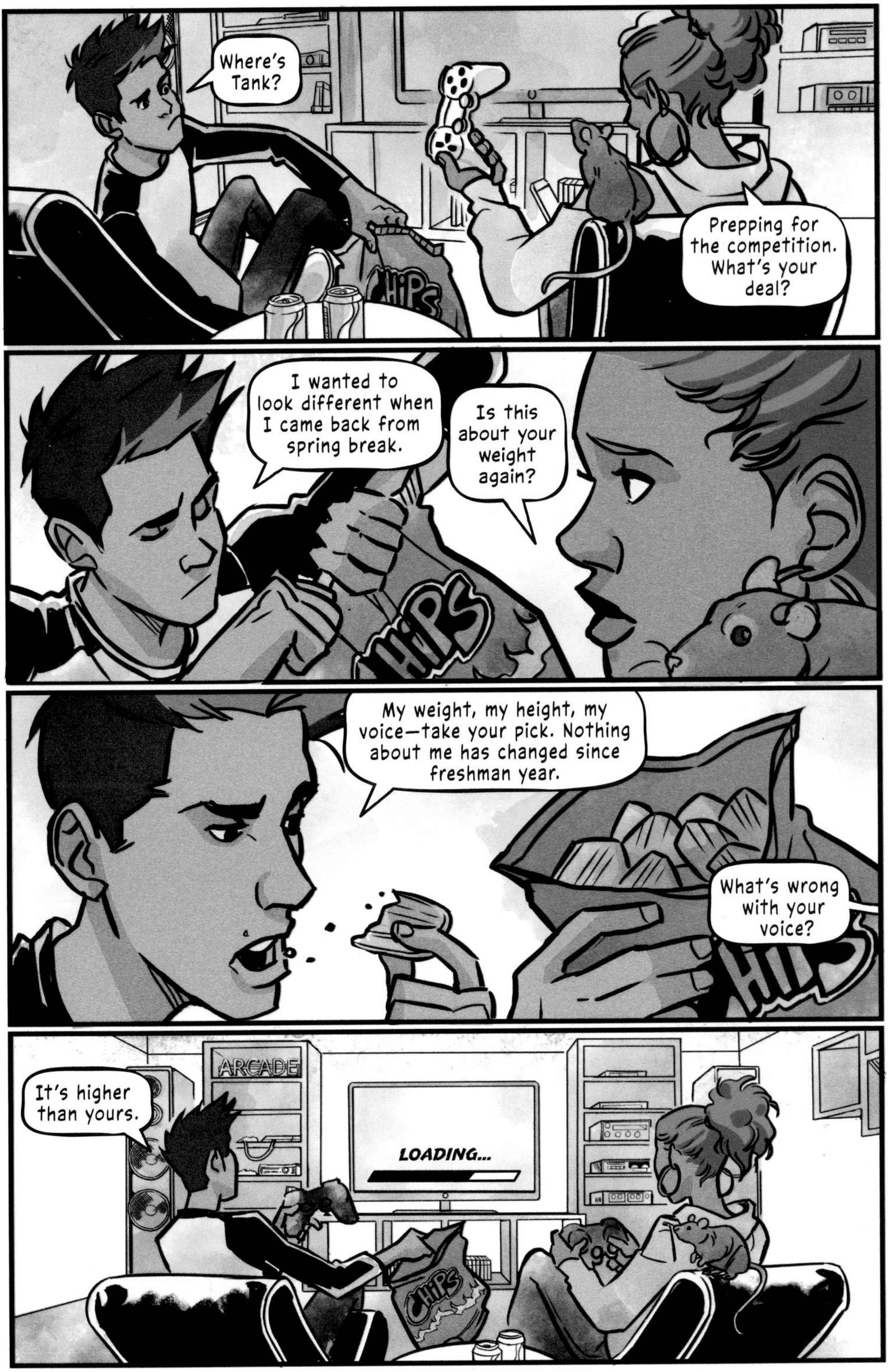
Where's Tank?
Prepping for the competition. What's your deal?
CHIPS
I wanted to look different when I came back from spring break.
Is this about your weight again?
My weight, my height, my voice—take your pick. Nothing about me has changed since freshman year.
What's wrong with your voice?
It's higher than yours.
ARCADE
LOADING...
CHIPS

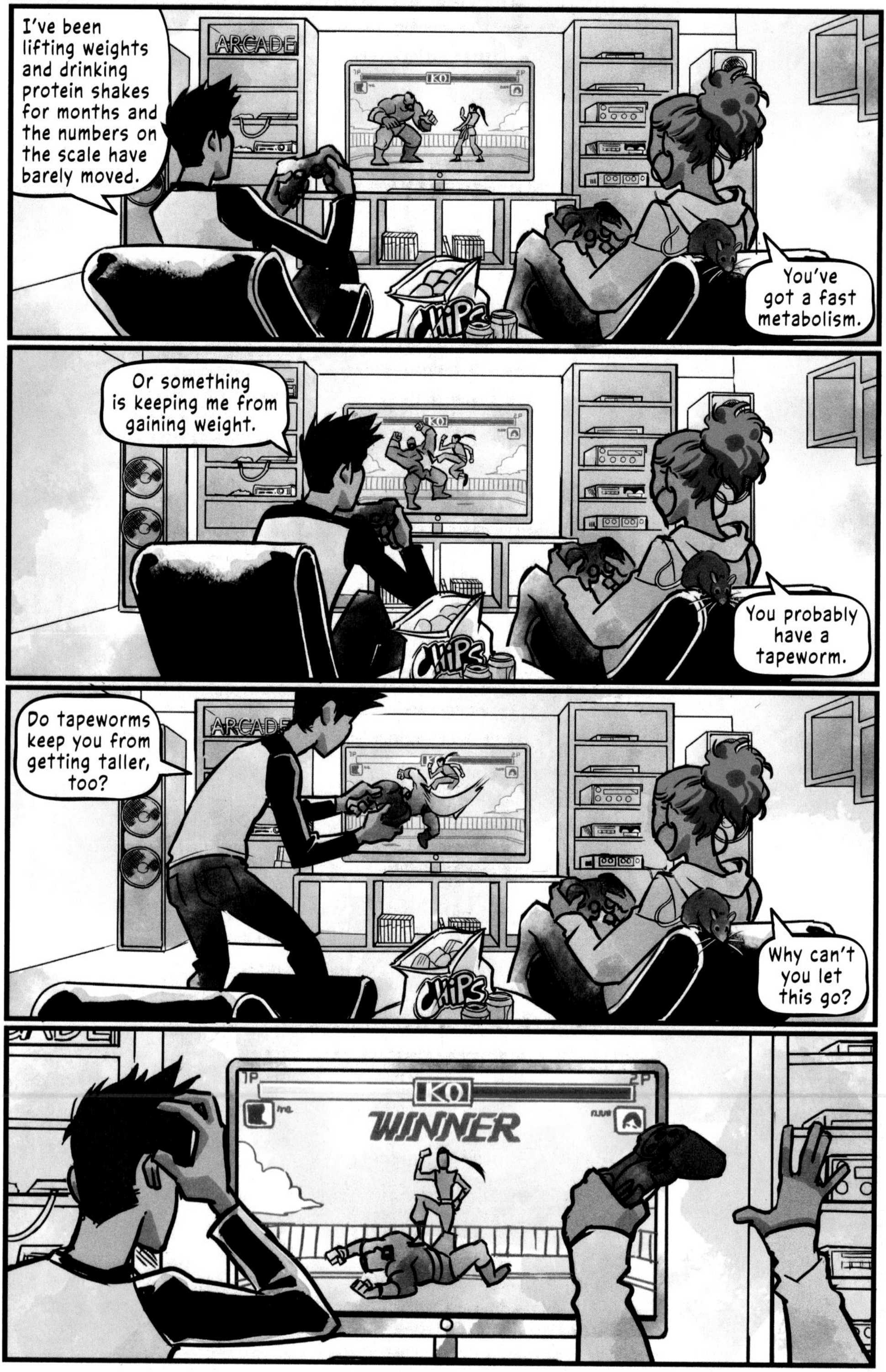
I've been lifting weights and drinking protein shakes for months and the numbers on the scale have barely moved.
ARCADE
KO
You've got a fast metabolism.
CHIPS
Or something is keeping me from gaining weight.
KO
You probably have a tapeworm.
CHIPS
Do tapeworms keep you from getting taller, too?
ARCADE
Why can't you let this go?
CHIPS
1P
KO
2P
WINNER

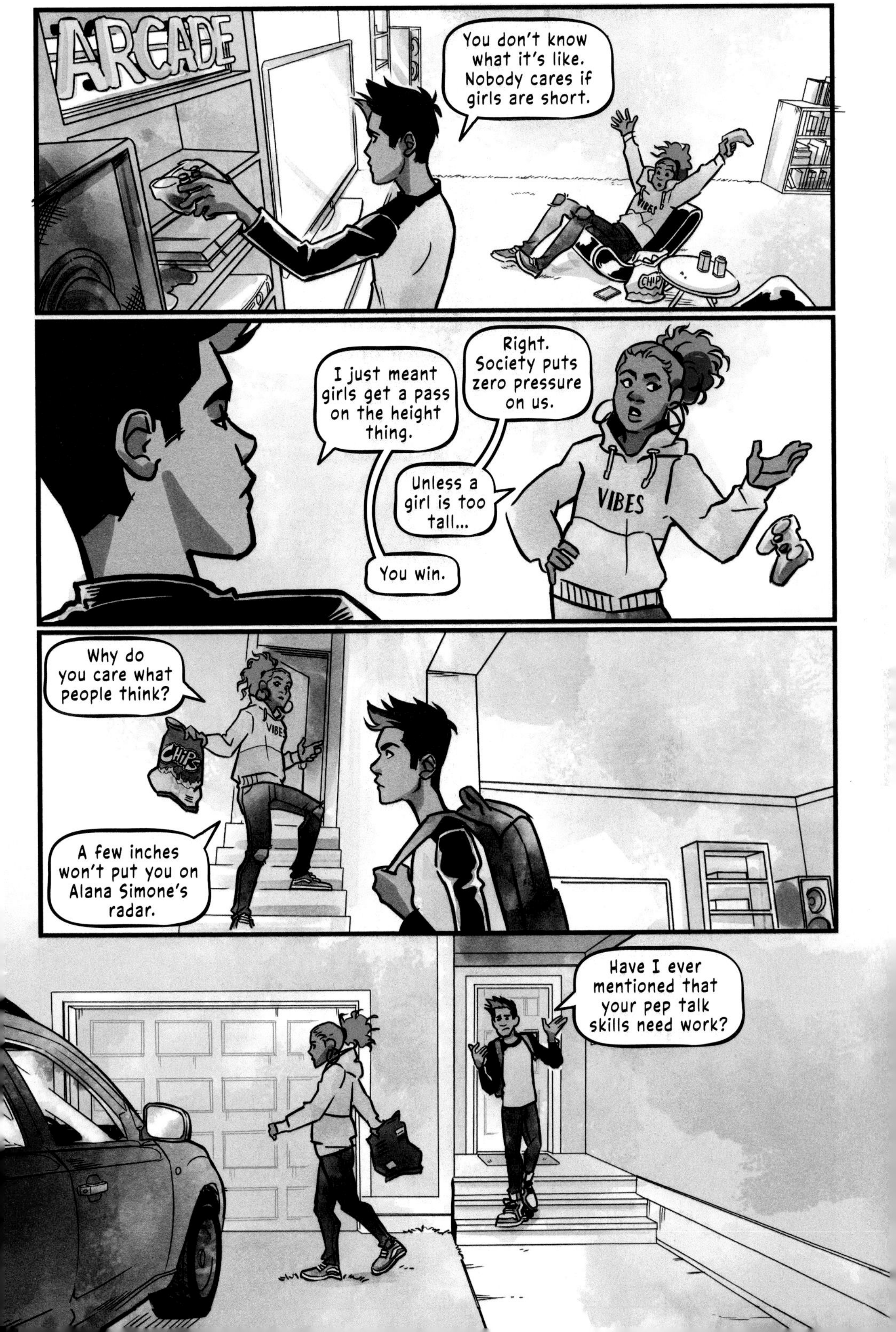
ARCADE
You don't know what it's like. Nobody cares if girls are short.
VIBES
CHIPS
I just meant girls get a pass on the height thing.
Right. Society puts zero pressure on us.
Unless a girl is too tall...
You win.
VIBES
Why do you care what people think?
CHIPS
VIBES
A few inches won't put you on Alana Simone's radar.
Have I ever mentioned that your pep talk skills need work?

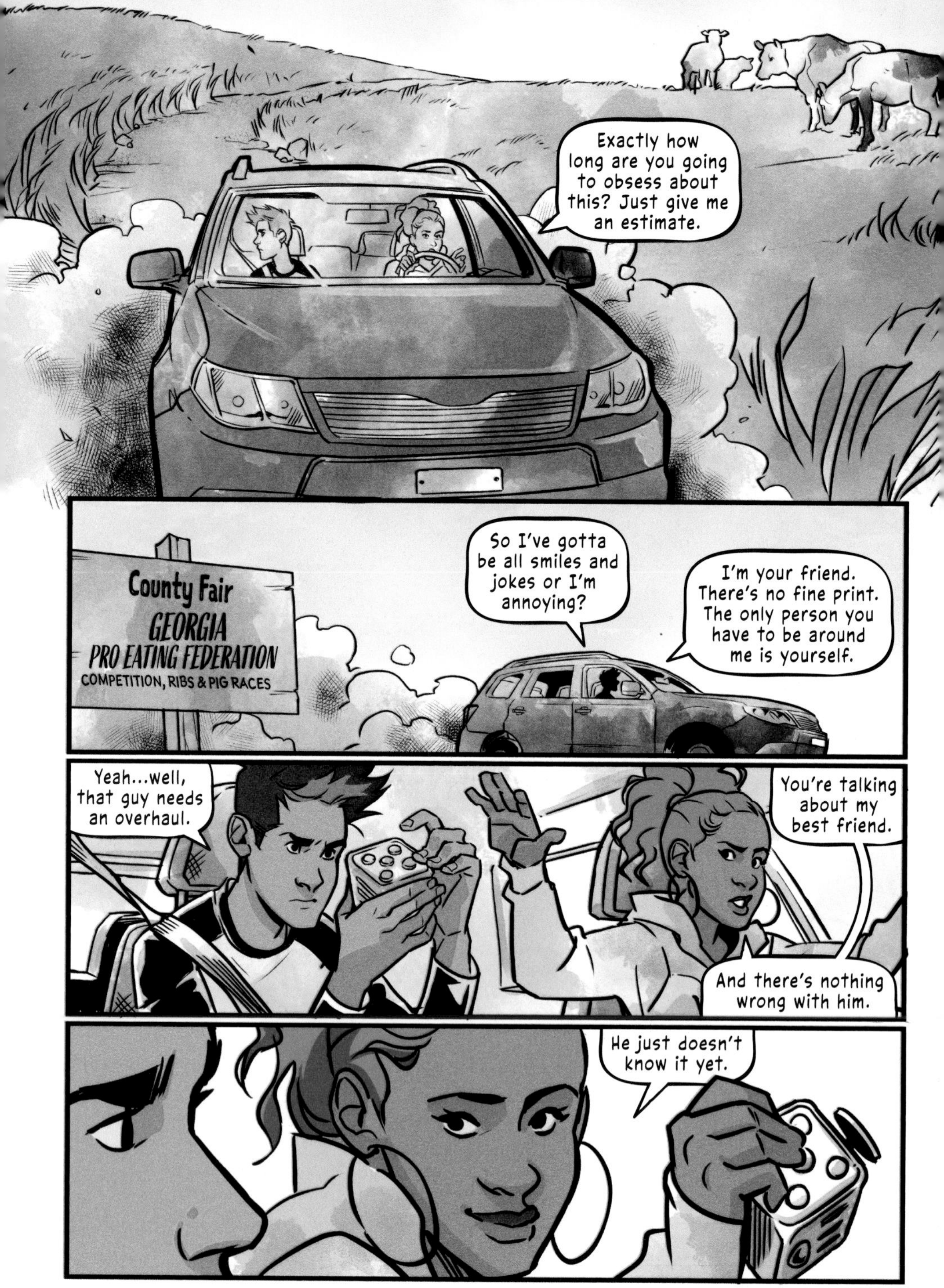
Exactly how long are you going to obsess about this? Just give me an estimate.
County Fair
GEORGIA
PRO EATING FEDERATION
COMPETITION, RIBS & PIG RACES
So I've gotta be all smiles and jokes or I'm annoying?
I'm your friend. There's no fine print. The only person you have to be around me is yourself.
Yeah...well, that guy needs an overhaul.
You're talking about my best friend.
And there's nothing wrong with him.
He just doesn't know it yet.

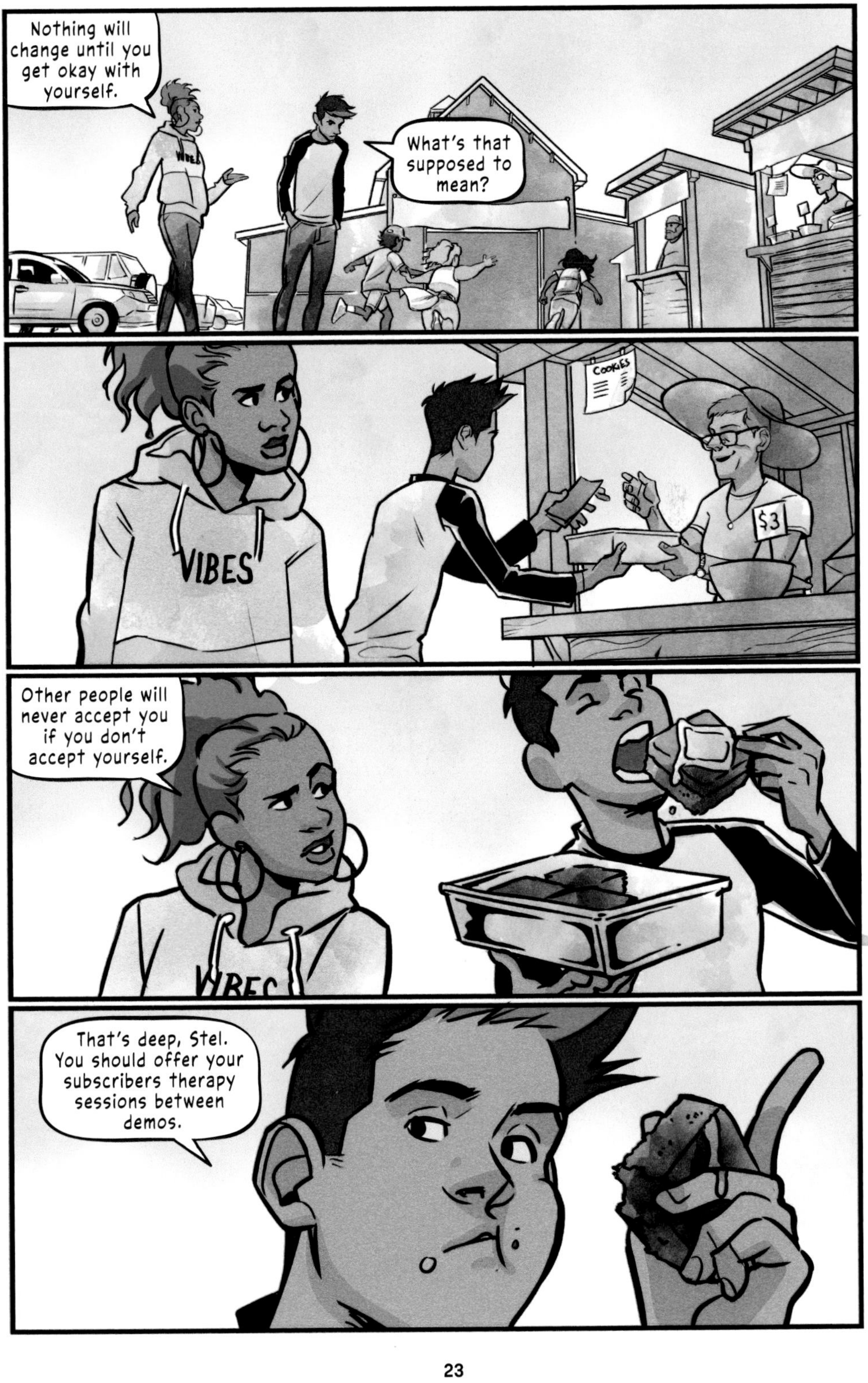
Nothing will change until you get okay with yourself.
What's that supposed to mean?
COOKIES
$3
Other people will never accept you if you don't accept yourself.
That's deep, Stel. You should offer your subscribers therapy sessions between demos.

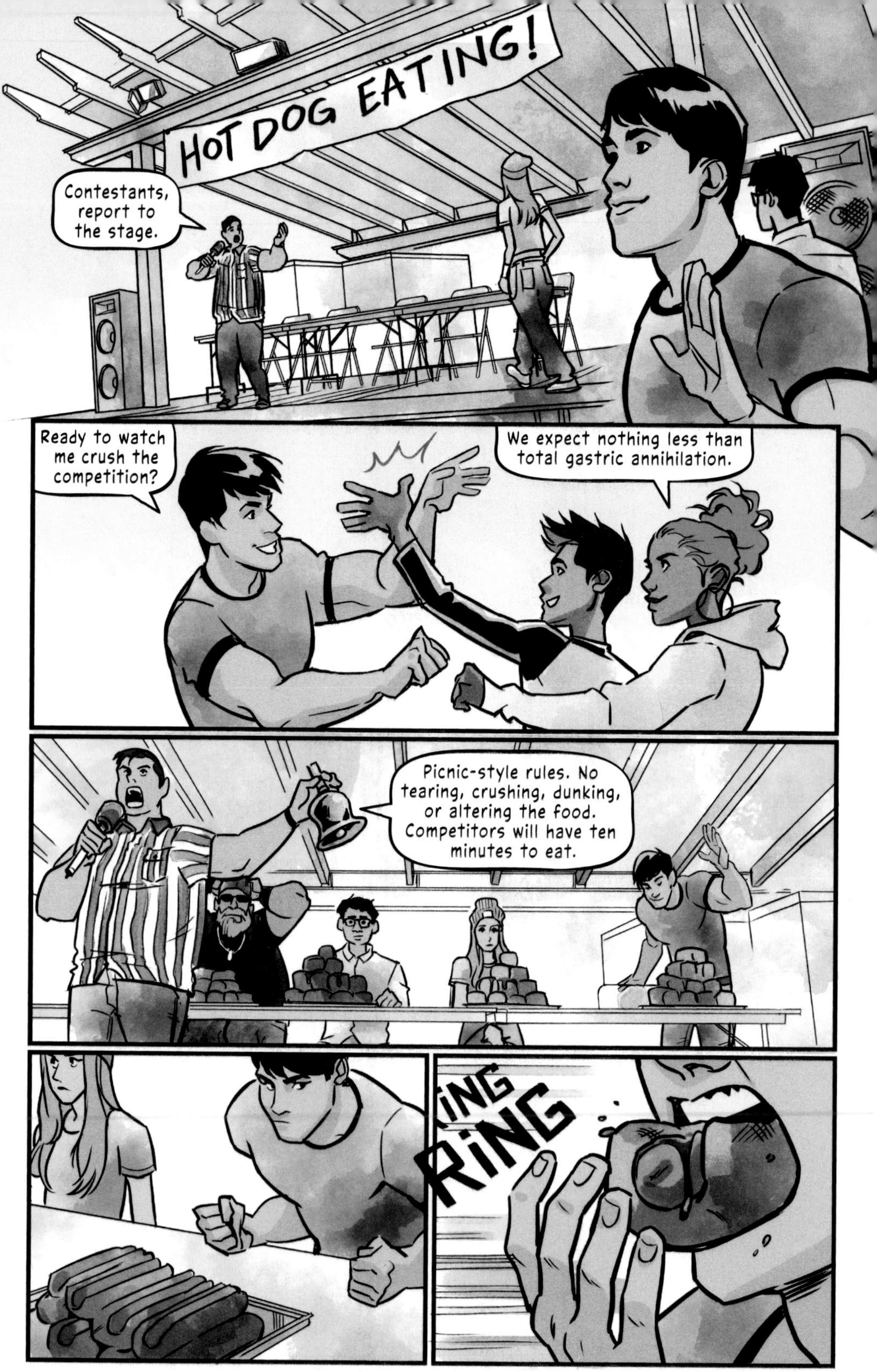
HOT DOG EATING!
Contestants, report to the stage.
Ready to watch me crush the competition?
We expect nothing less than total gastric annihilation.
Picnic-style rules. No tearing, crushing, dunking, or altering the food. Competitors will have ten minutes to eat.
RING RING

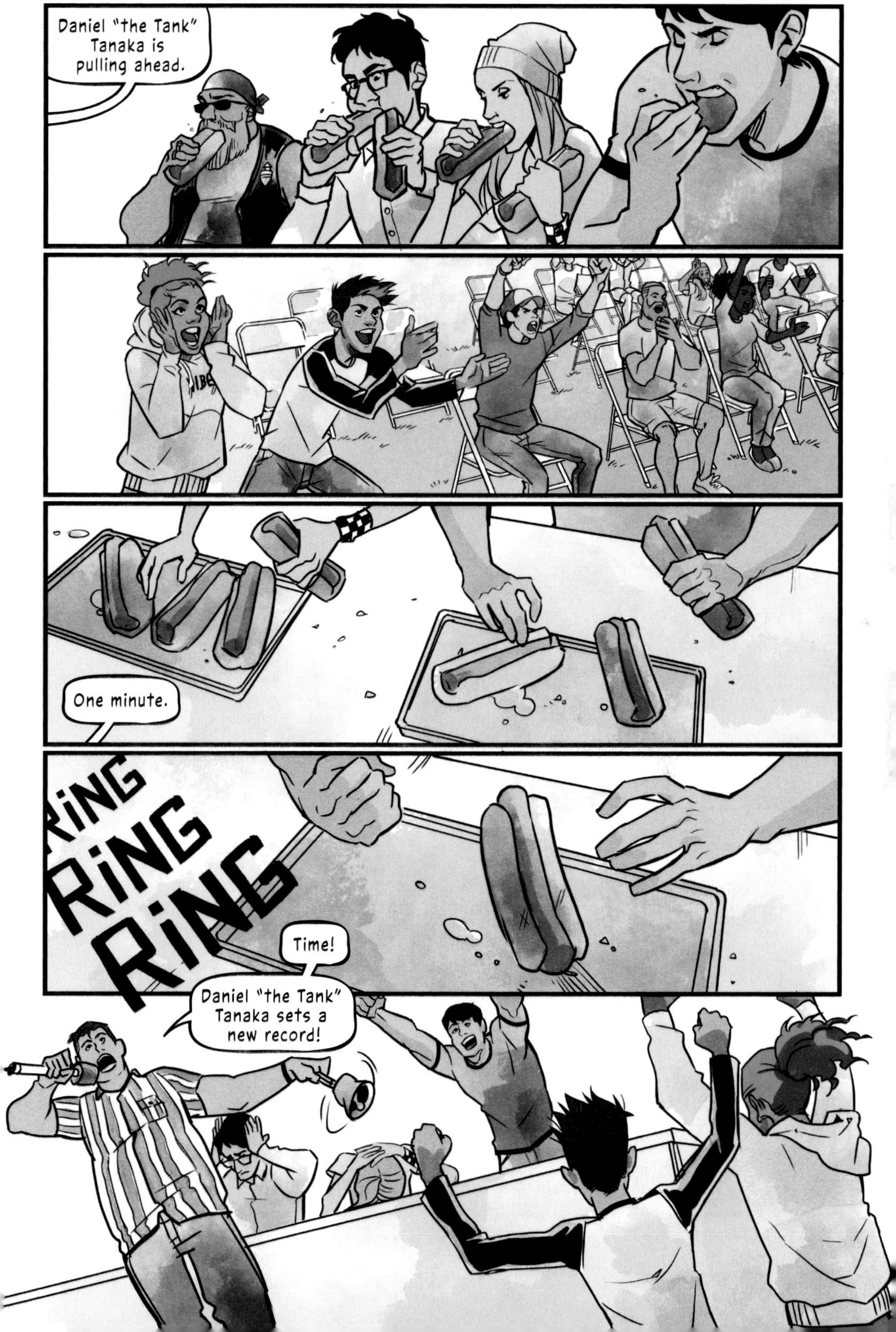
Daniel "the Tank" Tanaka is pulling ahead.
One minute.
RING
RING
RING
Time!
Daniel "the Tank" Tanaka sets a new record!

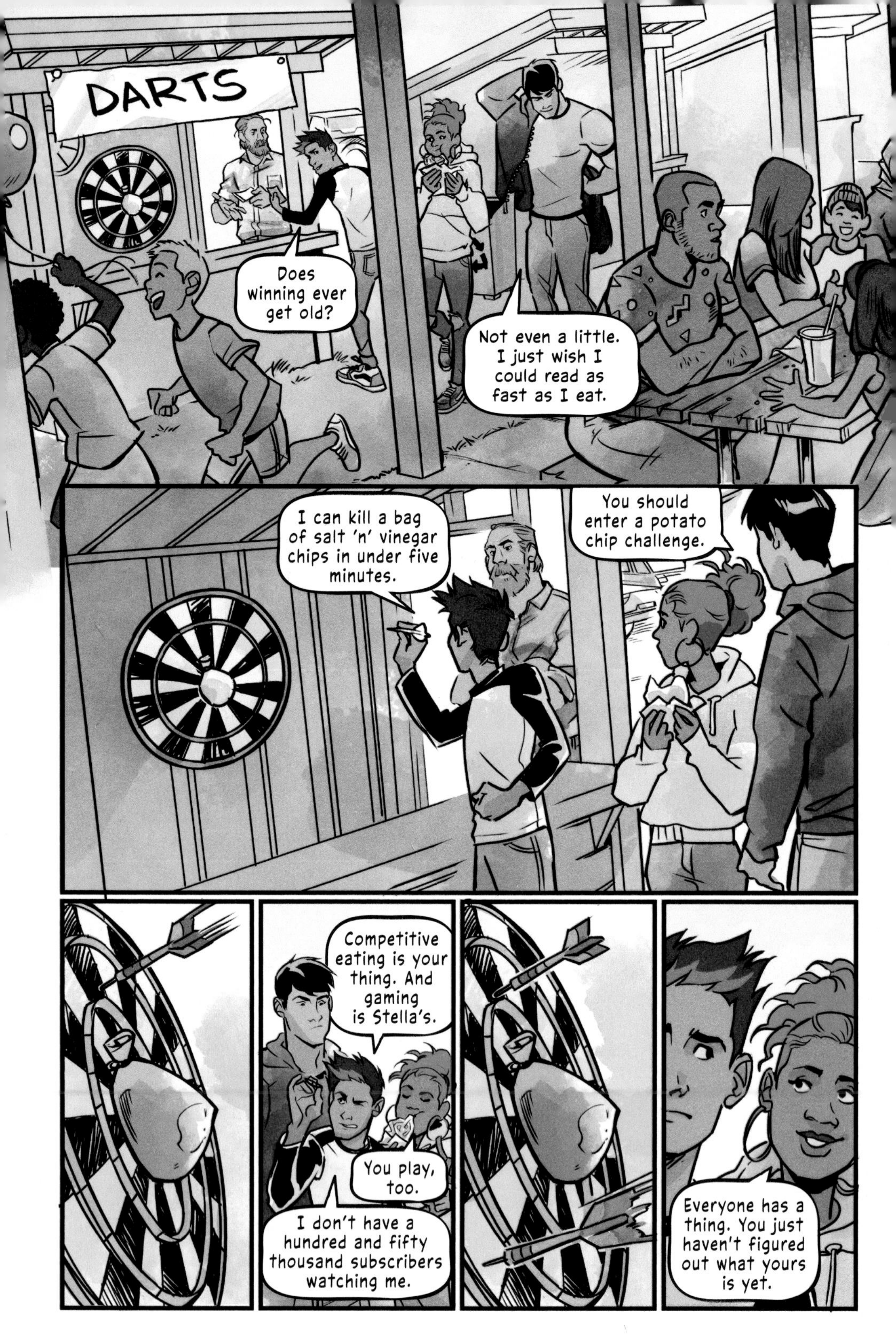
DARTS
Does winning ever get old?
Not even a little. I just wish I could read as fast as I eat.
I can kill a bag of salt 'n' vinegar chips in under five minutes.
You should enter a potato chip challenge.
Competitive eating is your thing. And gaming is Stella's.
You play, too.
I don't have a hundred and fifty thousand subscribers watching me.
Everyone has a thing. You just haven't figured out what yours is yet.

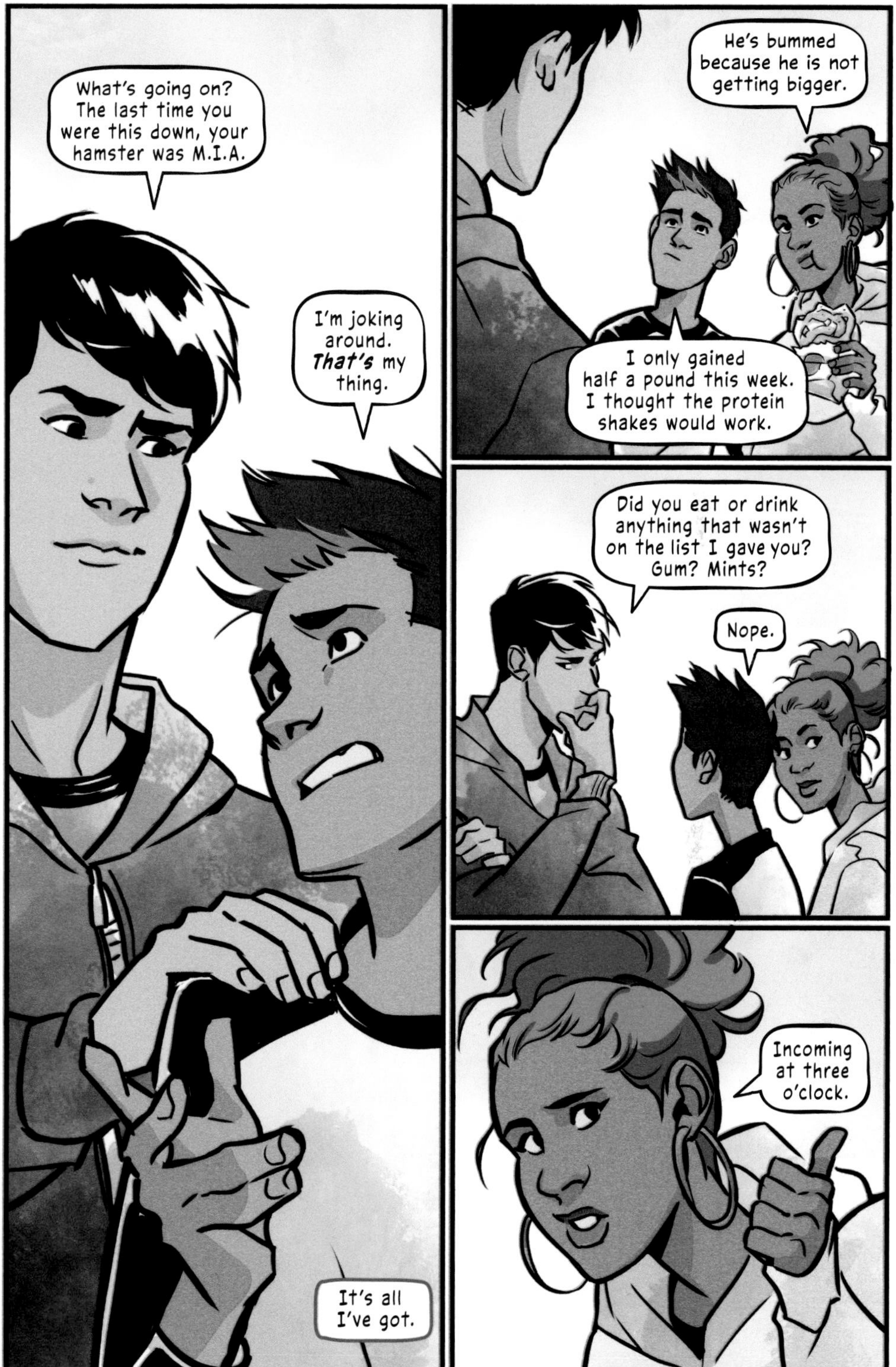
What's going on? The last time you were this down, your hamster was M.I.A.
I'm joking around. *That's* my thing.
It's all I've got.
He's bummed because he is not getting bigger.
I only gained half a pound this week. I thought the protein shakes would work.
Did you eat or drink anything that wasn't on the list I gave you? Gum? Mints?
Nope.
Incoming at three o'clock.

CHAPTER 3: CHOSEN ONES

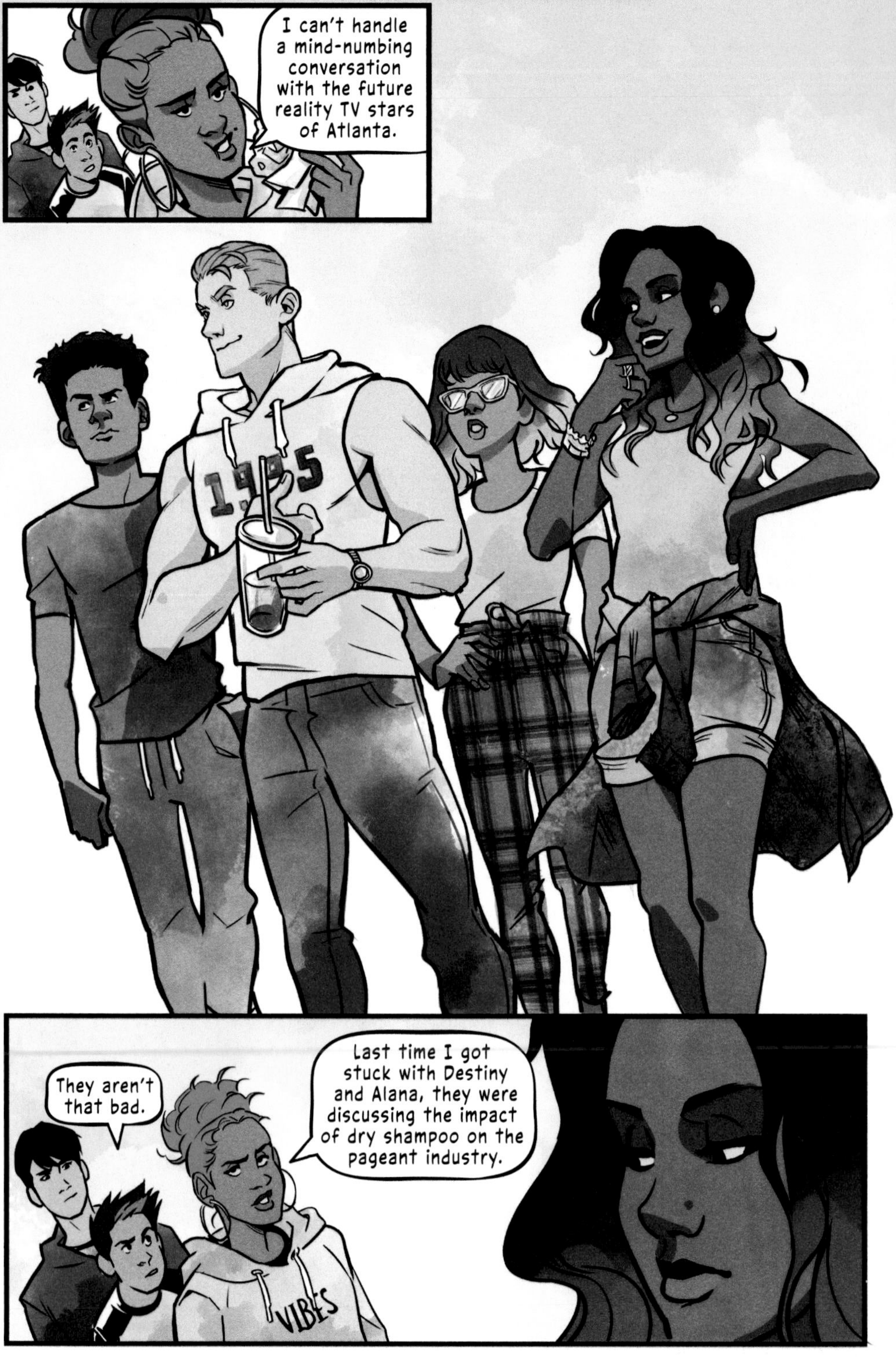
I can't handle a mind-numbing conversation with the future reality TV stars of Atlanta.
They aren't that bad.
Last time I got stuck with Destiny and Alana, they were discussing the impact of dry shampoo on the pageant industry.
VIBES

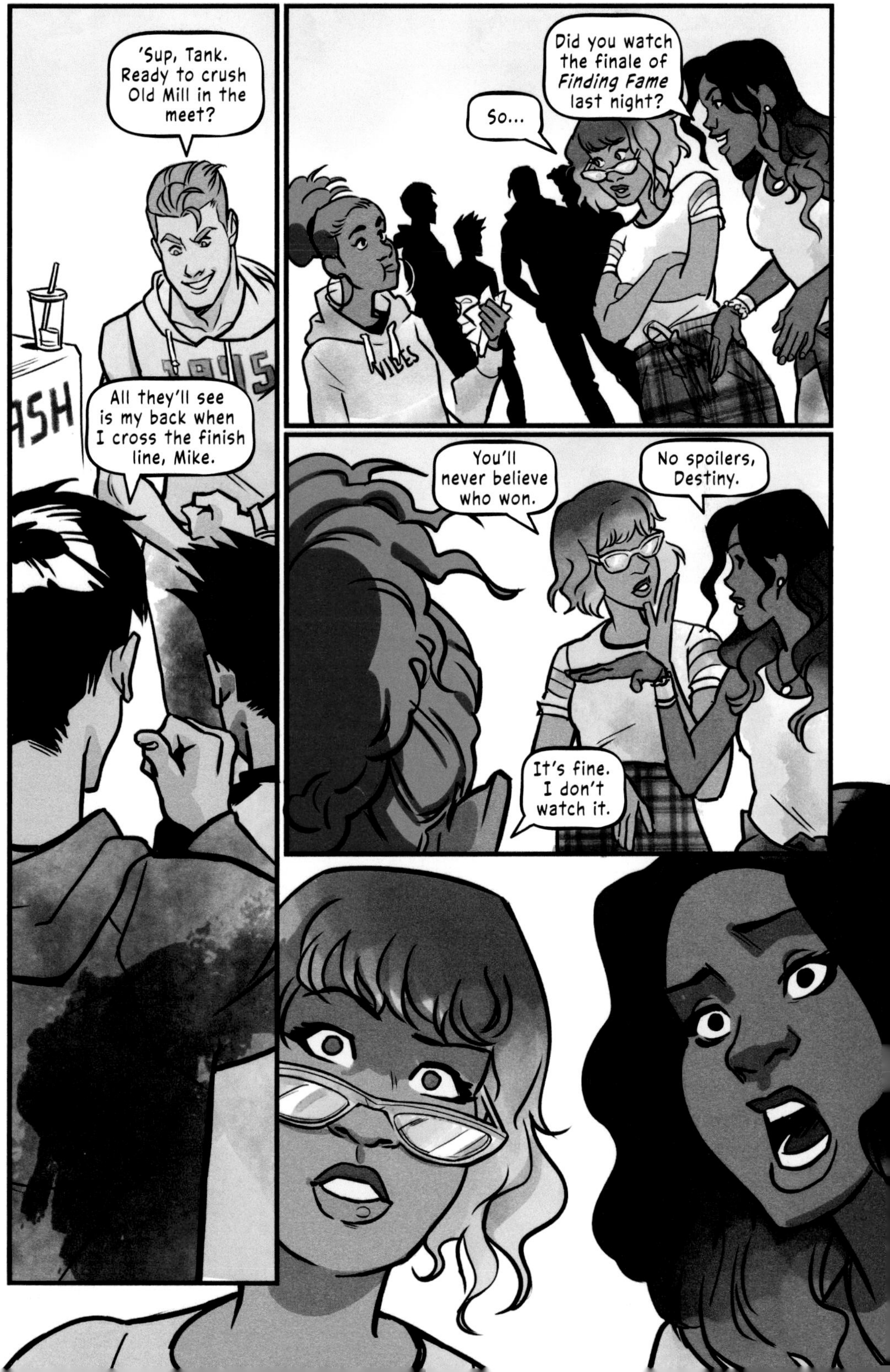
'Sup, Tank. Ready to crush Old Mill in the meet?
All they'll see is my back when I cross the finish line, Mike.
So...
Did you watch the finale of *Finding Fame* last night?
You'll never believe who won.
No spoilers, Destiny.
It's fine. I don't watch it.

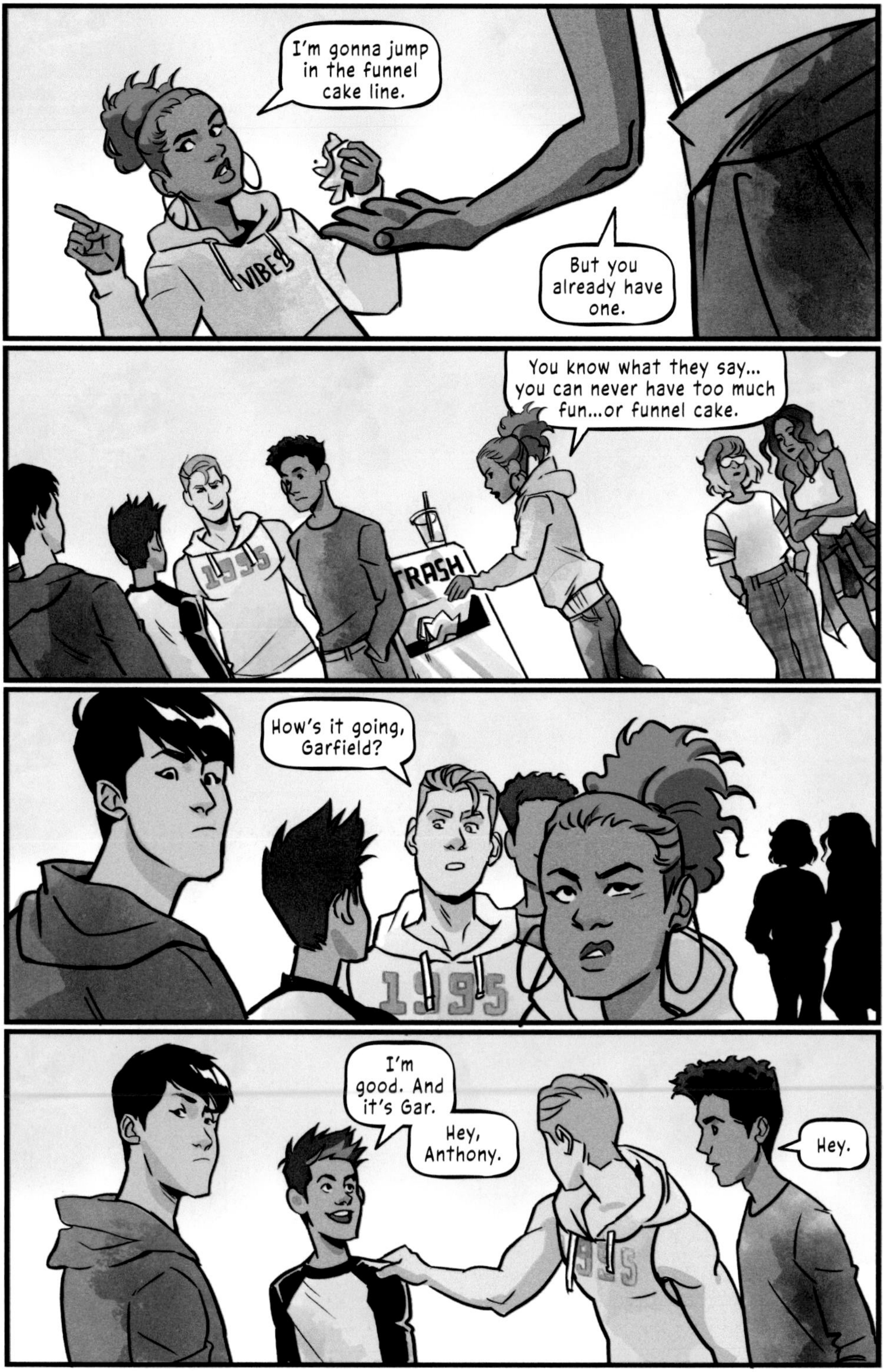
I'm gonna jump in the funnel cake line.
But you already have one.
You know what they say... you can never have too much fun...or funnel cake.
TRASH
VIBES
1995
How's it going, Garfield?
I'm good. And it's Gar.
Hey, Anthony.
Hey.

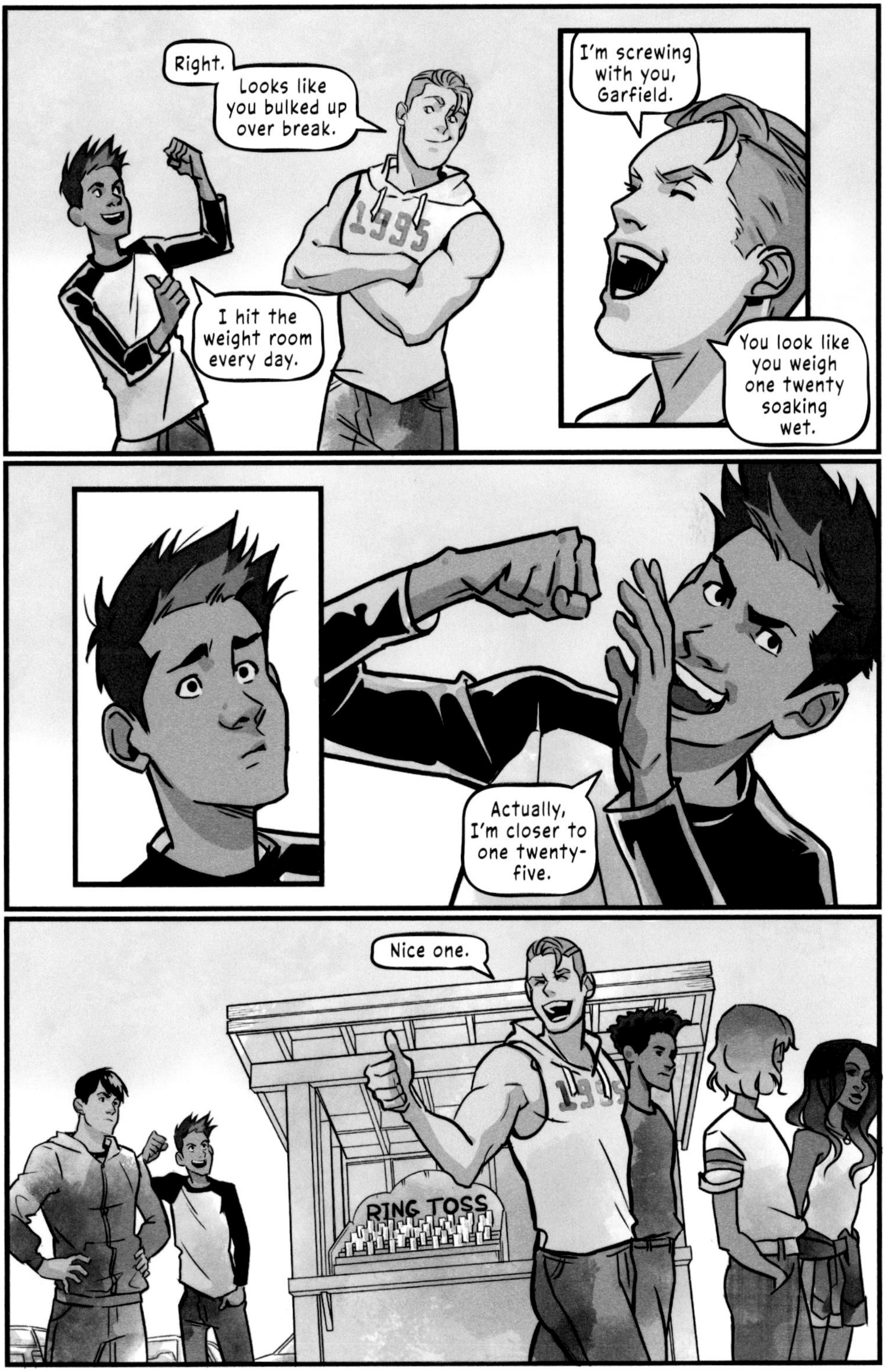
Right.
Looks like you bulked up over break.
I hit the weight room every day.
I'm screwing with you, Garfield.
You look like you weigh one twenty soaking wet.
Actually, I'm closer to one twenty-five.
Nice one.
RING TOSS

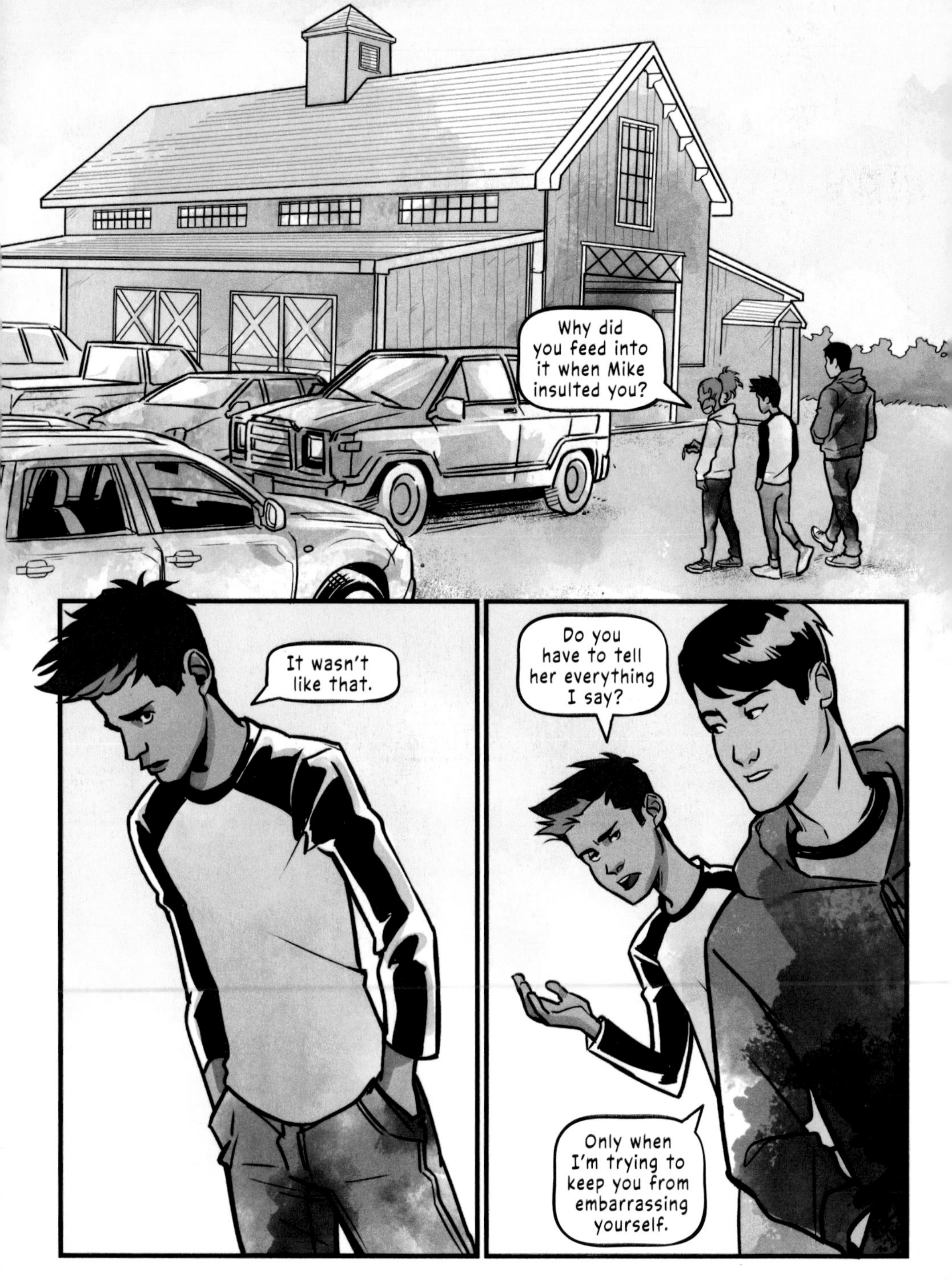
Why did you feed into it when Mike insulted you?
It wasn't like that.
Do you have to tell her everything I say?
Only when I'm trying to keep you from embarrassing yourself.

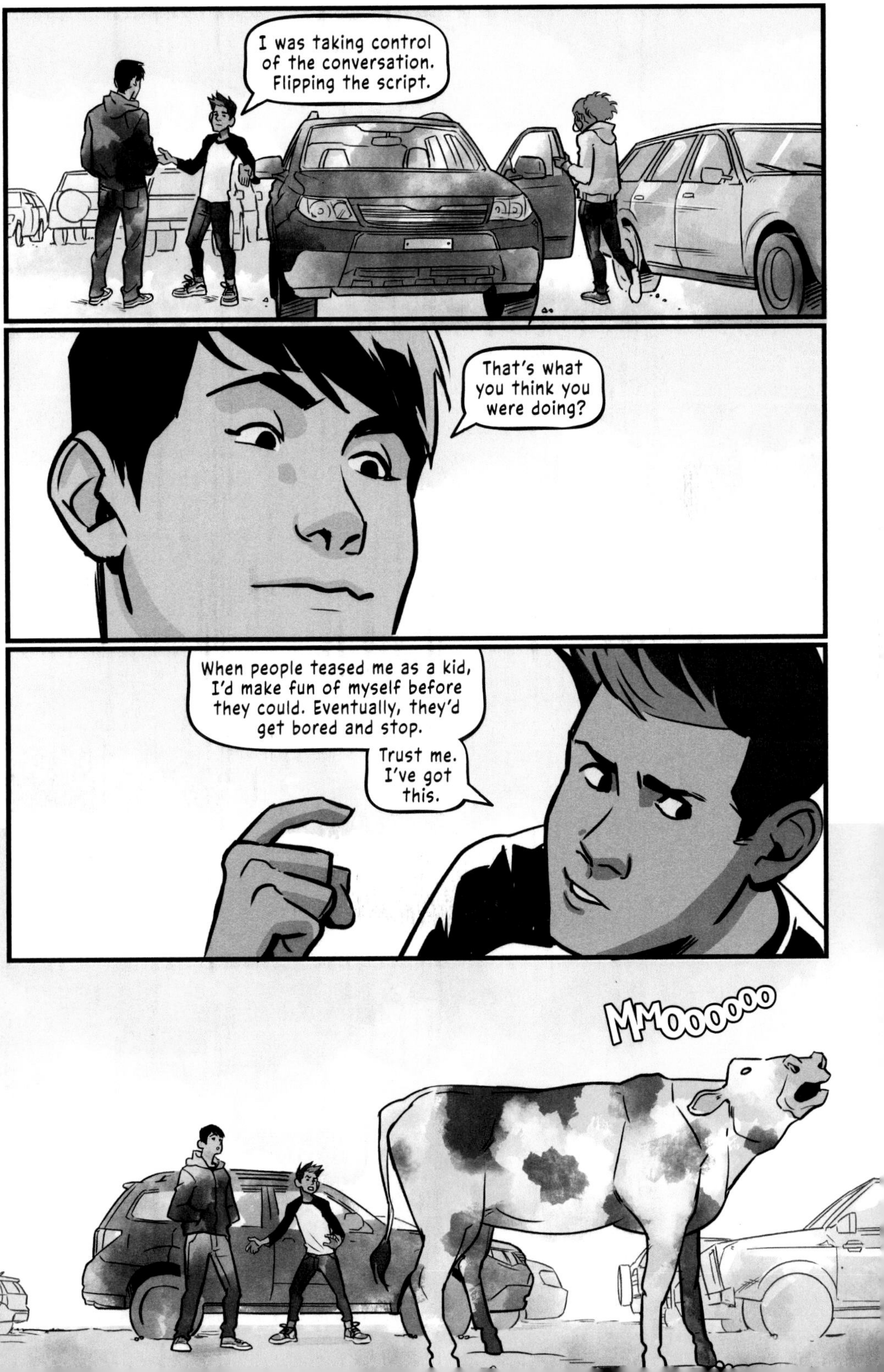
I was taking control of the conversation. Flipping the script.
That's what you think you were doing?
When people teased me as a kid, I'd make fun of myself before they could. Eventually, they'd get bored and stop.
Trust me. I've got this.
MMOOOOOO

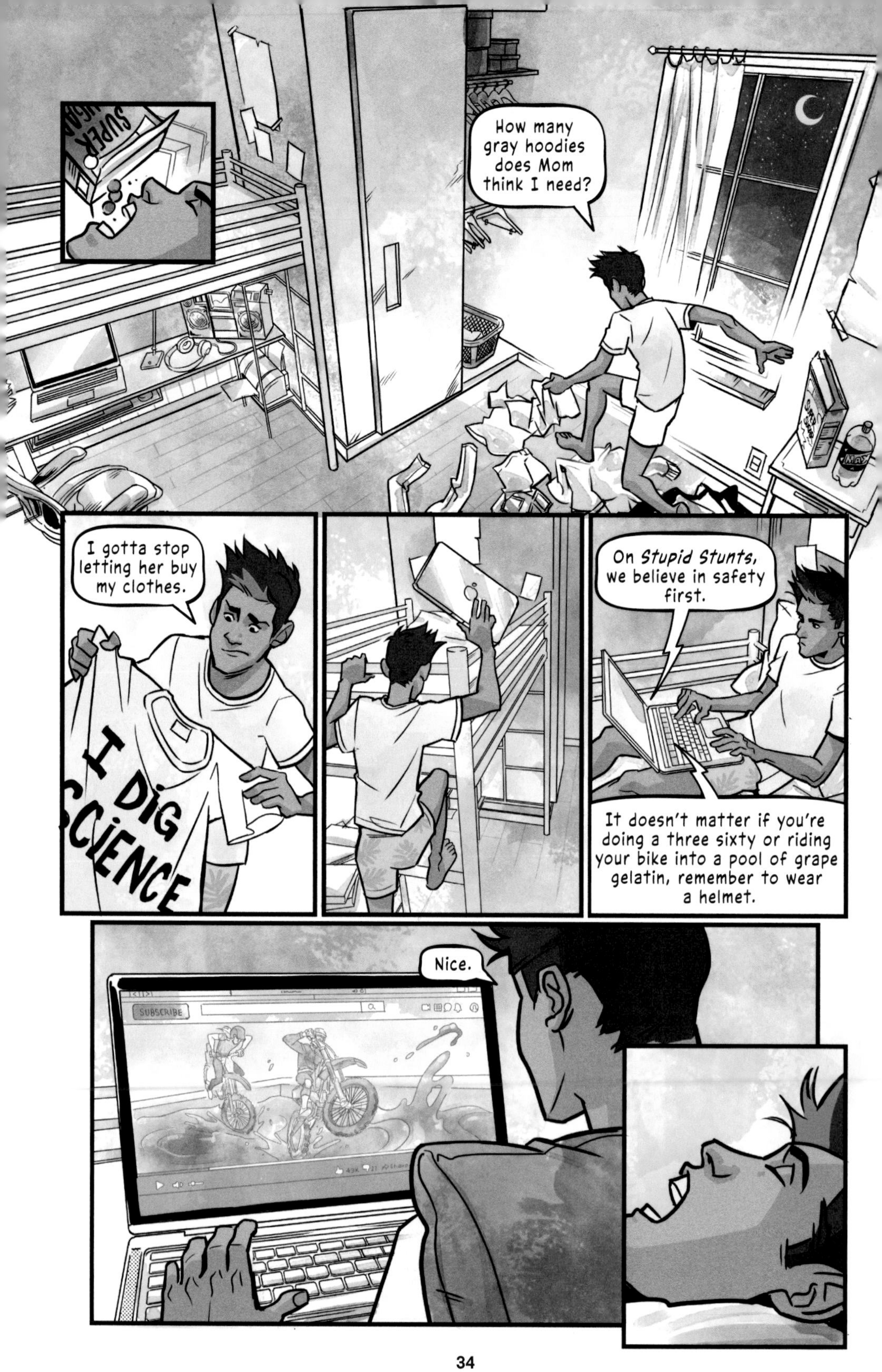
How many gray hoodies does Mom think I need?
I gotta stop letting her buy my clothes.
I DIG SCIENCE
On *Stupid Stunts*, we believe in safety first.
It doesn't matter if you're doing a three sixty or riding your bike into a pool of grape gelatin, remember to wear a helmet.
Nice.
SUBSCRIBE

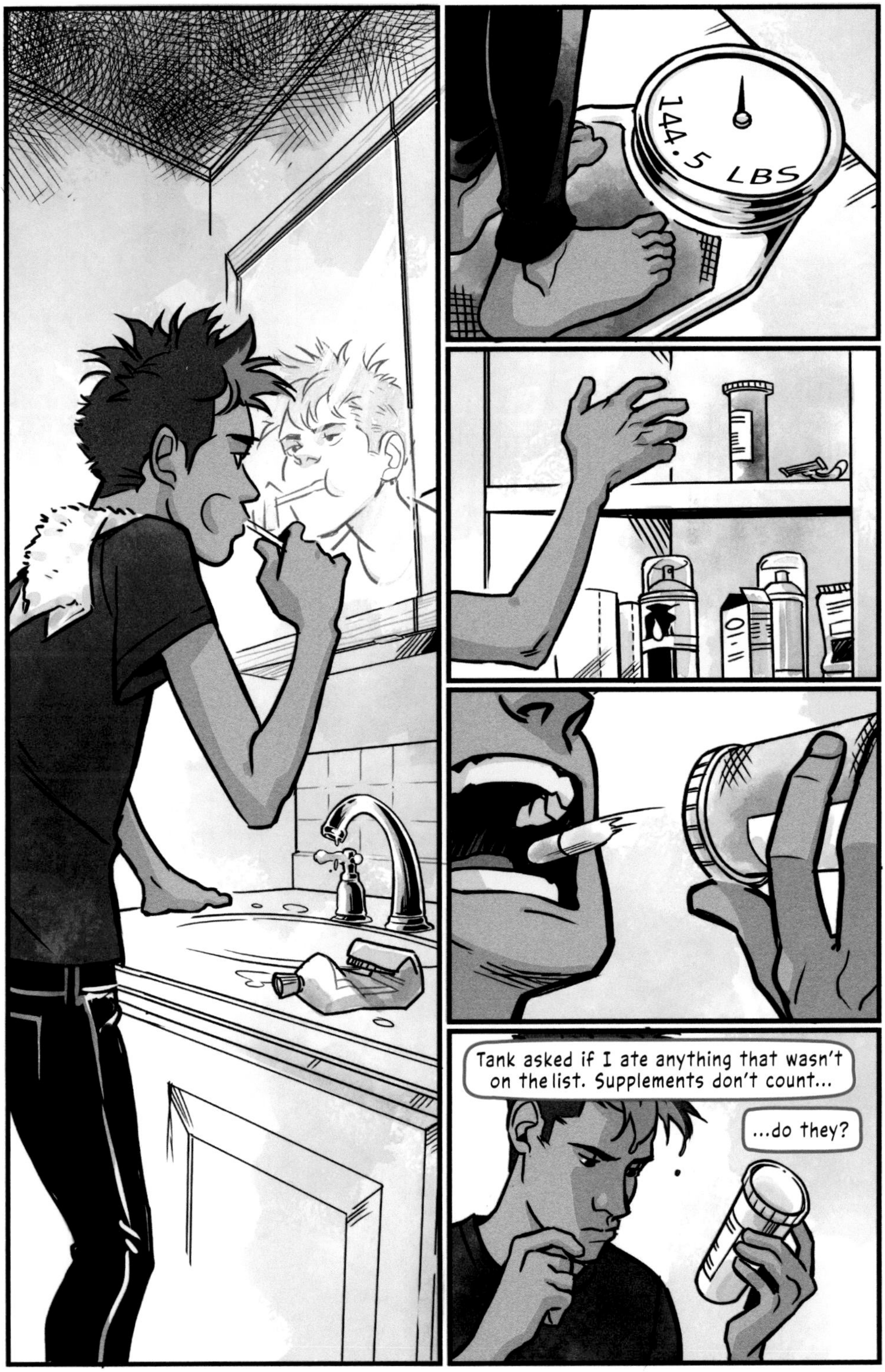
144.5 LBS
Tank asked if I ate anything that wasn't on the list. Supplements don't count...
...do they?

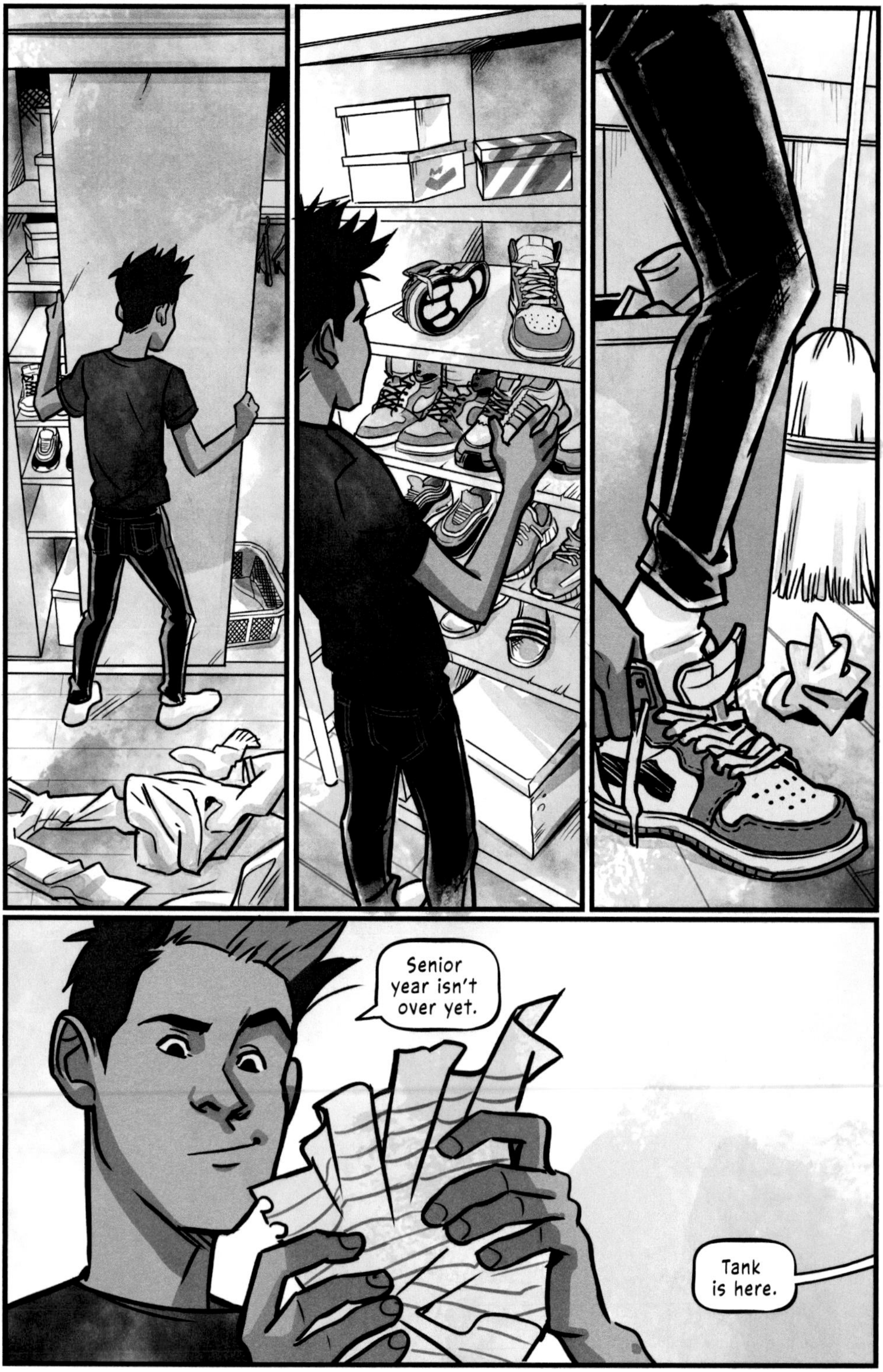
Senior year isn't over yet.
Tank is here.

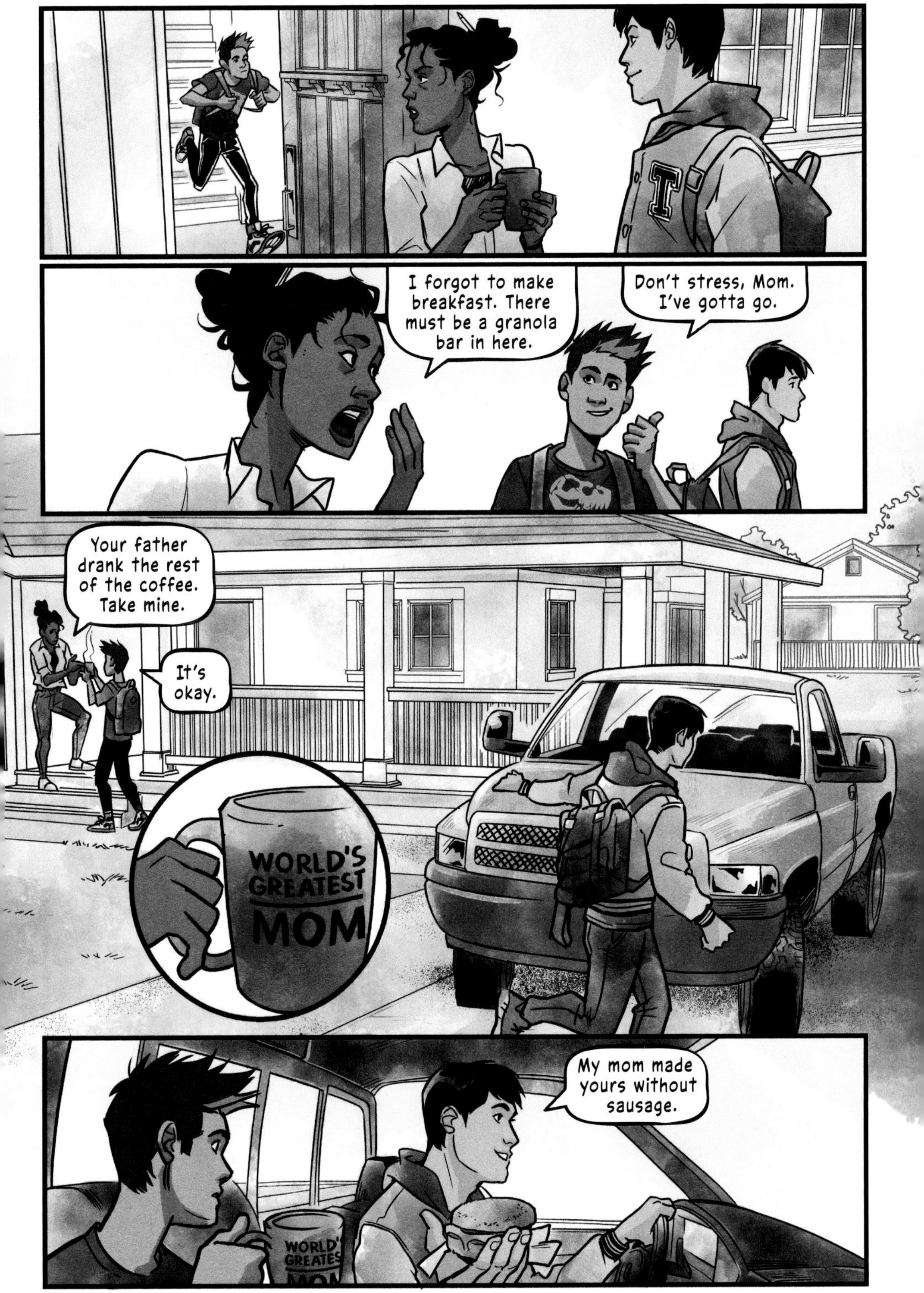
I forgot to make breakfast. There must be a granola bar in here.
Don't stress, Mom. I've gotta go.
Your father drank the rest of the coffee. Take mine.
It's okay.
WORLD'S GREATEST MOM
My mom made yours without sausage.
WORLD'S GREATES

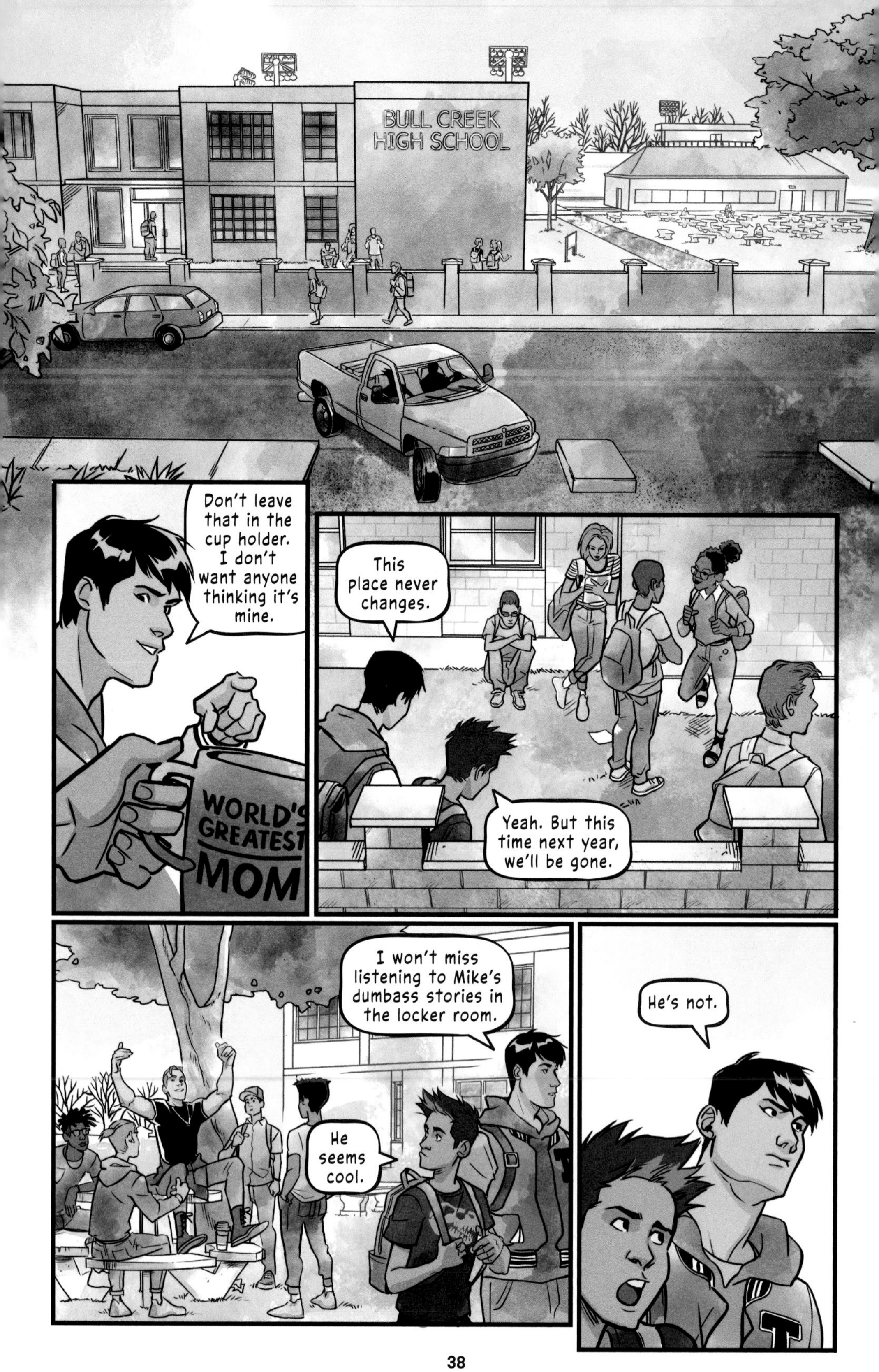
BULL CREEK
HIGH SCHOOL
Don't leave that in the cup holder. I don't want anyone thinking it's mine.
WORLD'S GREATEST MOM
This place never changes.
Yeah. But this time next year, we'll be gone.
I won't miss listening to Mike's dumbass stories in the locker room.
He seems cool.
He's not.

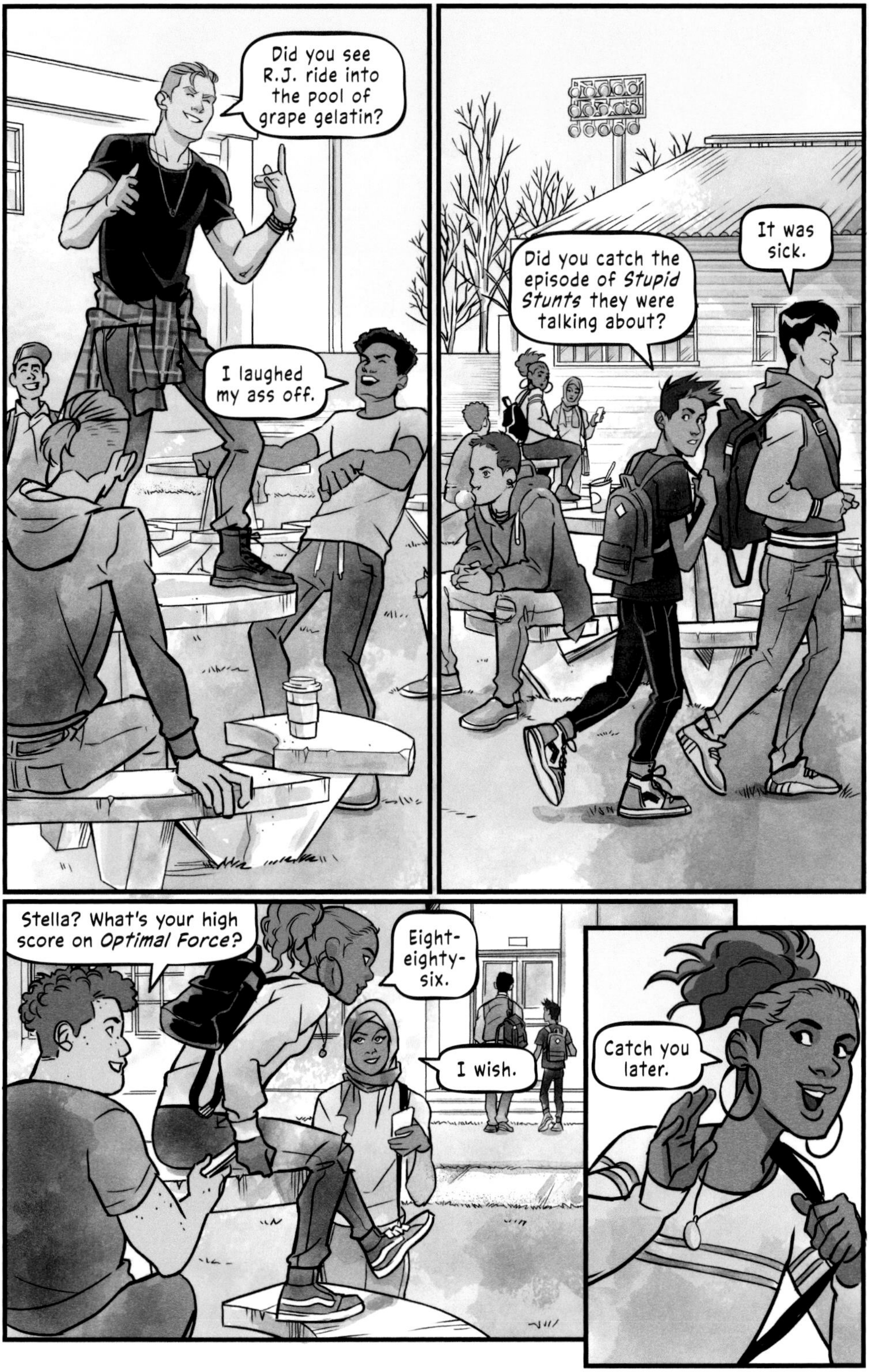
Did you see R.J. ride into the pool of grape gelatin?
I laughed my ass off.
Did you catch the episode of *Stupid Stunts* they were talking about?
It was sick.
Stella? What's your high score on *Optimal Force*?
Eight-eighty-six.
I wish.
Catch you later.

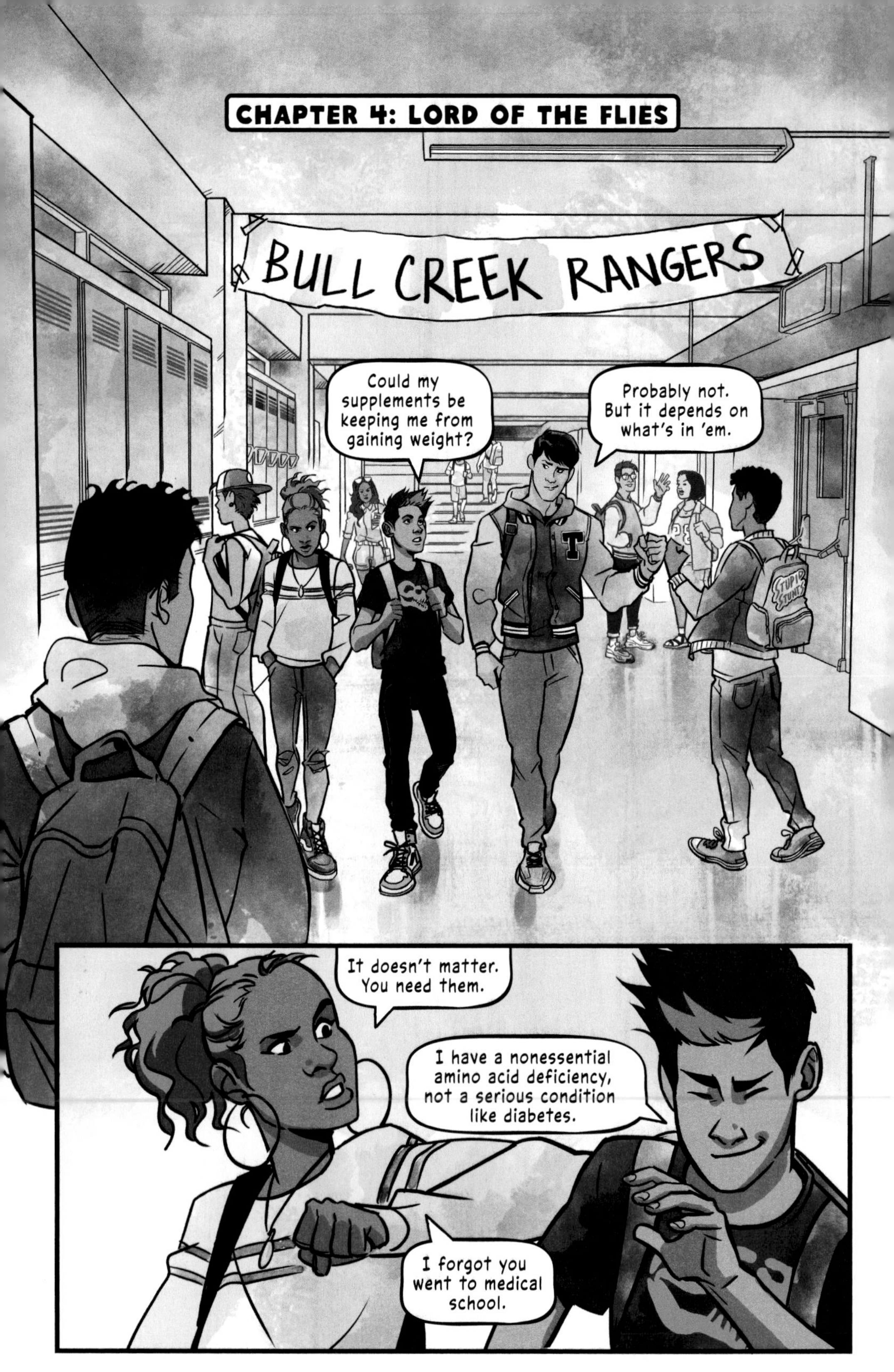
CHAPTER 4: LORD OF THE FLIES
BULL CREEK RANGERS
Could my supplements be keeping me from gaining weight?
Probably not. But it depends on what's in 'em.
It doesn't matter. You need them.
I have a nonessential amino acid deficiency, not a serious condition like diabetes.
I forgot you went to medical school.

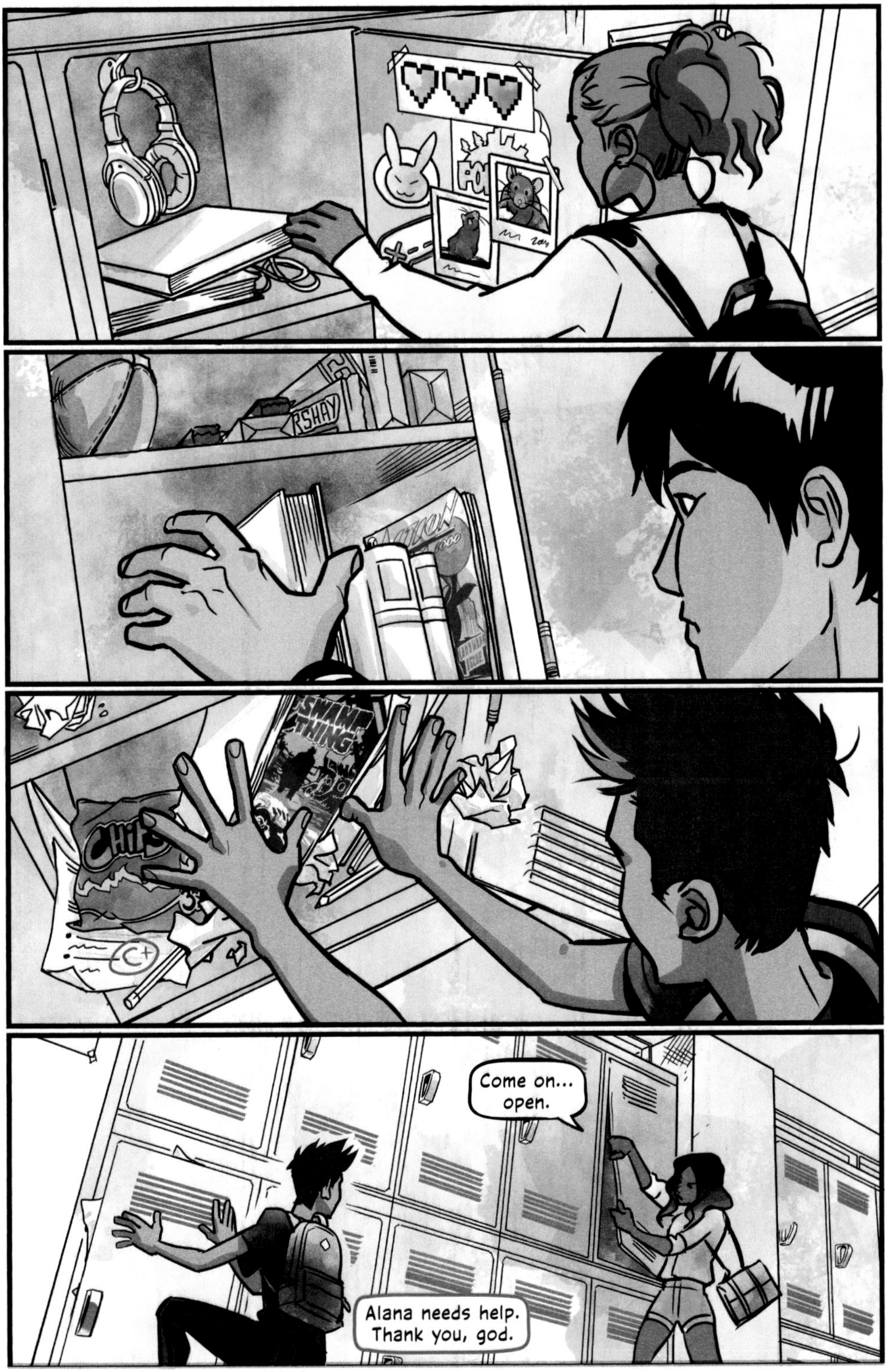
Come on... open.
Alana needs help. Thank you, god.

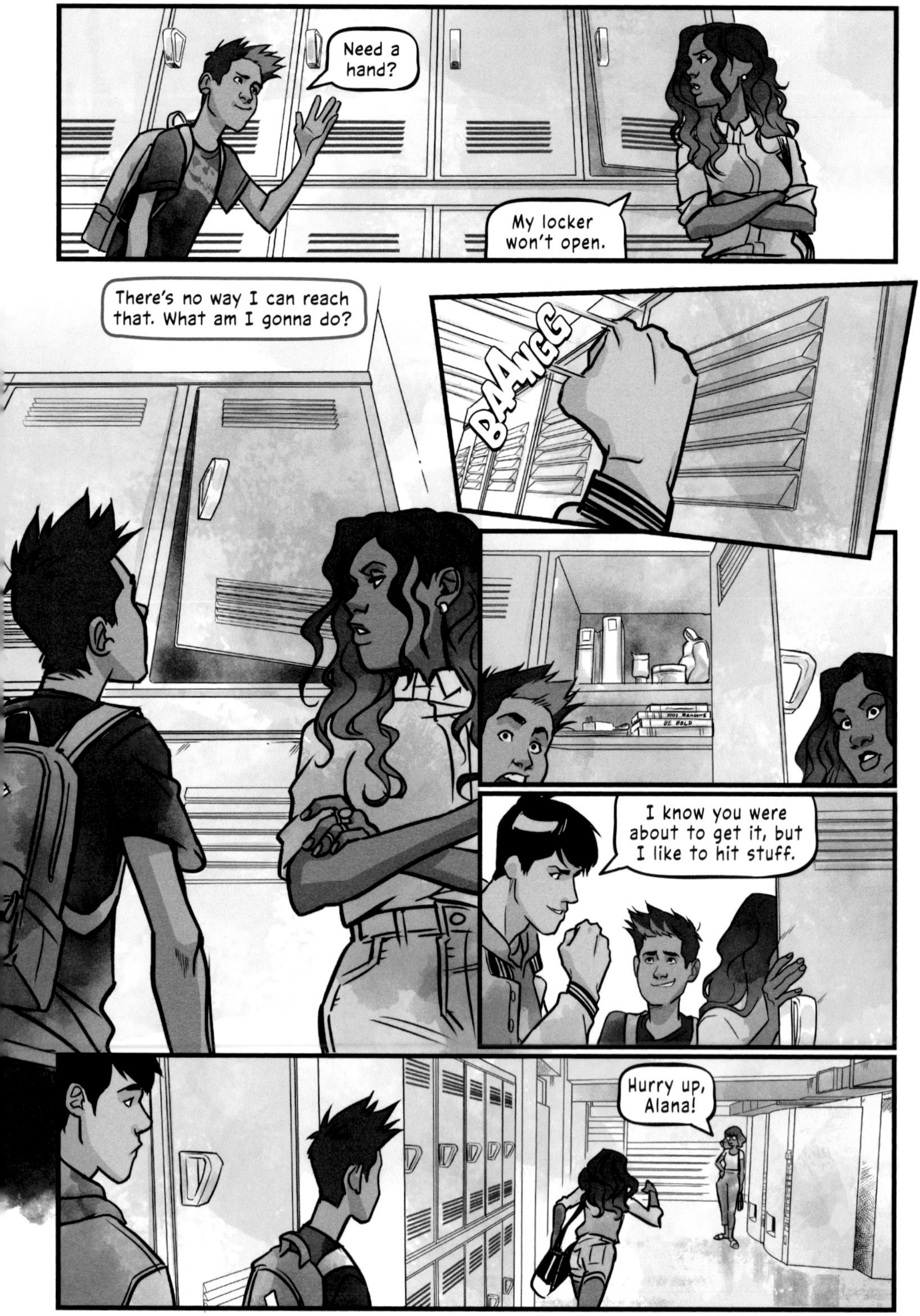
Need a hand?
My locker won't open.
There's no way I can reach that. What am I gonna do?
BAANGG
I know you were about to get it, but I like to hit stuff.
Hurry up, Alana!

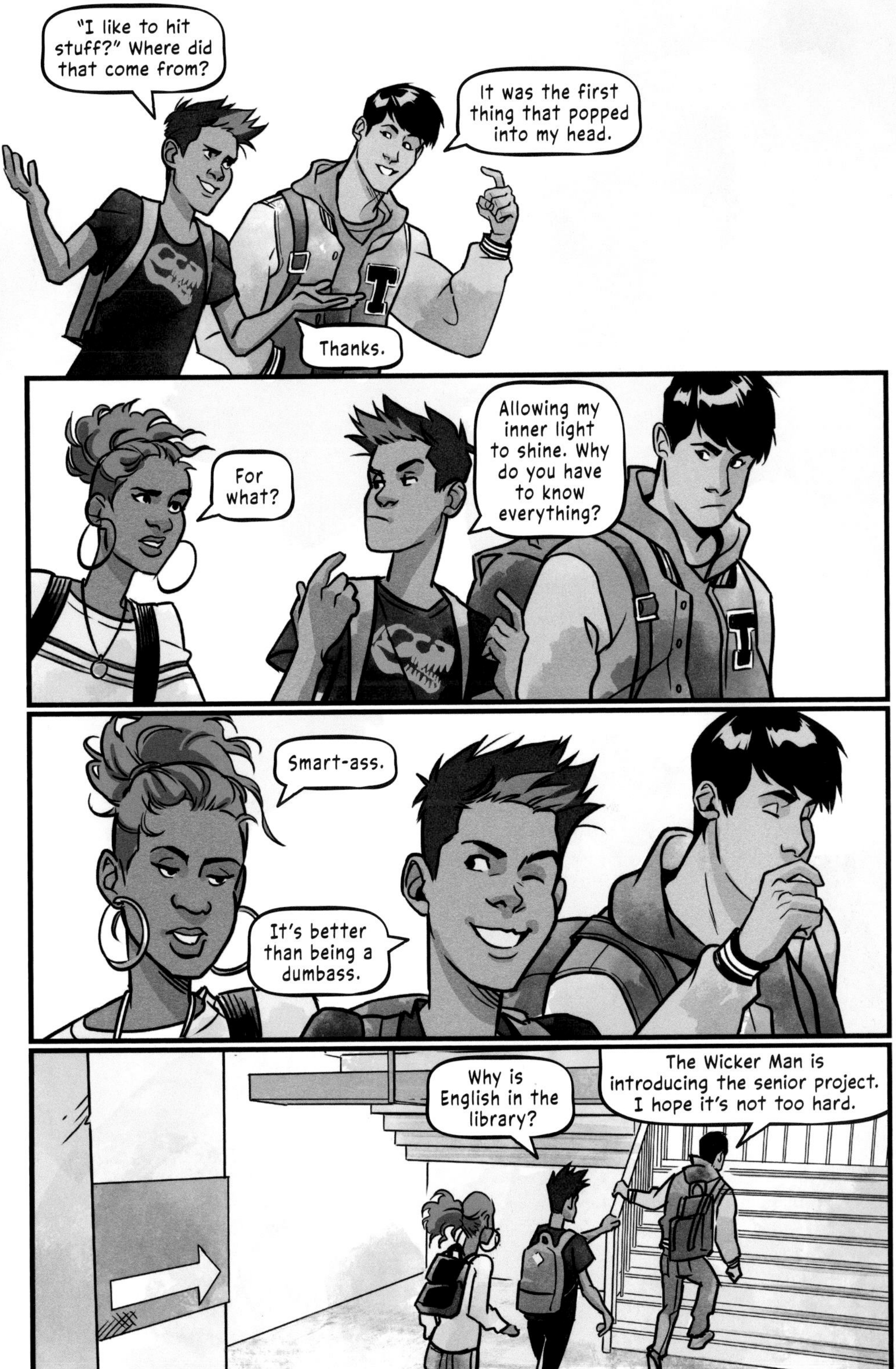
"I like to hit stuff?" Where did that come from?
It was the first thing that popped into my head.
Thanks.
For what?
Allowing my inner light to shine. Why do you have to know everything?
Smart-ass.
It's better than being a dumbass.
Why is English in the library?
The Wicker Man is introducing the senior project. I hope it's not too hard.

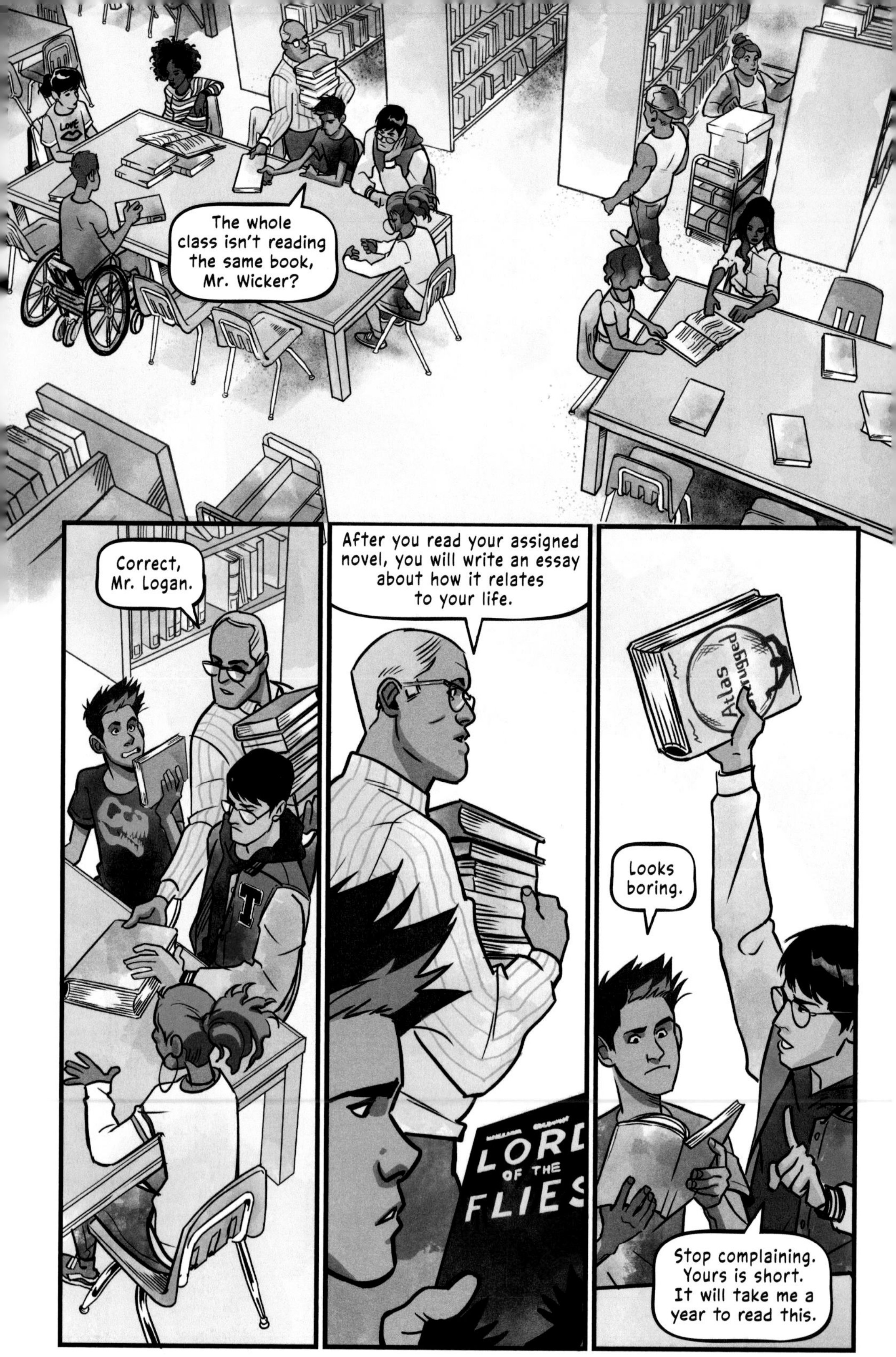
The whole class isn't reading the same book, Mr. Wicker?
Correct, Mr. Logan.
After you read your assigned novel, you will write an essay about how it relates to your life.
LORD OF THE FLIES
Atlas Shrugged
Looks boring.
Stop complaining. Yours is short. It will take me a year to read this.

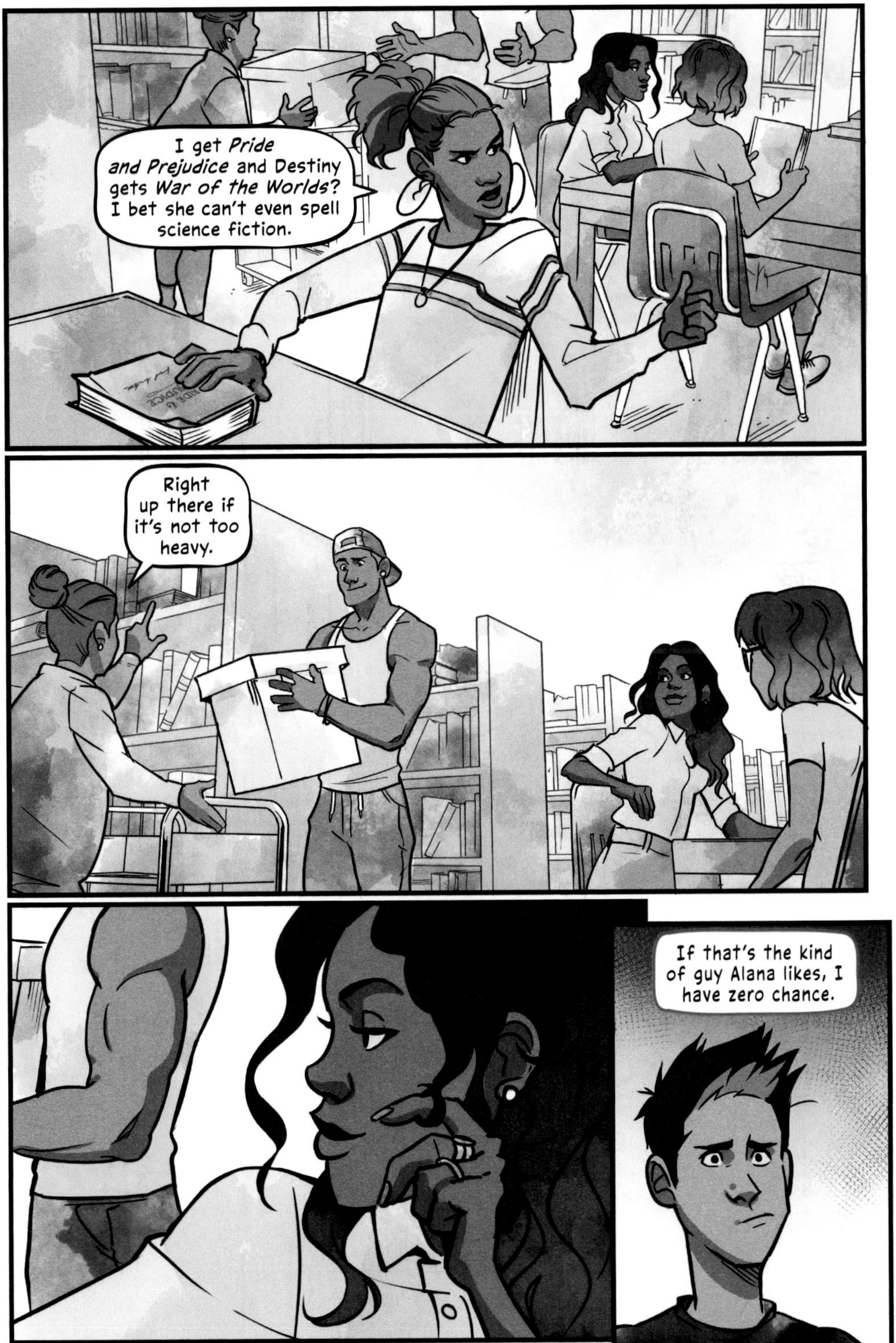
I get *Pride and Prejudice* and Destiny gets *War of the Worlds*? I bet she can't even spell science fiction.
Right up there if it's not too heavy.
If that's the kind of guy Alana likes, I have zero chance.

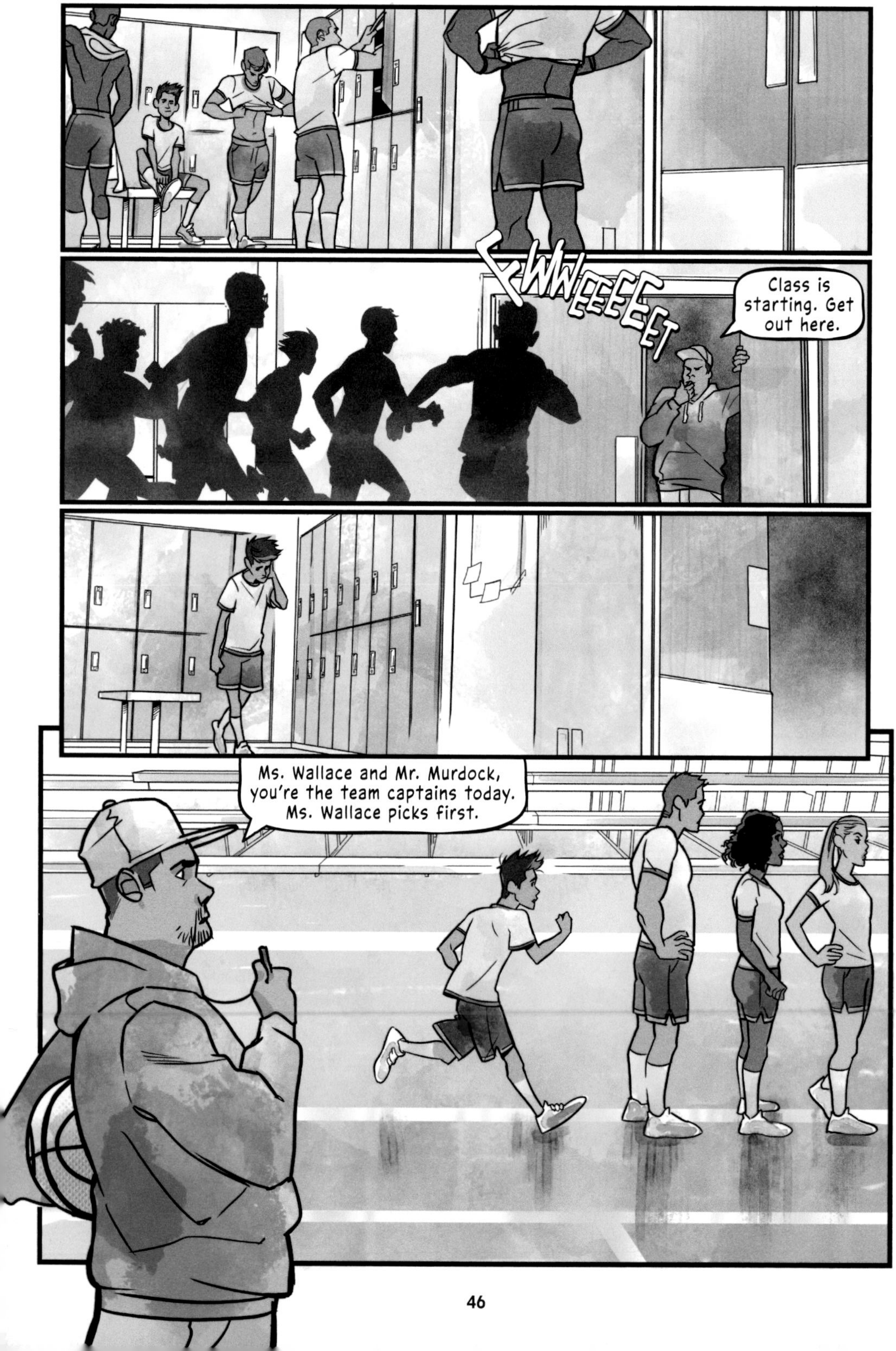
FWWEEEEEET
Class is starting. Get out here.
Ms. Wallace and Mr. Murdock, you're the team captains today. Ms. Wallace picks first.

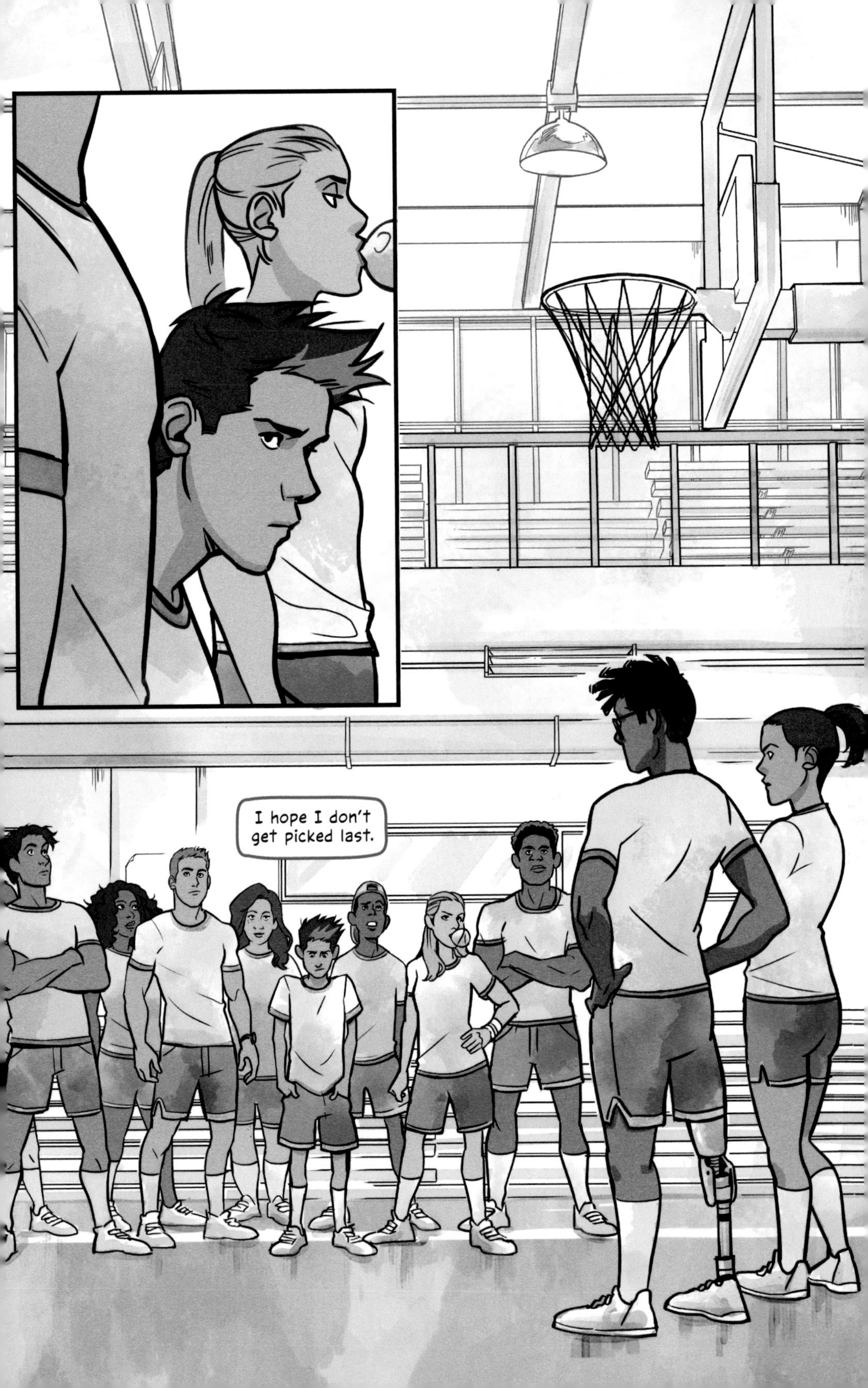
I hope I don't get picked last.

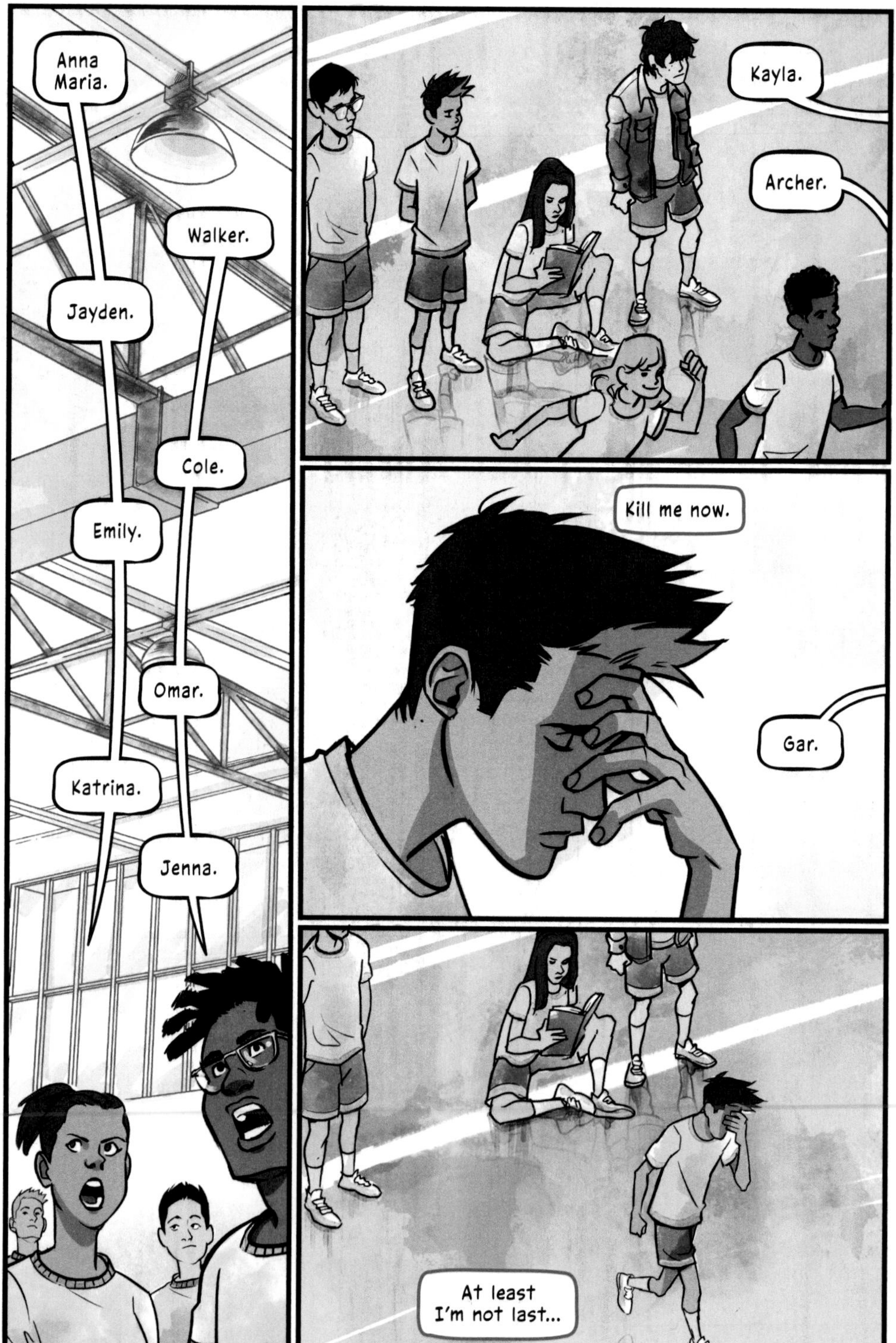
Anna Maria.
Walker.
Jayden.
Cole.
Emily.
Omar.
Katrina.
Jenna.
Kayla.
Archer.
Kill me now.
Gar.
At least I'm not last...

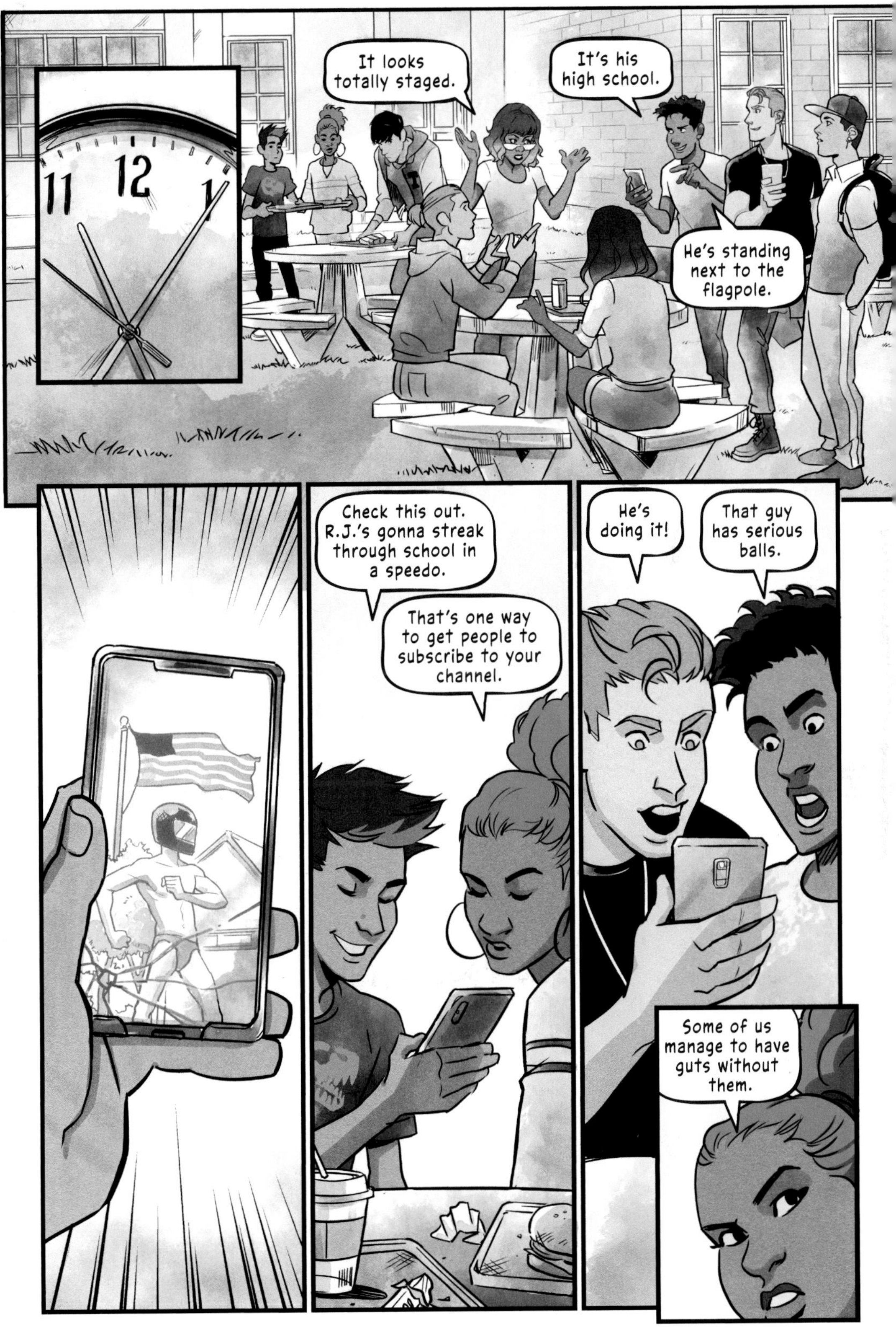
11
12
1
It looks totally staged.
It's his high school.
He's standing next to the flagpole.
Check this out. R.J.'s gonna streak through school in a speedo.
That's one way to get people to subscribe to your channel.
He's doing it!
That guy has serious balls.
Some of us manage to have guts without them.

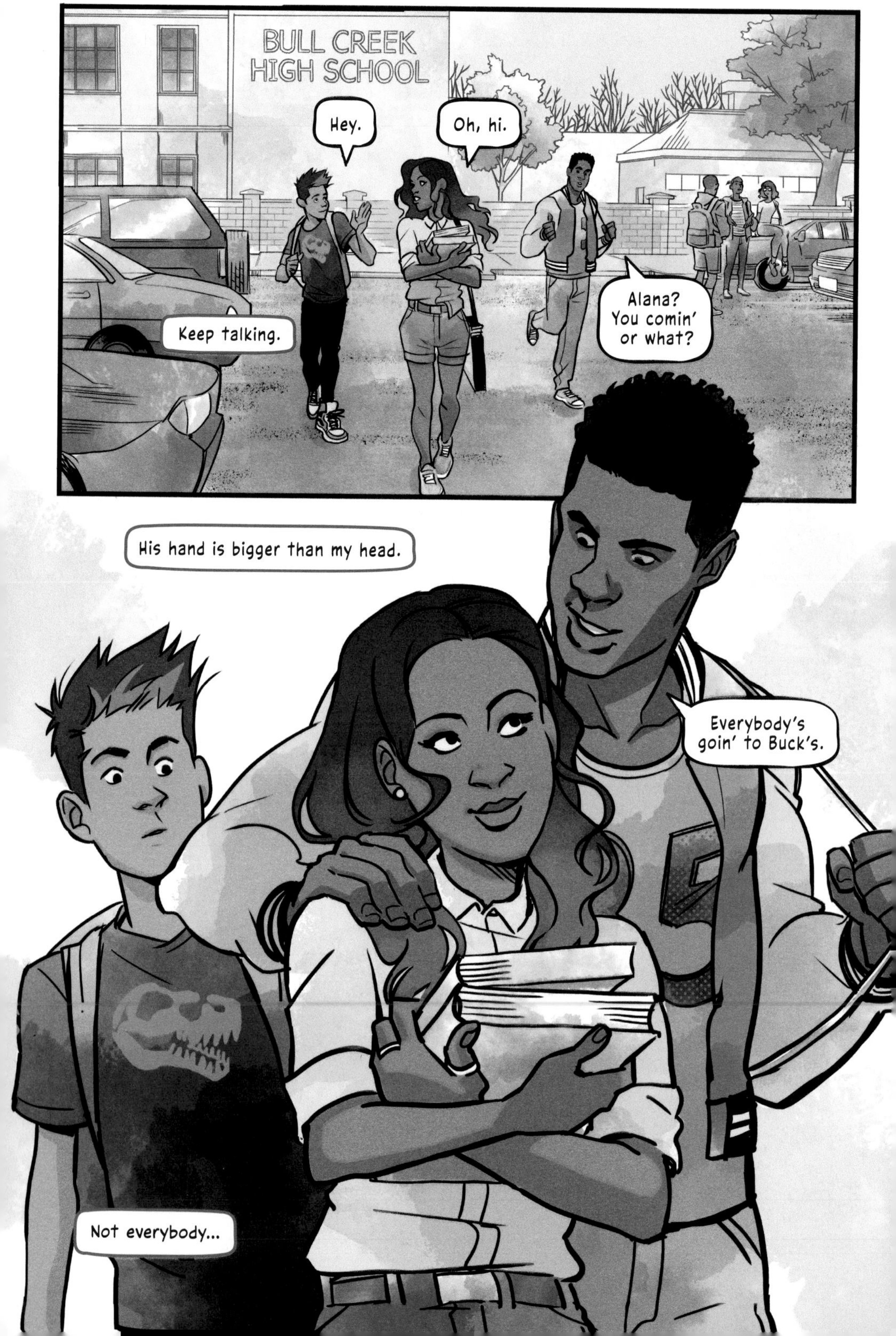
BULL CREEK HIGH SCHOOL
Hey.
Oh, hi.
Keep talking.
Alana? You comin' or what?
His hand is bigger than my head.
Everybody's goin' to Buck's.
Not everybody...

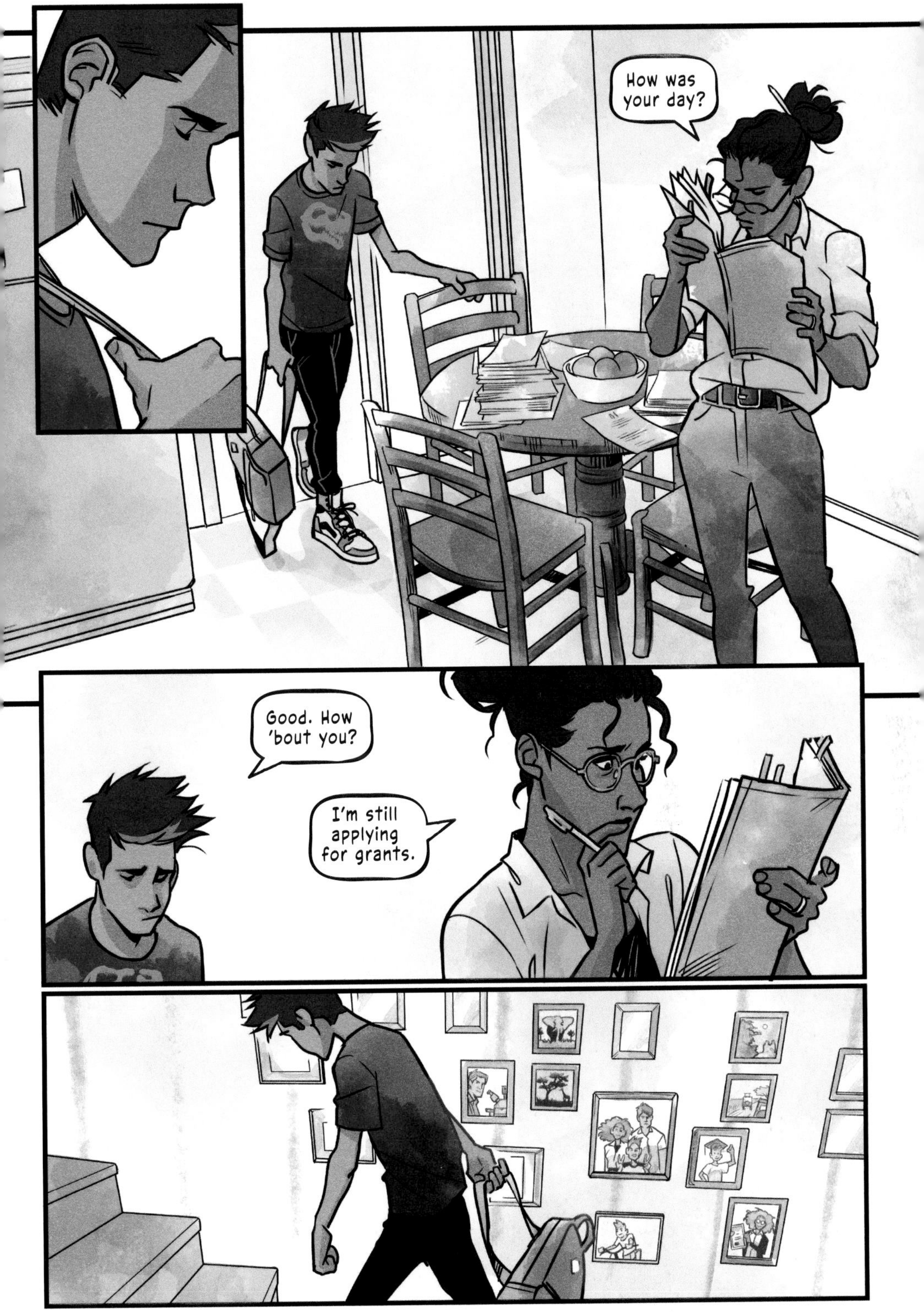
How was your day?
Good. How 'bout you?
I'm still applying for grants.

CHAPTER 5: UNKNOWN VARIABLE

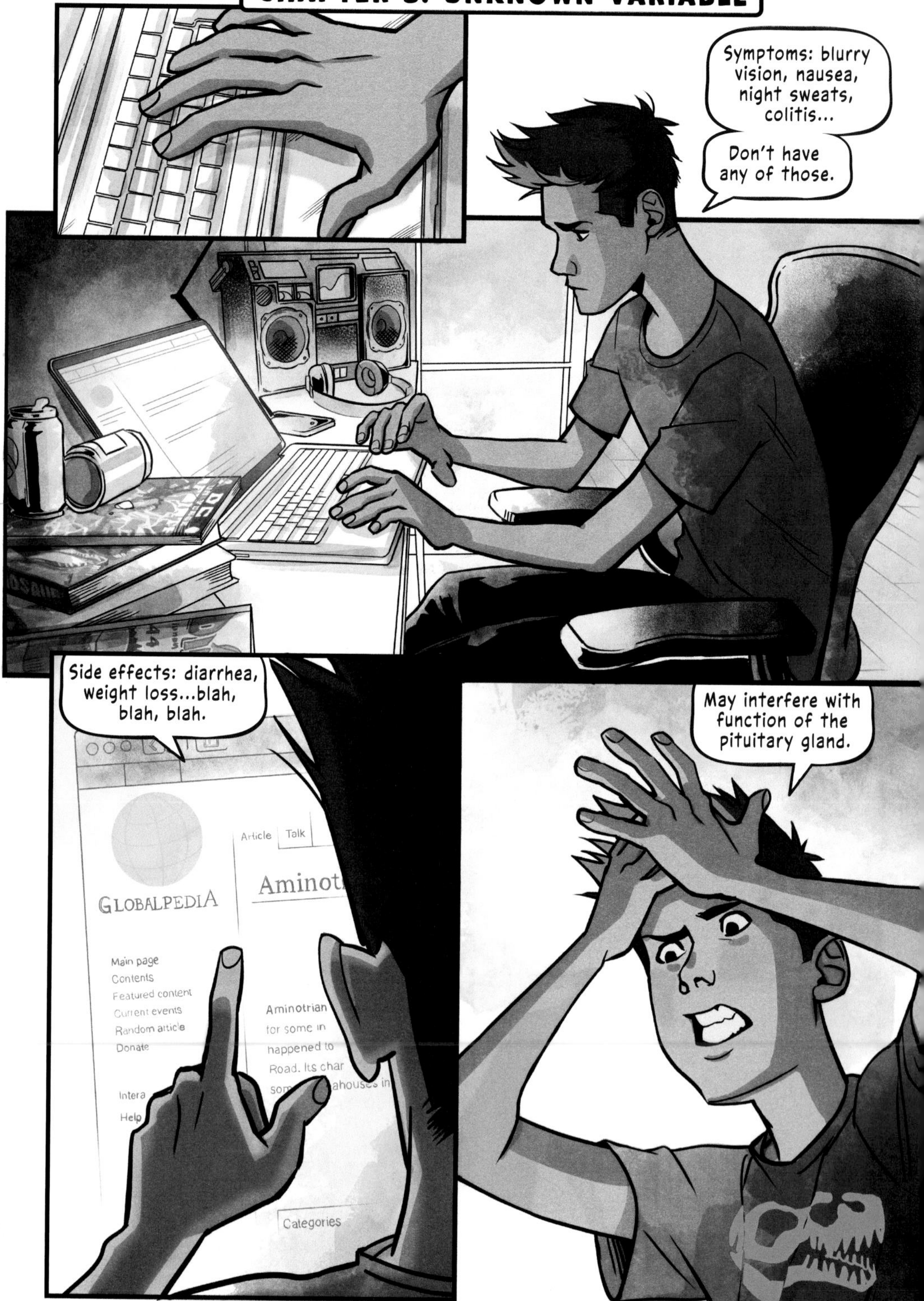

Symptoms: blurry vision, nausea, night sweats, colitis...
Don't have any of those.
Side effects: diarrhea, weight loss...blah, blah, blah.
GLOBALPEDIA
Article
Talk
Main page
Contents
Featured content
Current events
Random article
Donate
Categories
May interfere with function of the pituitary gland.

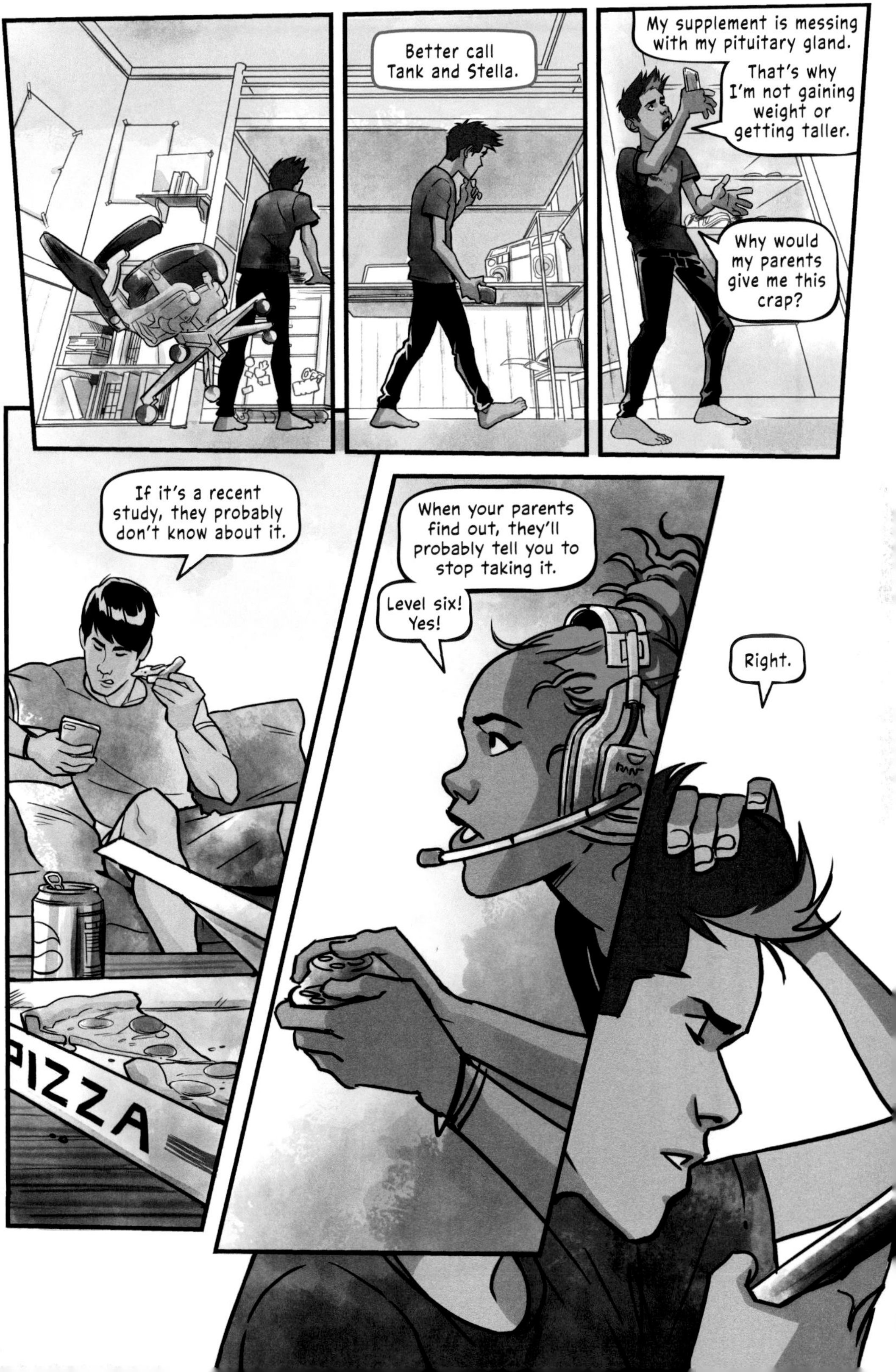
Better call Tank and Stella.
My supplement is messing with my pituitary gland.
That's why I'm not gaining weight or getting taller.
Why would my parents give me this crap?
If it's a recent study, they probably don't know about it.
When your parents find out, they'll probably tell you to stop taking it.
Level six! Yes!
Right.
PIZZA

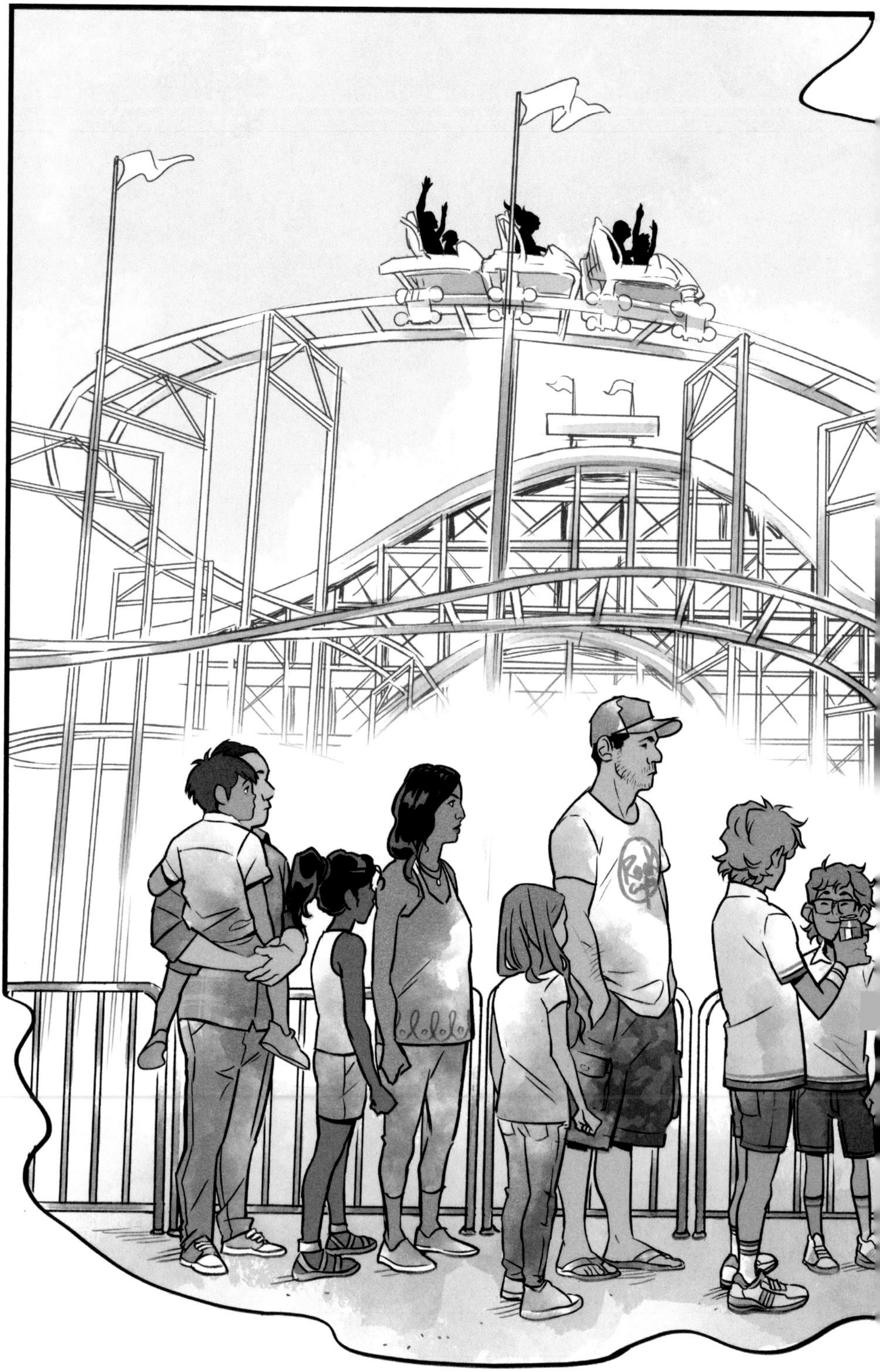

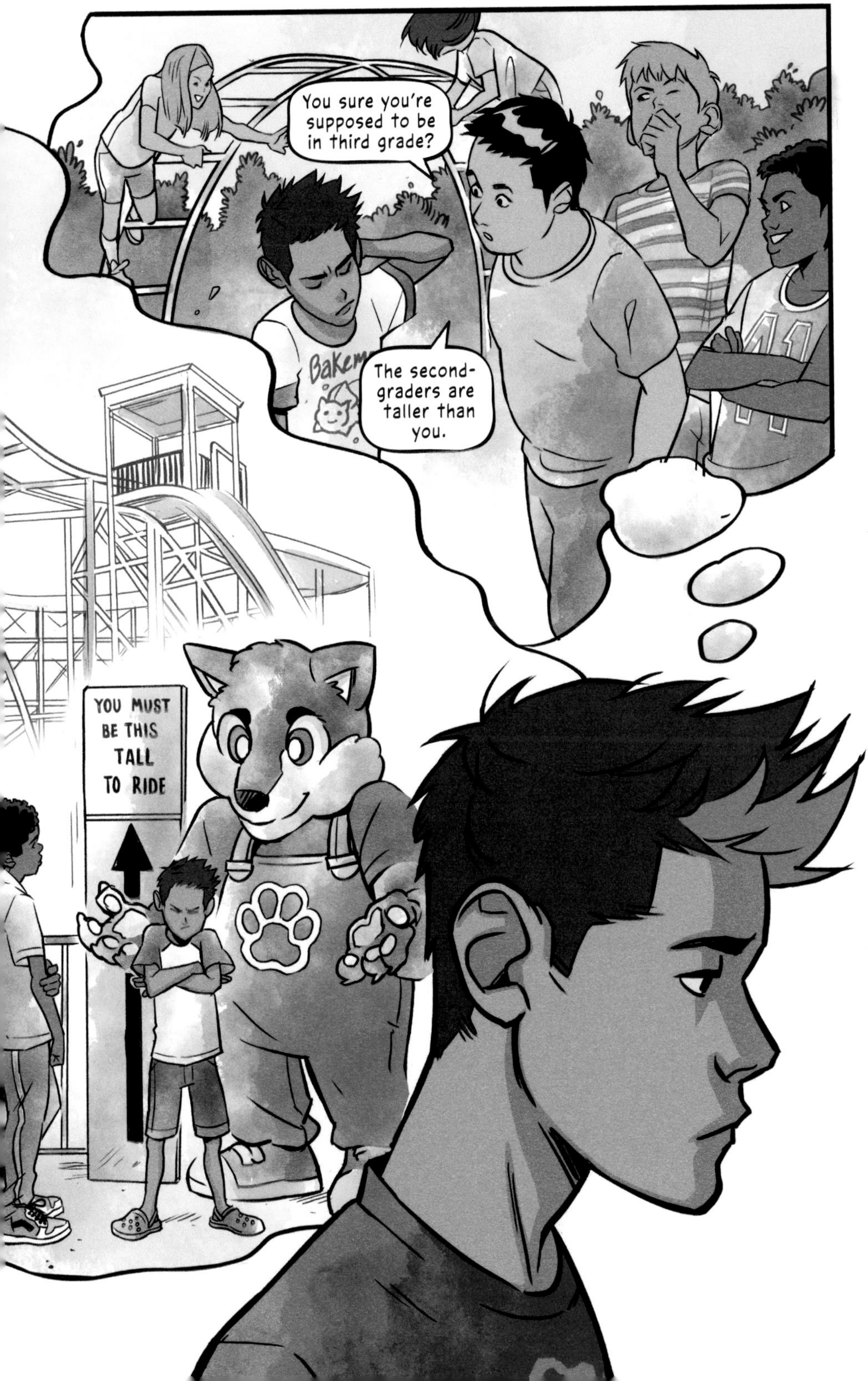
You sure you're supposed to be in third grade?
The second-graders are taller than you.
YOU MUST BE THIS TALL TO RIDE

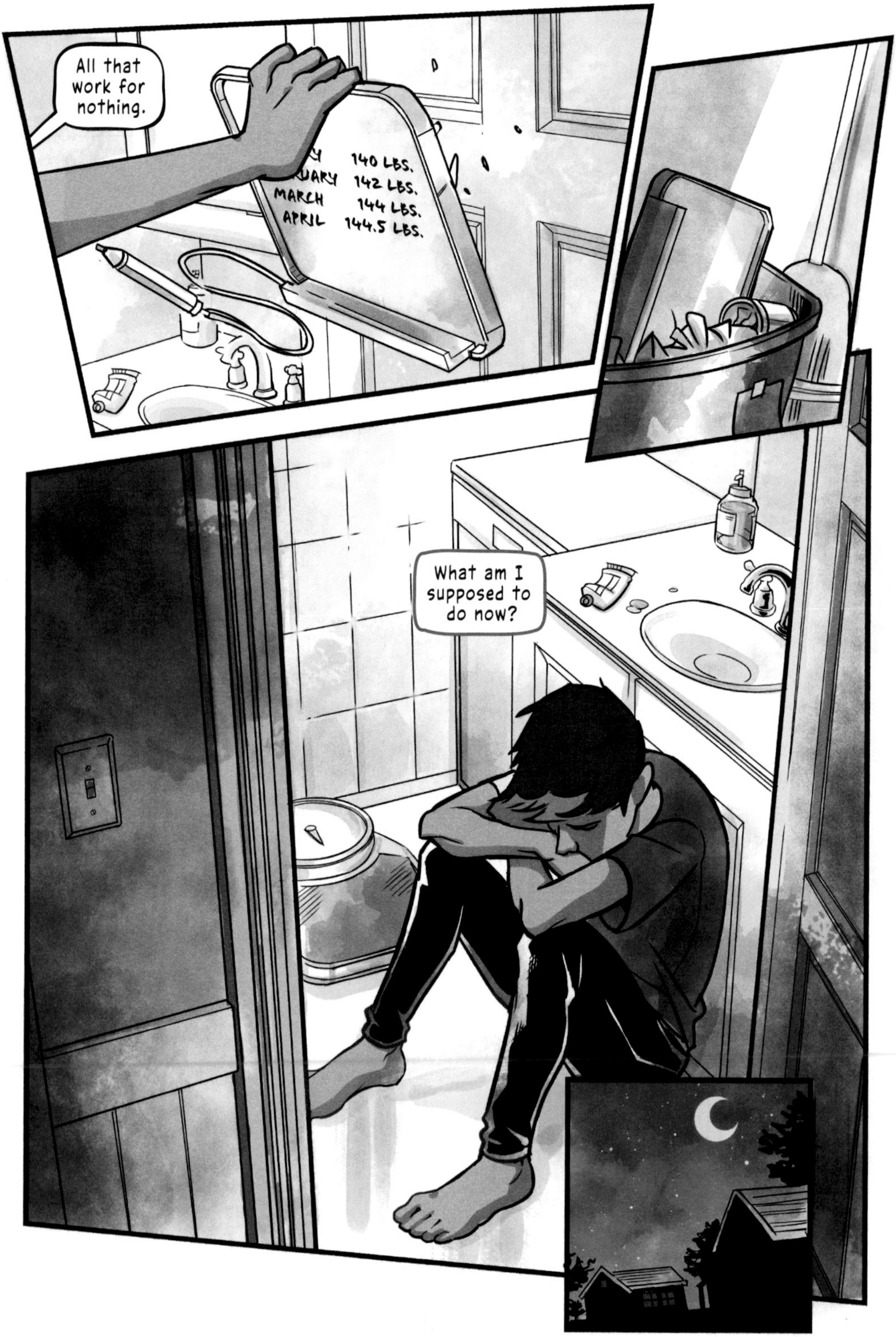
All that work for nothing.
140 LBS.
142 LBS.
MARCH 144 LBS.
APRIL 144.5 LBS.
What am I supposed to do now?

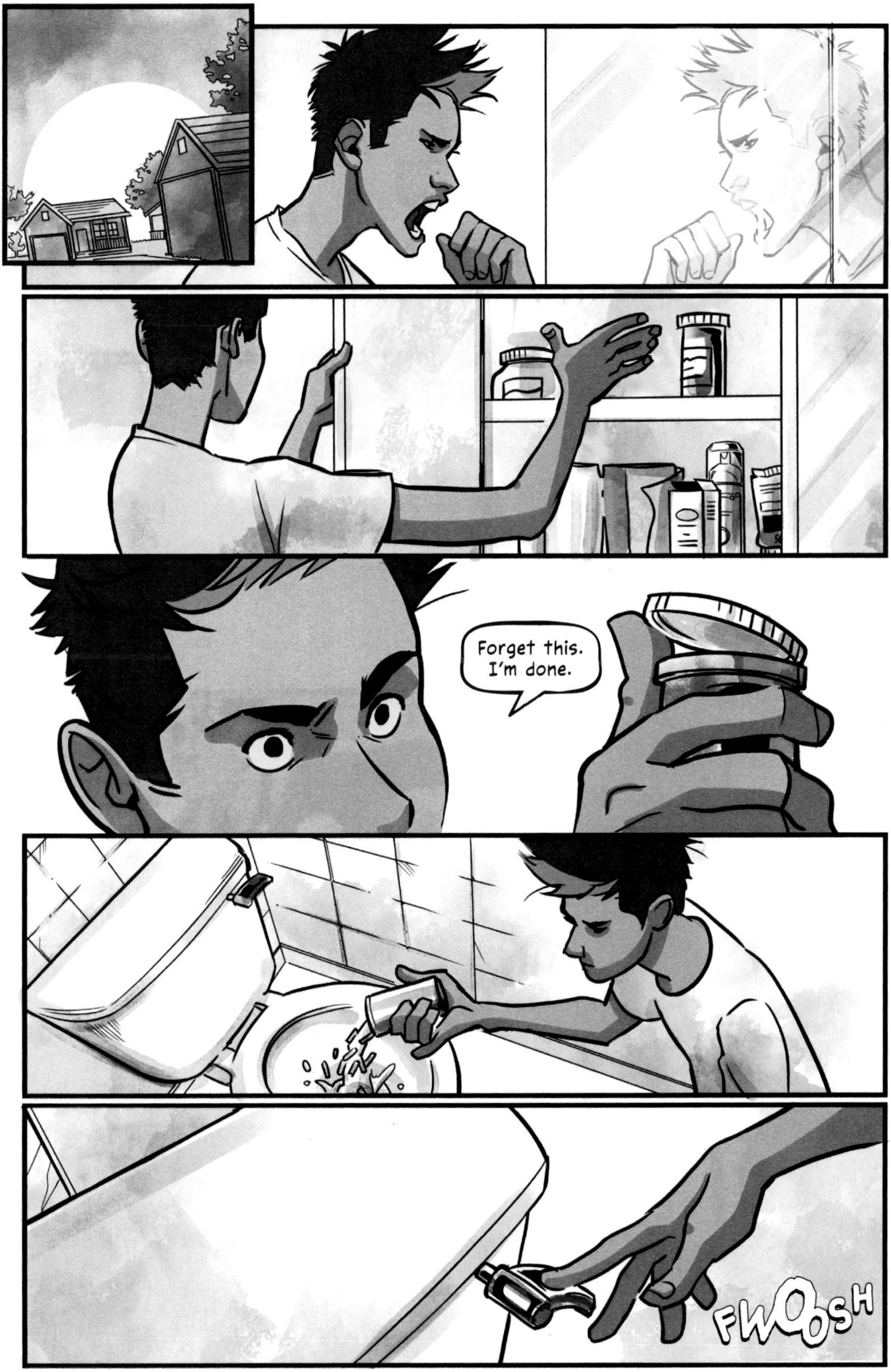
Forget this. I'm done.
FWOOSH

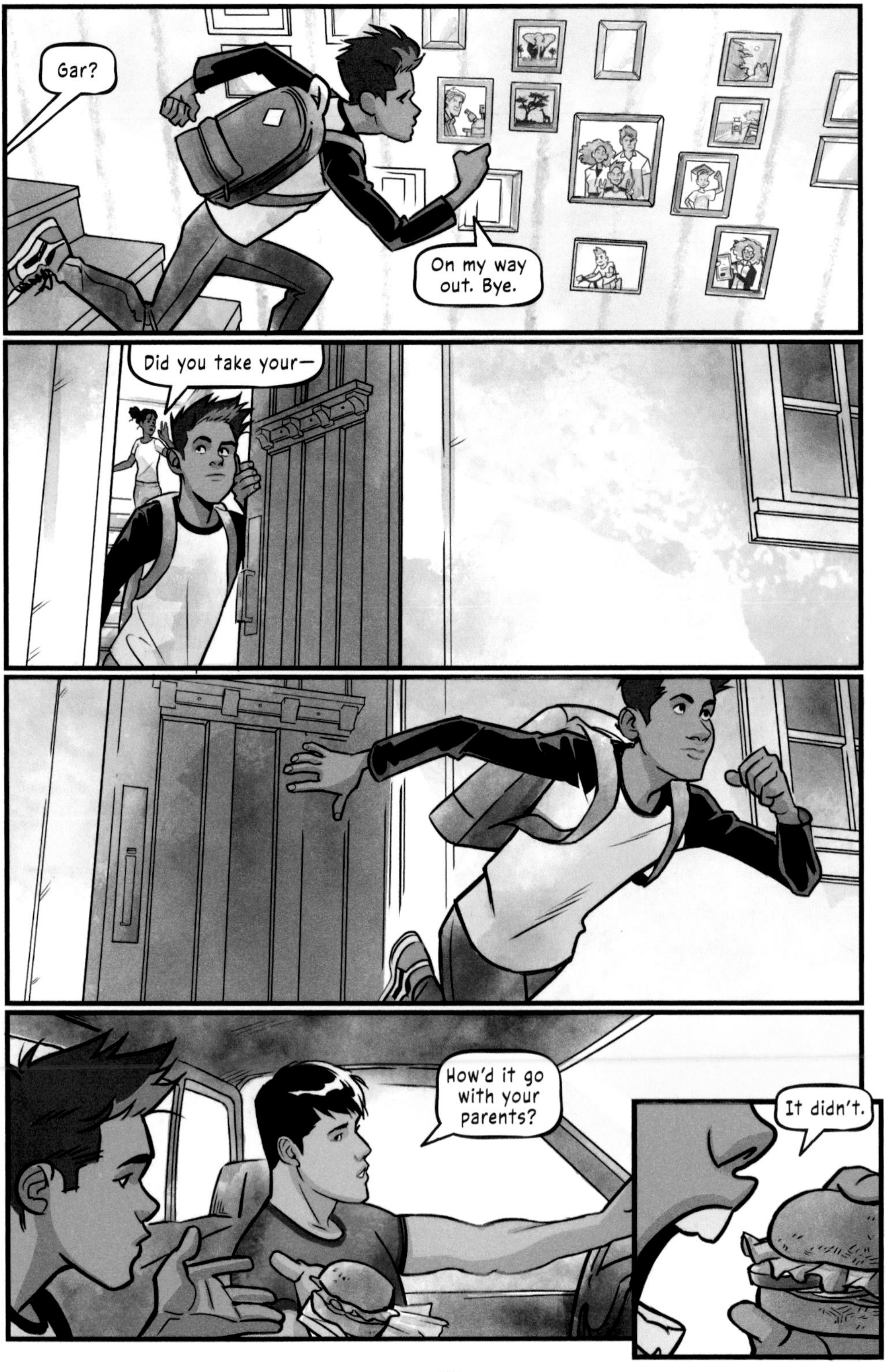
Gar?
On my way out. Bye.
Did you take your—
How'd it go with your parents?
It didn't.

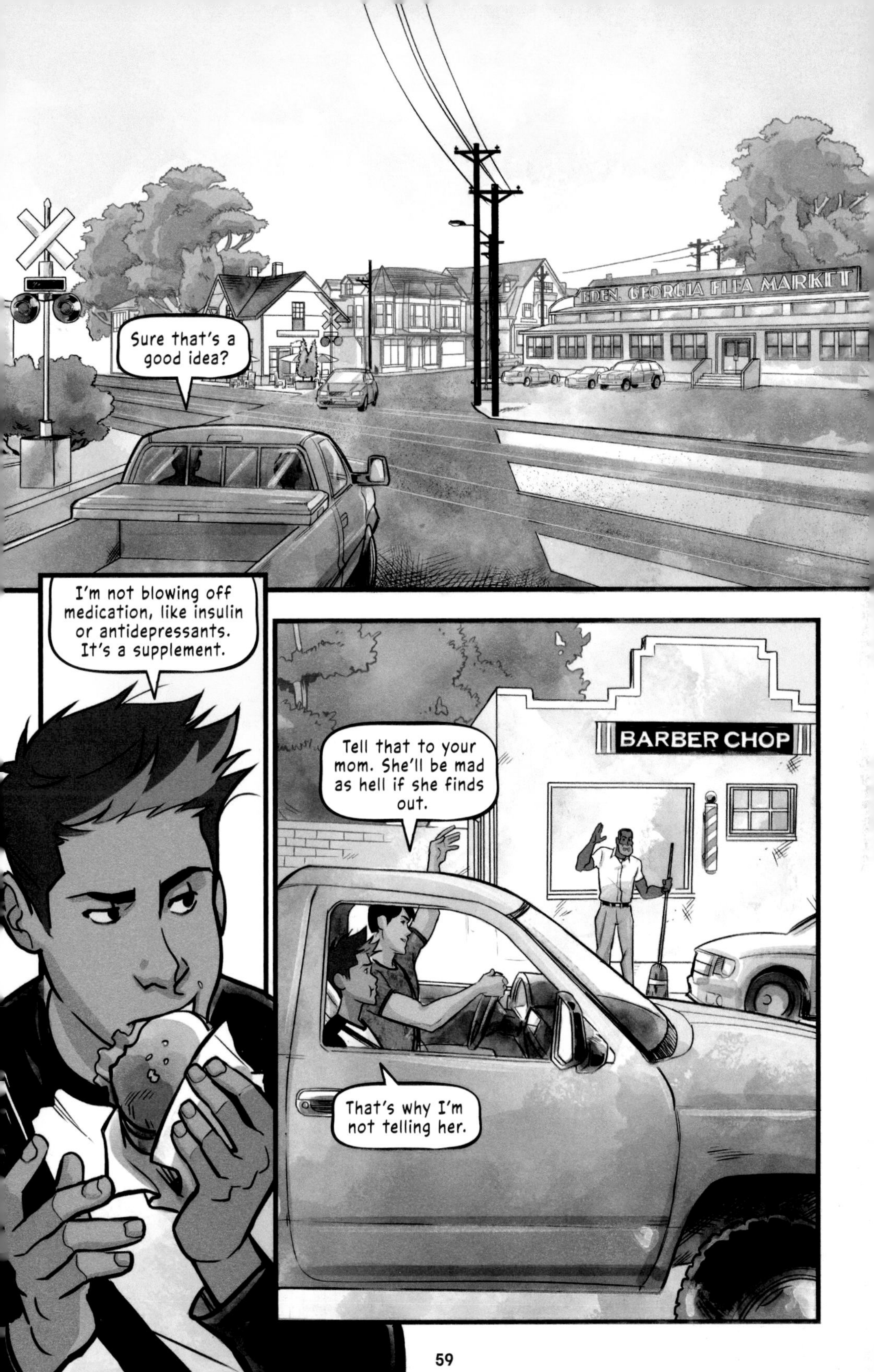
EDEN, GEORGIA FLEA MARKET
Sure that's a good idea?
I'm not blowing off medication, like insulin or antidepressants. It's a supplement.
BARBER CHOP
Tell that to your mom. She'll be mad as hell if she finds out.
That's why I'm not telling her.

CHAPTER 6: CAROLINA REAPER

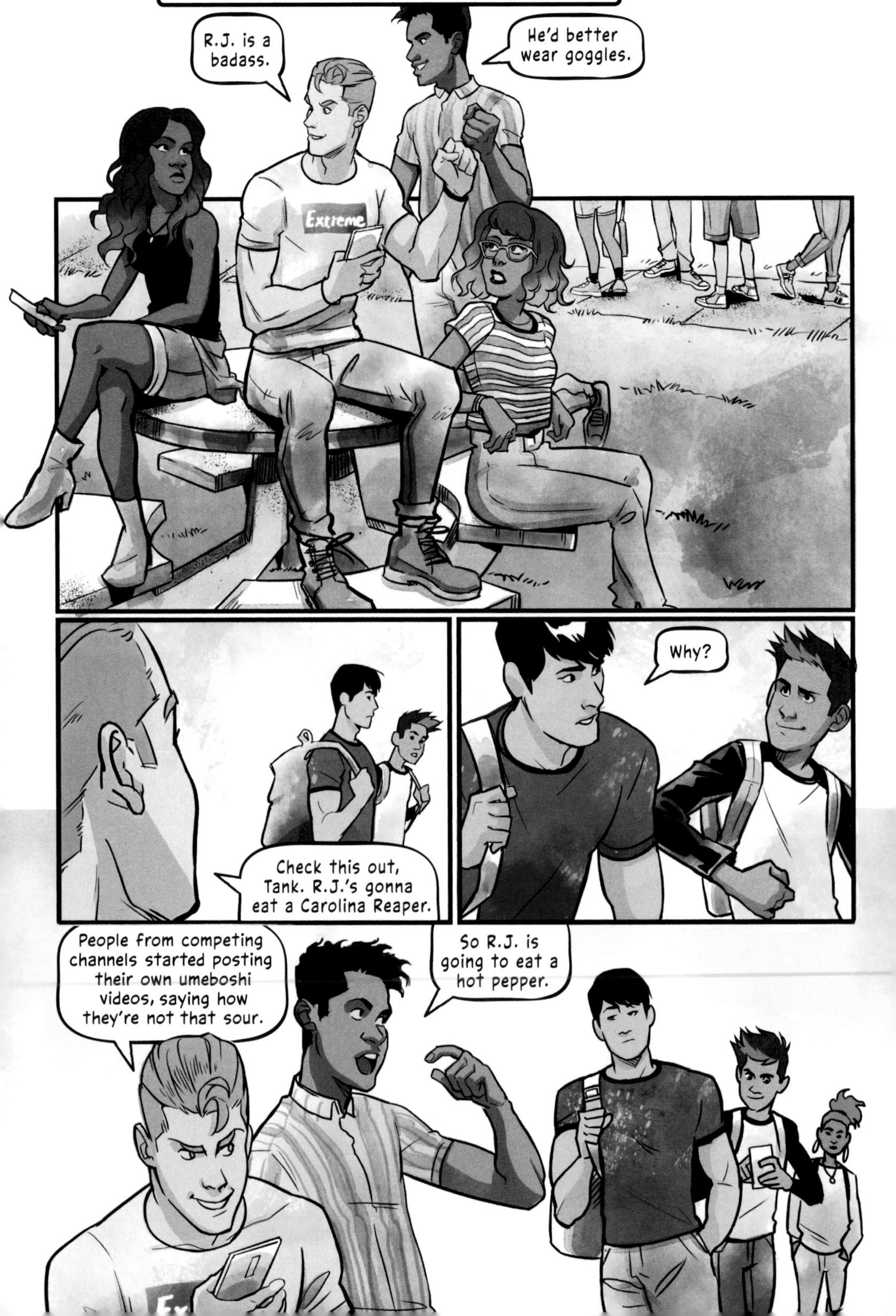
R.J. is a badass.
He'd better wear goggles.
Check this out, Tank. R.J.'s gonna eat a Carolina Reaper.
Why?
People from competing channels started posting their own umeboshi videos, saying how they're not that sour.
So R.J. is going to eat a hot pepper.
Extreme

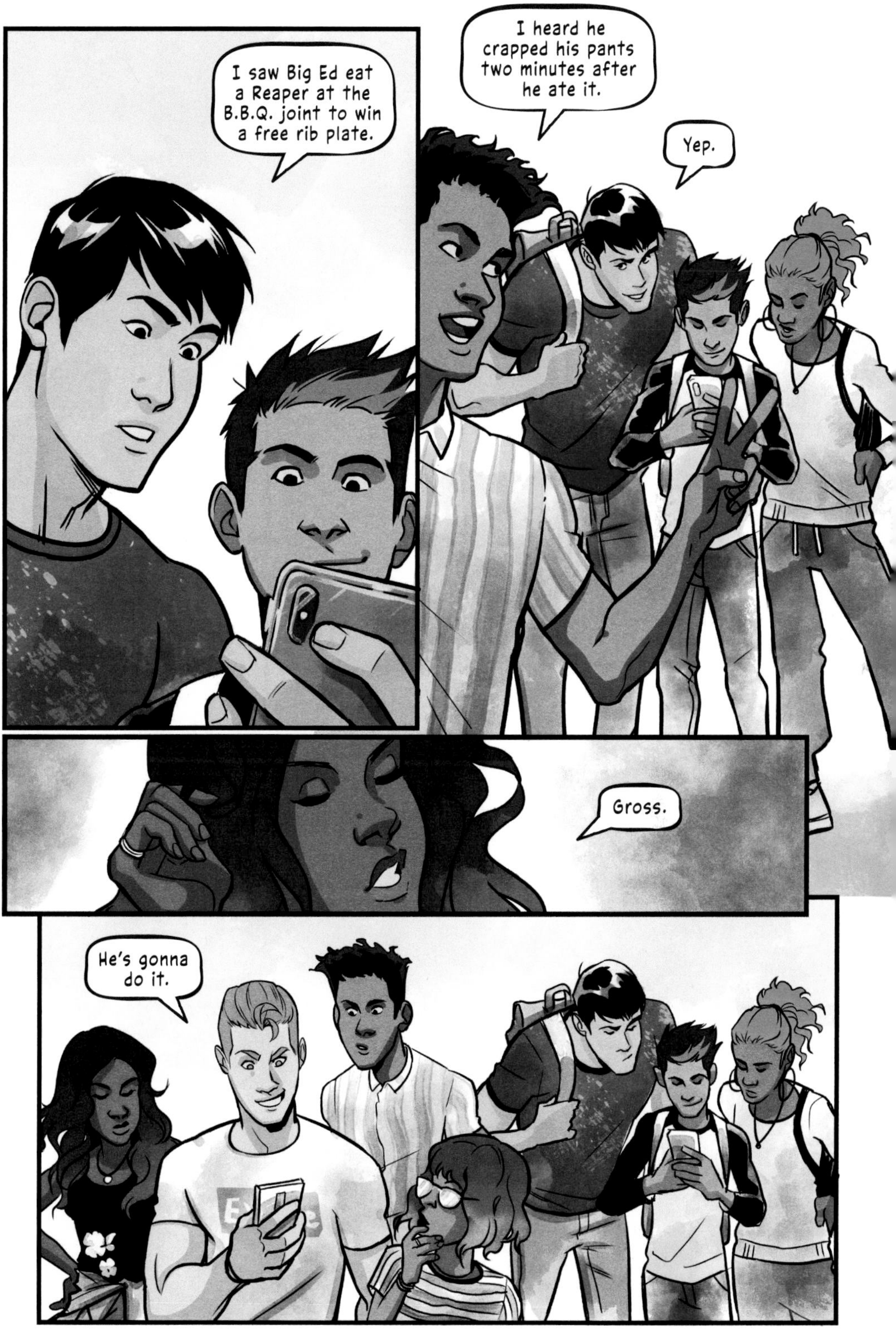
I saw Big Ed eat a Reaper at the B.B.Q. joint to win a free rib plate.
I heard he crapped his pants two minutes after he ate it.
Yep.
Gross.
He's gonna do it.

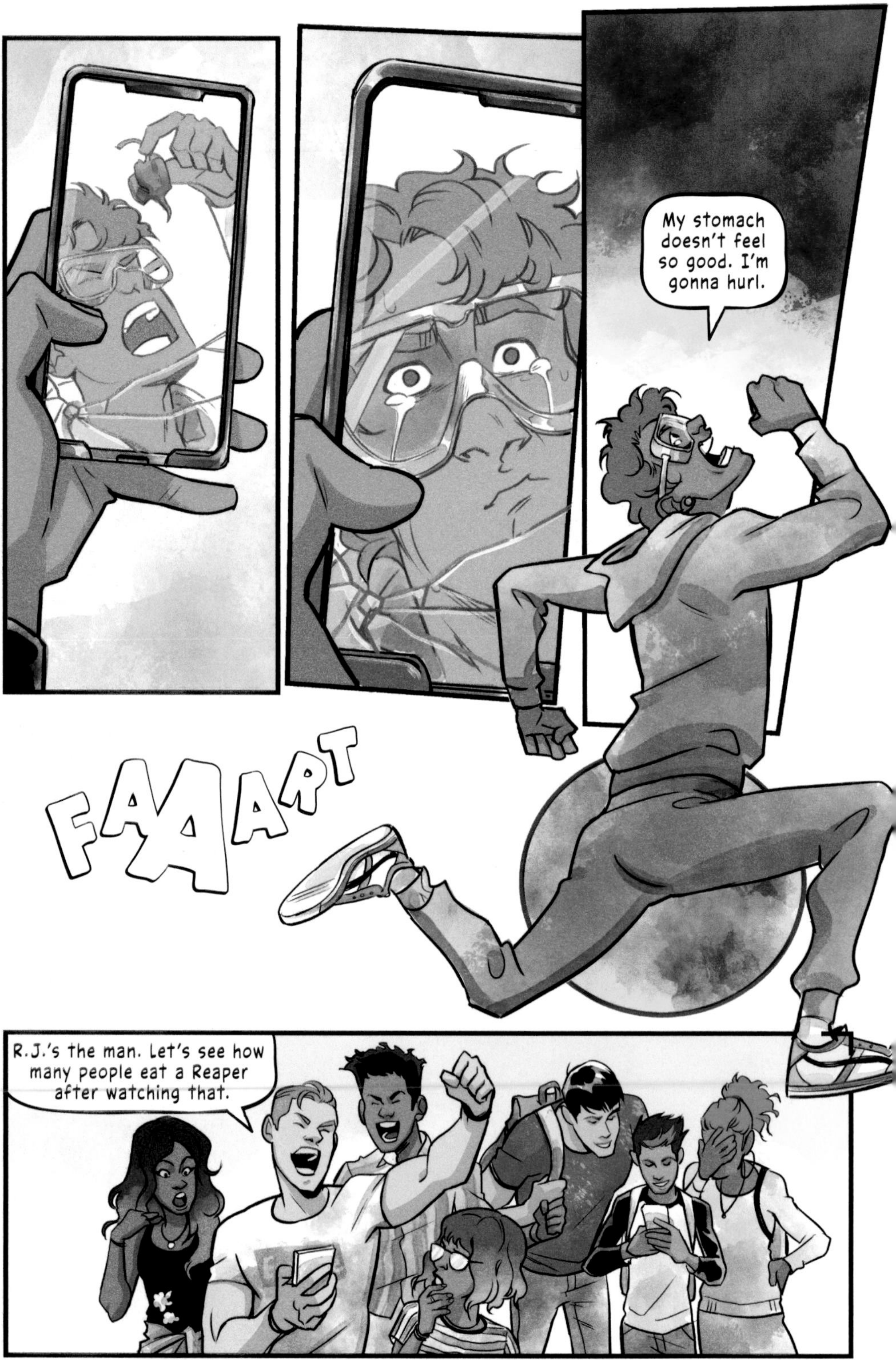
My stomach doesn't feel so good. I'm gonna hurl.
FAAAART
R.J.'s the man. Let's see how many people eat a Reaper after watching that.

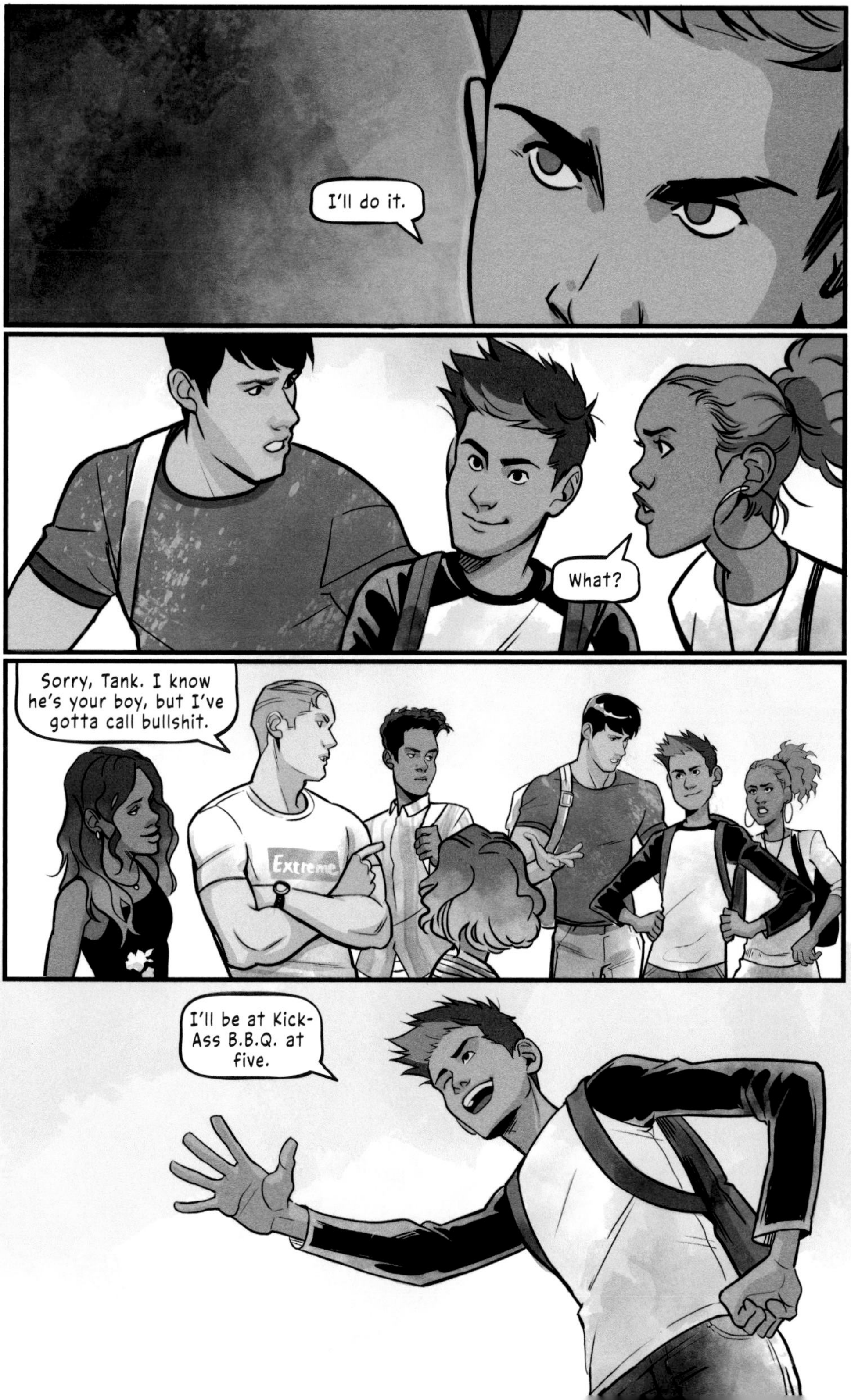
I'll do it.
What?
Sorry, Tank. I know he's your boy, but I've gotta call bullshit.
Extreme
I'll be at Kick-Ass B.B.Q. at five.

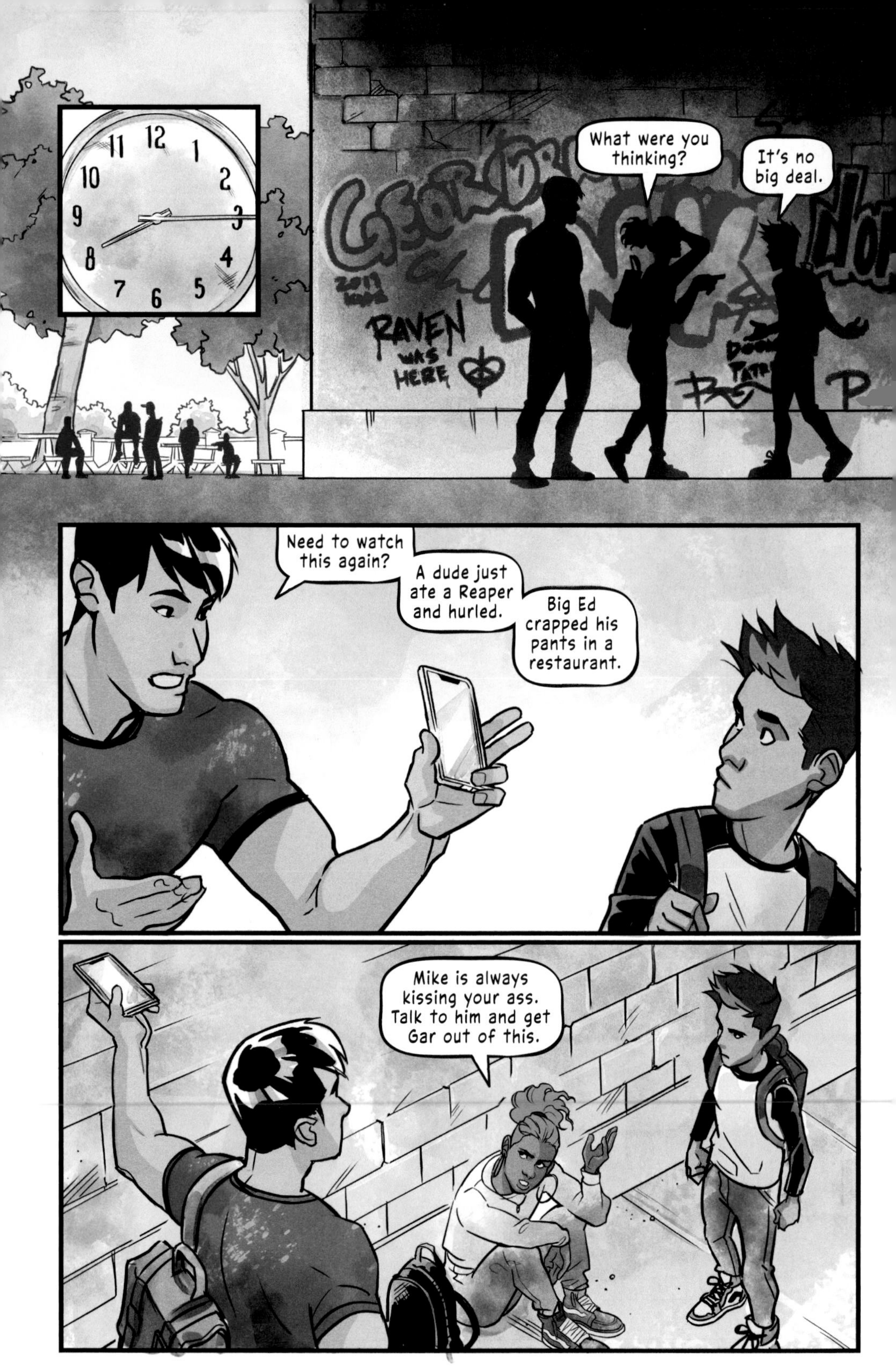

What were you thinking?
It's no big deal.
RAVEN WAS HERE
Need to watch this again?
A dude just ate a Reaper and hurled.
Big Ed crapped his pants in a restaurant.
Mike is always kissing your ass. Talk to him and get Gar out of this.

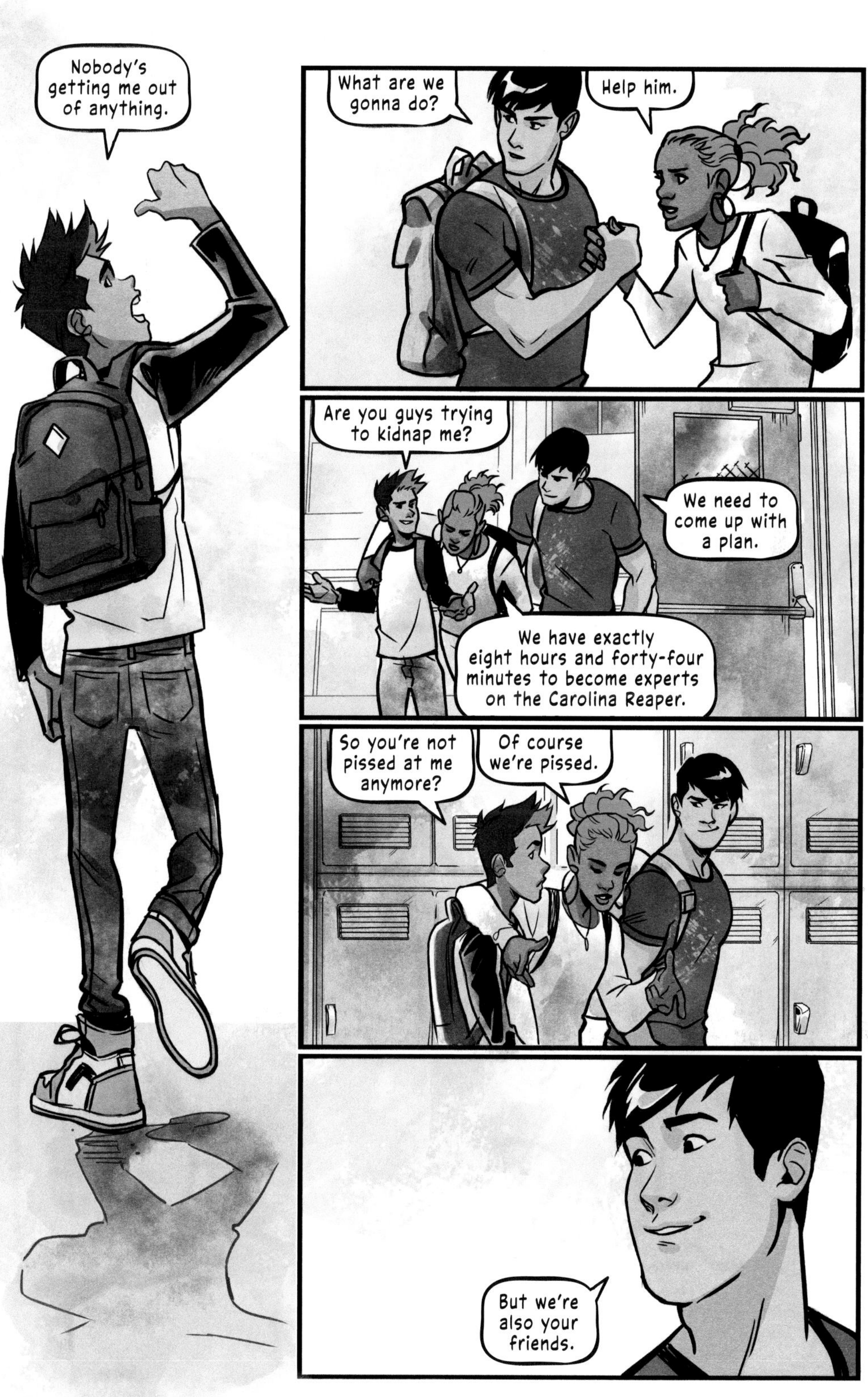
Nobody's getting me out of anything.
What are we gonna do?
Help him.
Are you guys trying to kidnap me?
We need to come up with a plan.
We have exactly eight hours and forty-four minutes to become experts on the Carolina Reaper.
So you're not pissed at me anymore?
Of course we're pissed.
But we're also your friends.

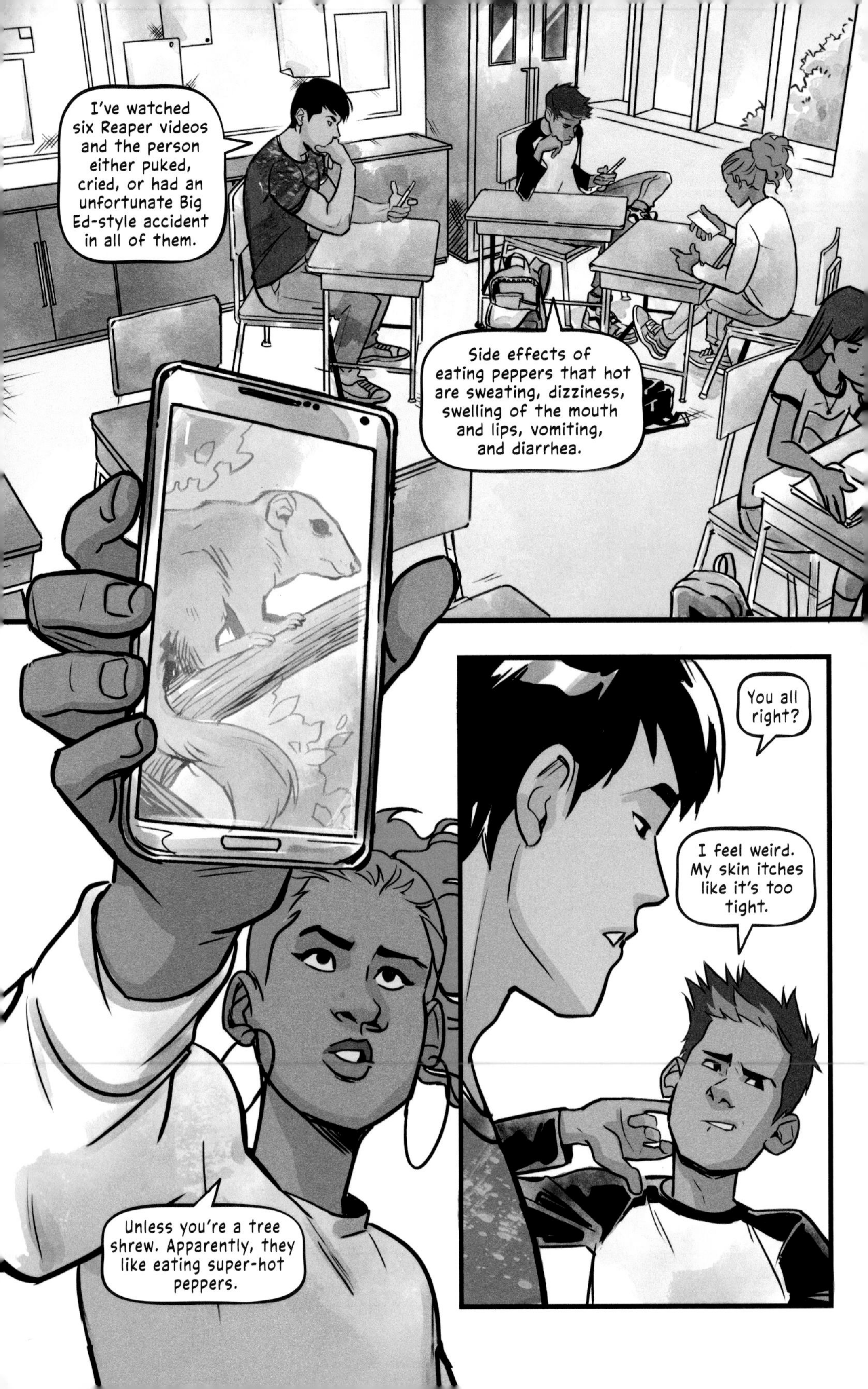
I've watched six Reaper videos and the person either puked, cried, or had an unfortunate Big Ed-style accident in all of them.
Side effects of eating peppers that hot are sweating, dizziness, swelling of the mouth and lips, vomiting, and diarrhea.
Unless you're a tree shrew. Apparently, they like eating super-hot peppers.
You all right?
I feel weird. My skin itches like it's too tight.

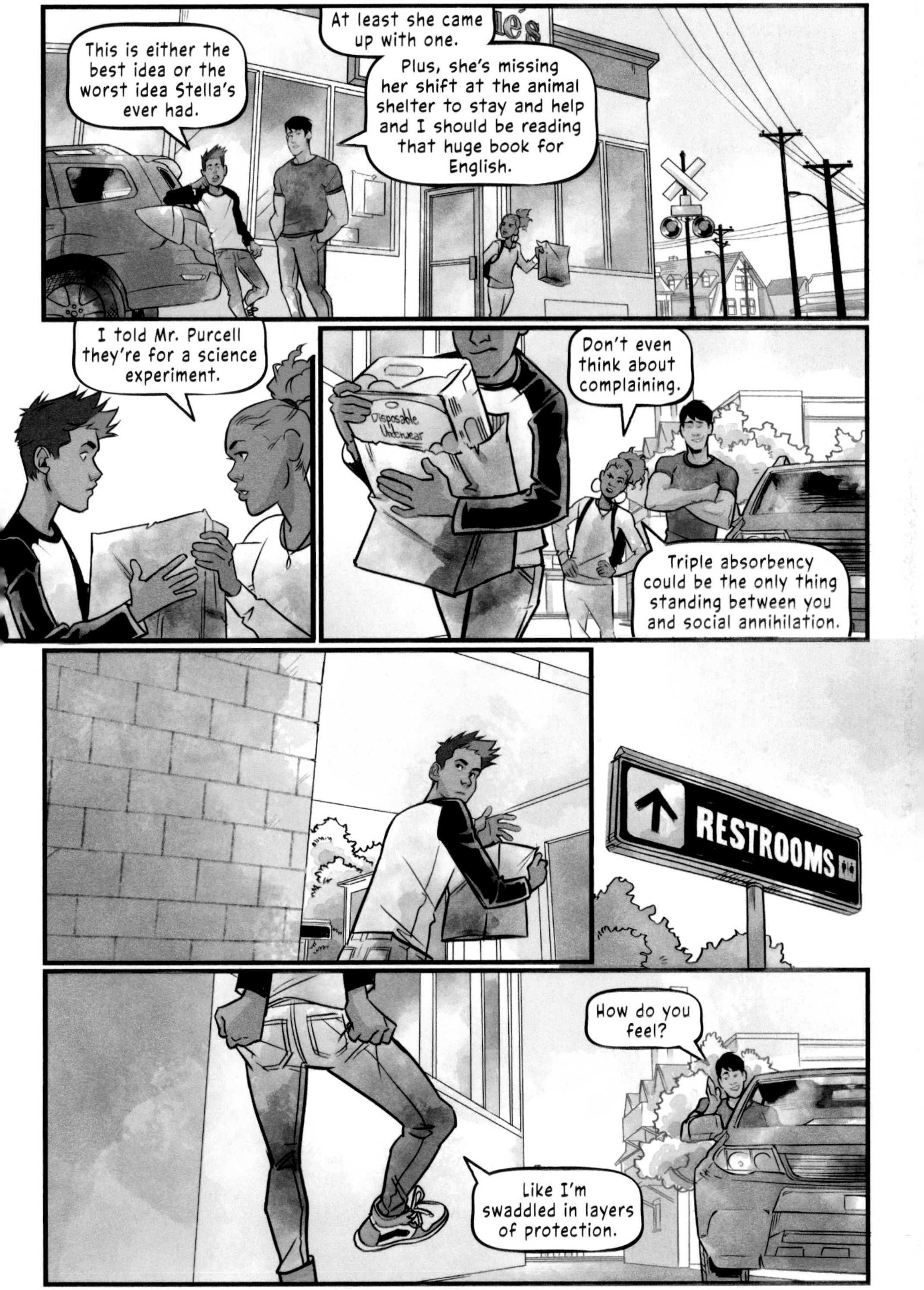
This is either the best idea or the worst idea Stella's ever had.
At least she came up with one.
Plus, she's missing her shift at the animal shelter to stay and help and I should be reading that huge book for English.
I told Mr. Purcell they're for a science experiment.
Disposable Underwear
Don't even think about complaining.
Triple absorbency could be the only thing standing between you and social annihilation.
RESTROOMS
How do you feel?
Like I'm swaddled in layers of protection.

CHAPTER 7: FIGHT OR FLIGHT

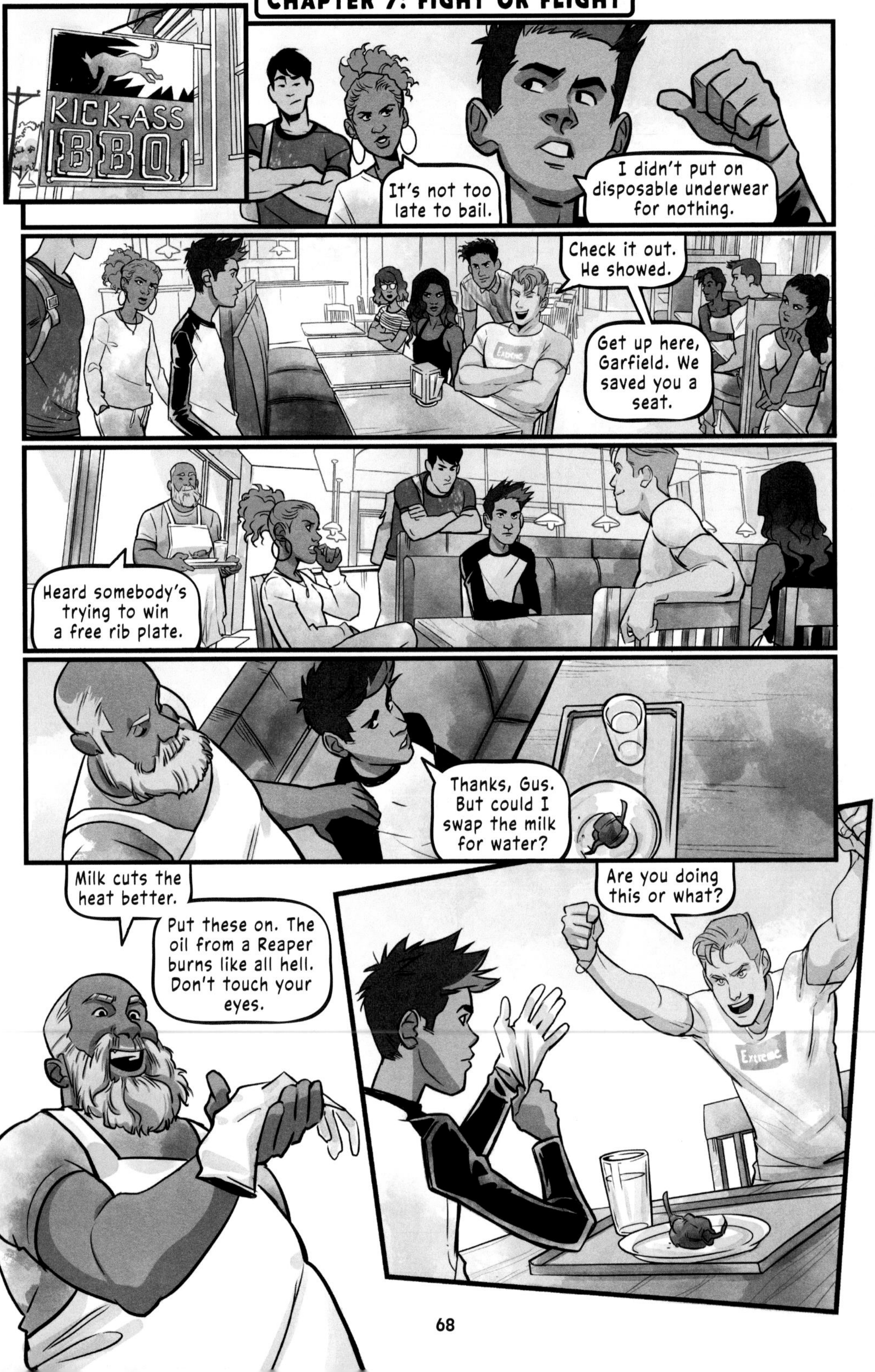
KICK-ASS BBQ
It's not too late to bail.
I didn't put on disposable underwear for nothing.
Check it out. He showed.
Get up here, Garfield. We saved you a seat.
Heard somebody's trying to win a free rib plate.
Thanks, Gus. But could I swap the milk for water?
Milk cuts the heat better.
Put these on. The oil from a Reaper burns like all hell. Don't touch your eyes.
Are you doing this or what?

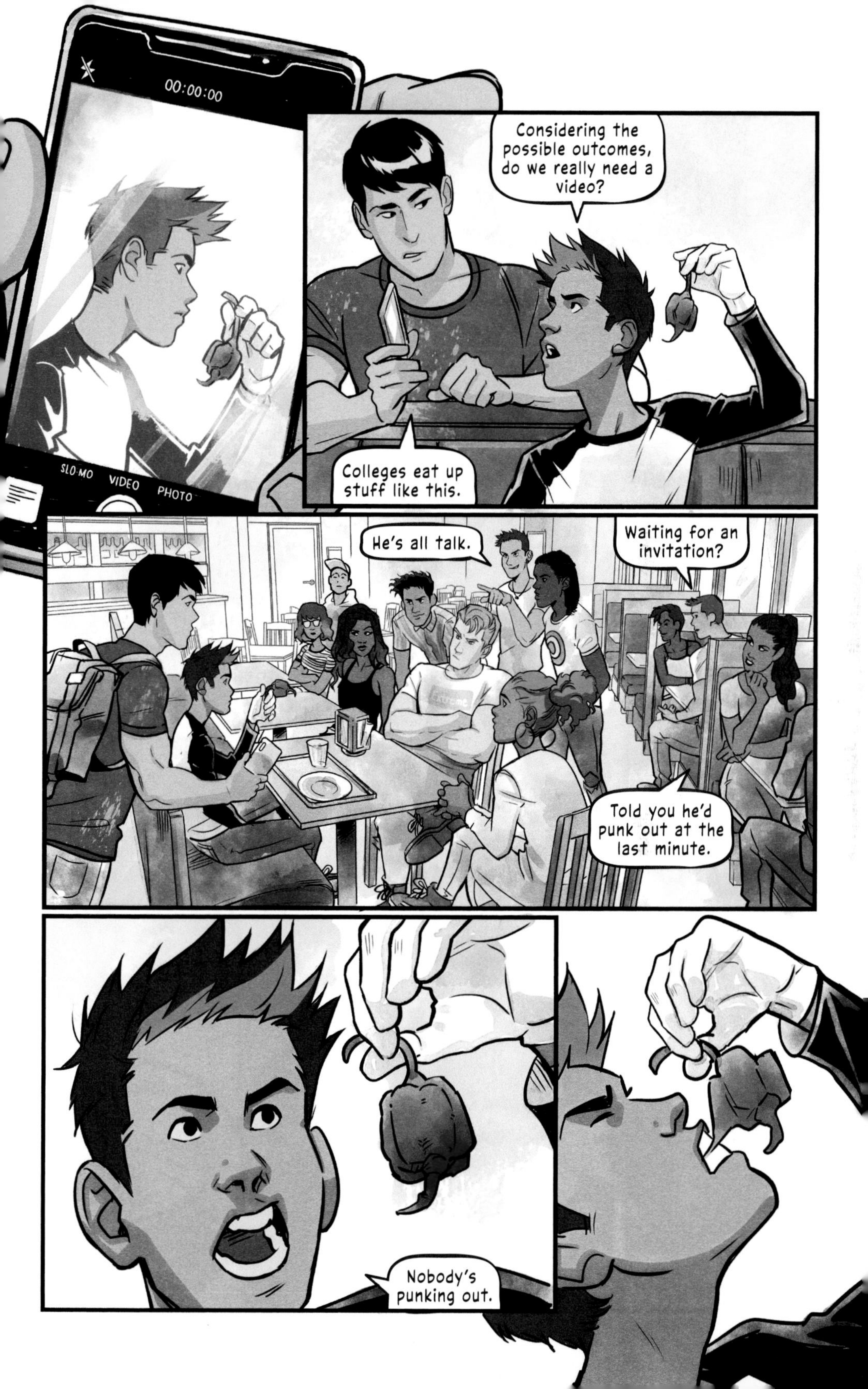

00:00:00
SLO-MO VIDEO PHOTO
Considering the possible outcomes, do we really need a video?
Colleges eat up stuff like this.
He's all talk.
Waiting for an invitation?
Told you he'd punk out at the last minute.
Nobody's punking out.

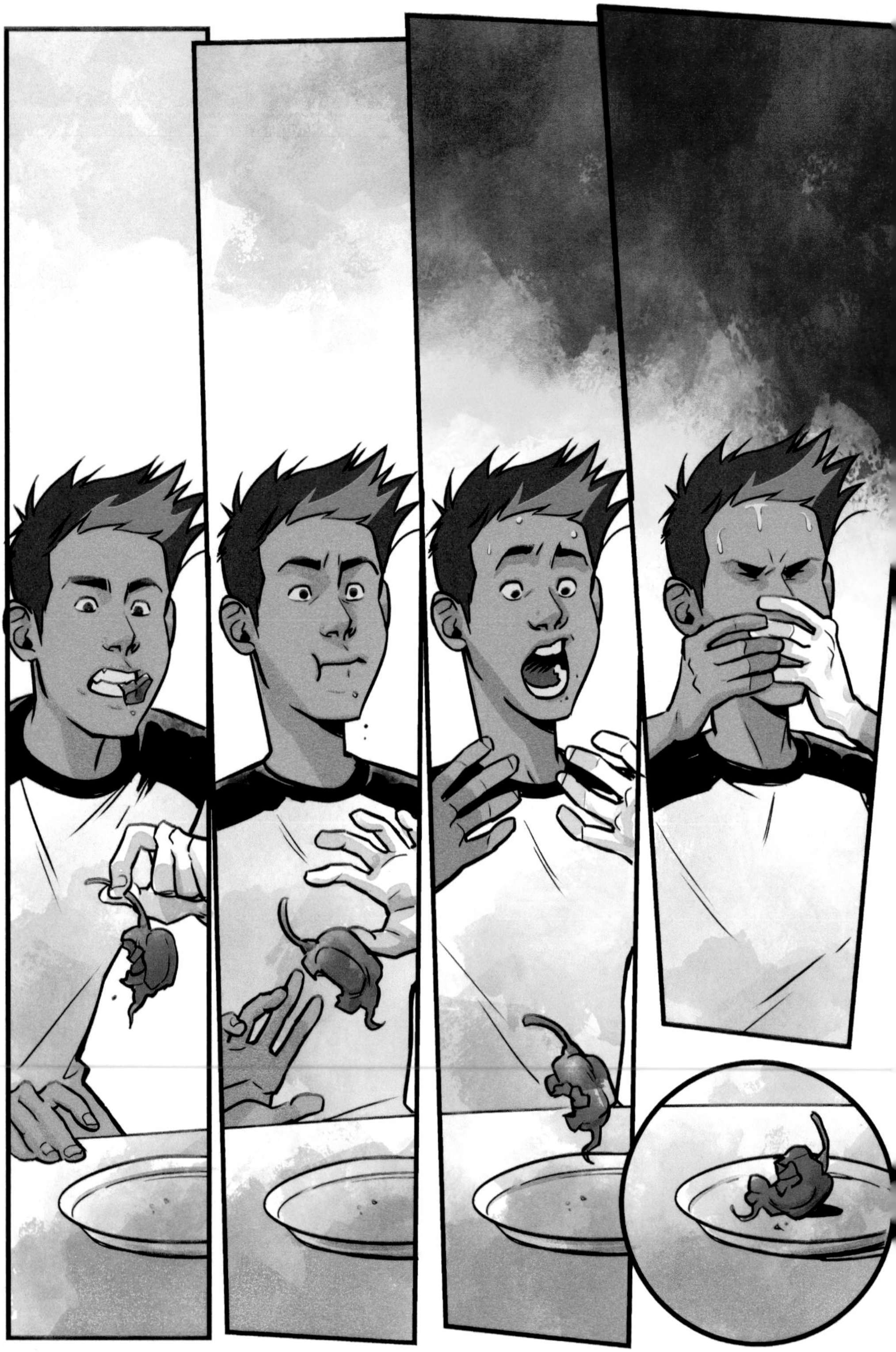

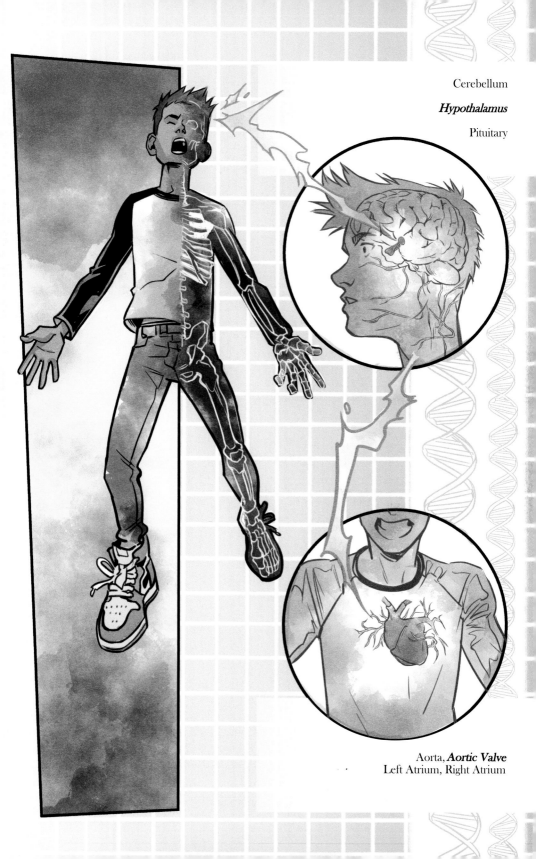

Cerebellum
Hypothalamus
Pituitary

Aorta, ***Aortic Valve***
Left Atrium, Right Atrium

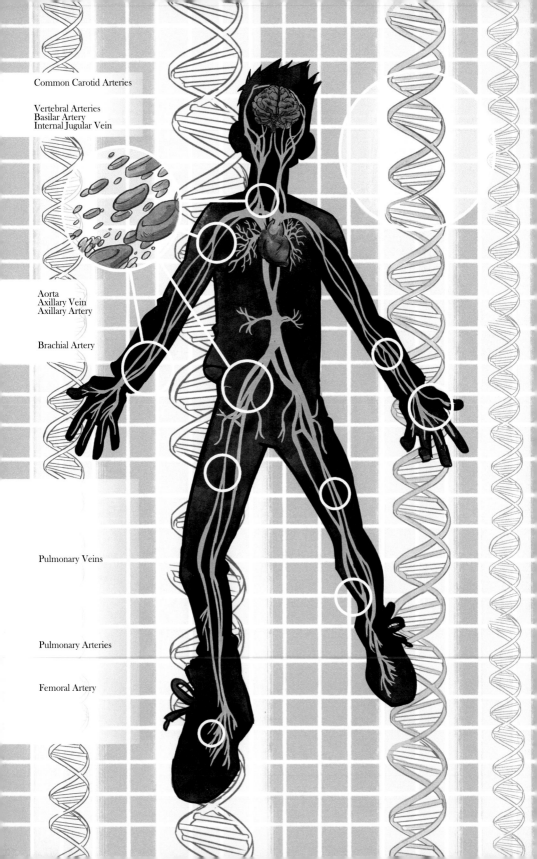

Common Carotid Arteries

Vertebral Arteries
Basilar Artery
Internal Jugular Vein

Aorta
Axillary Vein
Axillary Artery

Brachial Artery

Pulmonary Veins

Pulmonary Arteries

Femoral Artery

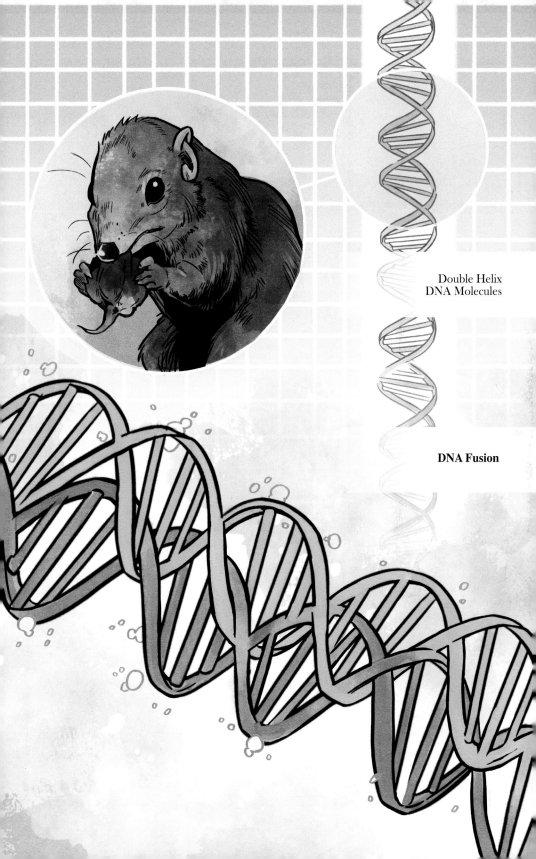

Double Helix
DNA Molecules

DNA Fusion

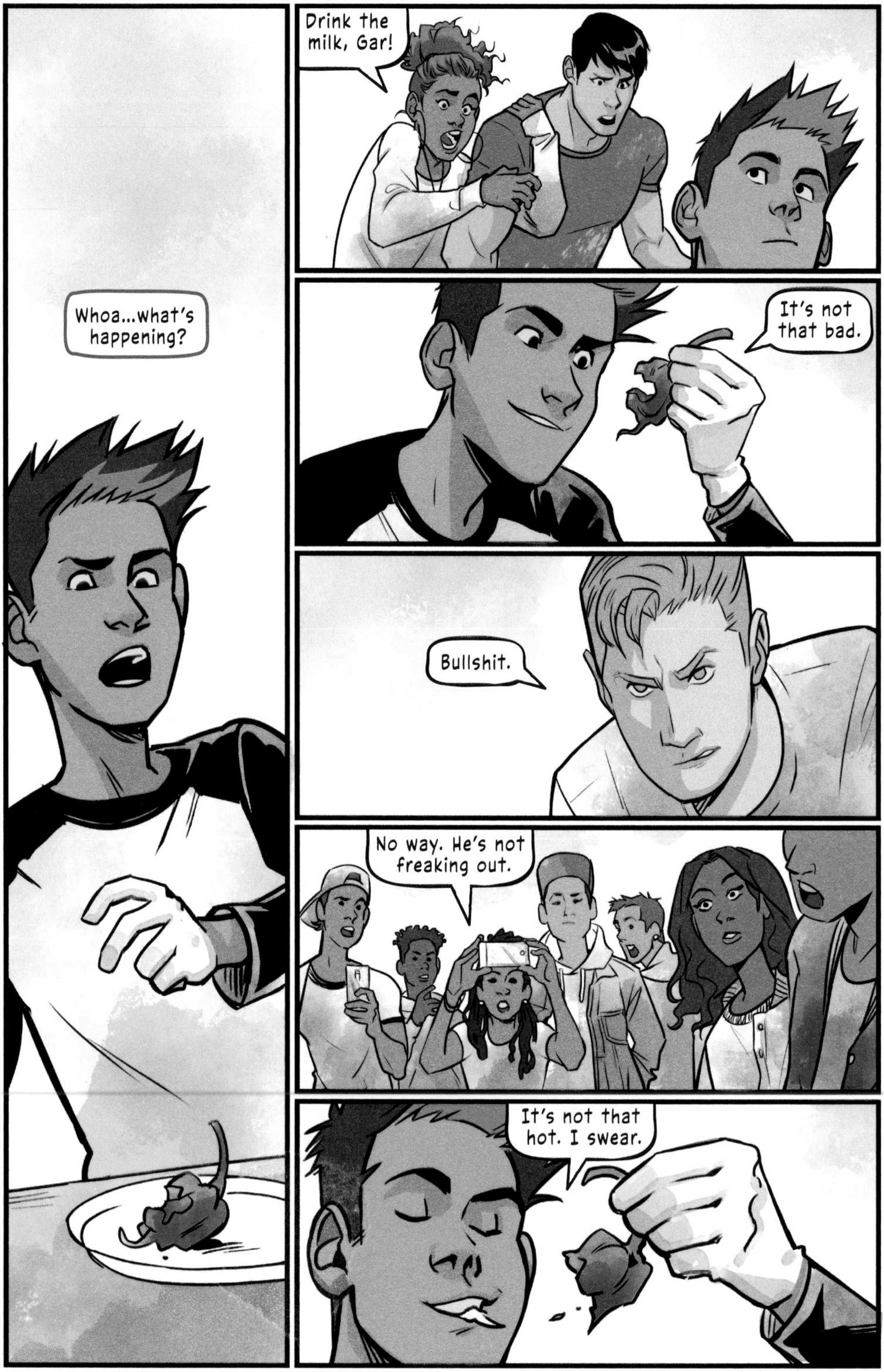
Drink the milk, Gar!
Whoa...what's happening?
It's not that bad.
Bullshit.
No way. He's not freaking out.
It's not that hot. I swear.

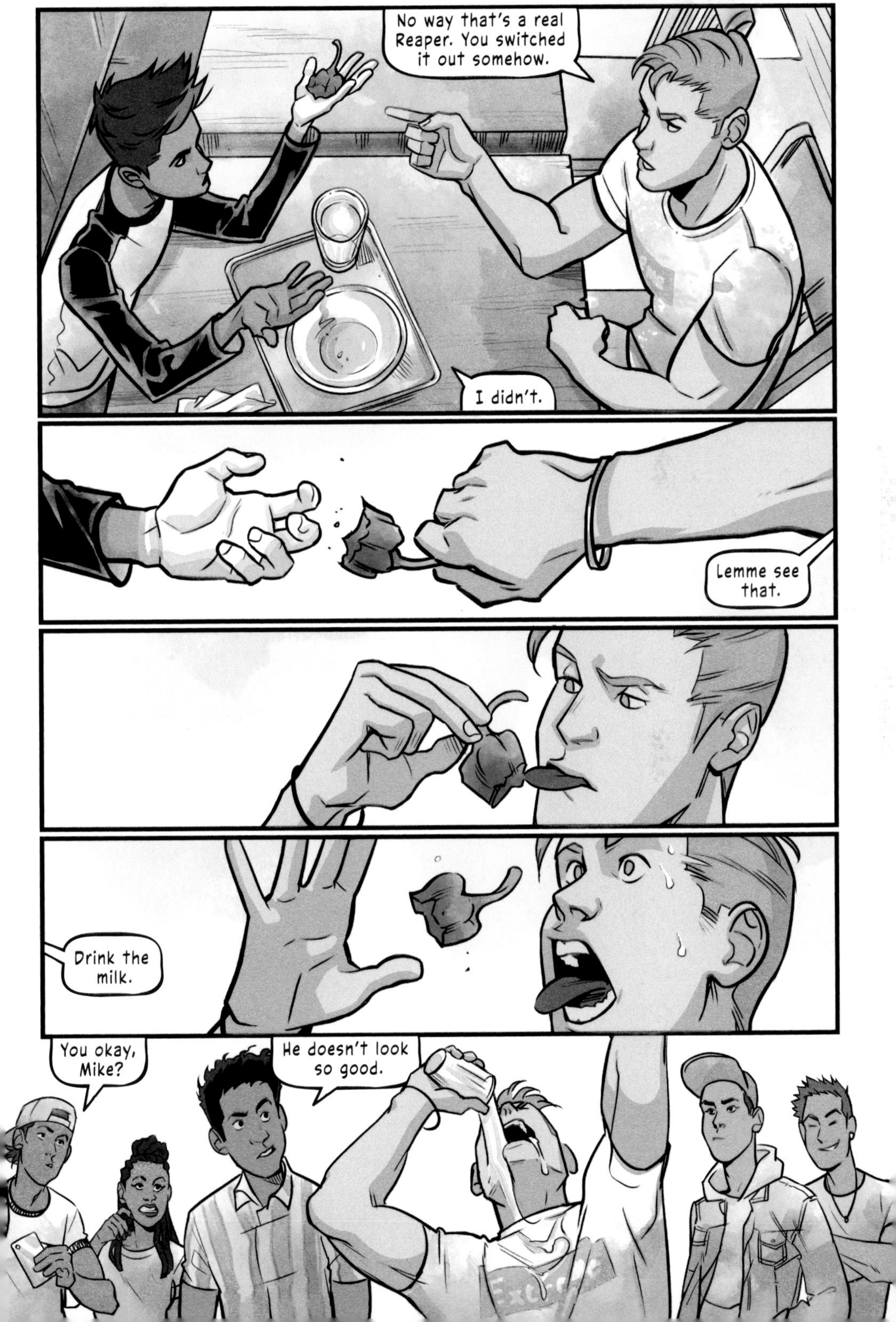
No way that's a real Reaper. You switched it out somehow.
I didn't.
Lemme see that.
Drink the milk.
You okay, Mike?
He doesn't look so good.

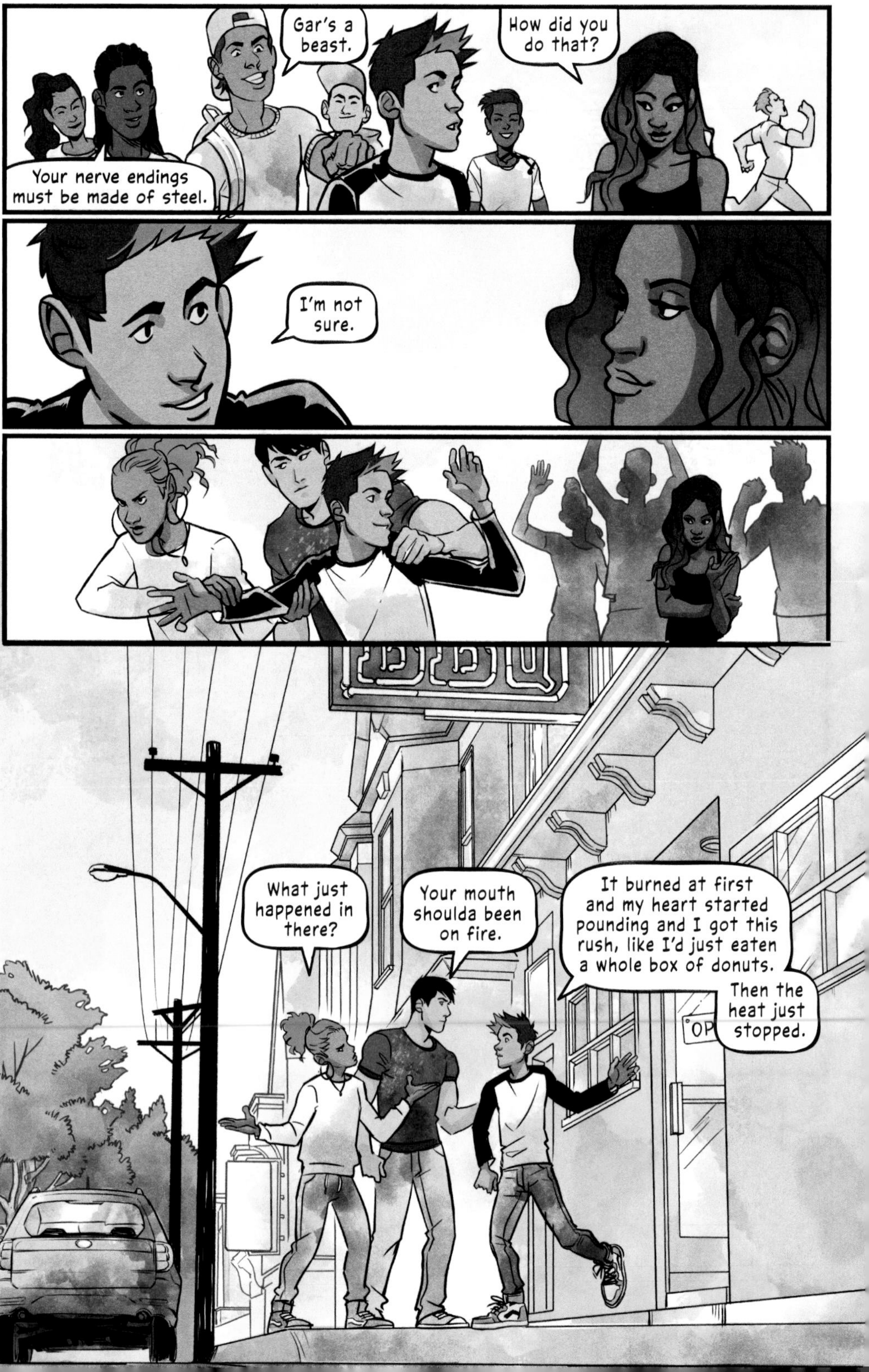
Gar's a beast.
How did you do that?
Your nerve endings must be made of steel.
I'm not sure.
What just happened in there?
Your mouth shoulda been on fire.
It burned at first and my heart started pounding and I got this rush, like I'd just eaten a whole box of donuts.
Then the heat just stopped.

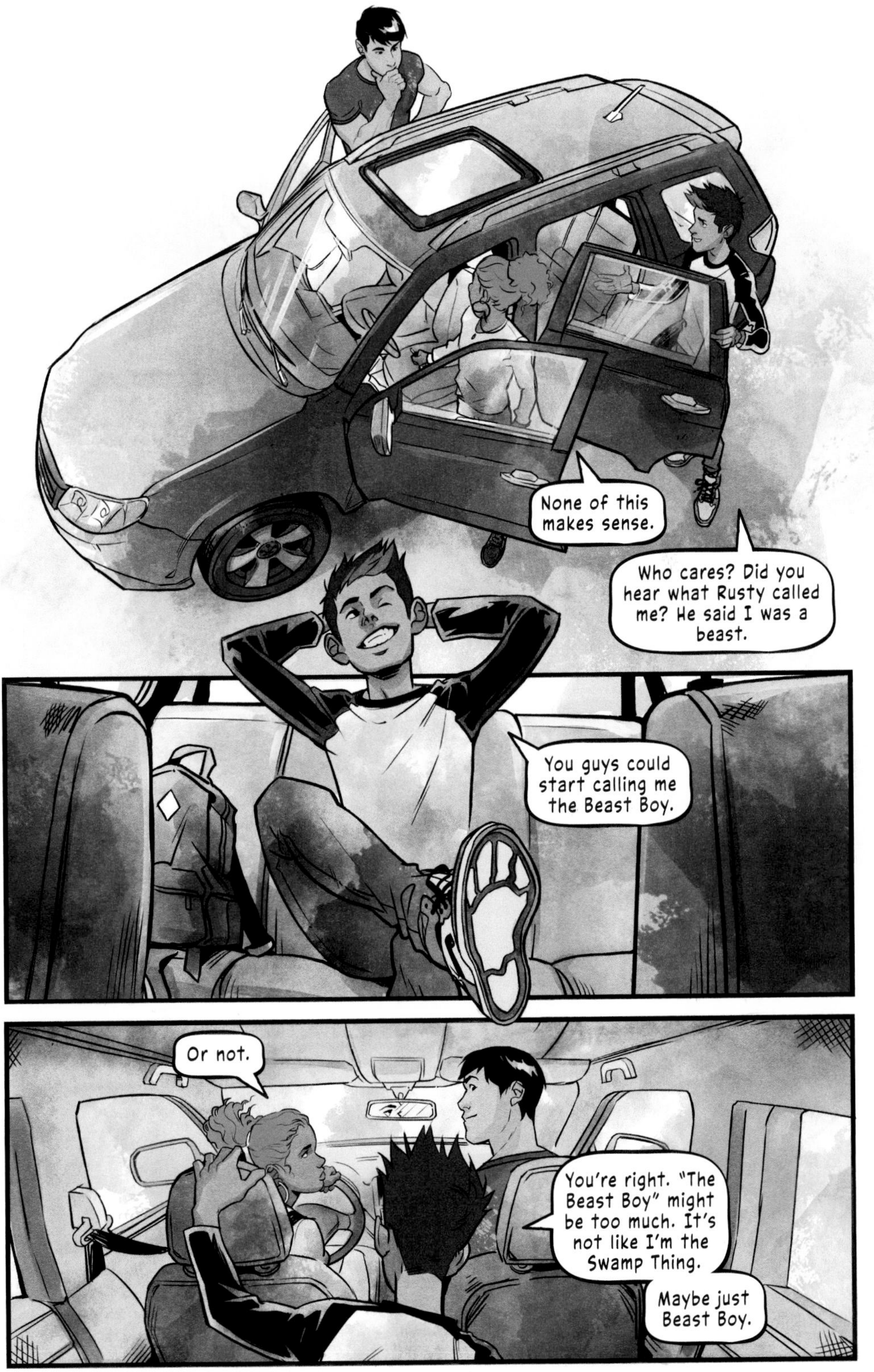
None of this makes sense.
Who cares? Did you hear what Rusty called me? He said I was a beast.
You guys could start calling me the Beast Boy.
Or not.
You're right. "The Beast Boy" might be too much. It's not like I'm the Swamp Thing.
Maybe just Beast Boy.

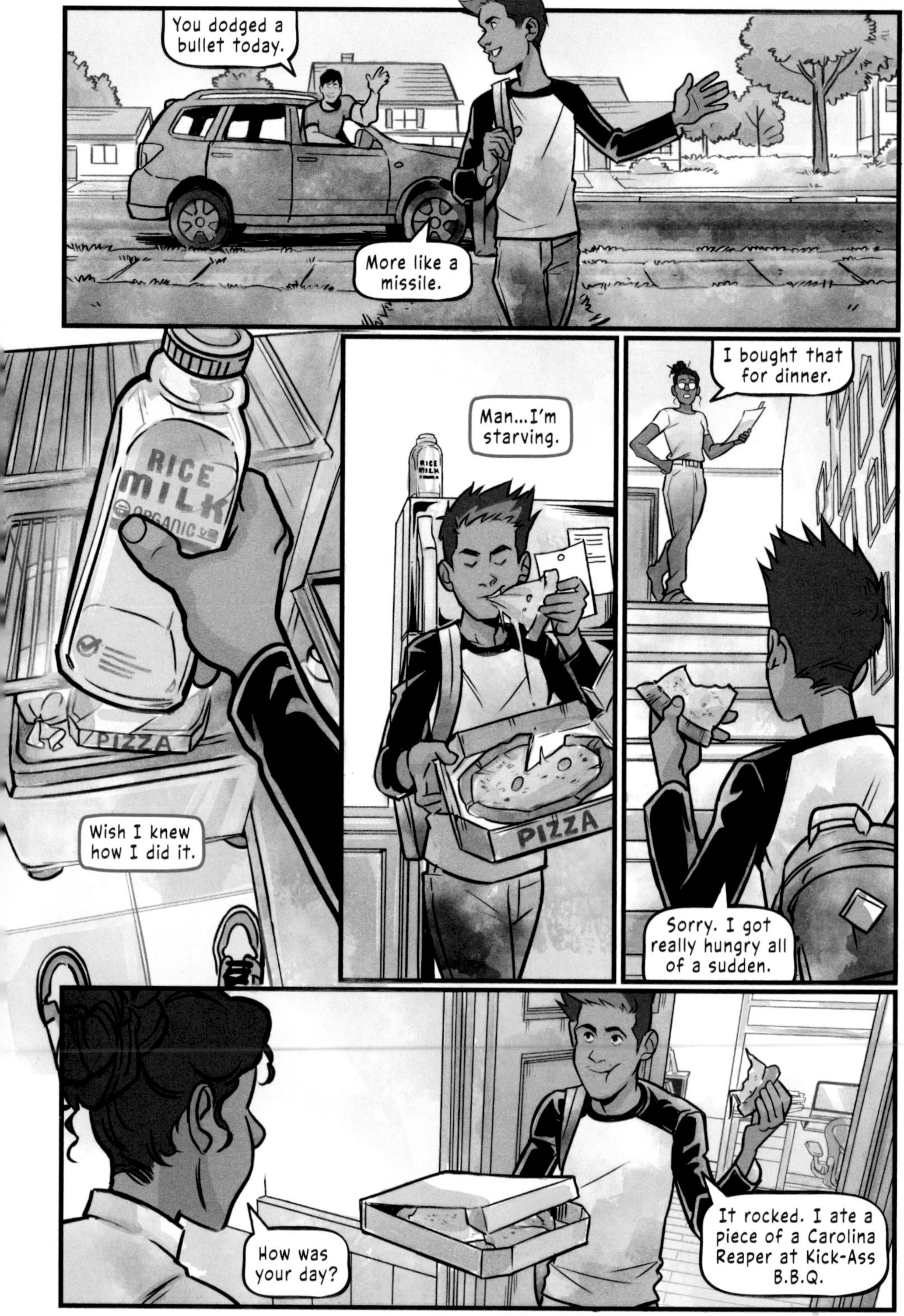
You dodged a bullet today.
More like a missile.
RICE MILK ORGANIC
PIZZA
Wish I knew how I did it.
Man...I'm starving.
PIZZA
I bought that for dinner.
Sorry. I got really hungry all of a sudden.
How was your day?
It rocked. I ate a piece of a Carolina Reaper at Kick-Ass B.B.Q.

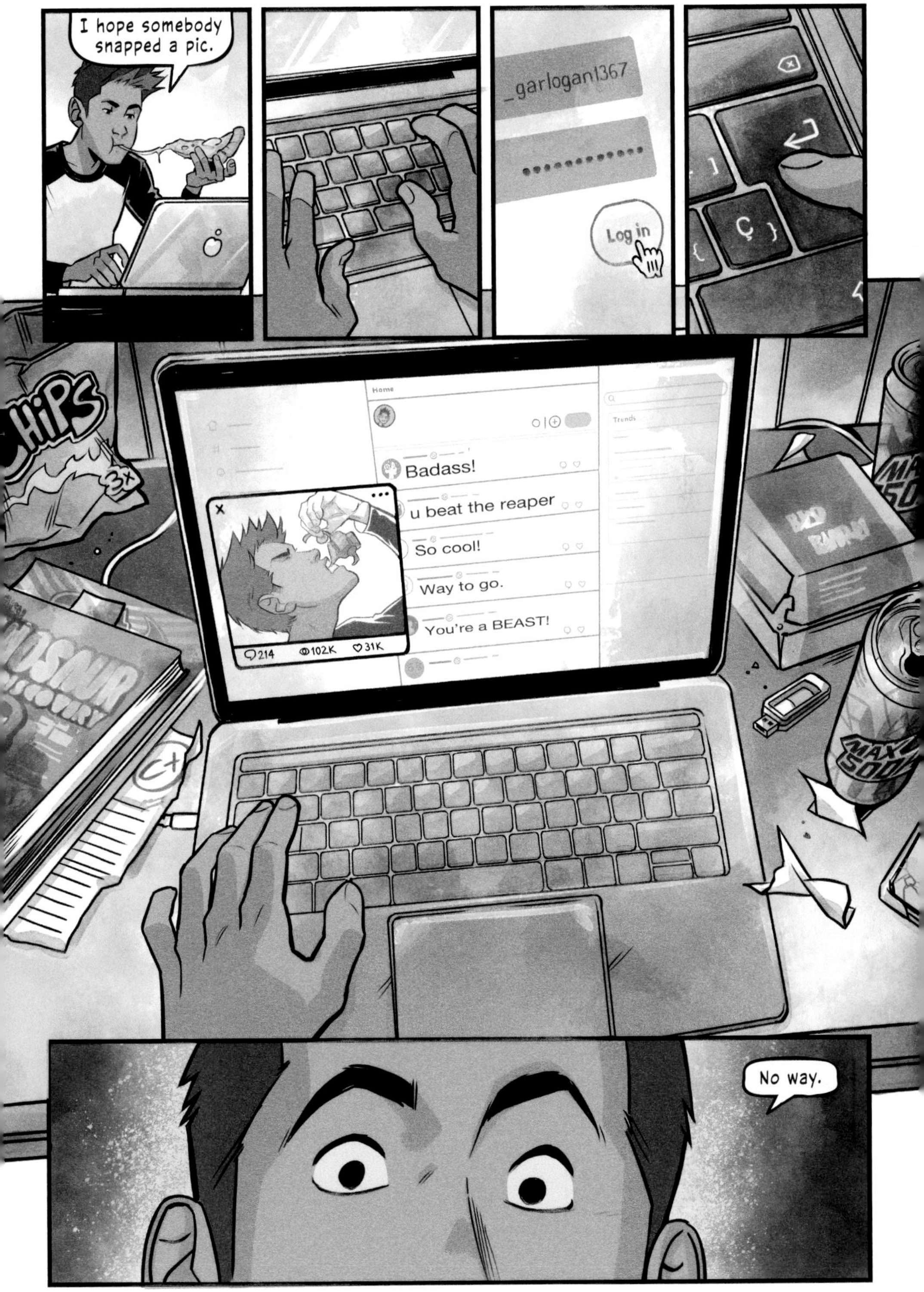
I hope somebody snapped a pic.
_garlogan1367
Log in
Home
Trends
Badass!
u beat the reaper
So cool!
Way to go.
You're a BEAST!
214
102K
31K
CHIPS
No way.

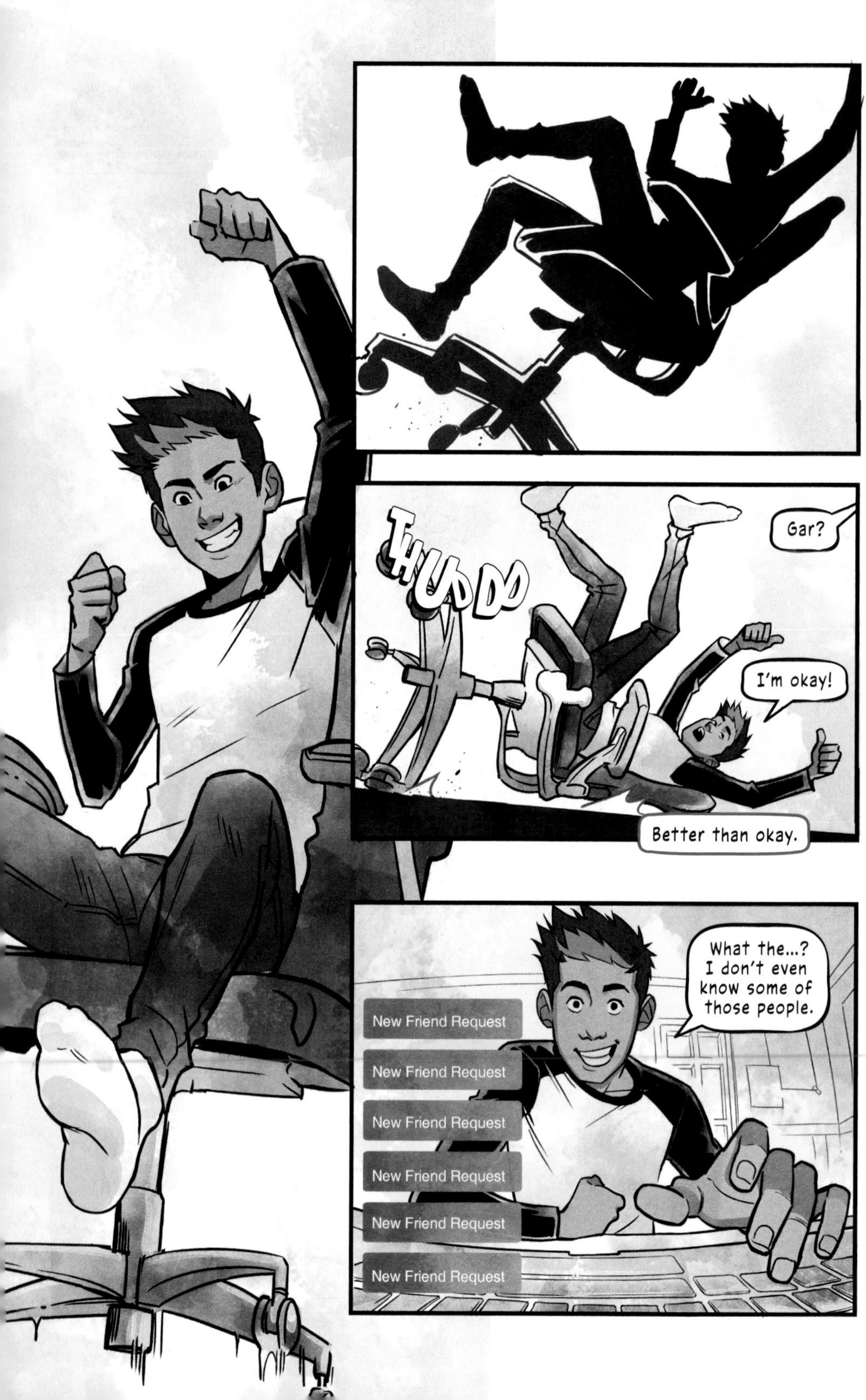
THUDD
Gar?
I'm okay!
Better than okay.
New Friend Request
New Friend Request
New Friend Request
New Friend Request
New Friend Request
New Friend Request
What the...? I don't even know some of those people.

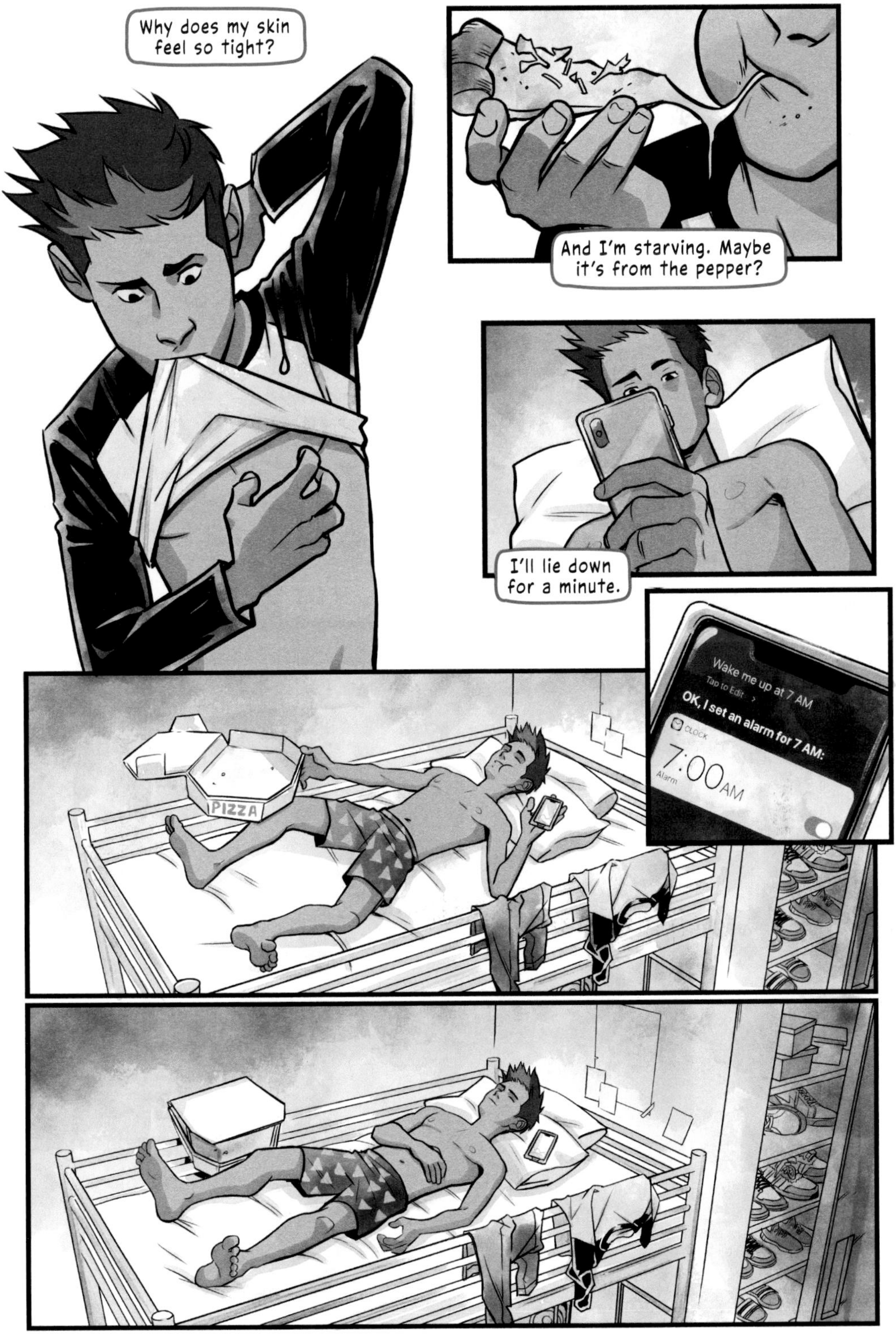
Why does my skin feel so tight?
And I'm starving. Maybe it's from the pepper?
I'll lie down for a minute.
Wake me up at 7 AM
Tap to Edit >
OK, I set an alarm for 7 AM:
CLOCK
7:00AM
Alarm
PIZZA

CHAPTER 8: GAR 2.0

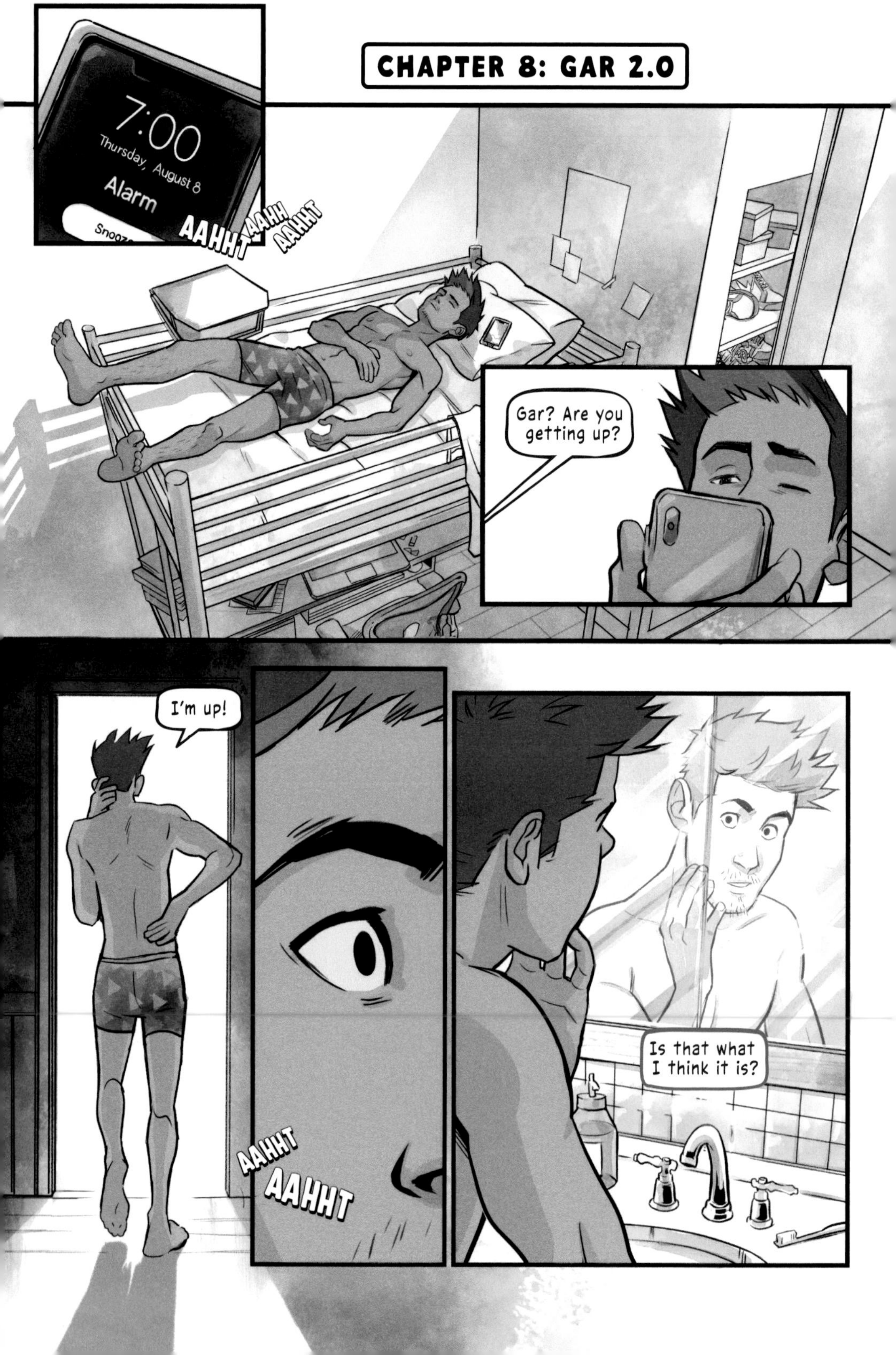
7:00
Thursday, August 8
Alarm
AAHHT AAHH AAHHT
Gar? Are you getting up?
I'm up!
AAHHT AAHHT
Is that what I think it is?

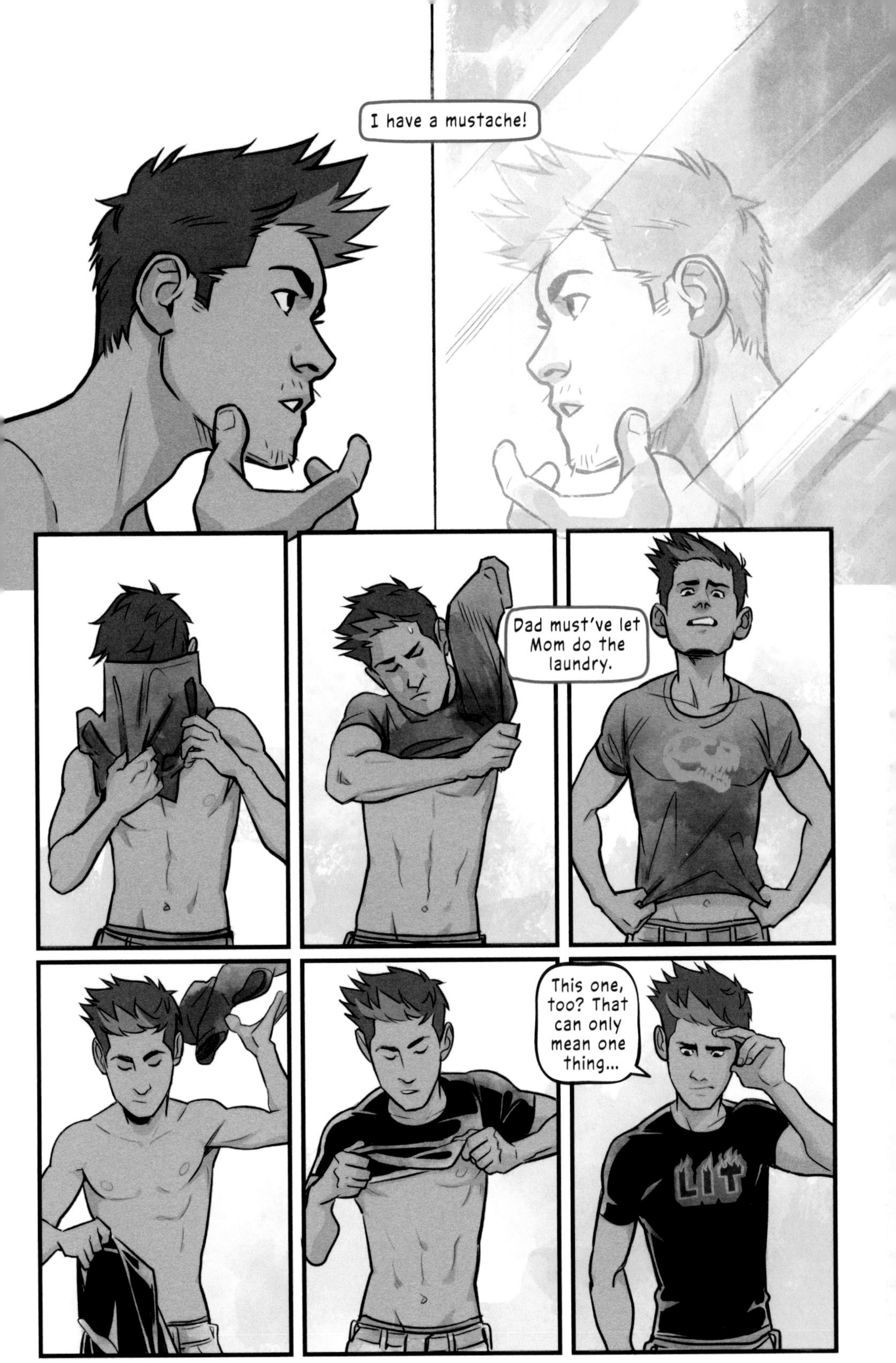
I have a mustache!
Dad must've let Mom do the laundry.
LIT
This one, too? That can only mean one thing...

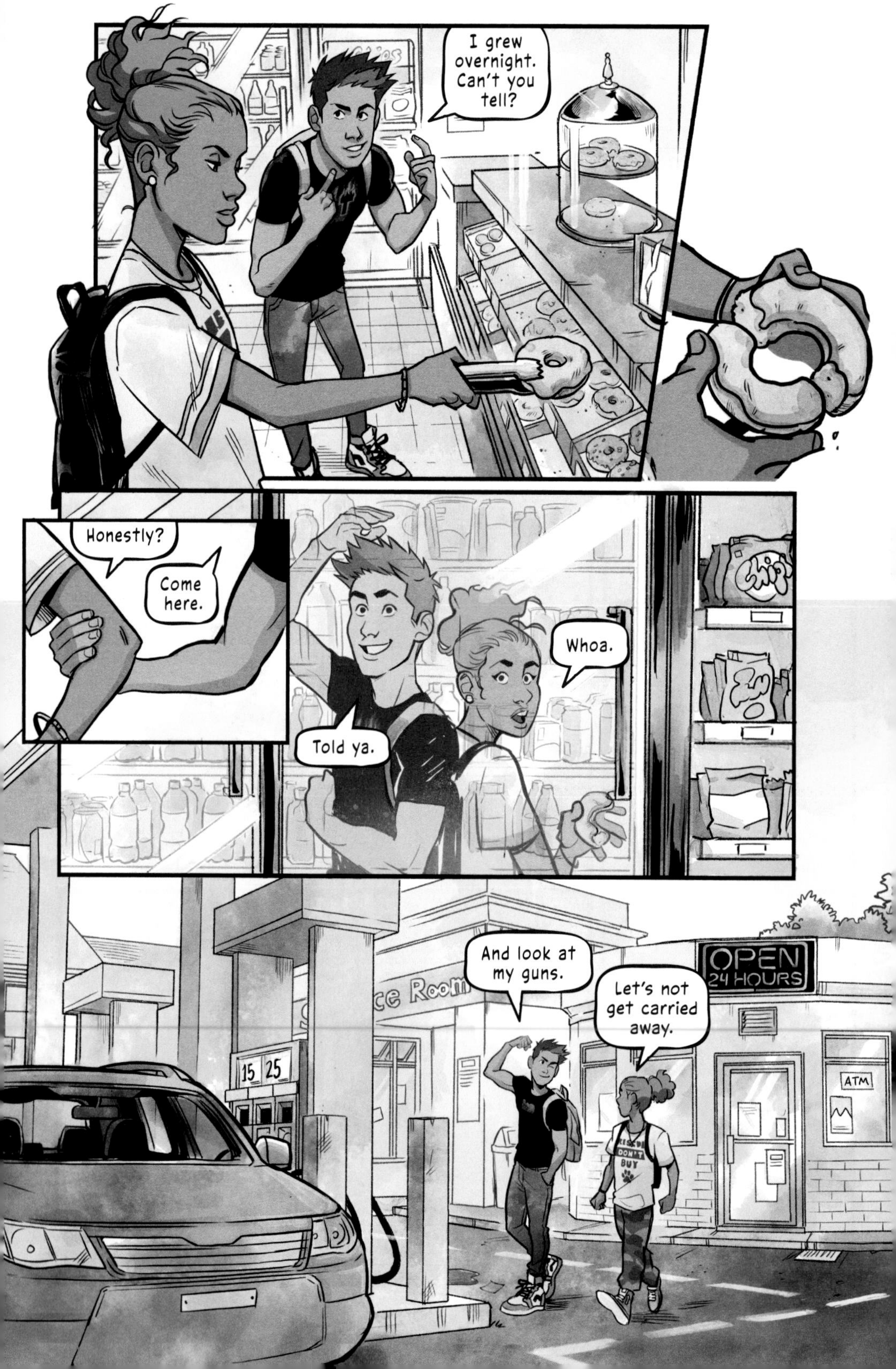

I grew overnight. Can't you tell?
Honestly?
Come here.
Whoa.
Told ya.
And look at my guns.
Let's not get carried away.
OPEN 24 HOURS
ATM

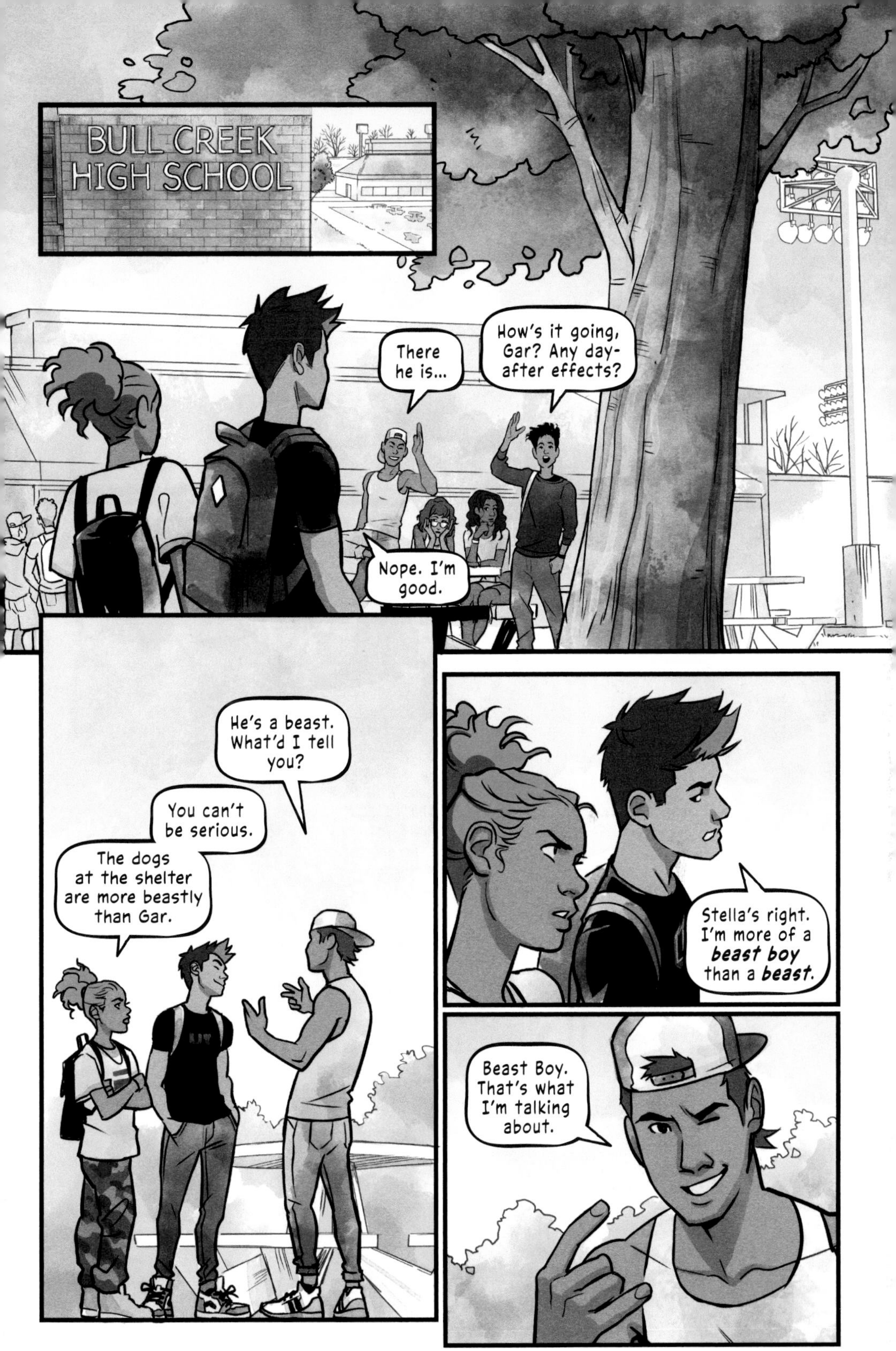
BULL CREEK HIGH SCHOOL
There he is...
How's it going, Gar? Any day-after effects?
Nope. I'm good.
He's a beast. What'd I tell you?
You can't be serious.
The dogs at the shelter are more beastly than Gar.
Stella's right. I'm more of a ***beast boy*** than a ***beast***.
Beast Boy. That's what I'm talking about.

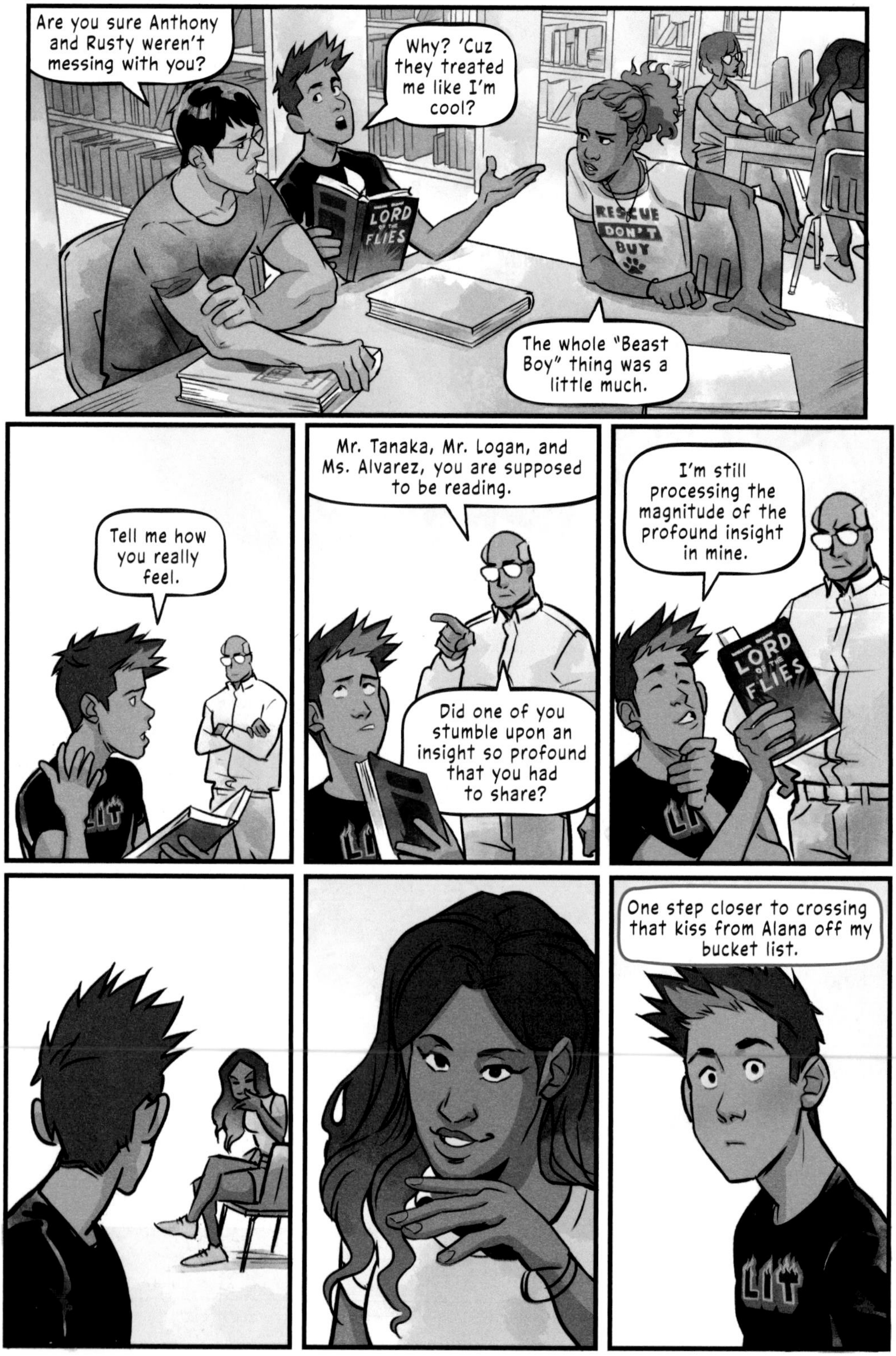
Are you sure Anthony and Rusty weren't messing with you?
Why? 'Cuz they treated me like I'm cool?
RESCUE DON'T BUY
The whole "Beast Boy" thing was a little much.
Tell me how you really feel.
Mr. Tanaka, Mr. Logan, and Ms. Alvarez, you are supposed to be reading.
Did one of you stumble upon an insight so profound that you had to share?
I'm still processing the magnitude of the profound insight in mine.
LORD OF THE FLIES
One step closer to crossing that kiss from Alana off my bucket list.

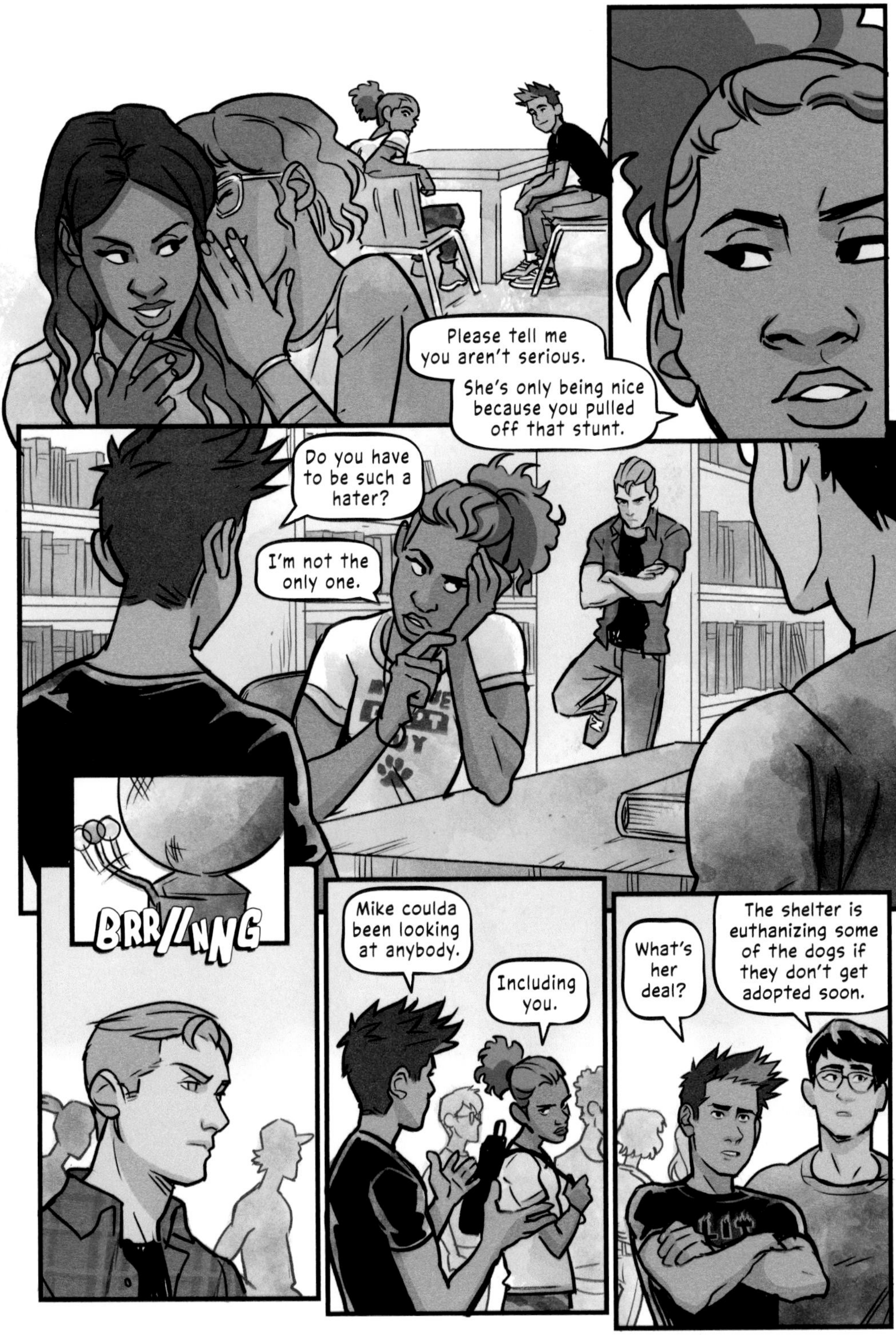

Please tell me you aren't serious.
She's only being nice because you pulled off that stunt.
Do you have to be such a hater?
I'm not the only one.
BRRIINNG
Mike coulda been looking at anybody.
Including you.
What's her deal?
The shelter is euthanizing some of the dogs if they don't get adopted soon.

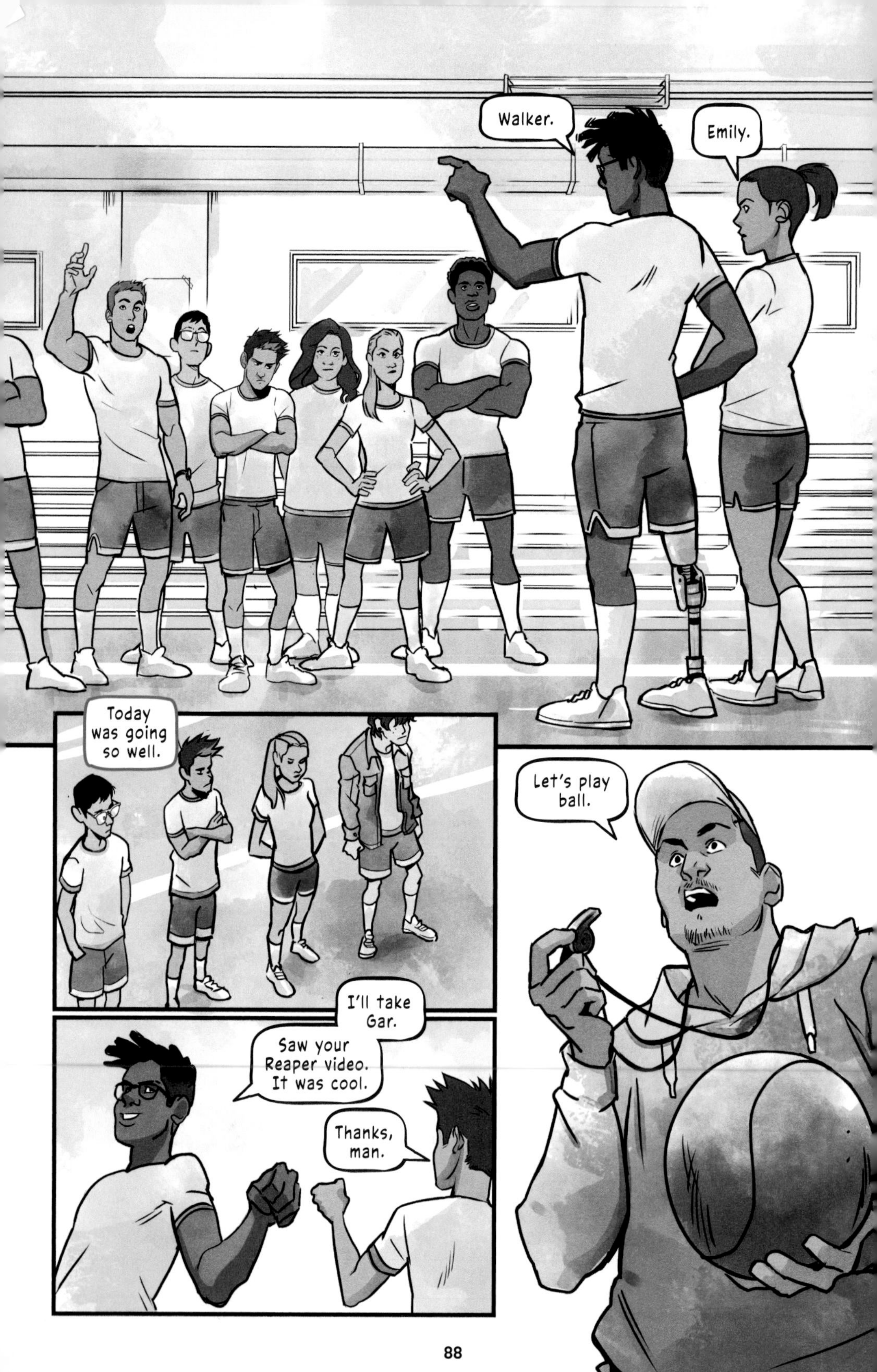
Walker.
Emily.
Today was going so well.
Let's play ball.
I'll take Gar.
Saw your Reaper video. It was cool.
Thanks, man.

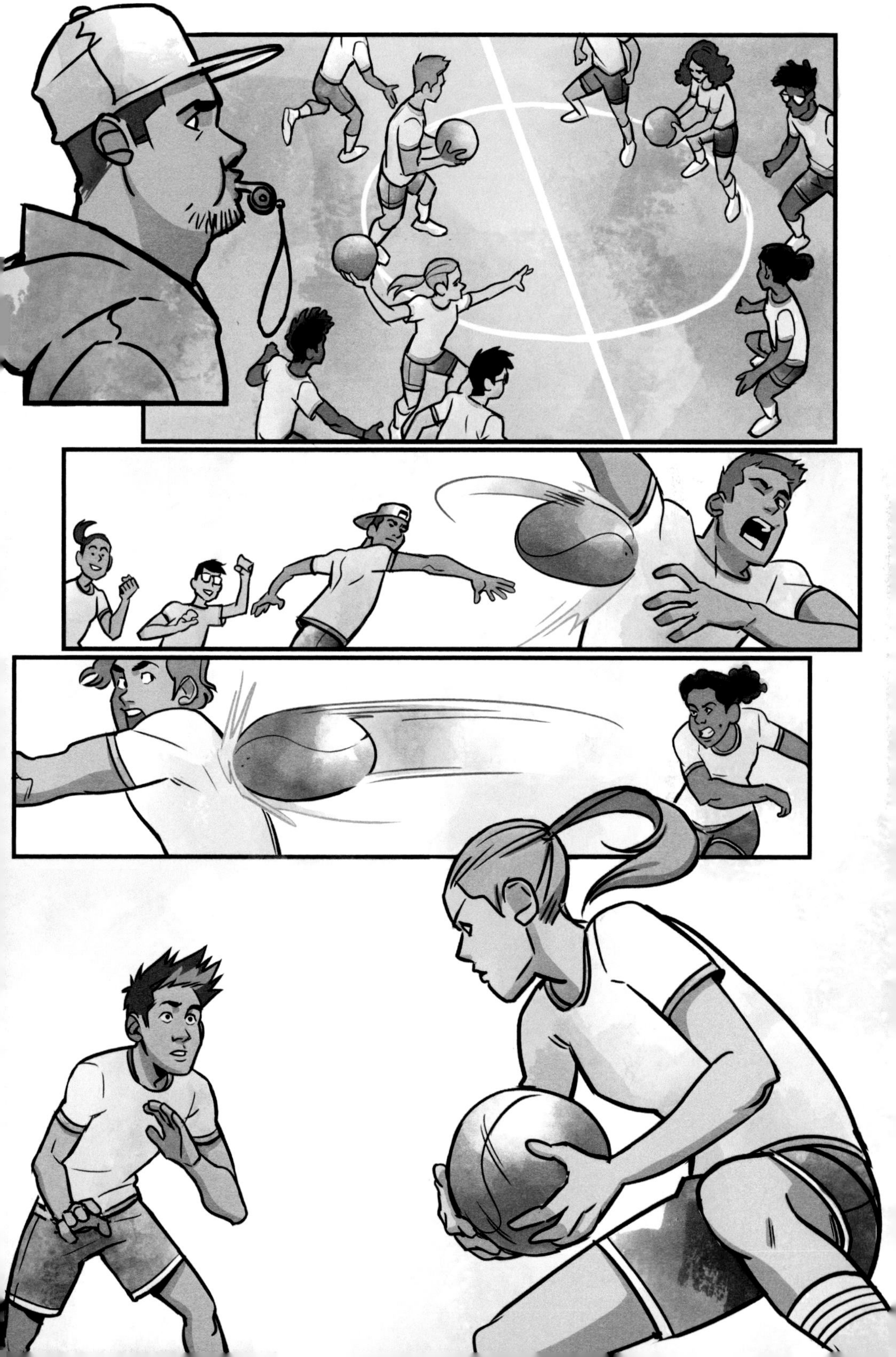

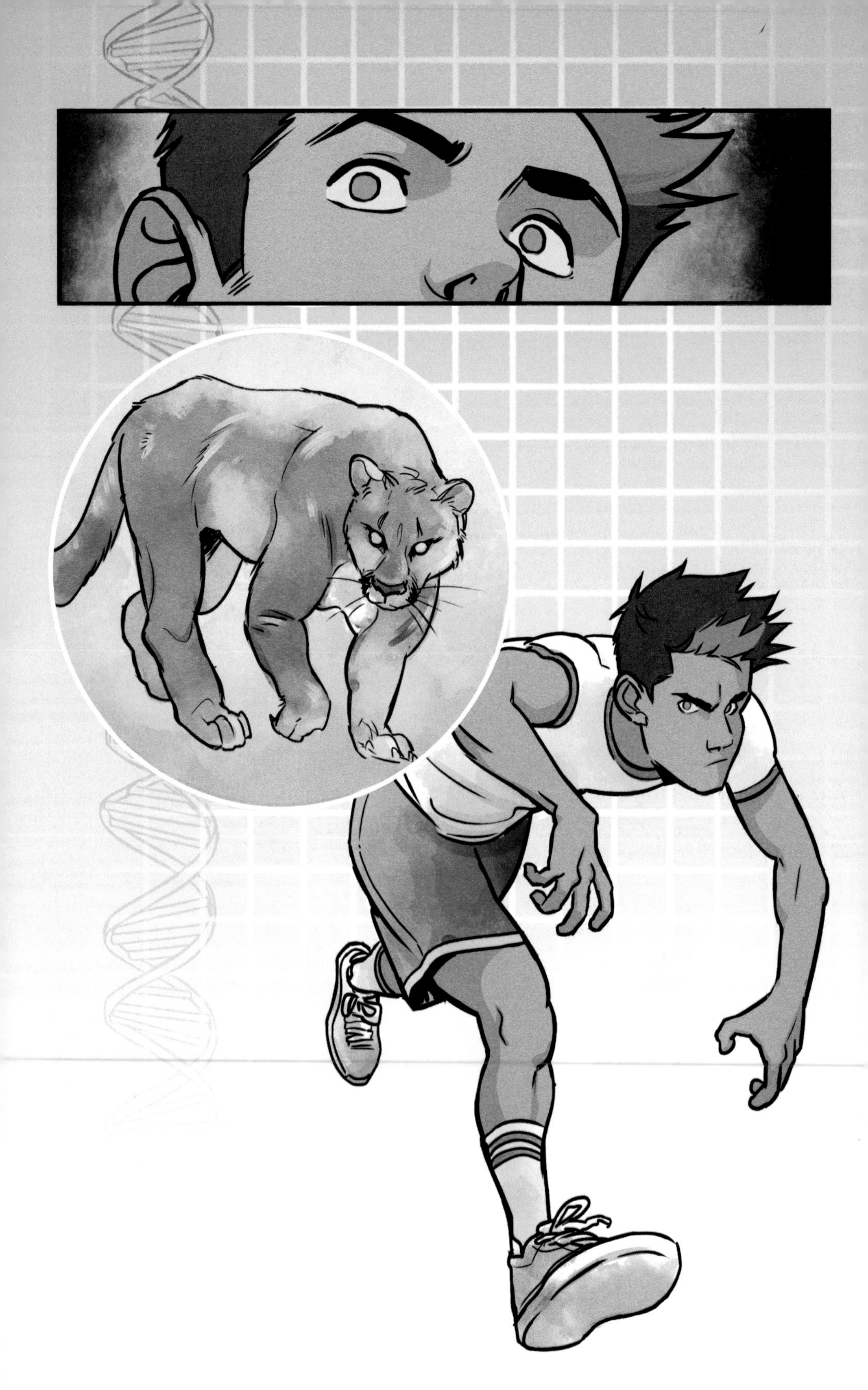

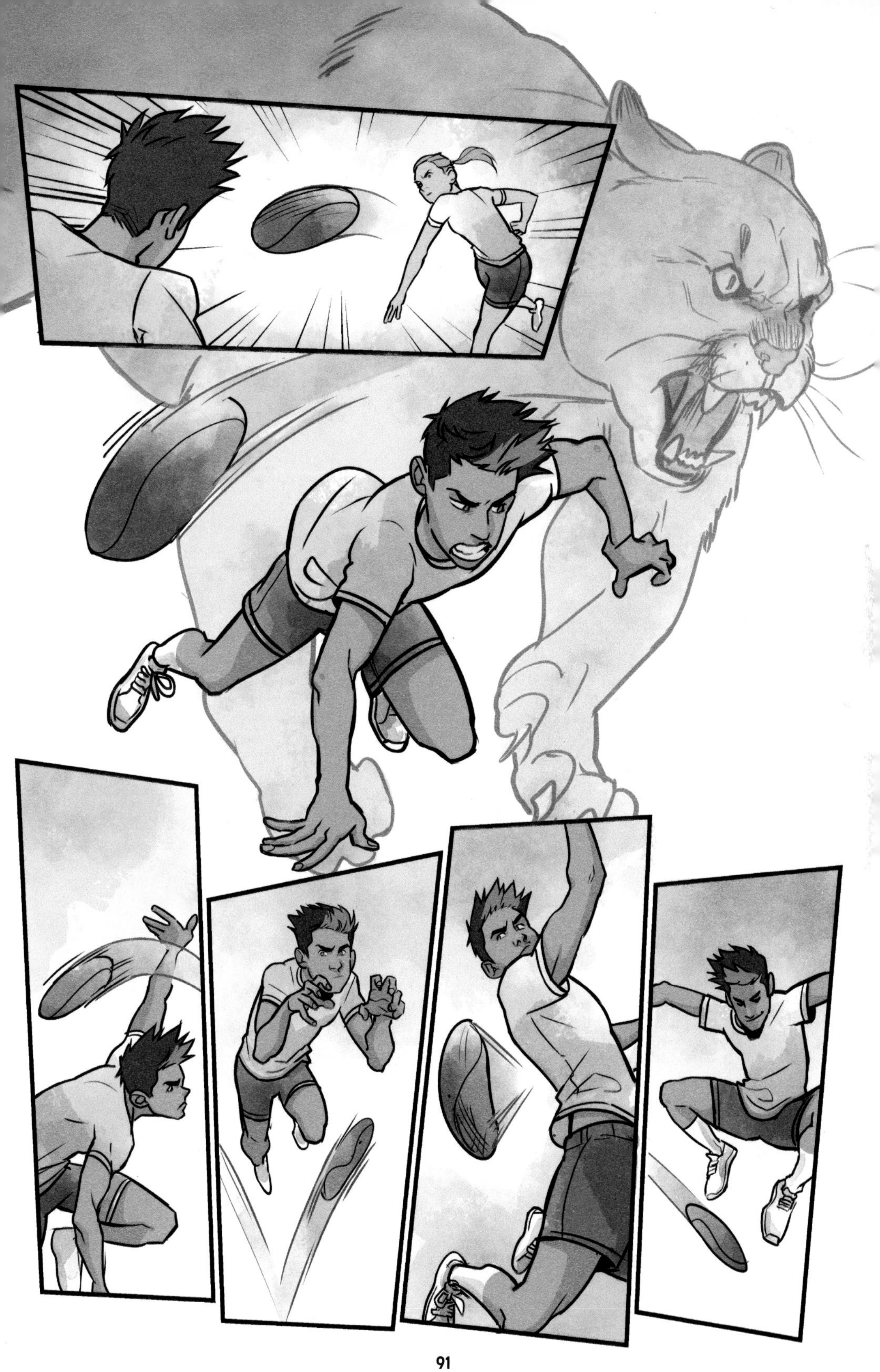

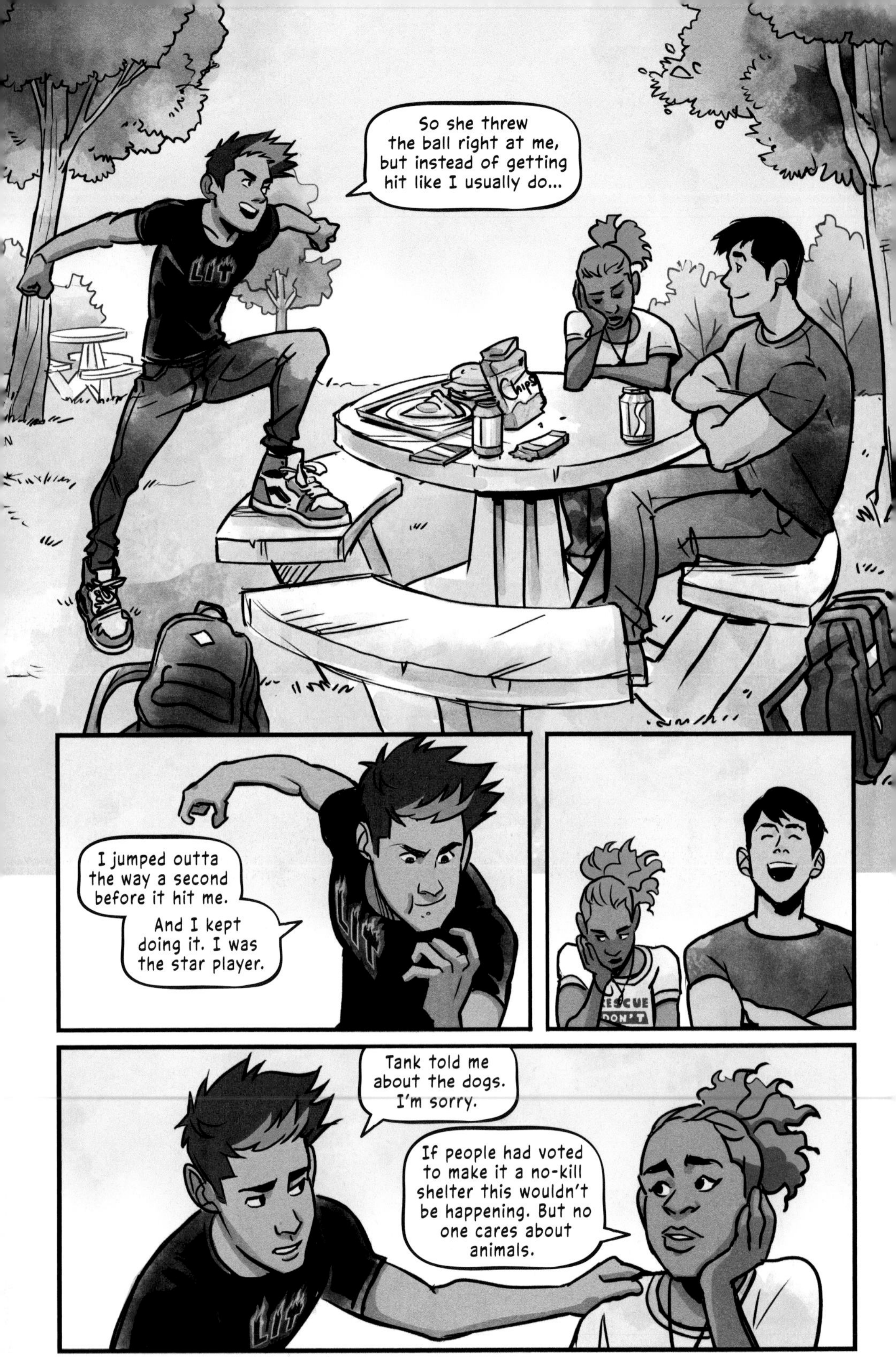
So she threw the ball right at me, but instead of getting hit like I usually do...
LIT
Chips
I jumped outta the way a second before it hit me.
And I kept doing it. I was the star player.
RESCUE DON'T
Tank told me about the dogs. I'm sorry.
If people had voted to make it a no-kill shelter this wouldn't be happening. But no one cares about animals.

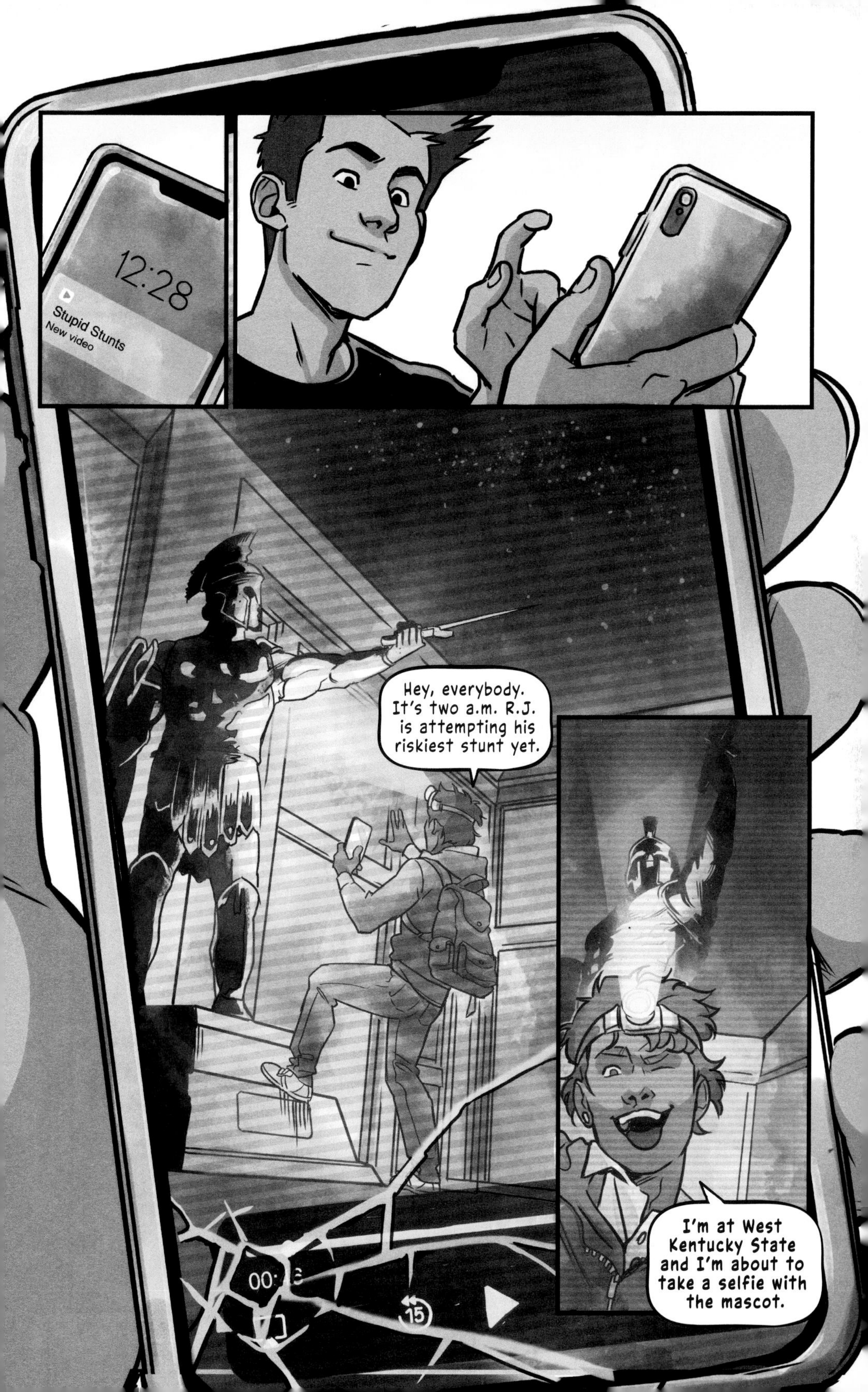
12:28
Stupid Stunts
New video
Hey, everybody. It's two a.m. R.J. is attempting his riskiest stunt yet.
I'm at West Kentucky State and I'm about to take a selfie with the mascot.

CHAPTER 9: EXTREME MEASURES

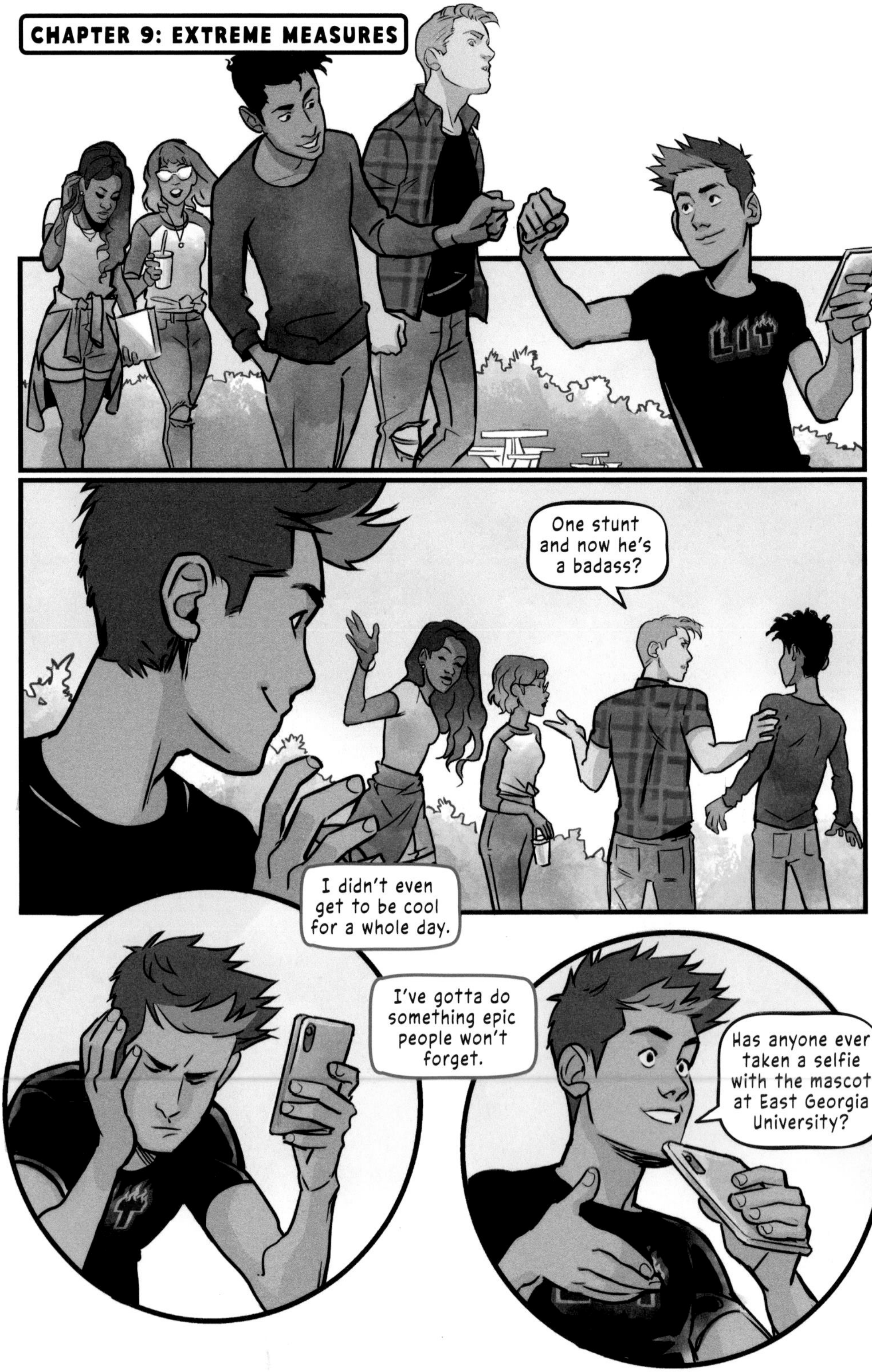
LIT
One stunt and now he's a badass?
I didn't even get to be cool for a whole day.
I've gotta do something epic people won't forget.
Has anyone ever taken a selfie with the mascot at East Georgia University?

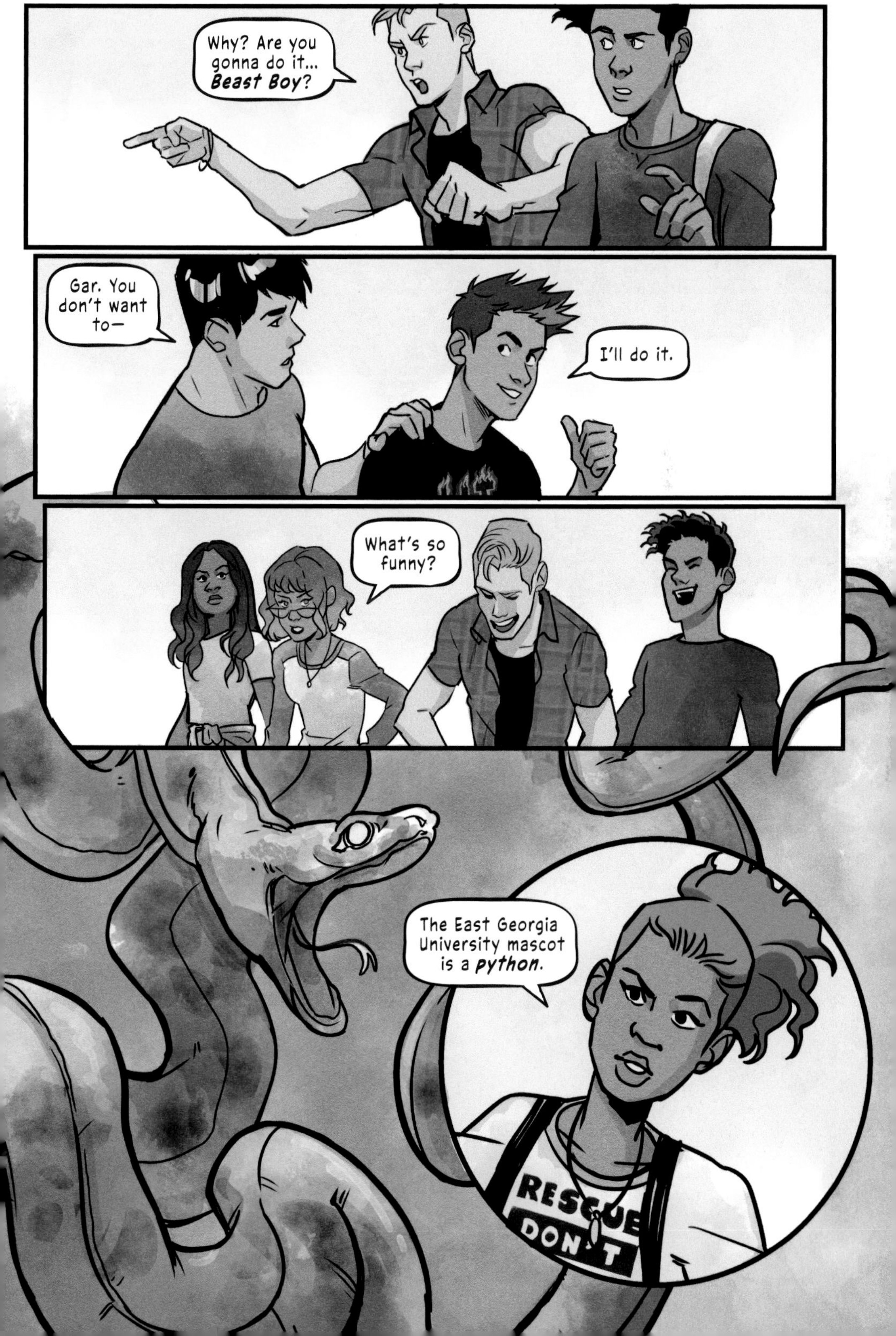
Why? Are you gonna do it... *Beast Boy*?
Gar. You don't want to—
I'll do it.
What's so funny?
The East Georgia University mascot is a *python*.
RESCUE DON'T

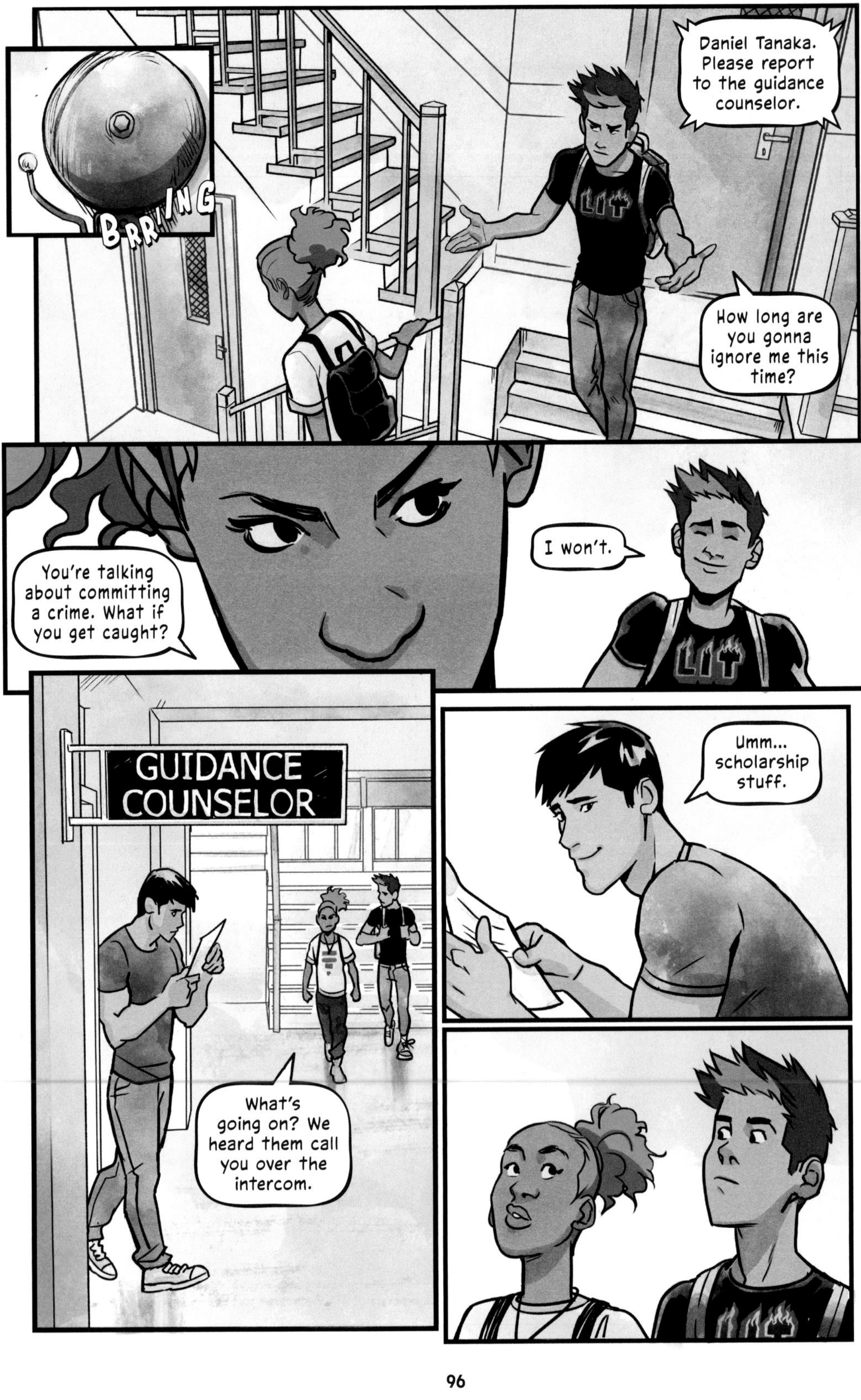
BRRING
Daniel Tanaka. Please report to the guidance counselor.
How long are you gonna ignore me this time?
You're talking about committing a crime. What if you get caught?
I won't.
GUIDANCE COUNSELOR
What's going on? We heard them call you over the intercom.
Umm... scholarship stuff.

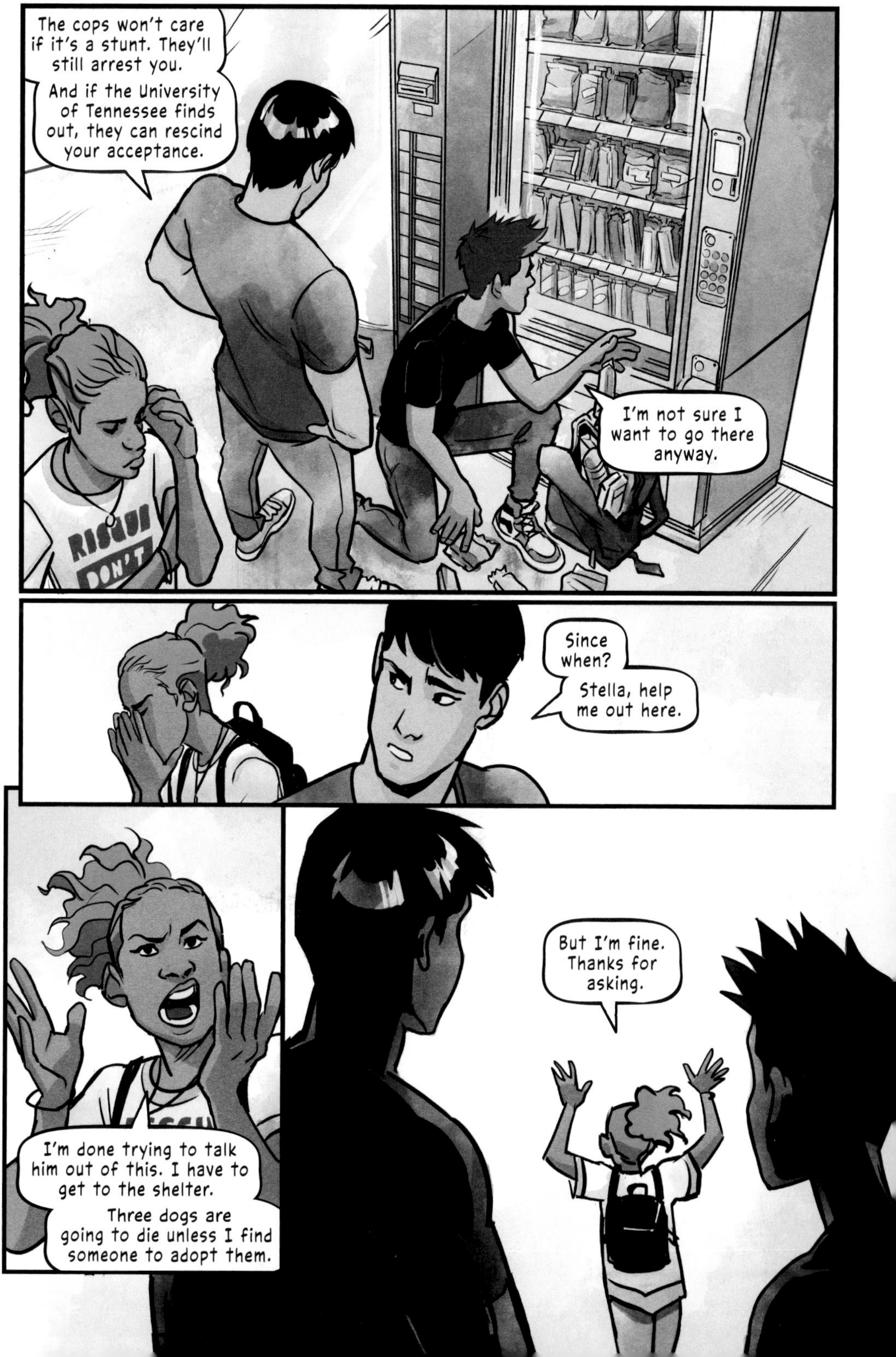
The cops won't care if it's a stunt. They'll still arrest you.
And if the University of Tennessee finds out, they can rescind your acceptance.
I'm not sure I want to go there anyway.
Since when?
Stella, help me out here.
I'm done trying to talk him out of this. I have to get to the shelter.
Three dogs are going to die unless I find someone to adopt them.
But I'm fine. Thanks for asking.

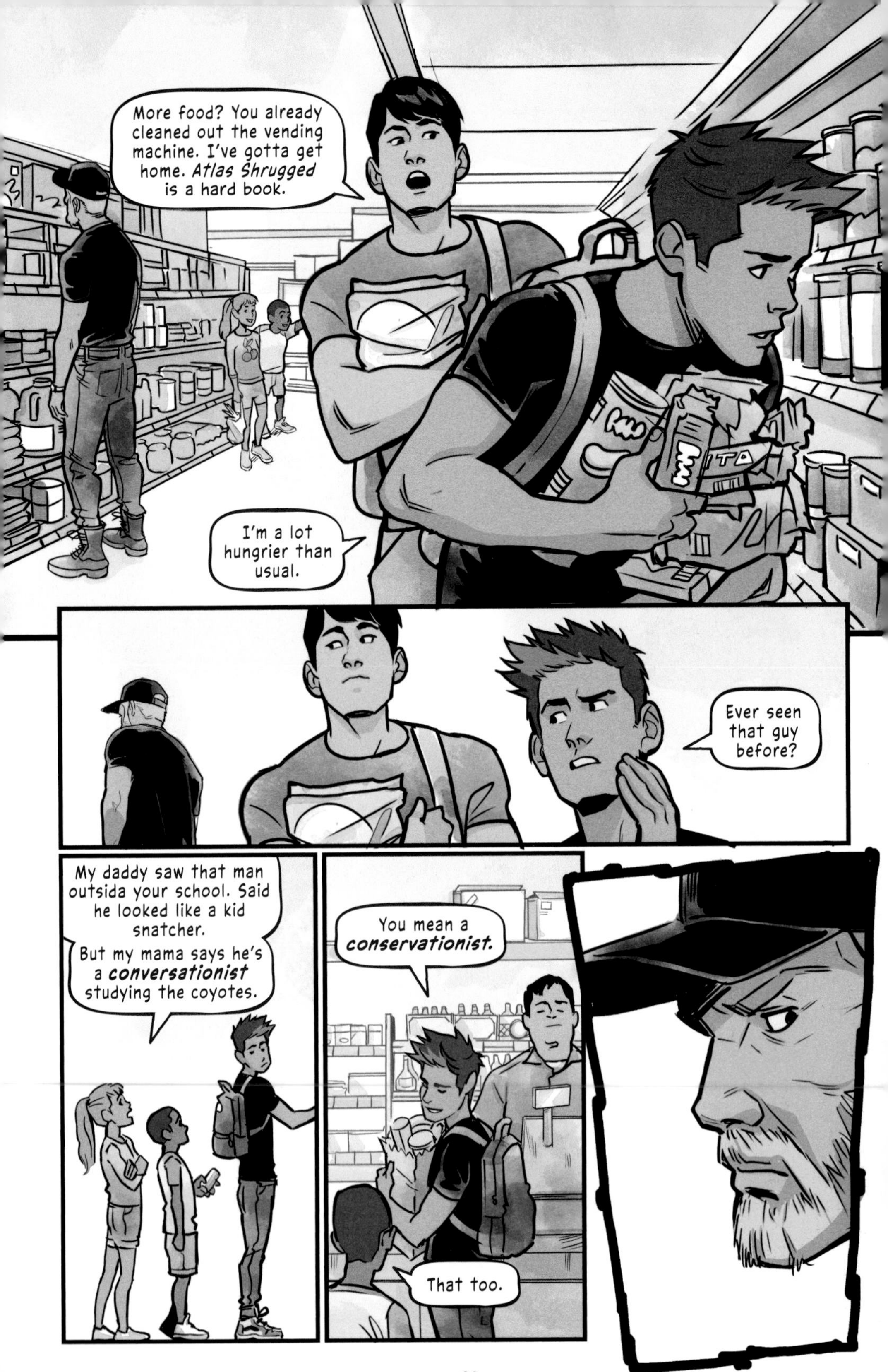
More food? You already cleaned out the vending machine. I've gotta get home. *Atlas Shrugged* is a hard book.
I'm a lot hungrier than usual.
Ever seen that guy before?
My daddy saw that man outsida your school. Said he looked like a kid snatcher.
But my mama says he's a **conversationist** studying the coyotes.
You mean a **conservationist.**
That too.

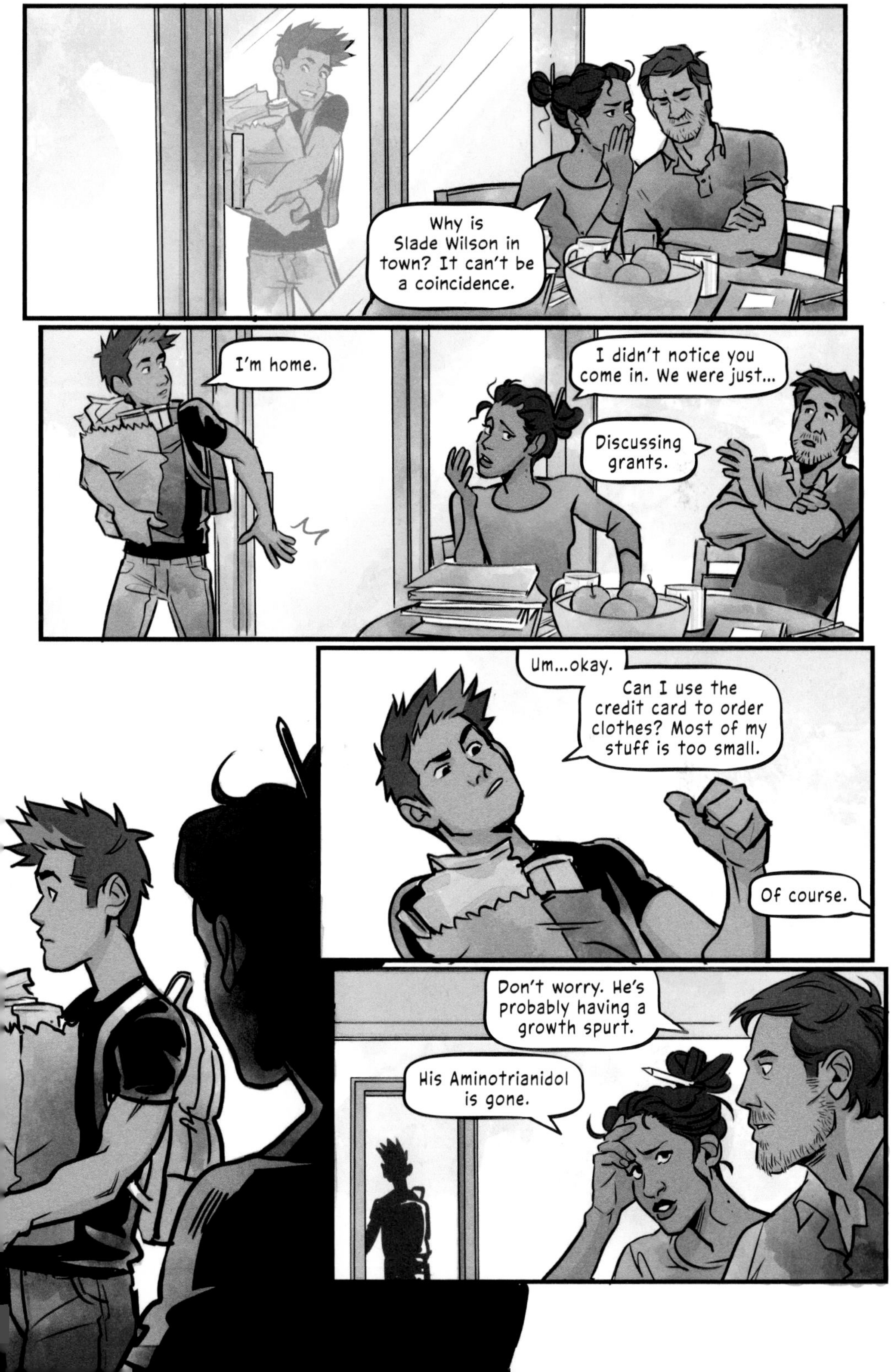
Why is Slade Wilson in town? It can't be a coincidence.
I'm home.
I didn't notice you come in. We were just...
Discussing grants.
Um...okay.
Can I use the credit card to order clothes? Most of my stuff is too small.
Of course.
Don't worry. He's probably having a growth spurt.
His Aminotrianidol is gone.

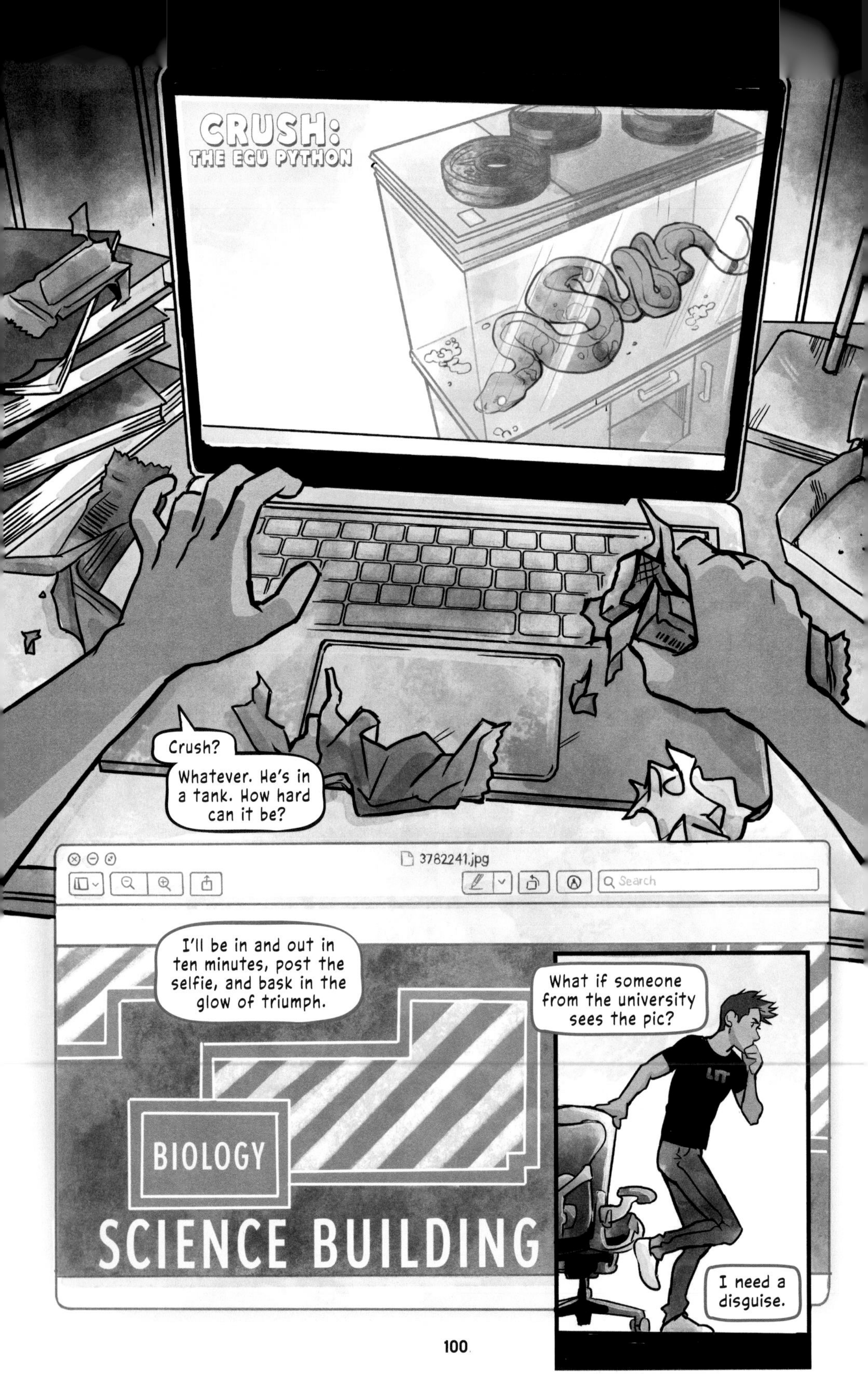
CRUSH:
THE EGU PYTHON
Crush?
Whatever. He's in a tank. How hard can it be?
3782241.jpg
Search
I'll be in and out in ten minutes, post the selfie, and bask in the glow of triumph.
BIOLOGY
SCIENCE BUILDING
What if someone from the university sees the pic?
I need a disguise.

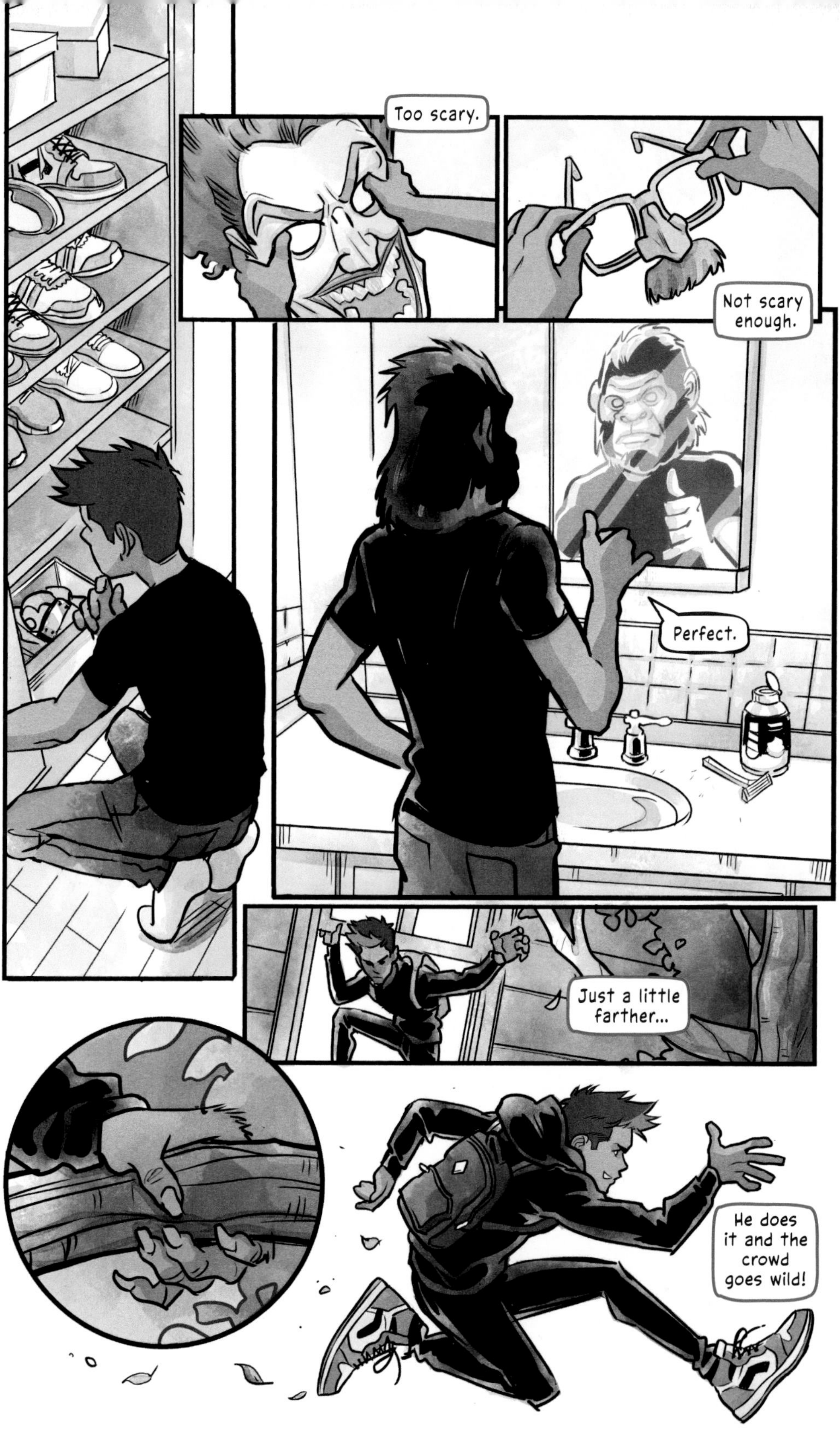
Too scary.
Not scary enough.
Perfect.
Just a little farther...
He does it and the crowd goes wild!

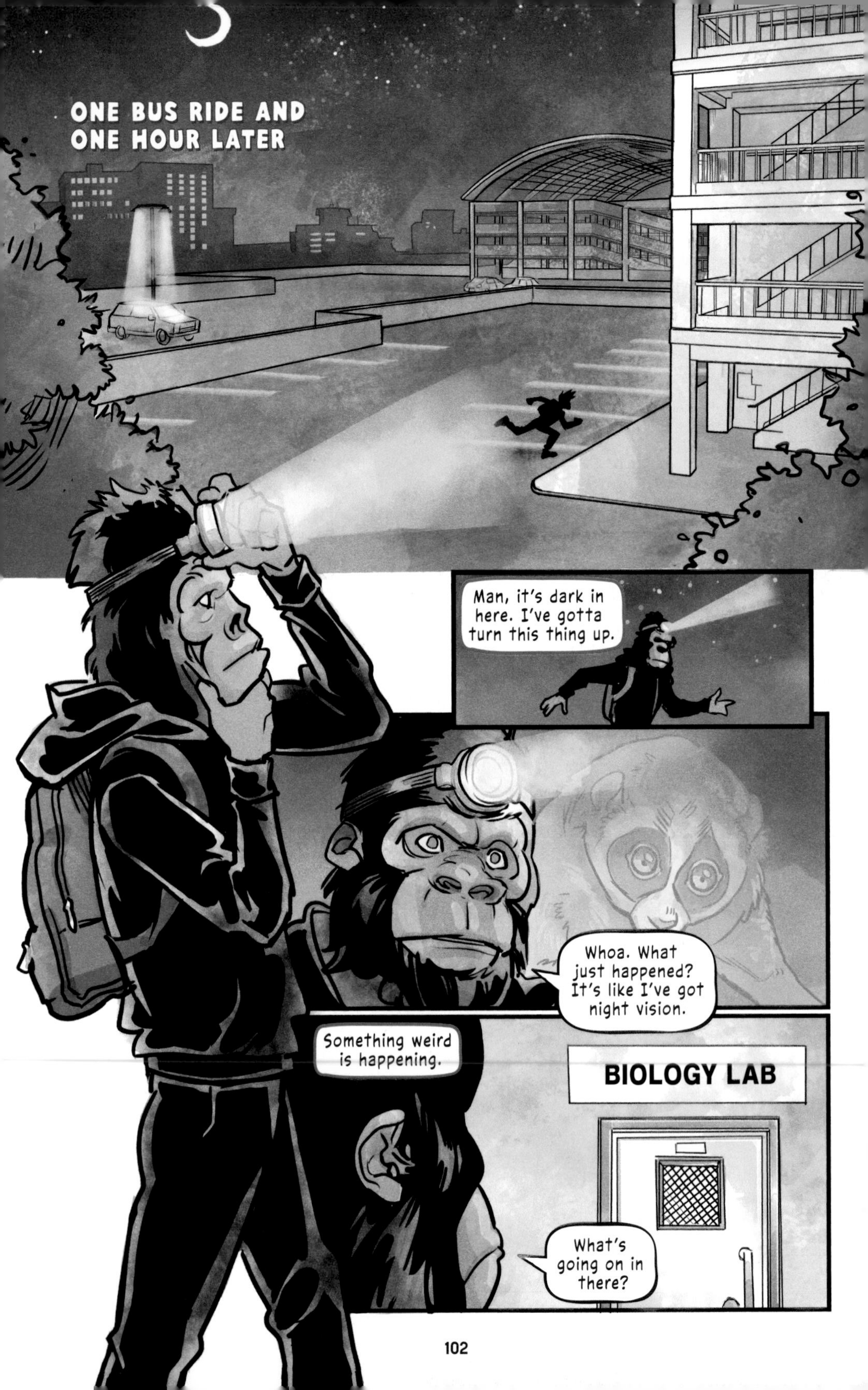
ONE BUS RIDE AND ONE HOUR LATER
Man, it's dark in here. I've gotta turn this thing up.
Whoa. What just happened? It's like I've got night vision.
Something weird is happening.
BIOLOGY LAB
What's going on in there?

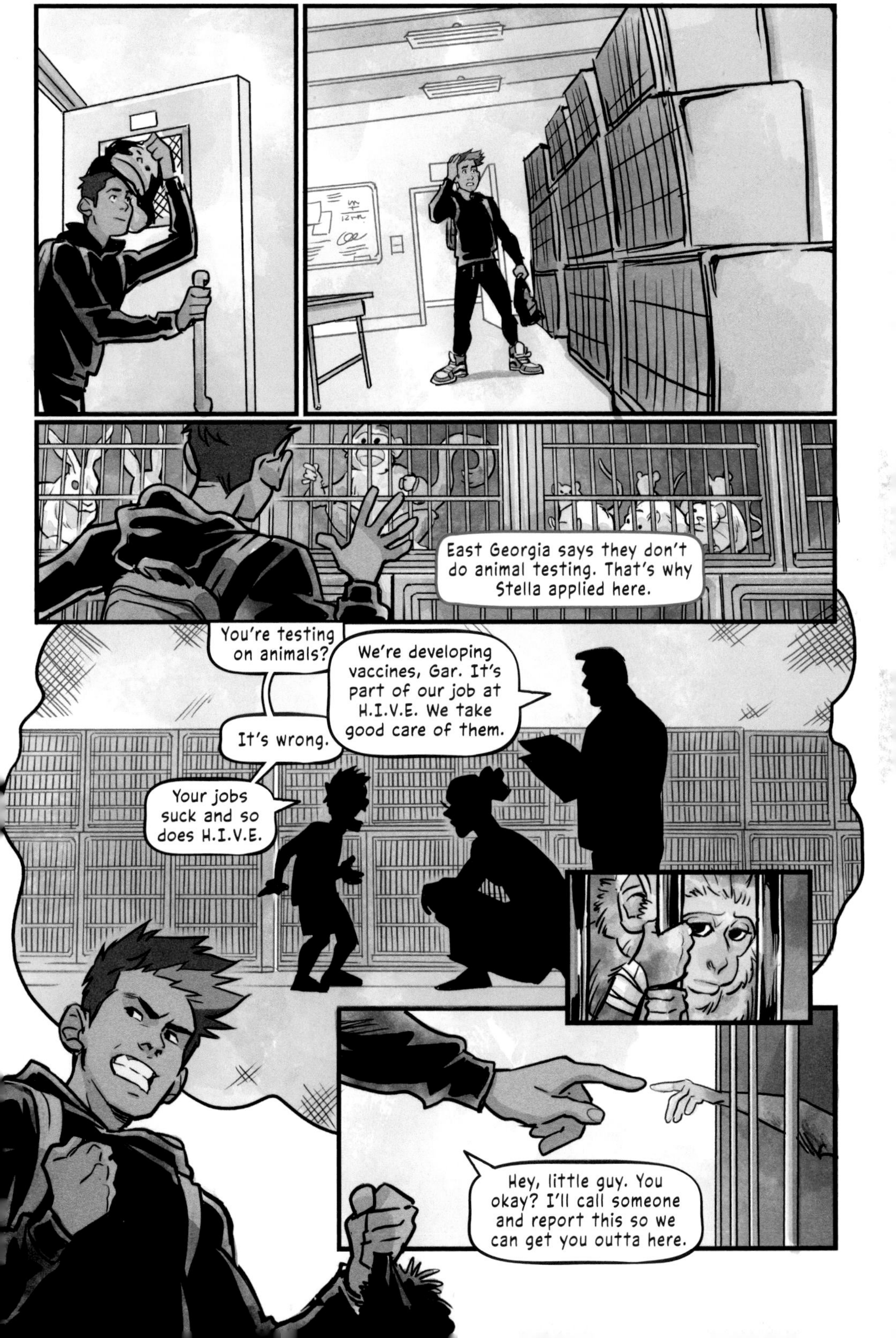
East Georgia says they don't do animal testing. That's why Stella applied here.
You're testing on animals?
We're developing vaccines, Gar. It's part of our job at H.I.V.E. We take good care of them.
It's wrong.
Your jobs suck and so does H.I.V.E.
Hey, little guy. You okay? I'll call someone and report this so we can get you outta here.

CHAPTER 10: SERIOUS CRUSH

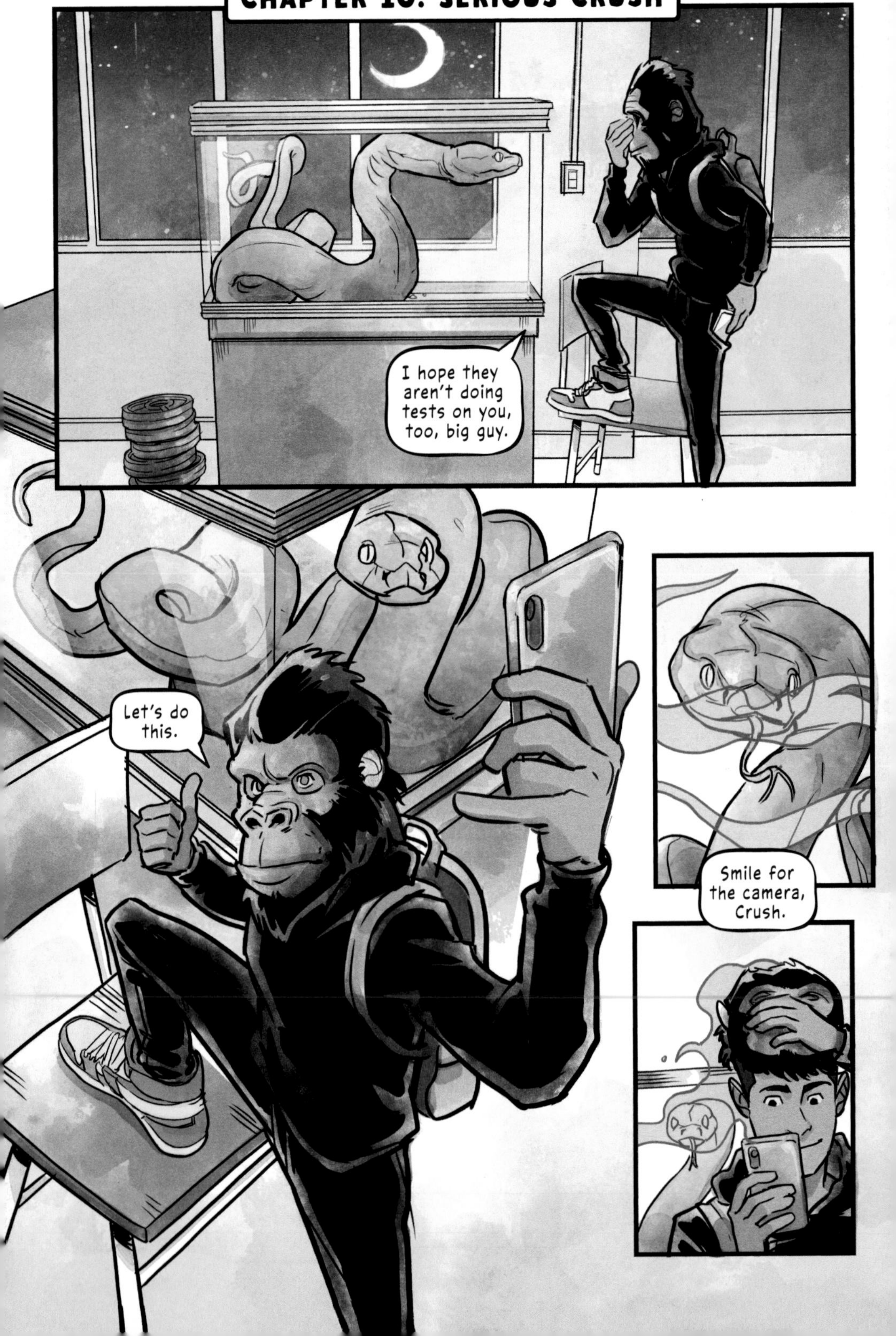
I hope they aren't doing tests on you, too, big guy.
Let's do this.
Smile for the camera, Crush.

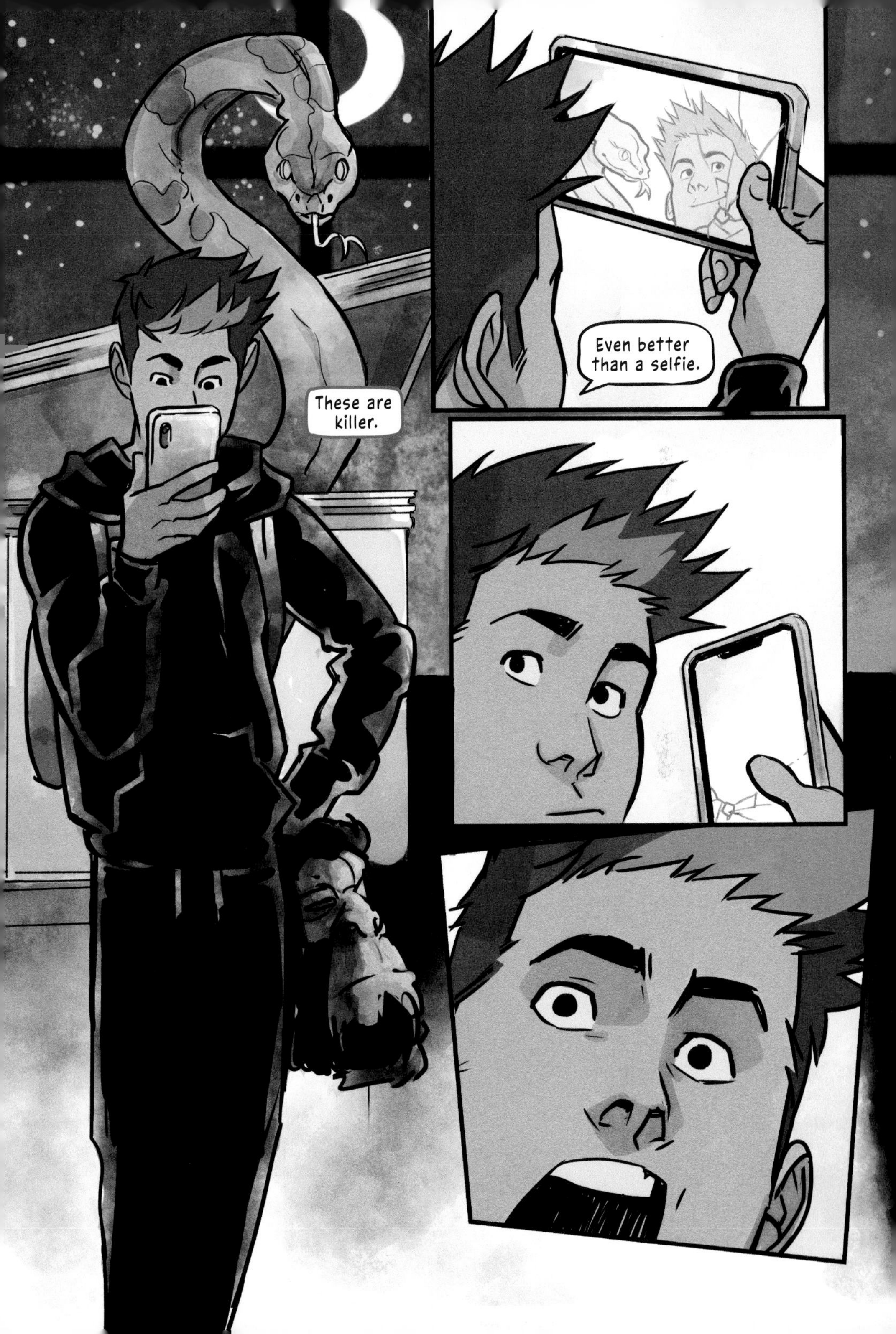
These are killer.
Even better than a selfie.

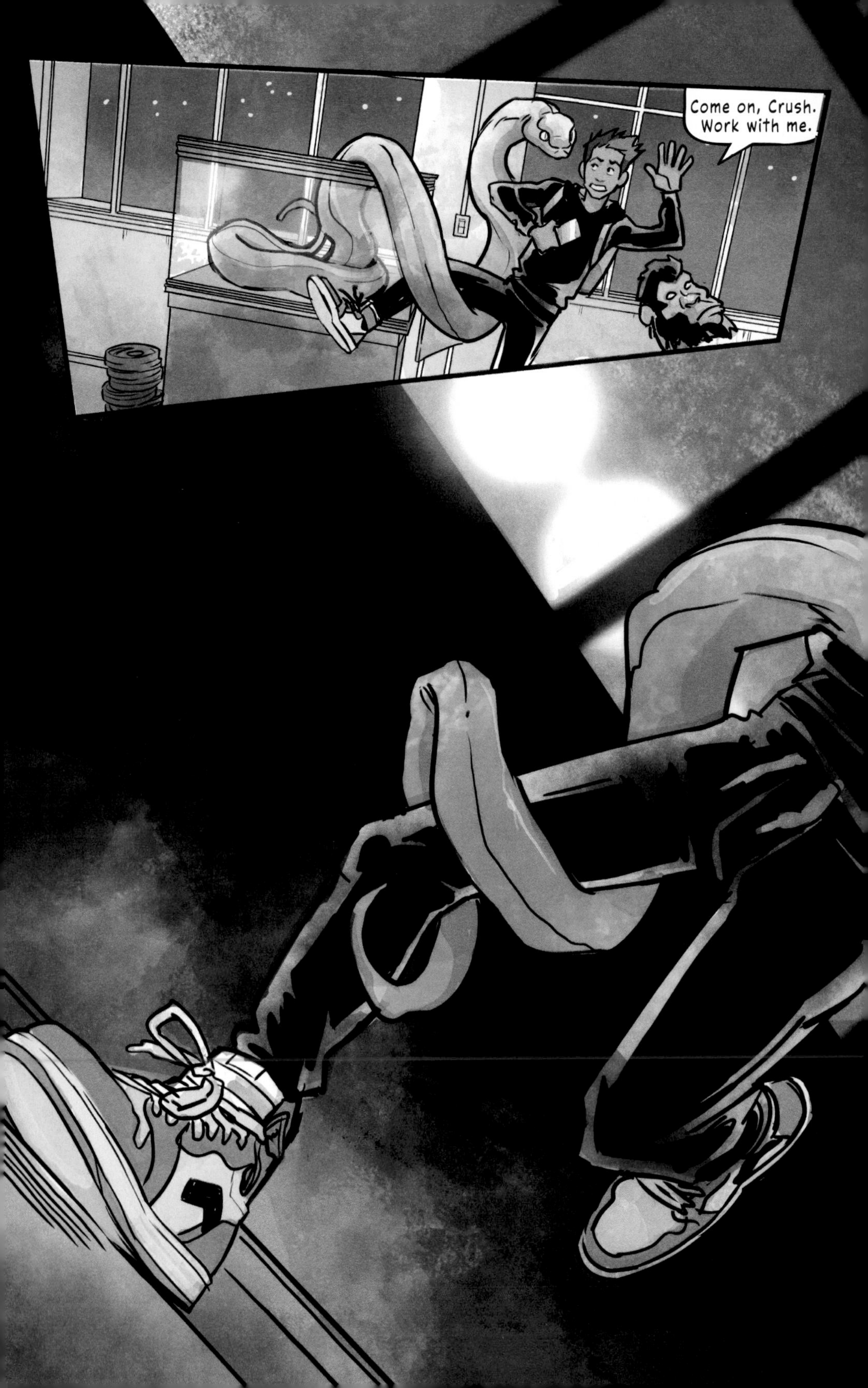
Come on, Crush. Work with me.

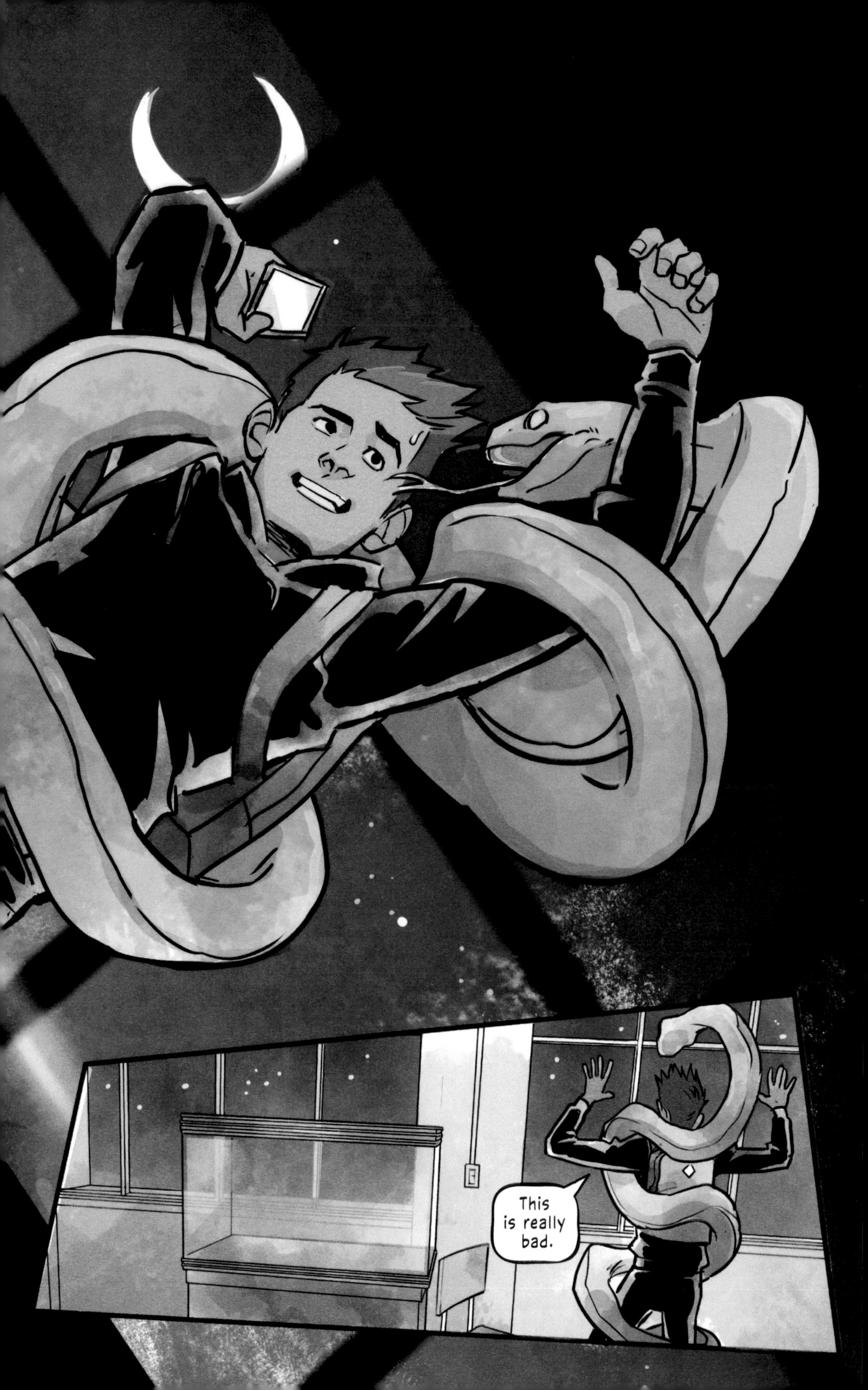
This is really bad.

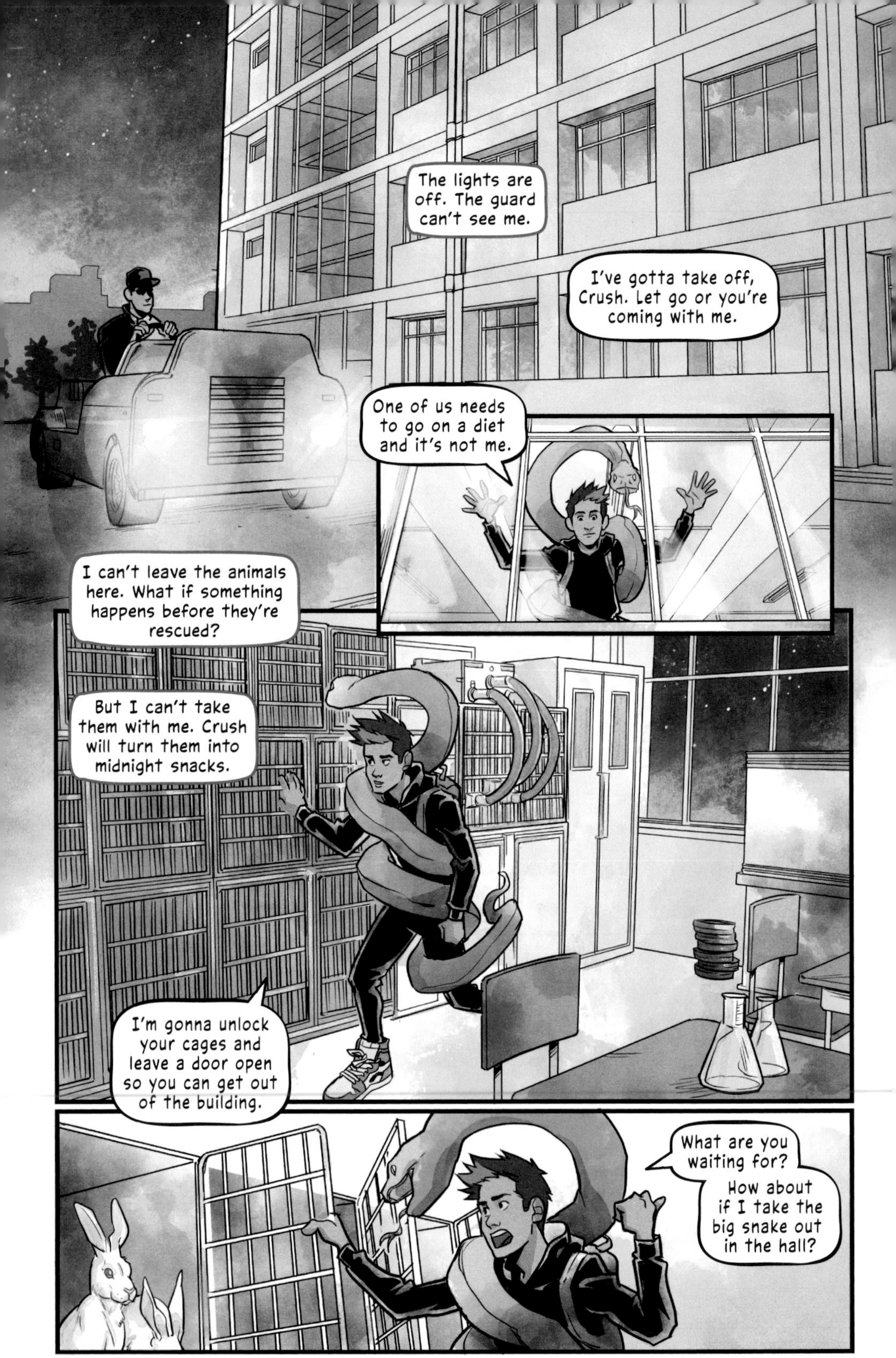
The lights are off. The guard can't see me.
I've gotta take off, Crush. Let go or you're coming with me.
One of us needs to go on a diet and it's not me.
I can't leave the animals here. What if something happens before they're rescued?
But I can't take them with me. Crush will turn them into midnight snacks.
I'm gonna unlock your cages and leave a door open so you can get out of the building.
What are you waiting for?
How about if I take the big snake out in the hall?

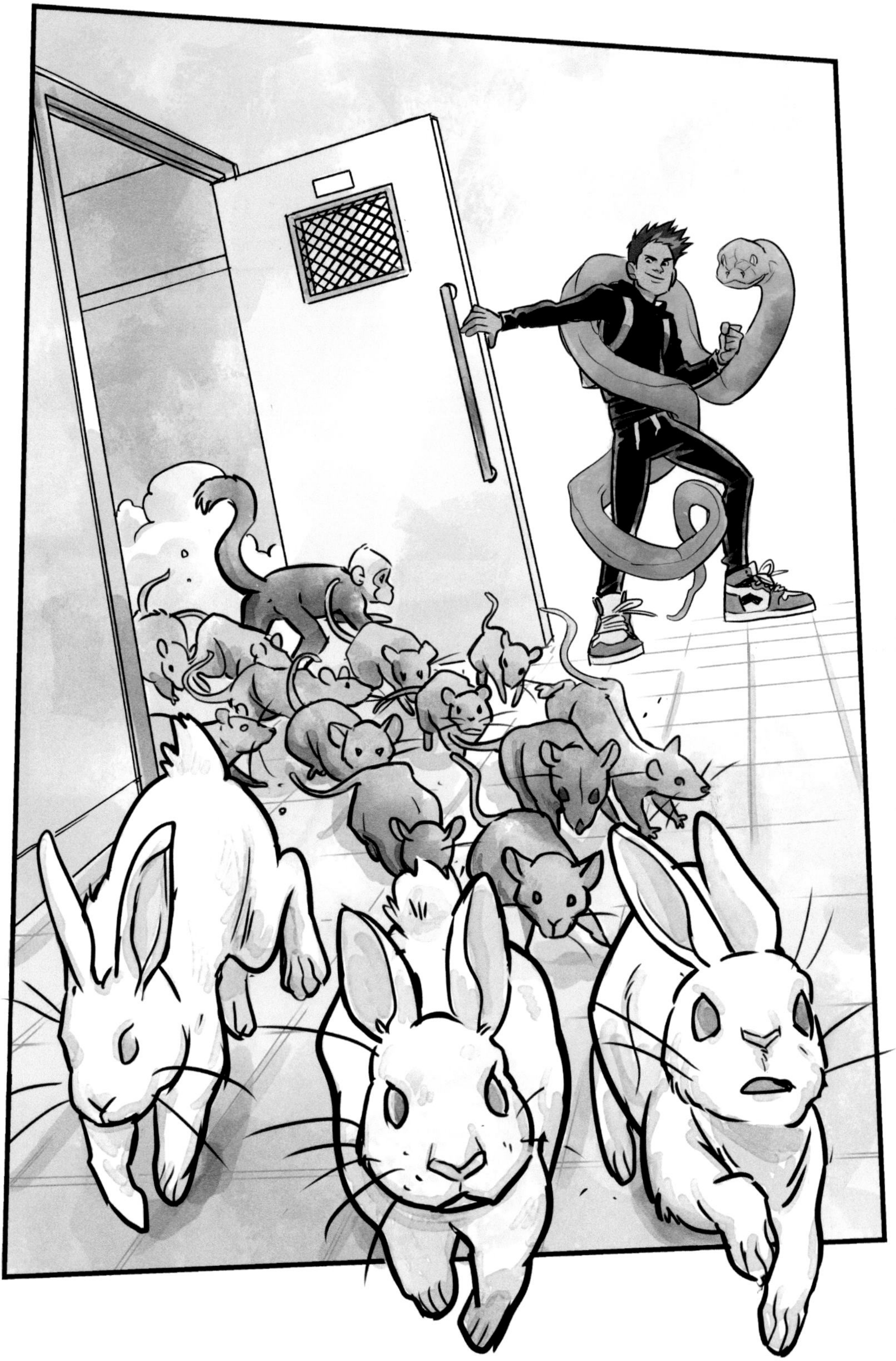

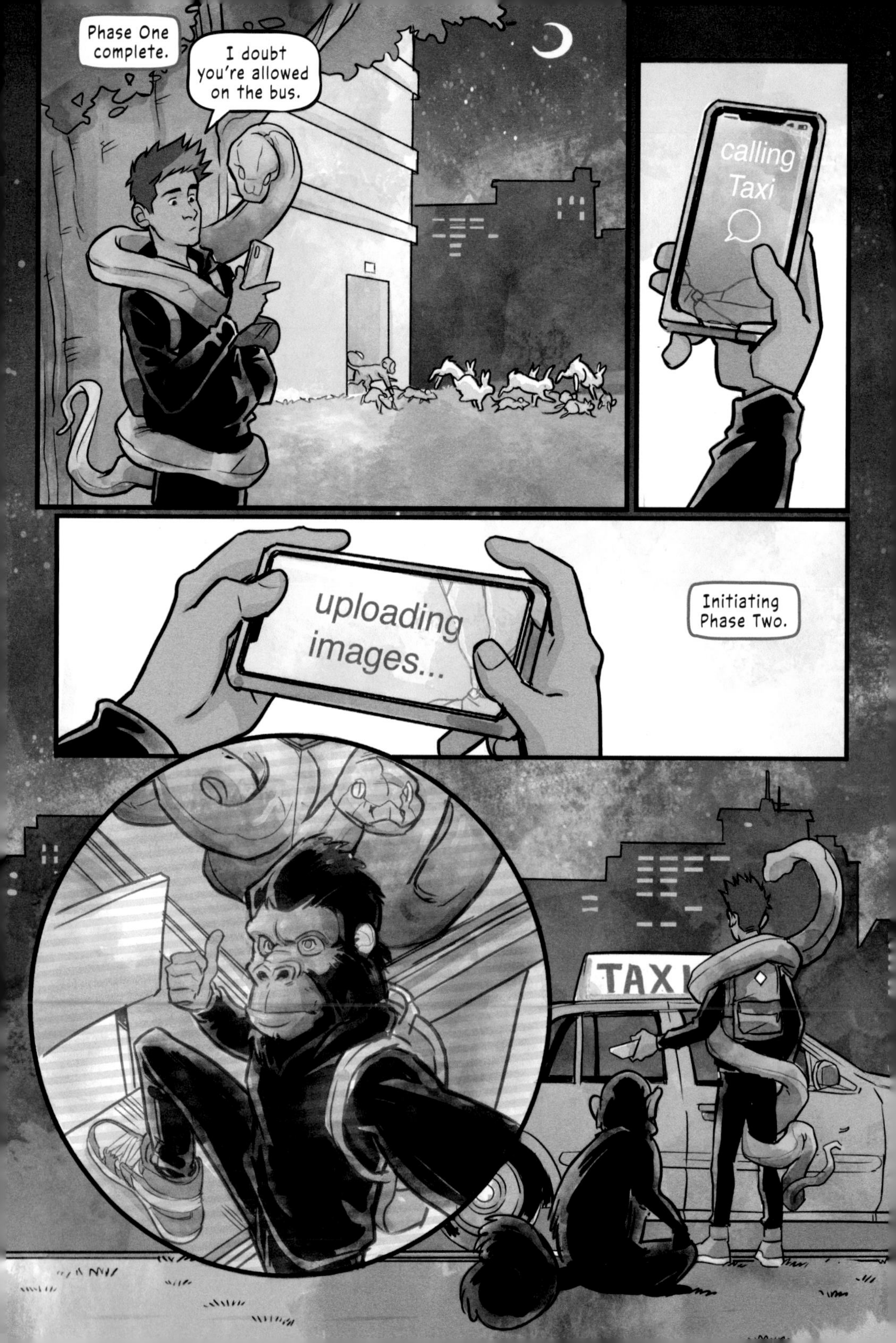
Phase One complete.
I doubt you're allowed on the bus.
calling Taxi
uploading images...
Initiating Phase Two.
TAXI

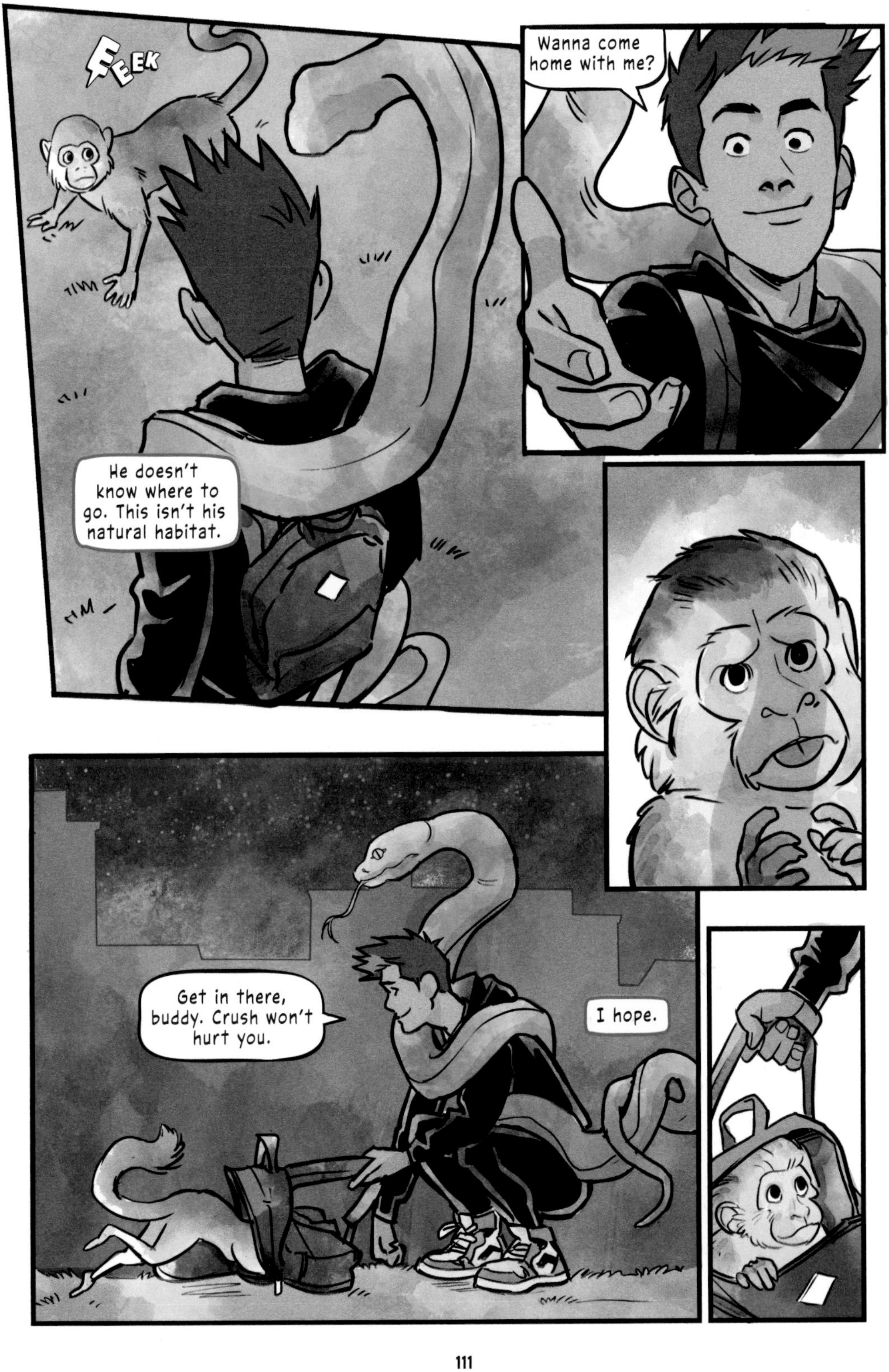
EEEK
Wanna come home with me?
He doesn't know where to go. This isn't his natural habitat.
Get in there, buddy. Crush won't hurt you.
I hope.

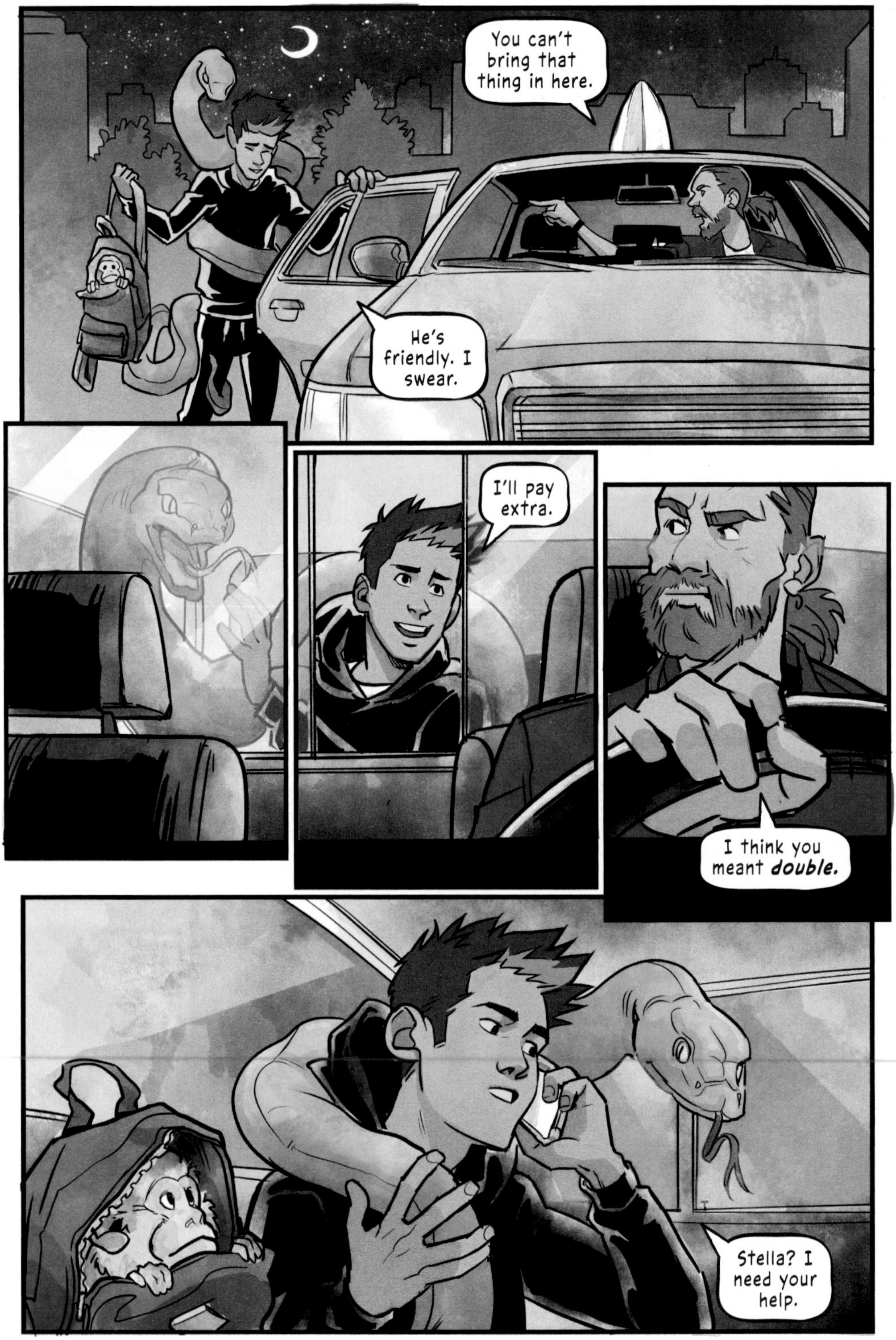
You can't bring that thing in here.
He's friendly. I swear.
I'll pay extra.
I think you meant *double.*
Stella? I need your help.

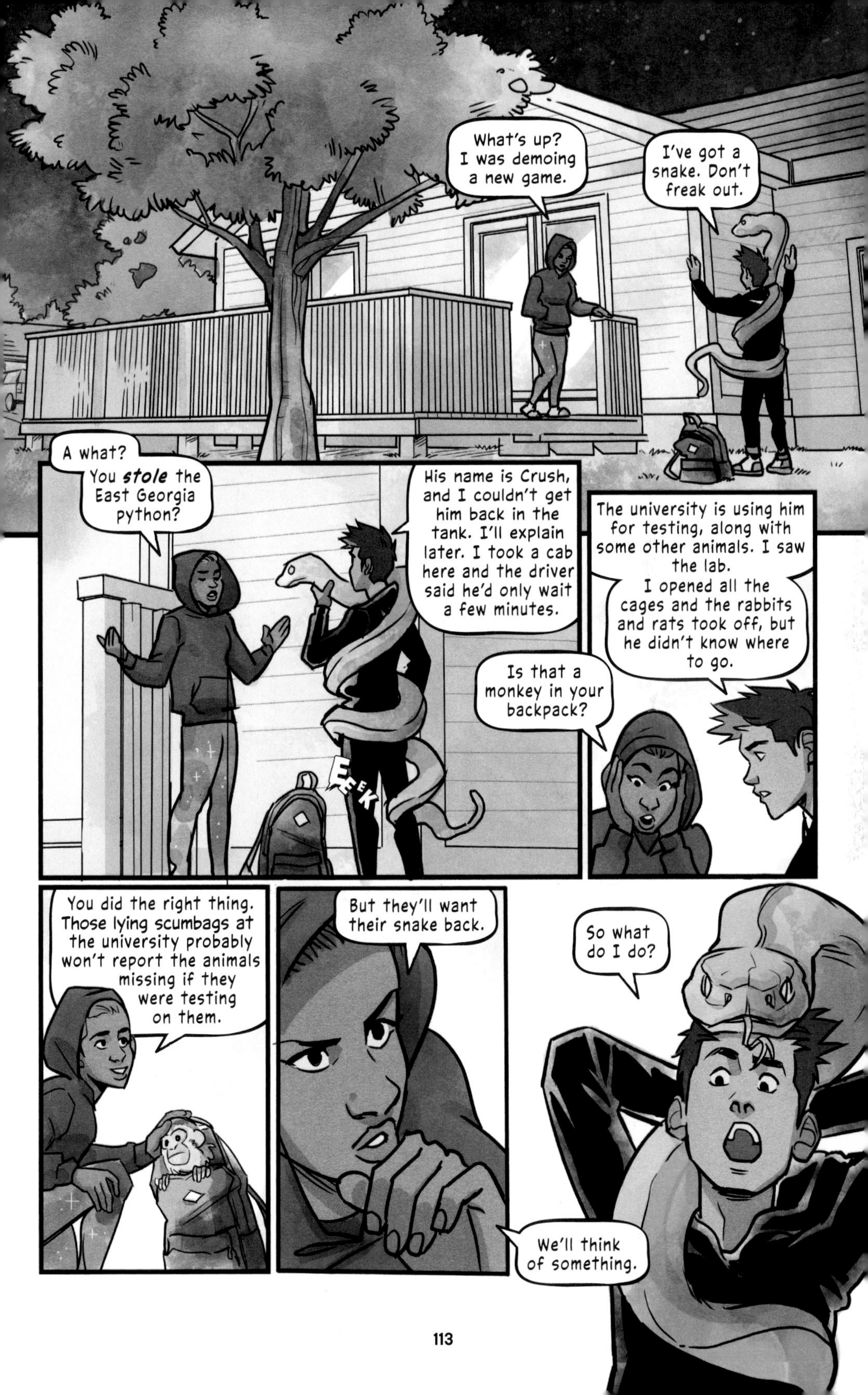
What's up? I was demoing a new game.
I've got a snake. Don't freak out.
A what?
You *stole* the East Georgia python?
His name is Crush, and I couldn't get him back in the tank. I'll explain later. I took a cab here and the driver said he'd only wait a few minutes.
EEEK
The university is using him for testing, along with some other animals. I saw the lab.
I opened all the cages and the rabbits and rats took off, but he didn't know where to go.
Is that a monkey in your backpack?
You did the right thing. Those lying scumbags at the university probably won't report the animals missing if they were testing on them.
But they'll want their snake back.
So what do I do?
We'll think of something.

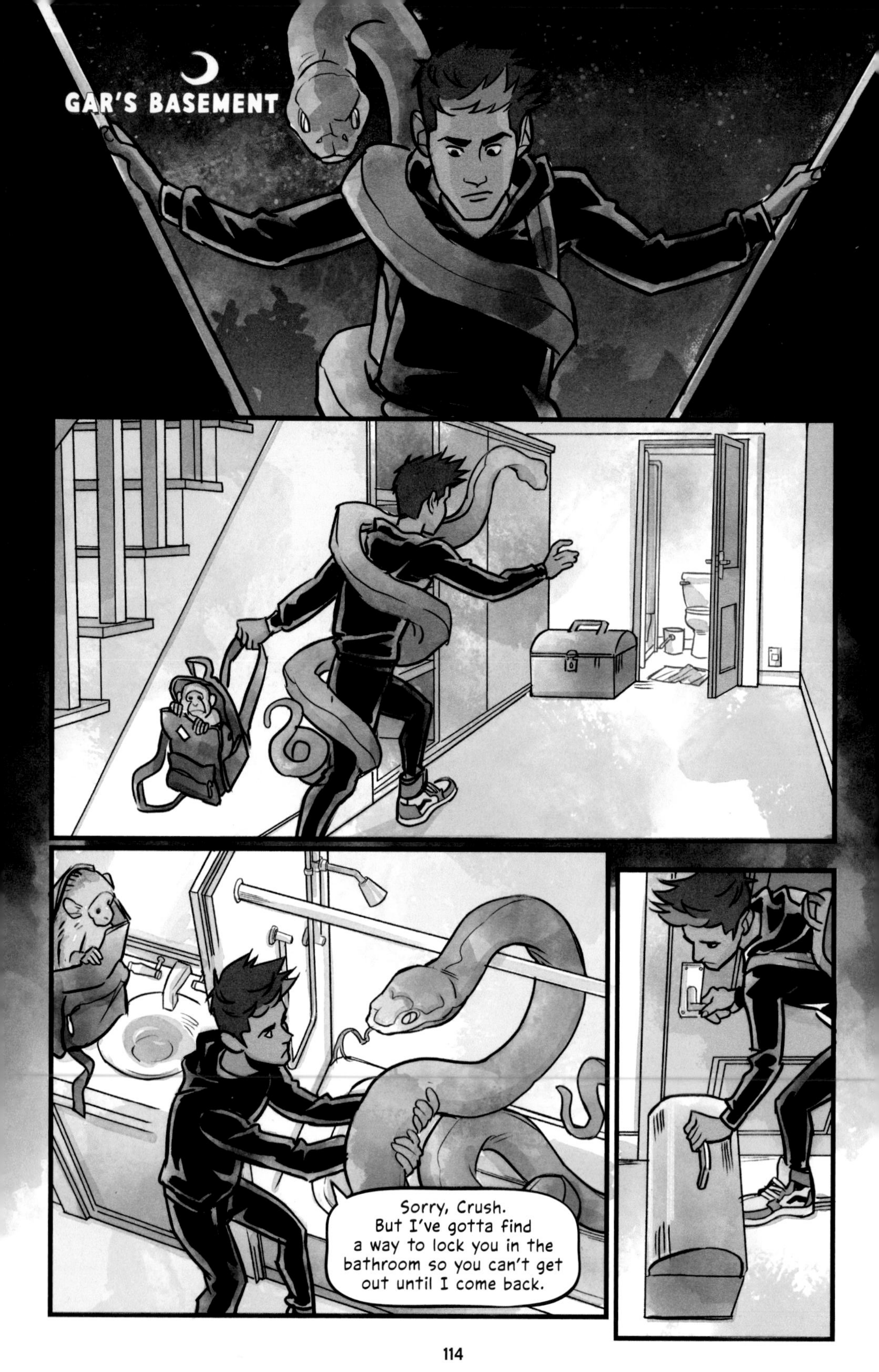
GAR'S BASEMENT
Sorry, Crush. But I've gotta find a way to lock you in the bathroom so you can't get out until I come back.

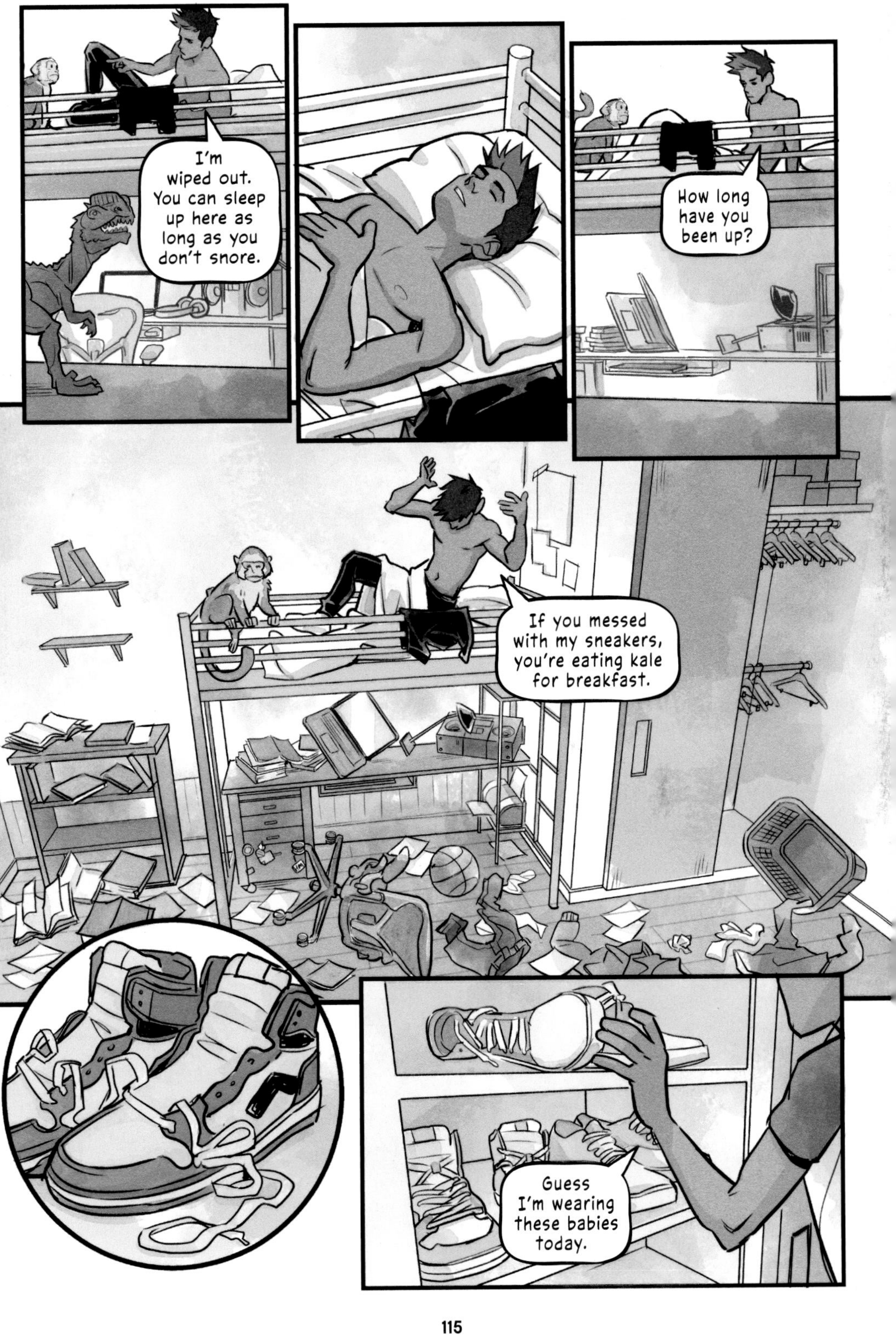
I'm wiped out. You can sleep up here as long as you don't snore.
How long have you been up?
If you messed with my sneakers, you're eating kale for breakfast.
Guess I'm wearing these babies today.

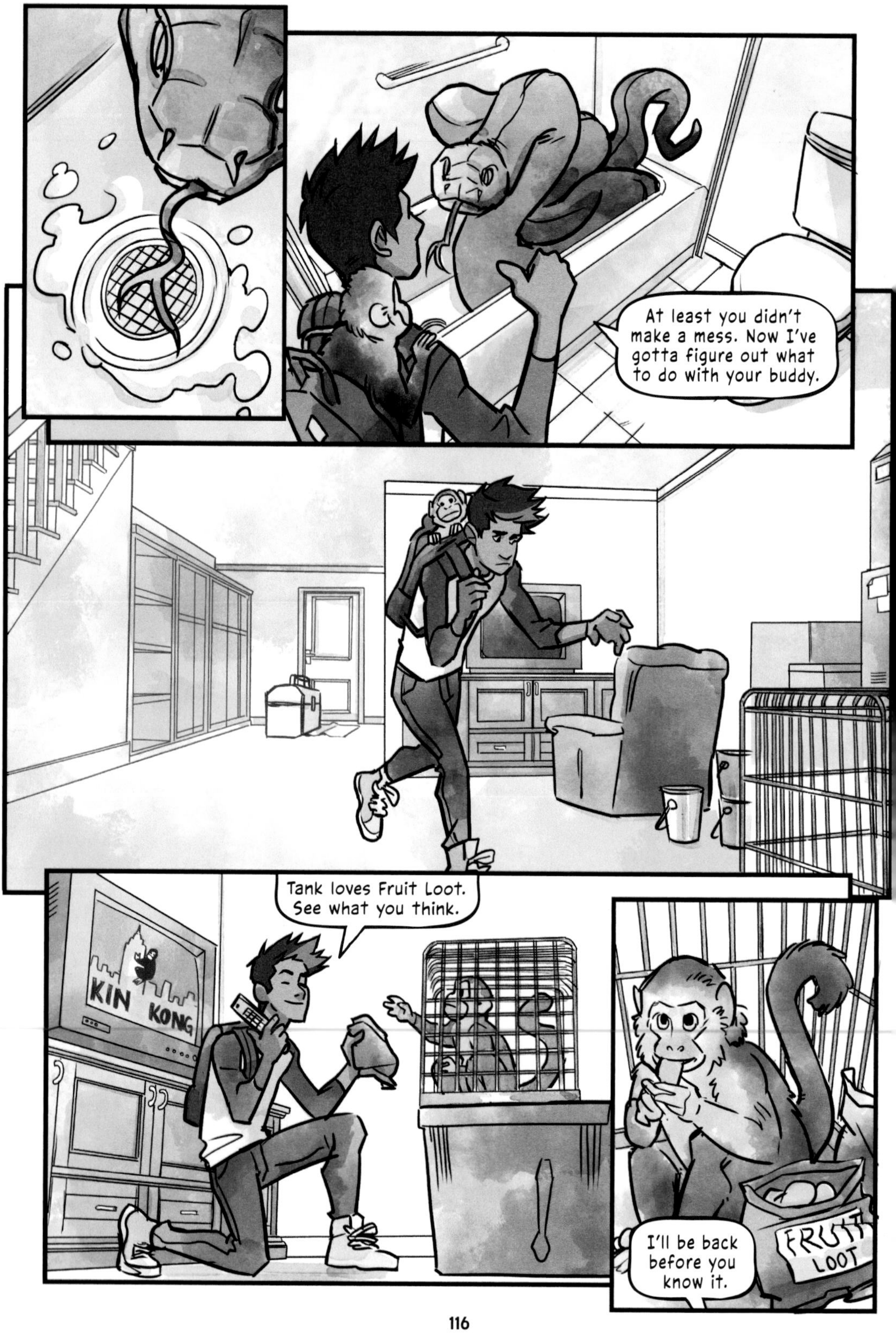
At least you didn't make a mess. Now I've gotta figure out what to do with your buddy.
KIN KONG
Tank loves Fruit Loot. See what you think.
I'll be back before you know it.
FRUIT LOOT

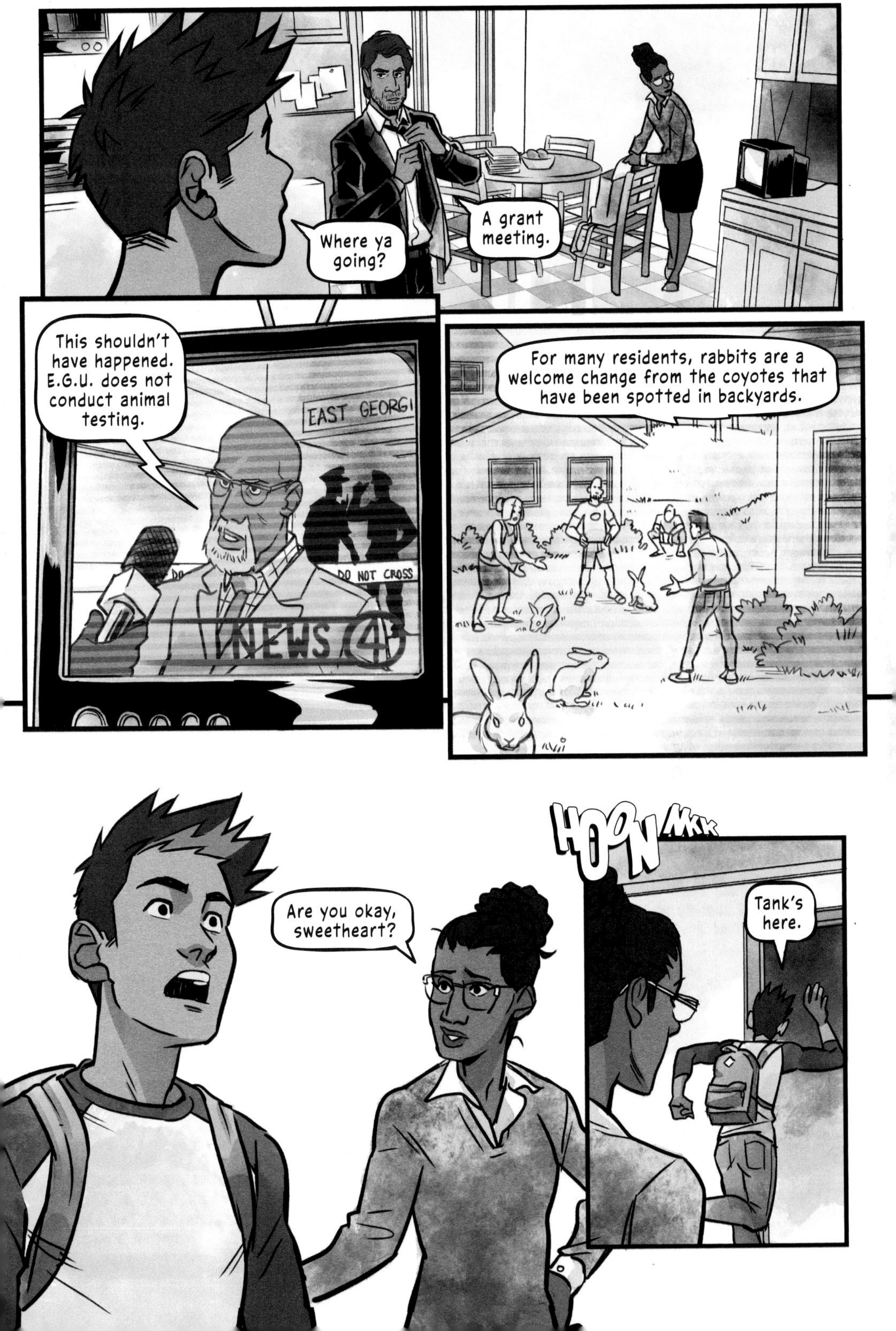
Where ya going?
A grant meeting.
This shouldn't have happened. E.G.U. does not conduct animal testing.
EAST GEORGI
DO NOT CROSS
NEWS 4
For many residents, rabbits are a welcome change from the coyotes that have been spotted in backyards.
Are you okay, sweetheart?
HOONKK
Tank's here.

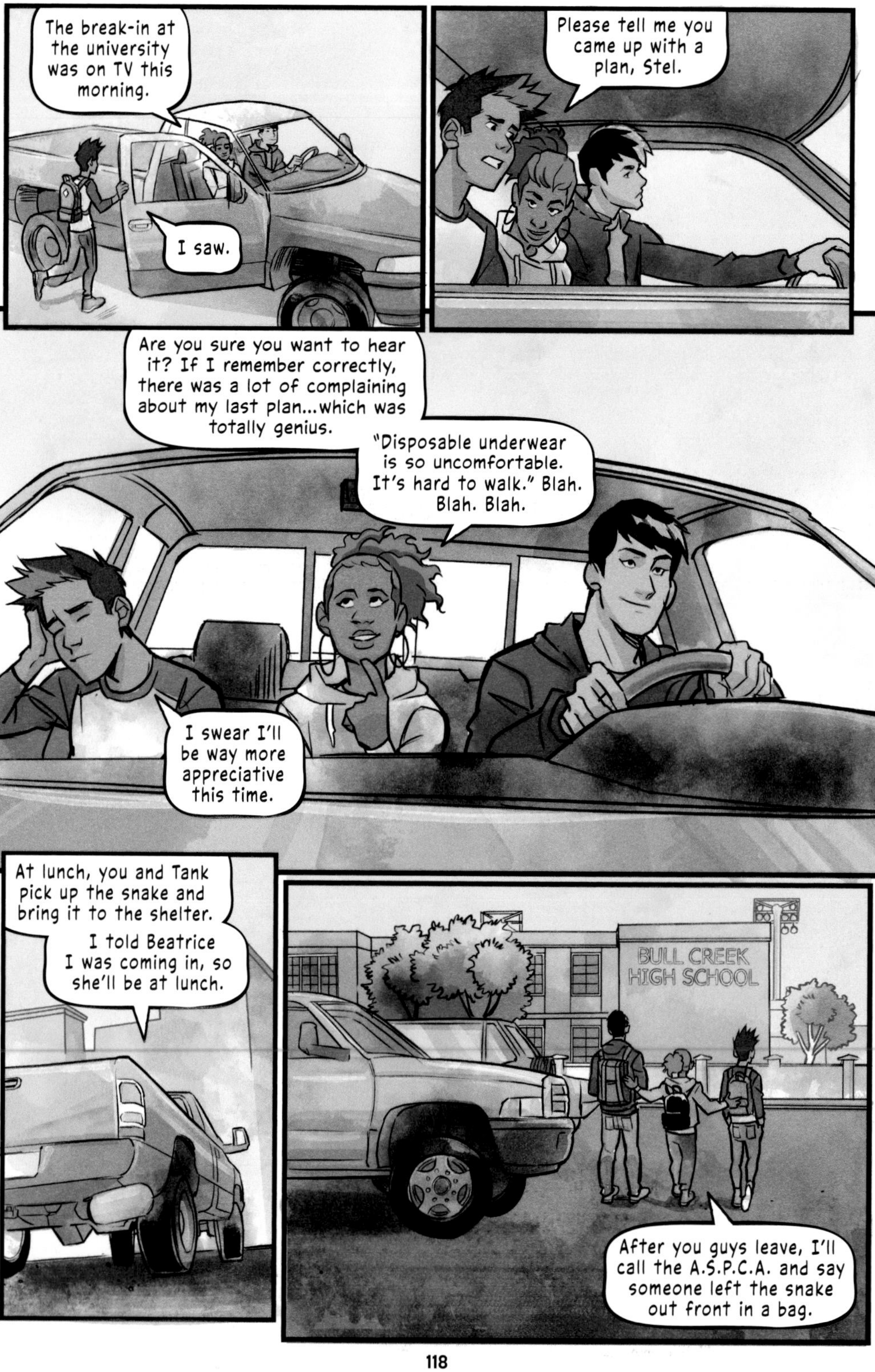

The break-in at the university was on TV this morning.
I saw.
Please tell me you came up with a plan, Stel.
Are you sure you want to hear it? If I remember correctly, there was a lot of complaining about my last plan...which was totally genius.
"Disposable underwear is so uncomfortable. It's hard to walk." Blah. Blah. Blah.
I swear I'll be way more appreciative this time.
At lunch, you and Tank pick up the snake and bring it to the shelter.
I told Beatrice I was coming in, so she'll be at lunch.
BULL CREEK HIGH SCHOOL
After you guys leave, I'll call the A.S.P.C.A. and say someone left the snake out front in a bag.

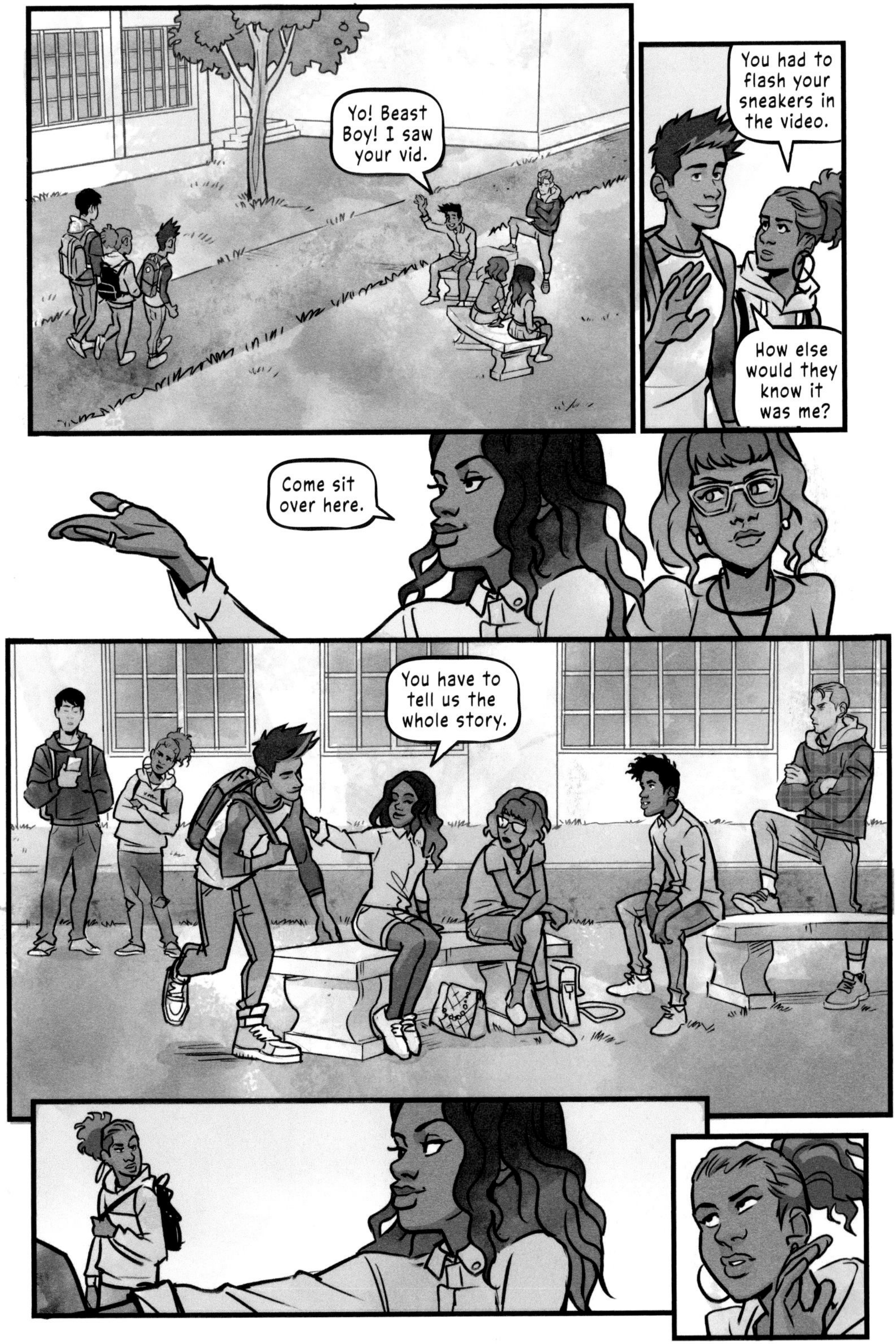
Yo! Beast Boy! I saw your vid.
You had to flash your sneakers in the video.
How else would they know it was me?
Come sit over here.
You have to tell us the whole story.

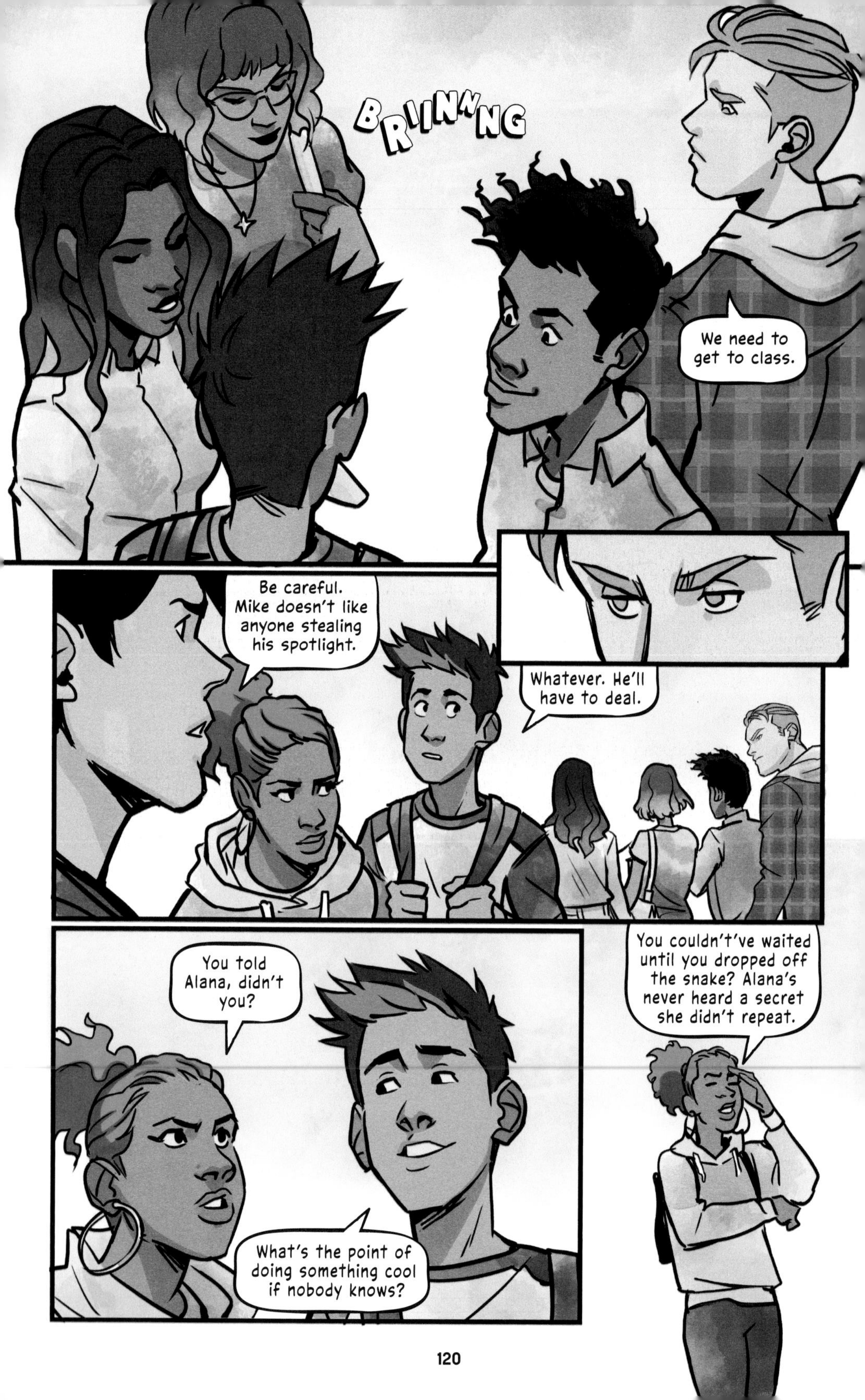
BRIINNNG
We need to get to class.
Be careful. Mike doesn't like anyone stealing his spotlight.
Whatever. He'll have to deal.
You told Alana, didn't you?
What's the point of doing something cool if nobody knows?
You couldn't've waited until you dropped off the snake? Alana's never heard a secret she didn't repeat.

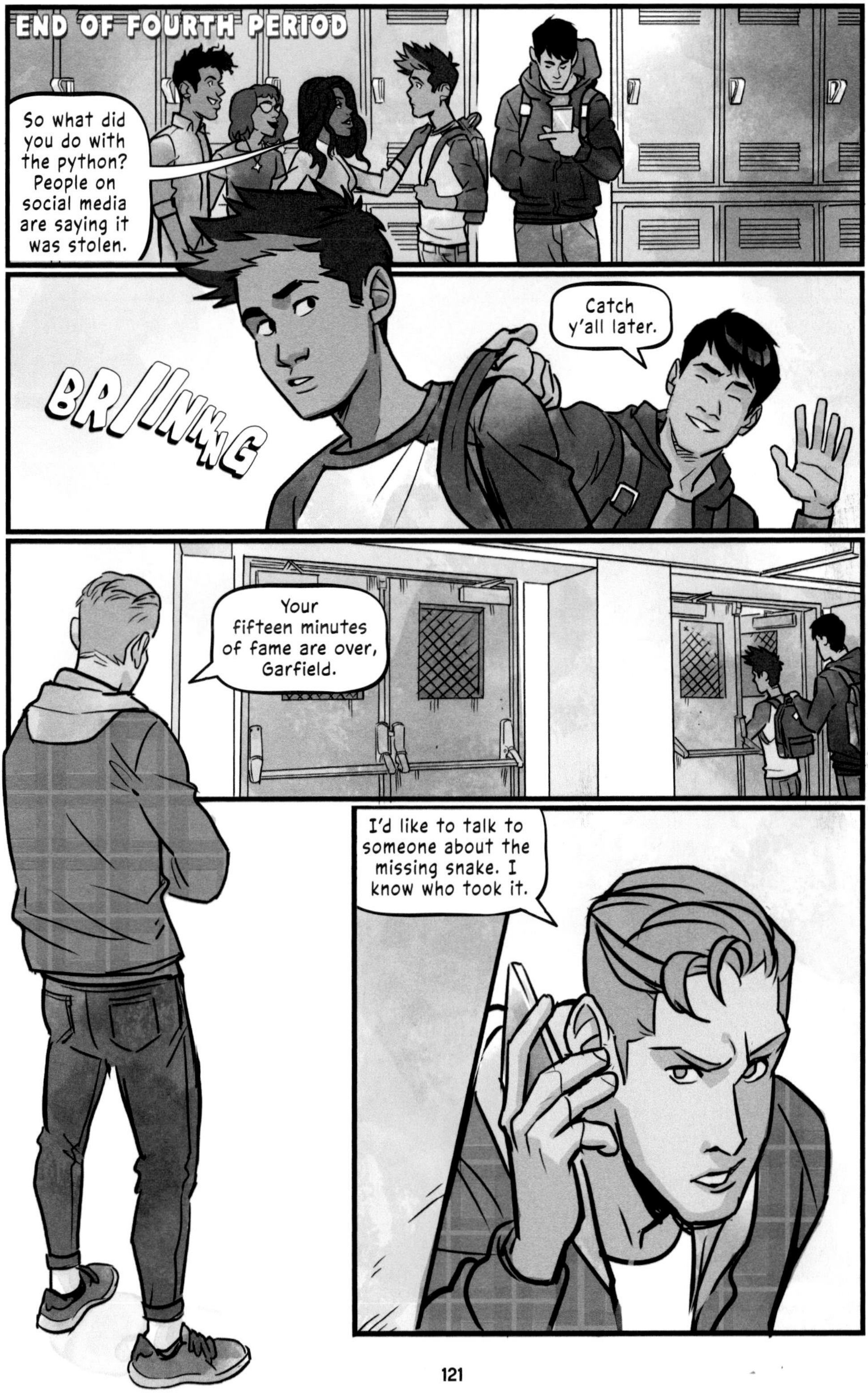
END OF FOURTH PERIOD
So what did you do with the python? People on social media are saying it was stolen.
Catch y'all later.
BRIIINNNG
Your fifteen minutes of fame are over, Garfield.
I'd like to talk to someone about the missing snake. I know who took it.

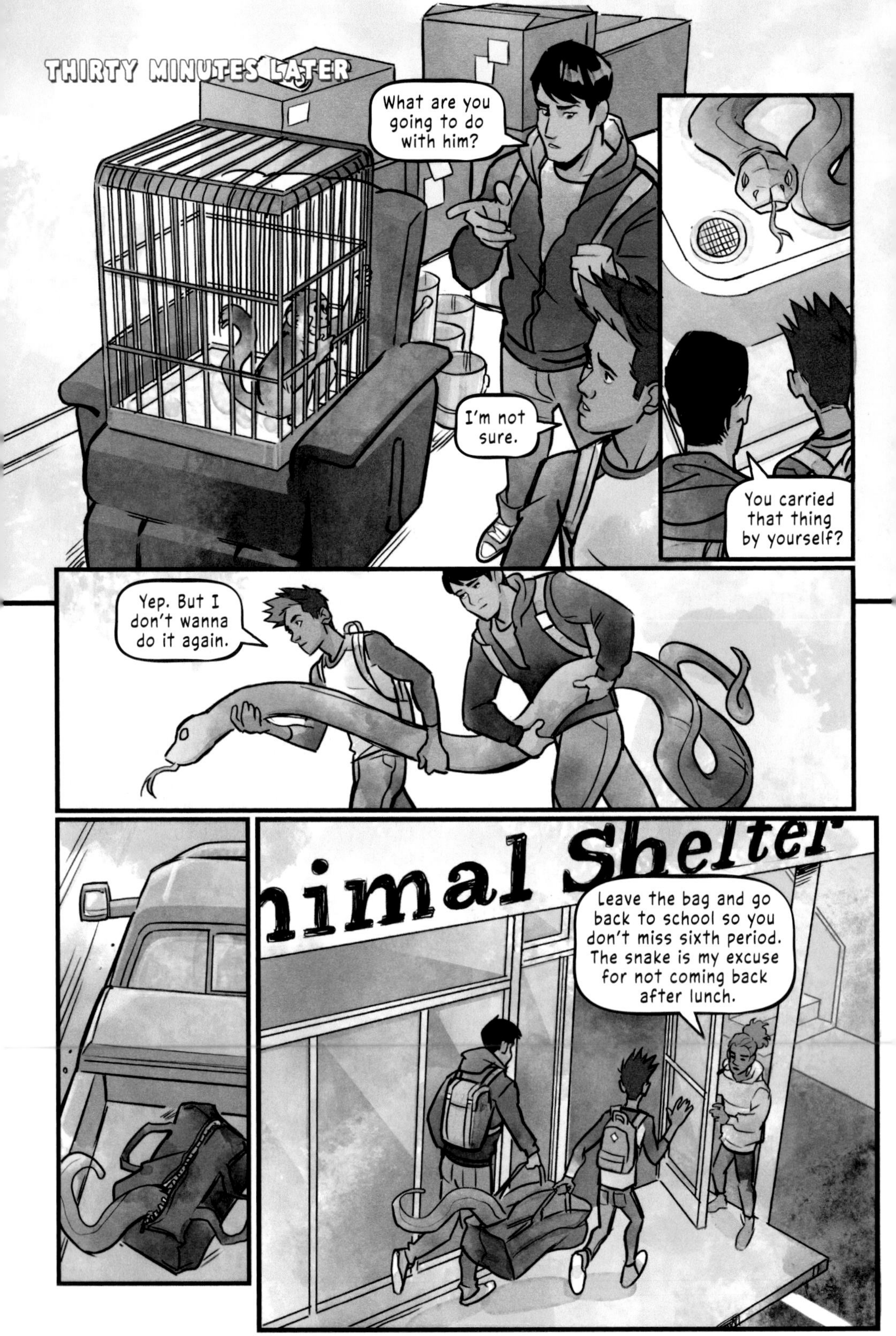
THIRTY MINUTES LATER
What are you going to do with him?
I'm not sure.
You carried that thing by yourself?
Yep. But I don't wanna do it again.
nimal Shelter
Leave the bag and go back to school so you don't miss sixth period. The snake is my excuse for not coming back after lunch.

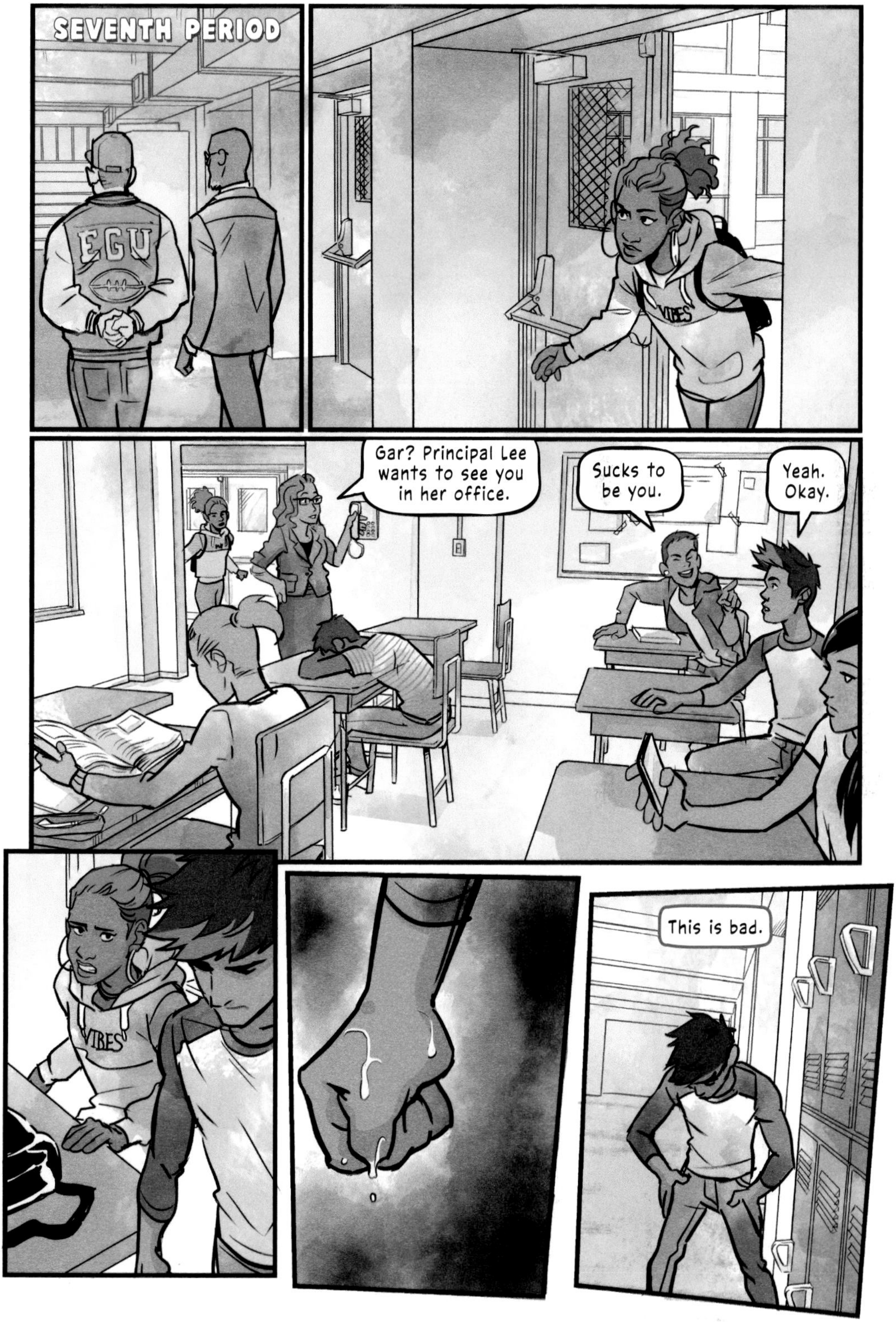
SEVENTH PERIOD
EGU
VIBES
Gar? Principal Lee wants to see you in her office.
Sucks to be you.
Yeah. Okay.
VIBES
This is bad.

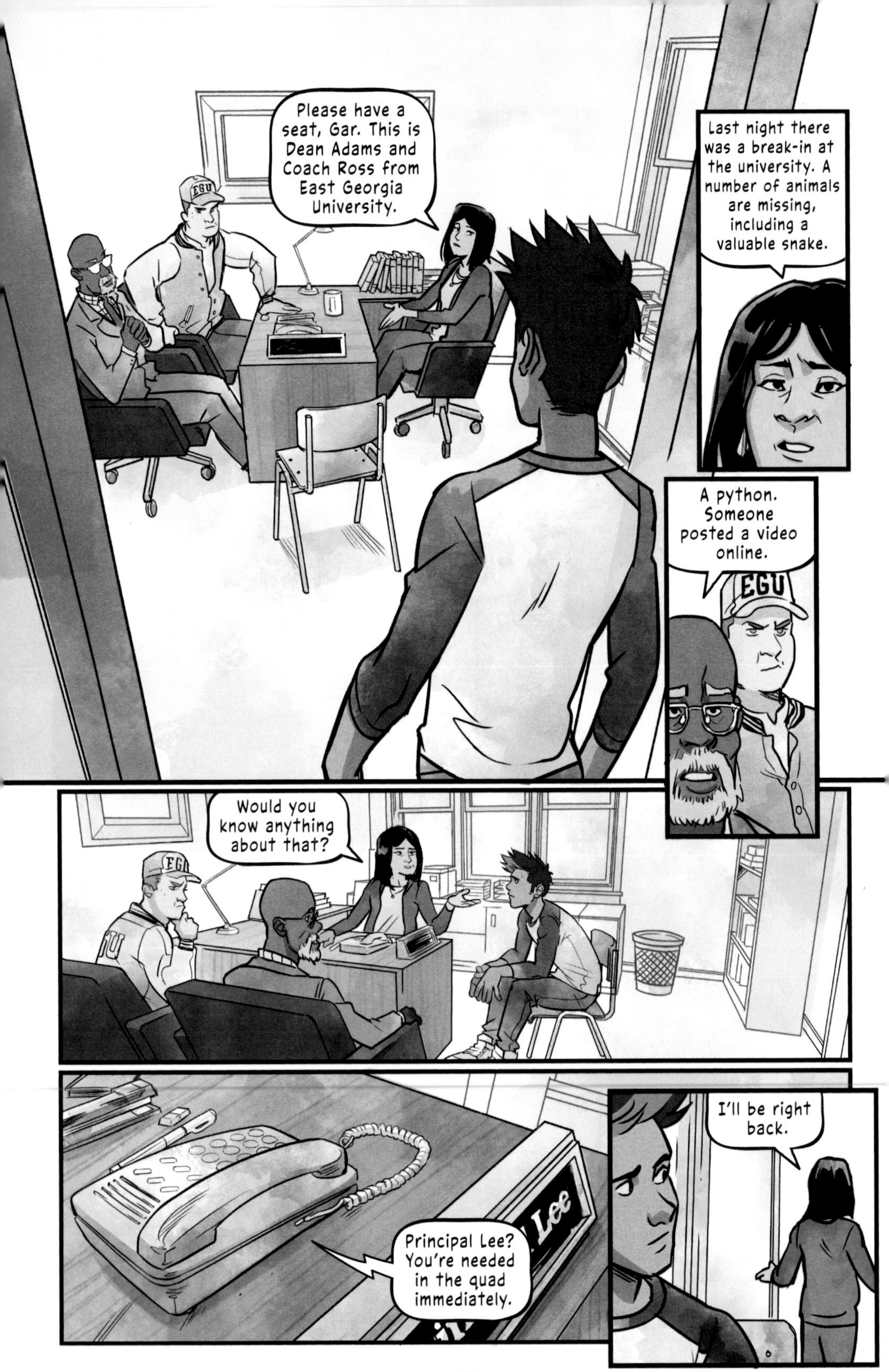
Please have a seat, Gar. This is Dean Adams and Coach Ross from East Georgia University.
Last night there was a break-in at the university. A number of animals are missing, including a valuable snake.
A python. Someone posted a video online.
Would you know anything about that?
Principal Lee? You're needed in the quad immediately.
I'll be right back.

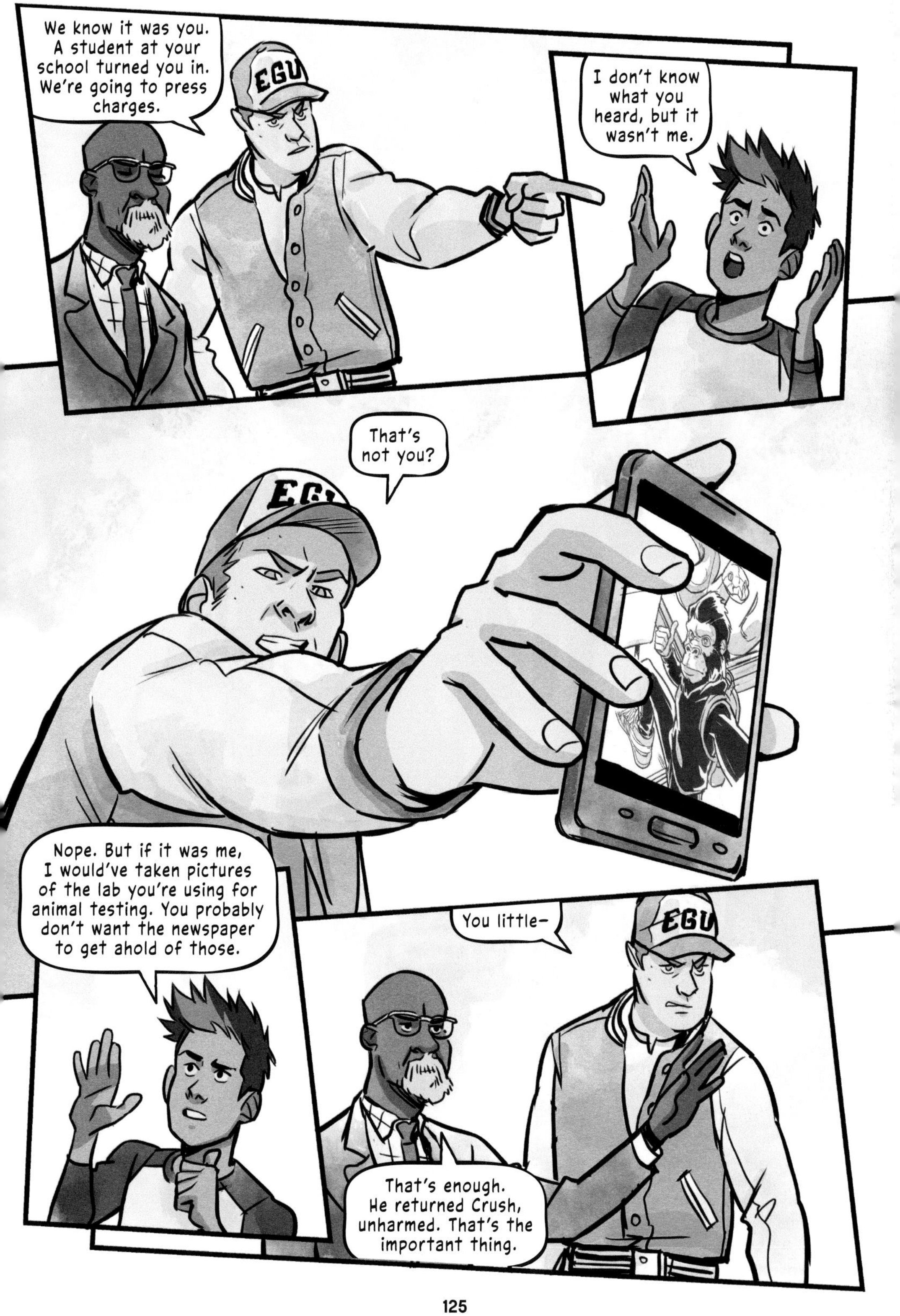
We know it was you. A student at your school turned you in. We're going to press charges.
EGU
I don't know what you heard, but it wasn't me.
That's not you?
EGU
Nope. But if it was me, I would've taken pictures of the lab you're using for animal testing. You probably don't want the newspaper to get ahold of those.
You little–
EGU
That's enough. He returned Crush, unharmed. That's the important thing.

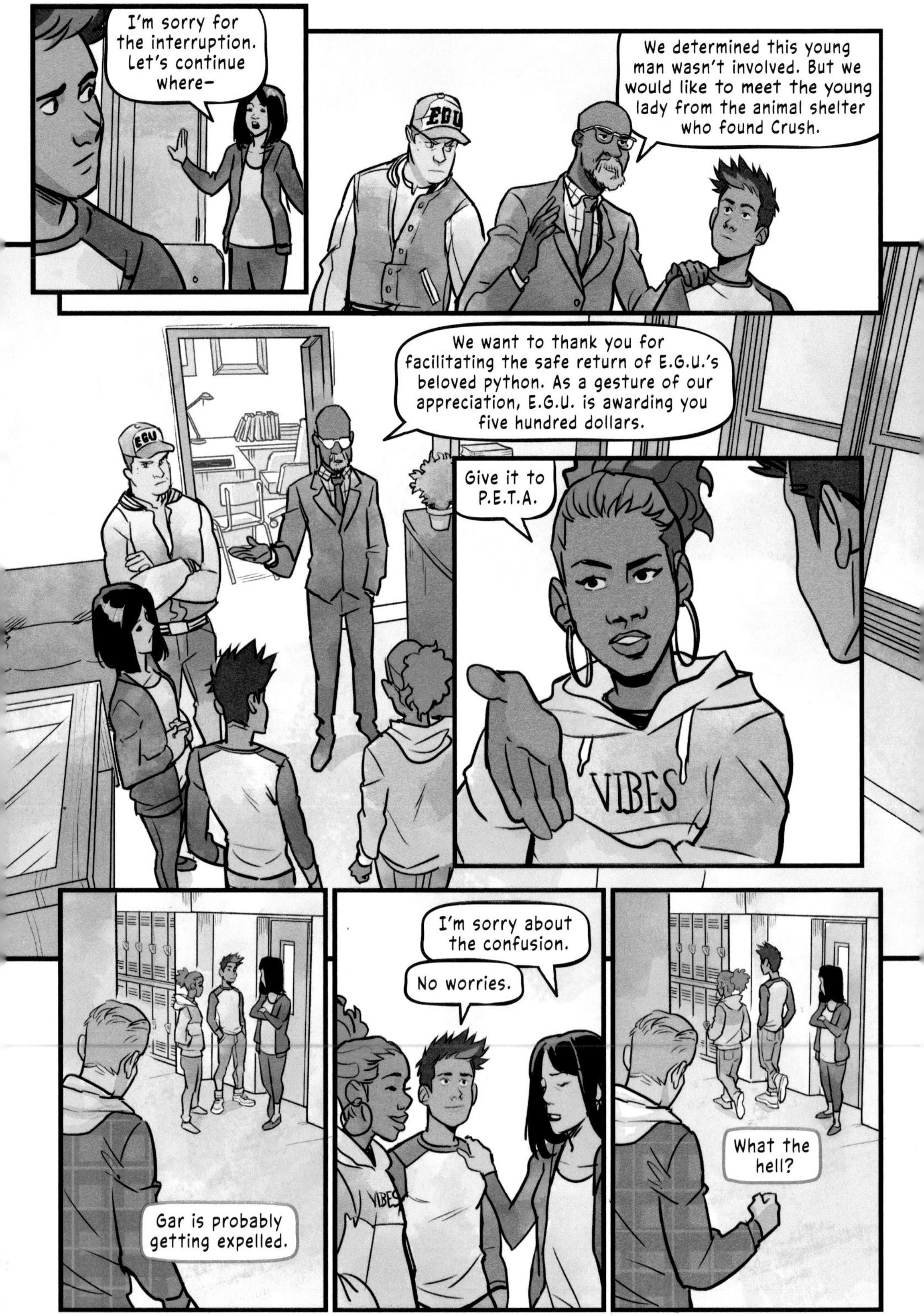
I'm sorry for the interruption. Let's continue where–
We determined this young man wasn't involved. But we would like to meet the young lady from the animal shelter who found Crush.
We want to thank you for facilitating the safe return of E.G.U.'s beloved python. As a gesture of our appreciation, E.G.U. is awarding you five hundred dollars.
Give it to P.E.T.A.
VIBES
Gar is probably getting expelled.
I'm sorry about the confusion.
No worries.
VIBES
What the hell?

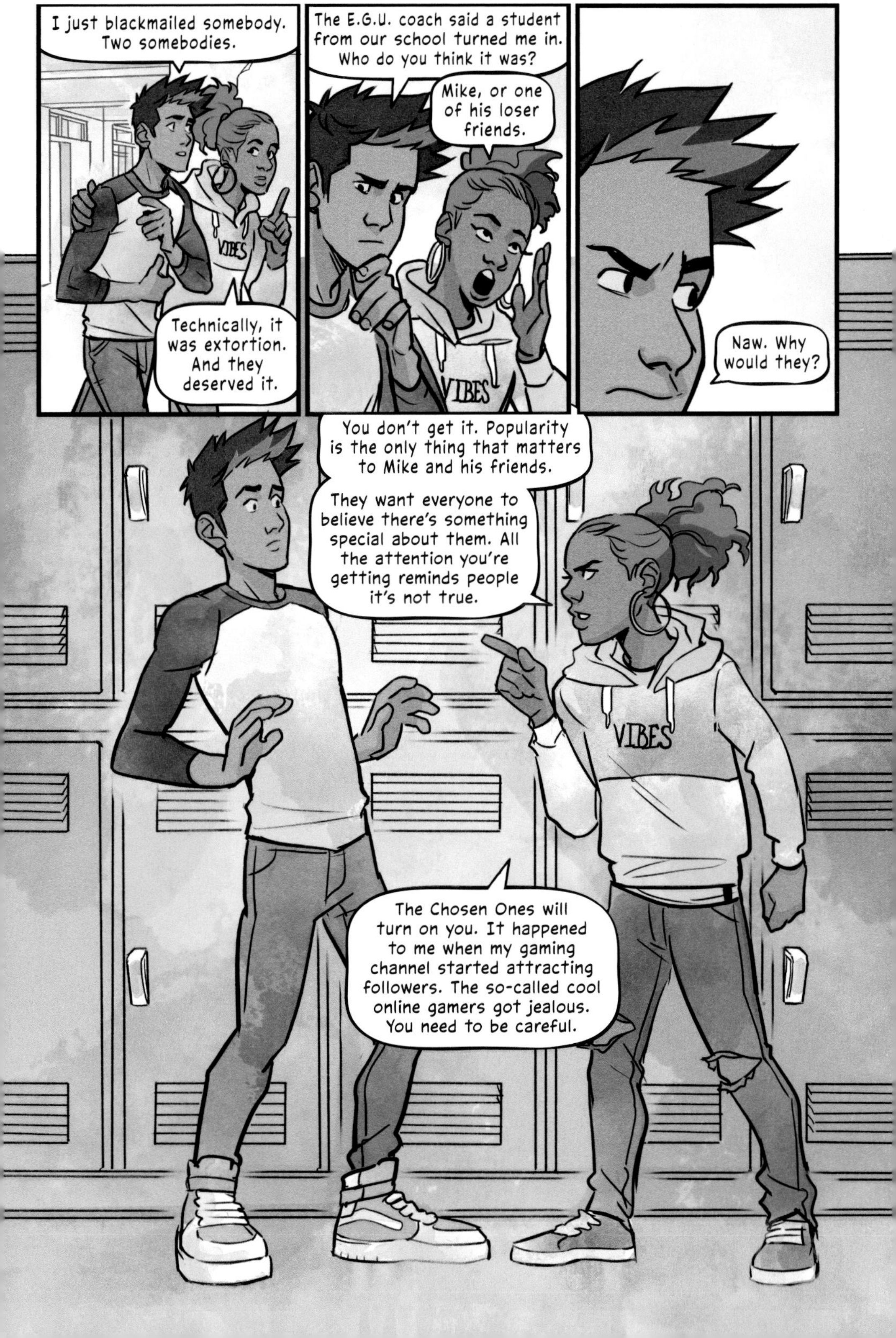
I just blackmailed somebody. Two somebodies.
Technically, it was extortion. And they deserved it.
The E.G.U. coach said a student from our school turned me in. Who do you think it was?
Mike, or one of his loser friends.
Naw. Why would they?
You don't get it. Popularity is the only thing that matters to Mike and his friends.
They want everyone to believe there's something special about them. All the attention you're getting reminds people it's not true.
The Chosen Ones will turn on you. It happened to me when my gaming channel started attracting followers. The so-called cool online gamers got jealous. You need to be careful.
VIBES

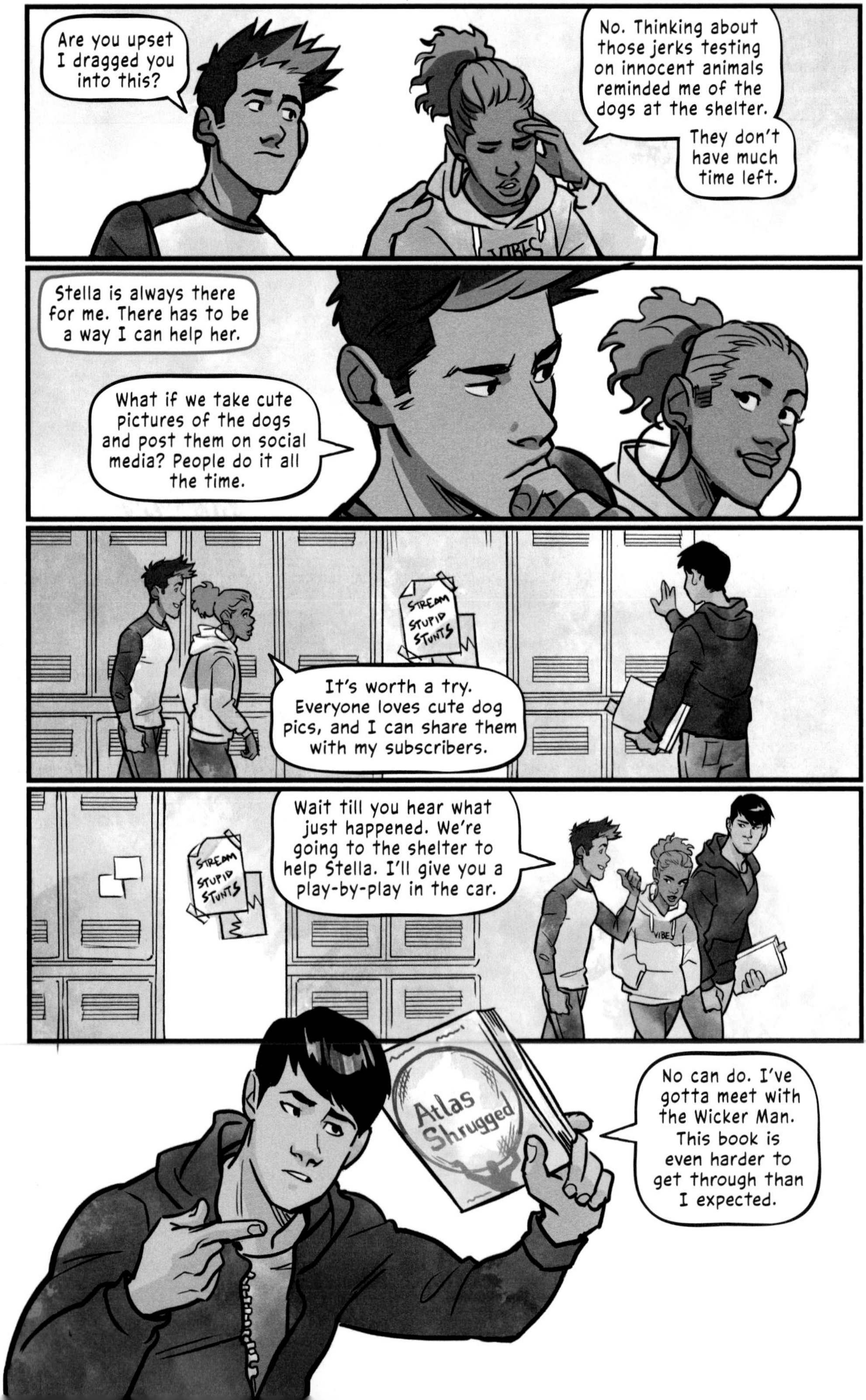
Are you upset I dragged you into this?
No. Thinking about those jerks testing on innocent animals reminded me of the dogs at the shelter.
They don't have much time left.
VIBES
Stella is always there for me. There has to be a way I can help her.
What if we take cute pictures of the dogs and post them on social media? People do it all the time.
STREAM STUPID STUNTS
It's worth a try. Everyone loves cute dog pics, and I can share them with my subscribers.
STREAM STUPID STUNTS
Wait till you hear what just happened. We're going to the shelter to help Stella. I'll give you a play-by-play in the car.
VIBES
Atlas Shrugged
No can do. I've gotta meet with the Wicker Man. This book is even harder to get through than I expected.

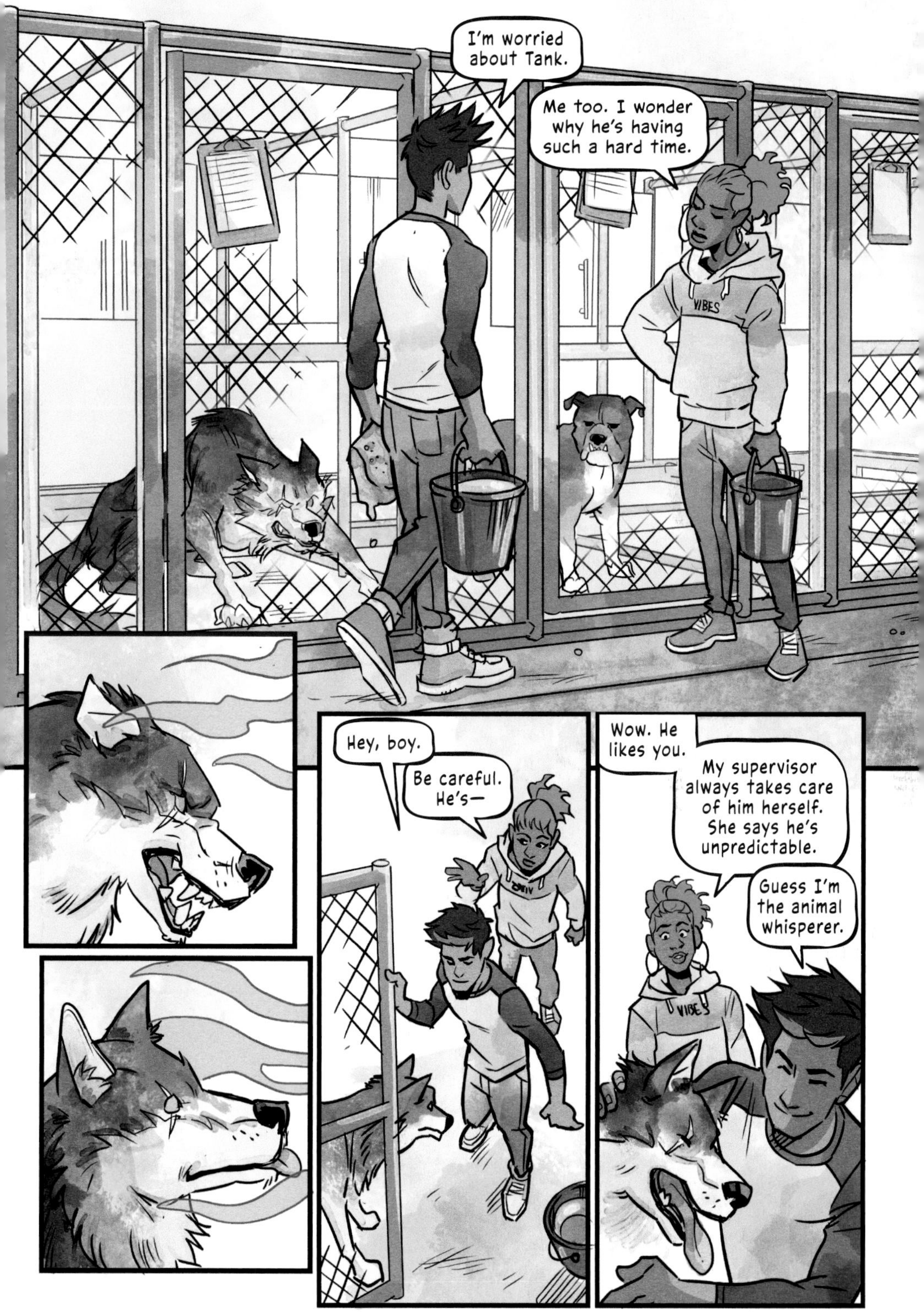
I'm worried about Tank.
Me too. I wonder why he's having such a hard time.
VIBES
Hey, boy.
Be careful. He's—
Wow. He likes you.
My supervisor always takes care of him herself. She says he's unpredictable.
Guess I'm the animal whisperer.
VIBES

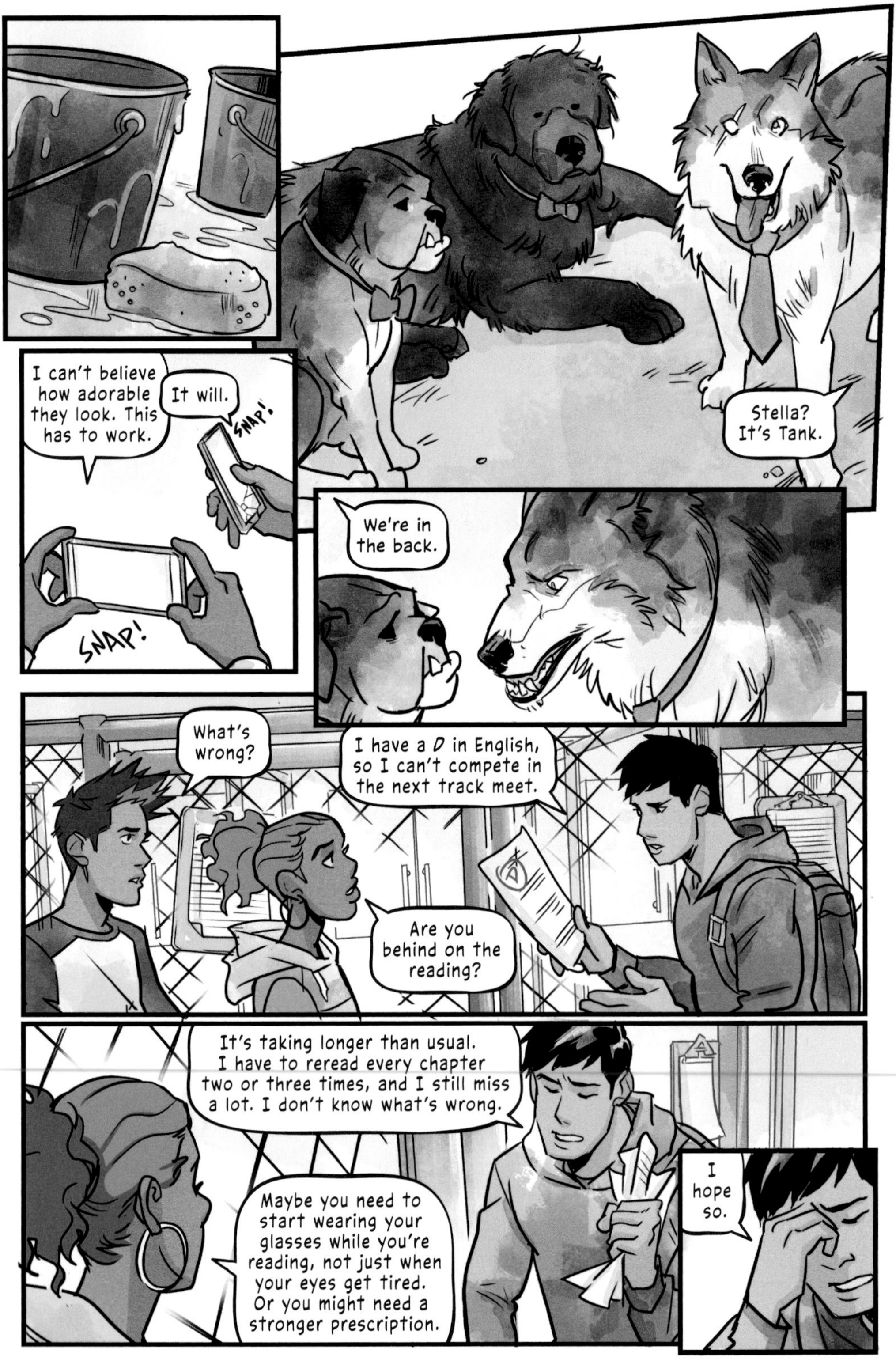
I can't believe how adorable they look. This has to work.
It will.
SNAP!
SNAP!
Stella? It's Tank.
We're in the back.
What's wrong?
I have a D in English, so I can't compete in the next track meet.
Are you behind on the reading?
It's taking longer than usual. I have to reread every chapter two or three times, and I still miss a lot. I don't know what's wrong.
Maybe you need to start wearing your glasses while you're reading, not just when your eyes get tired. Or you might need a stronger prescription.
I hope so.

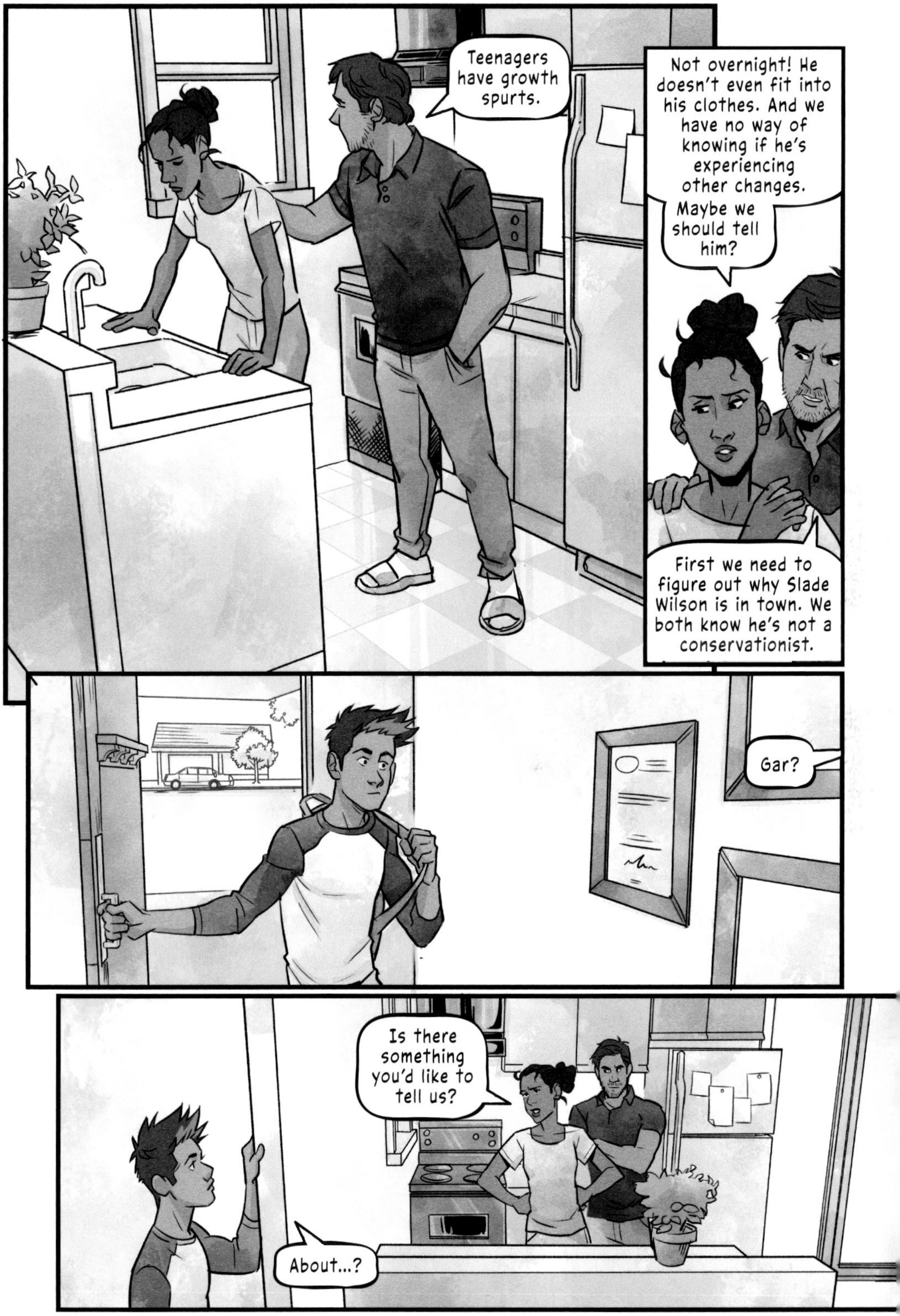

Teenagers have growth spurts.
Not overnight! He doesn't even fit into his clothes. And we have no way of knowing if he's experiencing other changes.
Maybe we should tell him?
First we need to figure out why Slade Wilson is in town. We both know he's not a conservationist.
Gar?
Is there something you'd like to tell us?
About...?

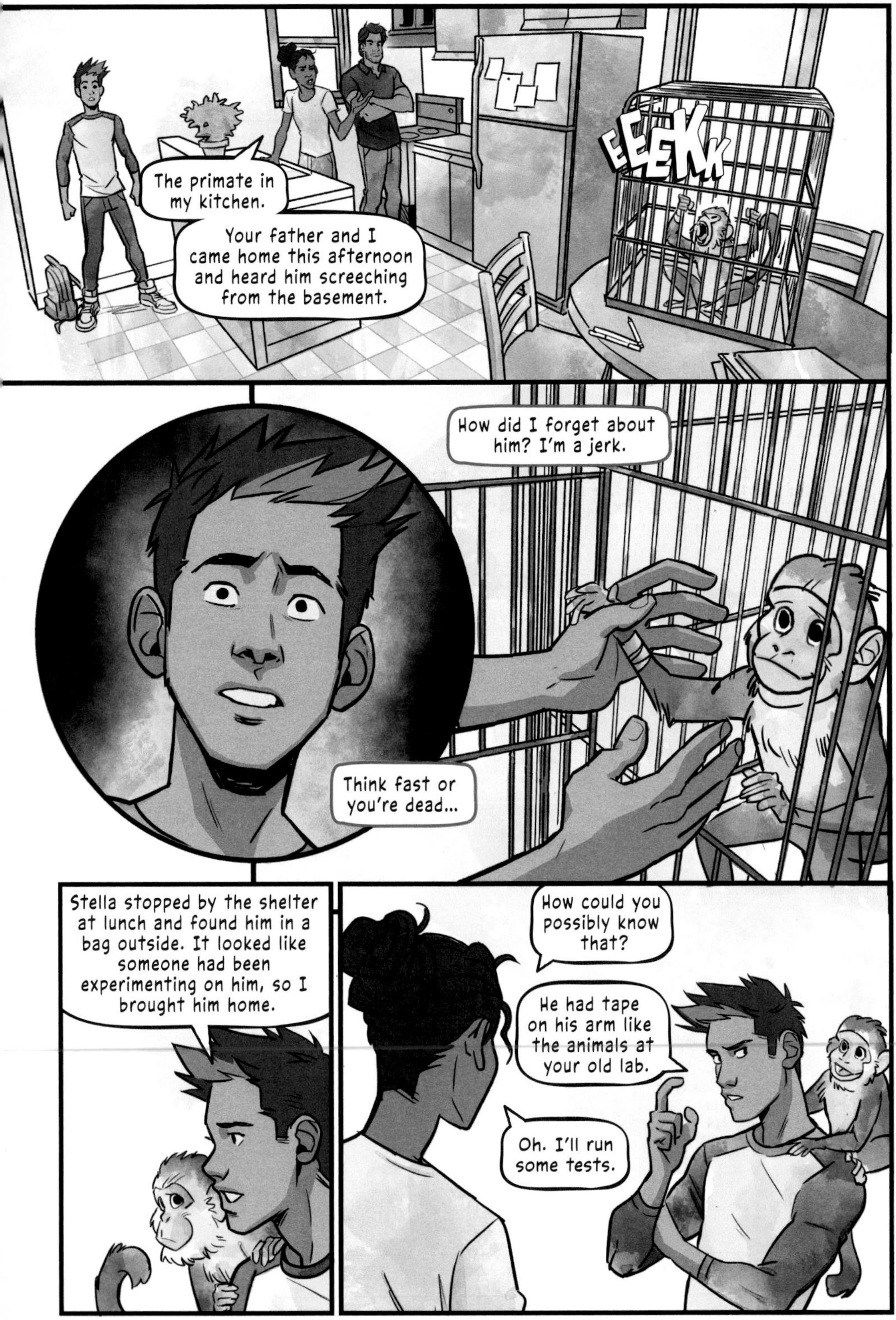
The primate in my kitchen.
Your father and I came home this afternoon and heard him screeching from the basement.
EEEKK
How did I forget about him? I'm a jerk.
Think fast or you're dead...
Stella stopped by the shelter at lunch and found him in a bag outside. It looked like someone had been experimenting on him, so I brought him home.
How could you possibly know that?
He had tape on his arm like the animals at your old lab.
Oh. I'll run some tests.

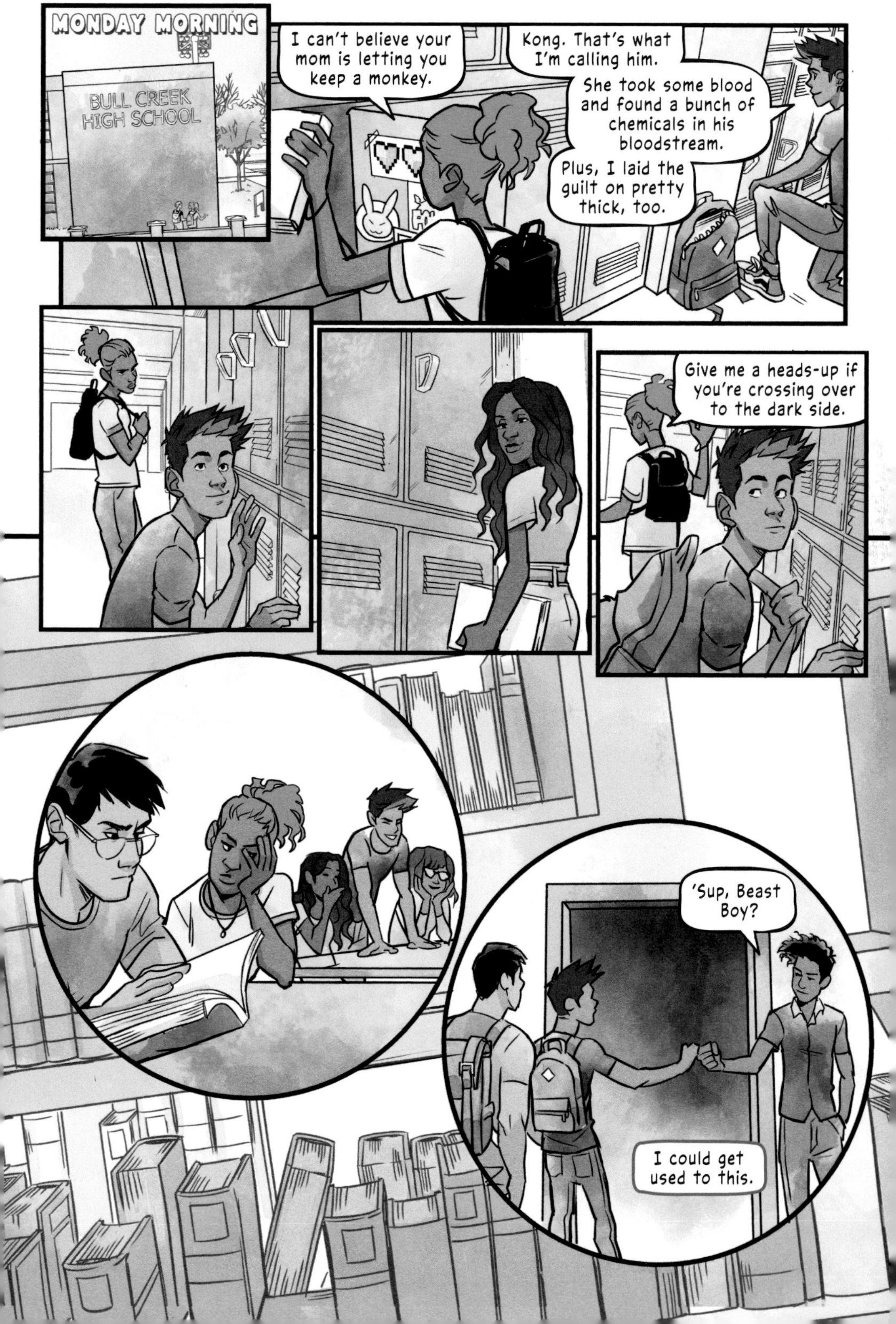
MONDAY MORNING
BULL CREEK HIGH SCHOOL
I can't believe your mom is letting you keep a monkey.
Kong. That's what I'm calling him.
She took some blood and found a bunch of chemicals in his bloodstream.
Plus, I laid the guilt on pretty thick, too.
Give me a heads-up if you're crossing over to the dark side.
'Sup, Beast Boy?
I could get used to this.

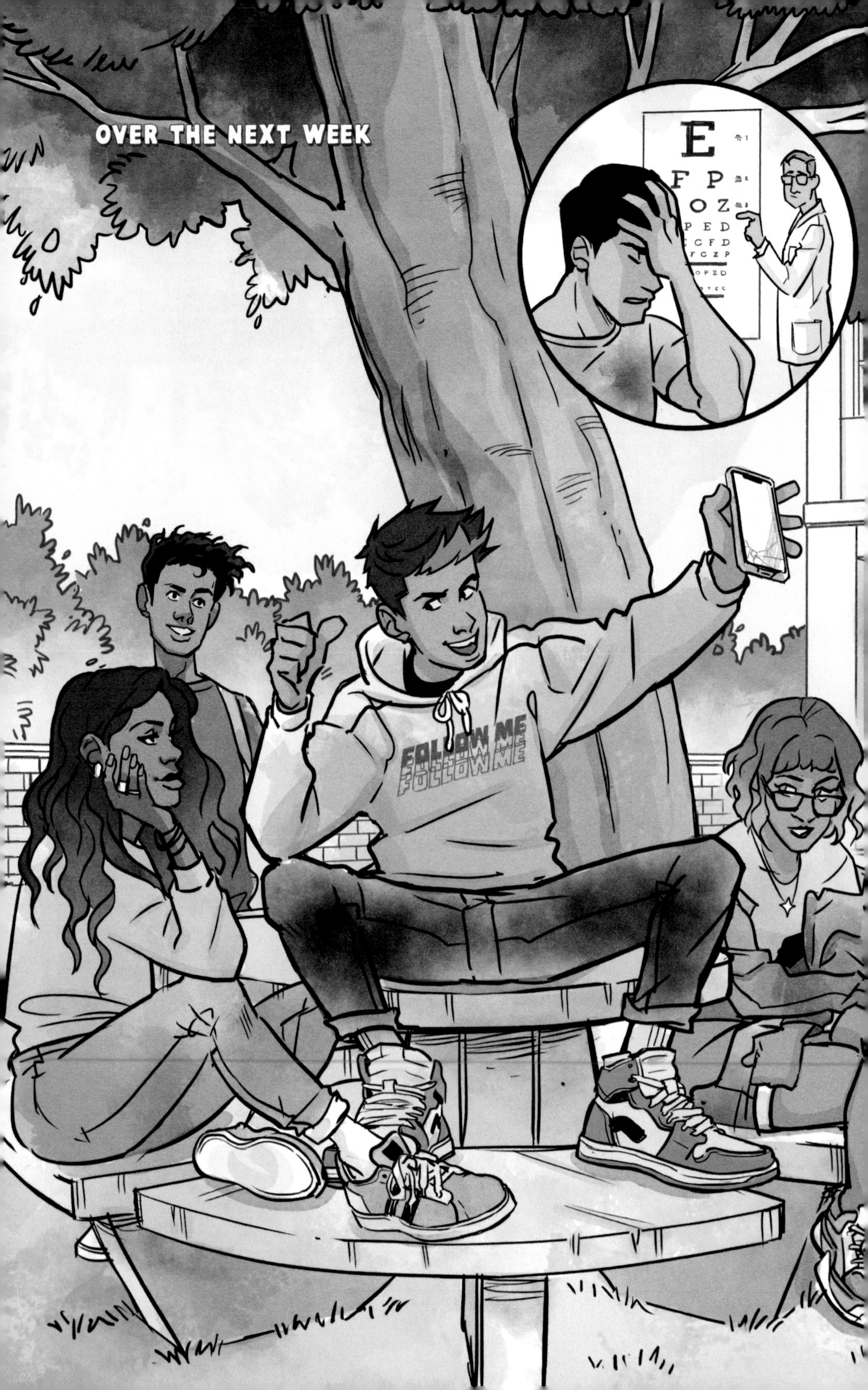
OVER THE NEXT WEEK
FOLLOW ME
FOLLOW ME
FOLLOW ME

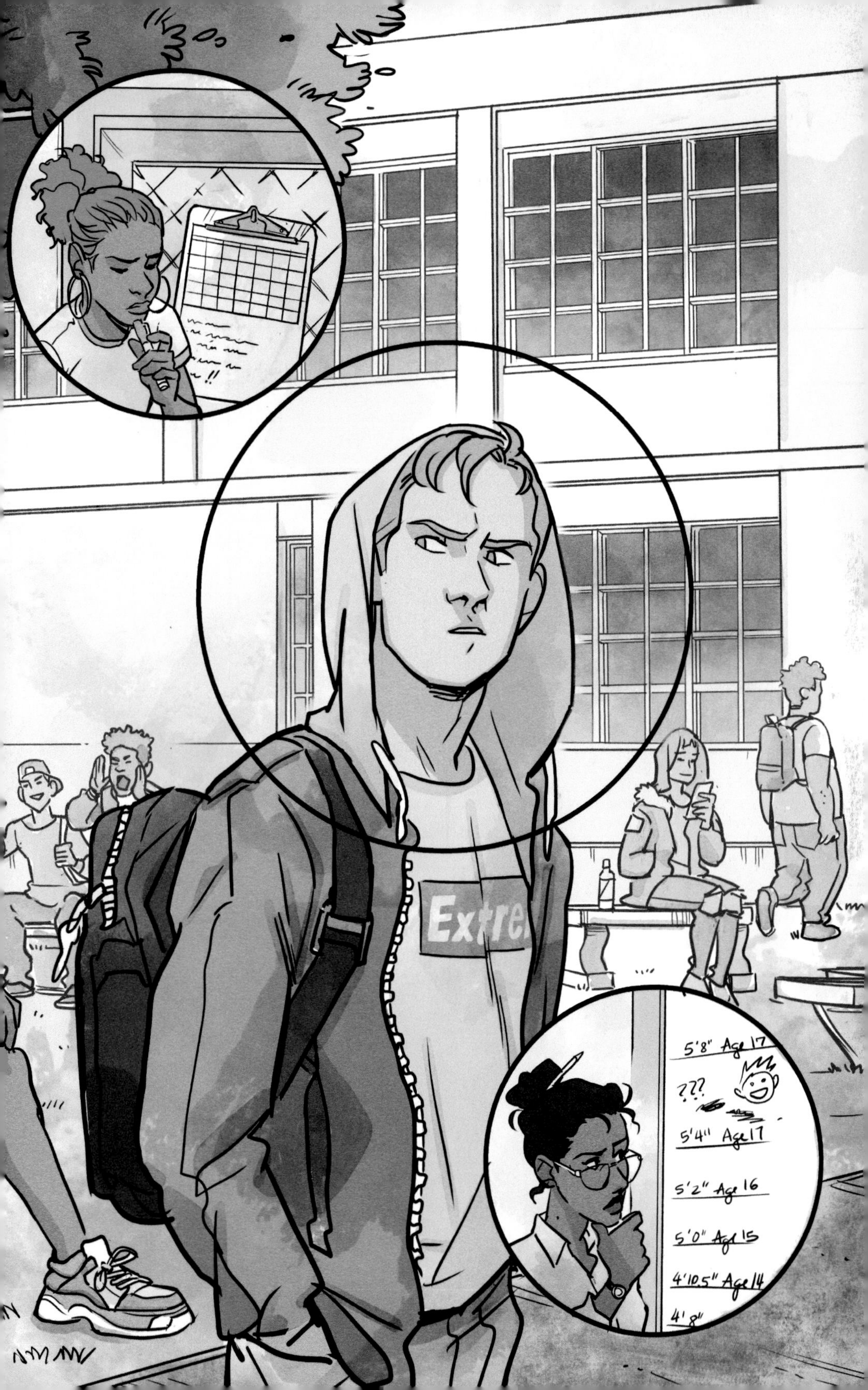
5'8" Age 17
???
5'4" Age 17
5'2" Age 16
5'0" Age 15
4'10.5" Age 14
4'8"

CHAPTER 13: RESCUE OPERATION

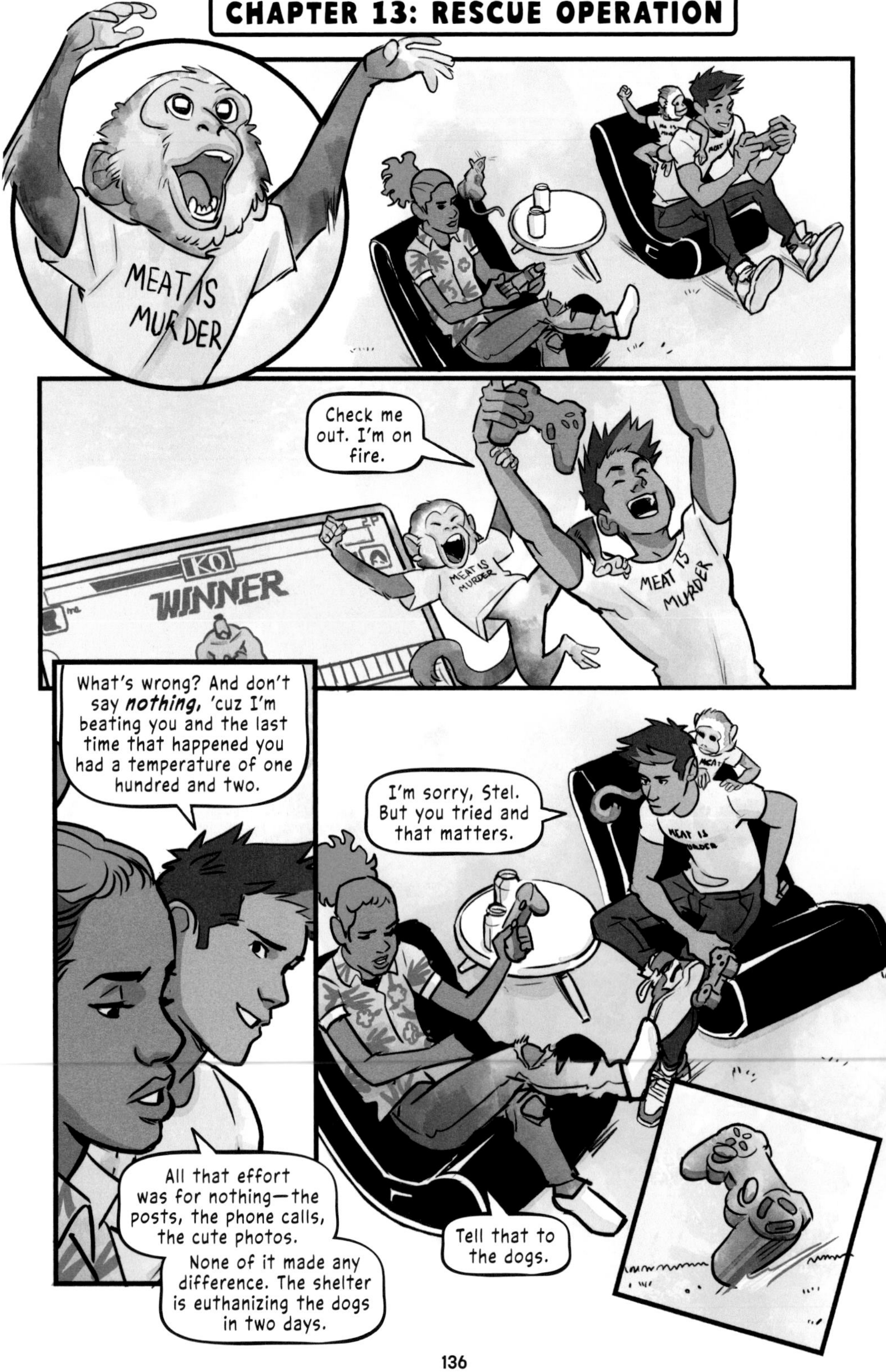
MEAT IS MURDER
Check me out. I'm on fire.
KO
WINNER
MEAT IS MURDER
MEAT IS MURDER
What's wrong? And don't say *nothing,* 'cuz I'm beating you and the last time that happened you had a temperature of one hundred and two.
I'm sorry, Stel. But you tried and that matters.
All that effort was for nothing—the posts, the phone calls, the cute photos.
None of it made any difference. The shelter is euthanizing the dogs in two days.
Tell that to the dogs.

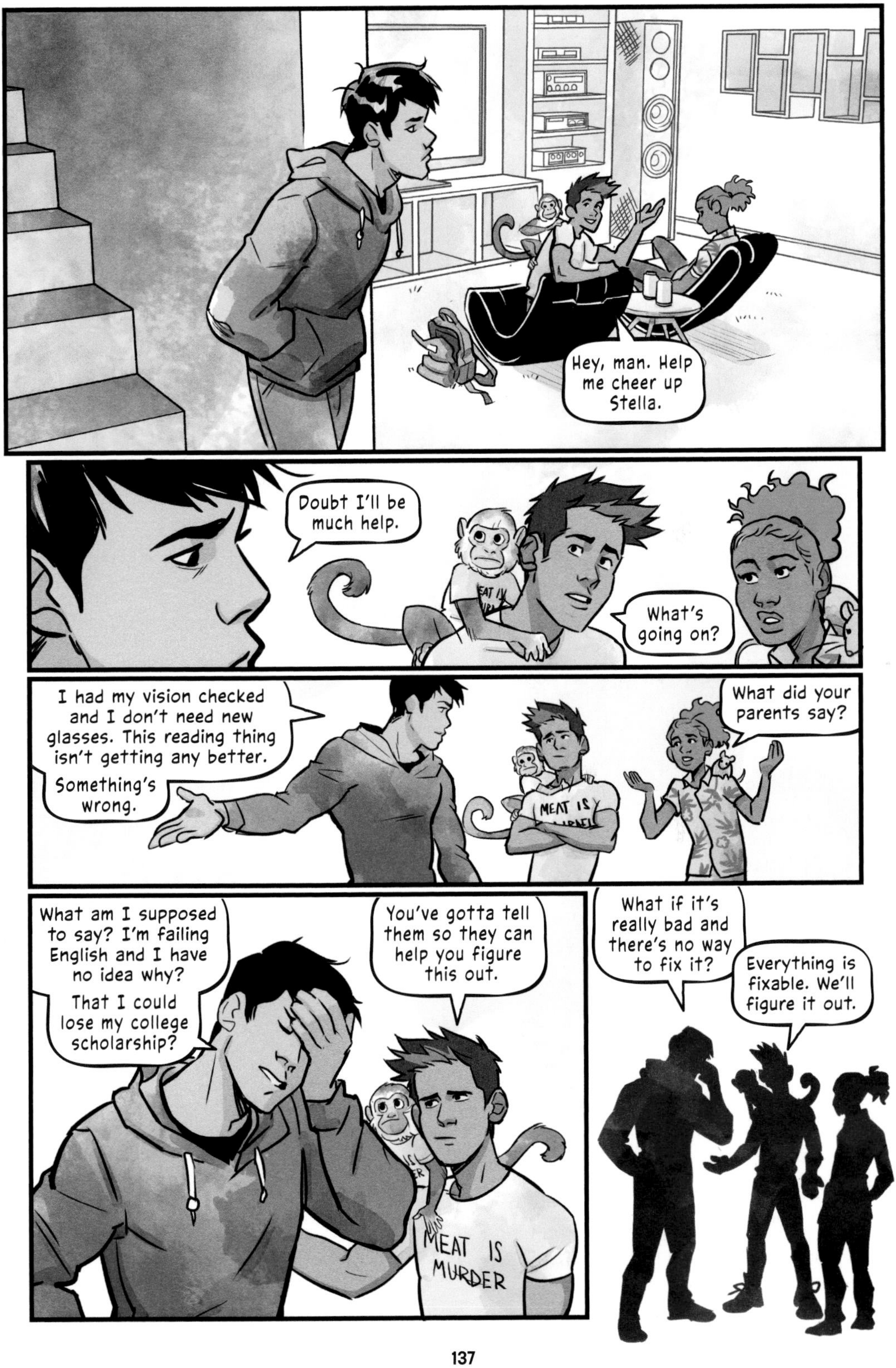
Hey, man. Help me cheer up Stella.
Doubt I'll be much help.
What's going on?
I had my vision checked and I don't need new glasses. This reading thing isn't getting any better.
Something's wrong.
What did your parents say?
What am I supposed to say? I'm failing English and I have no idea why?
That I could lose my college scholarship?
You've gotta tell them so they can help you figure this out.
MEAT IS MURDER
What if it's really bad and there's no way to fix it?
Everything is fixable. We'll figure it out.

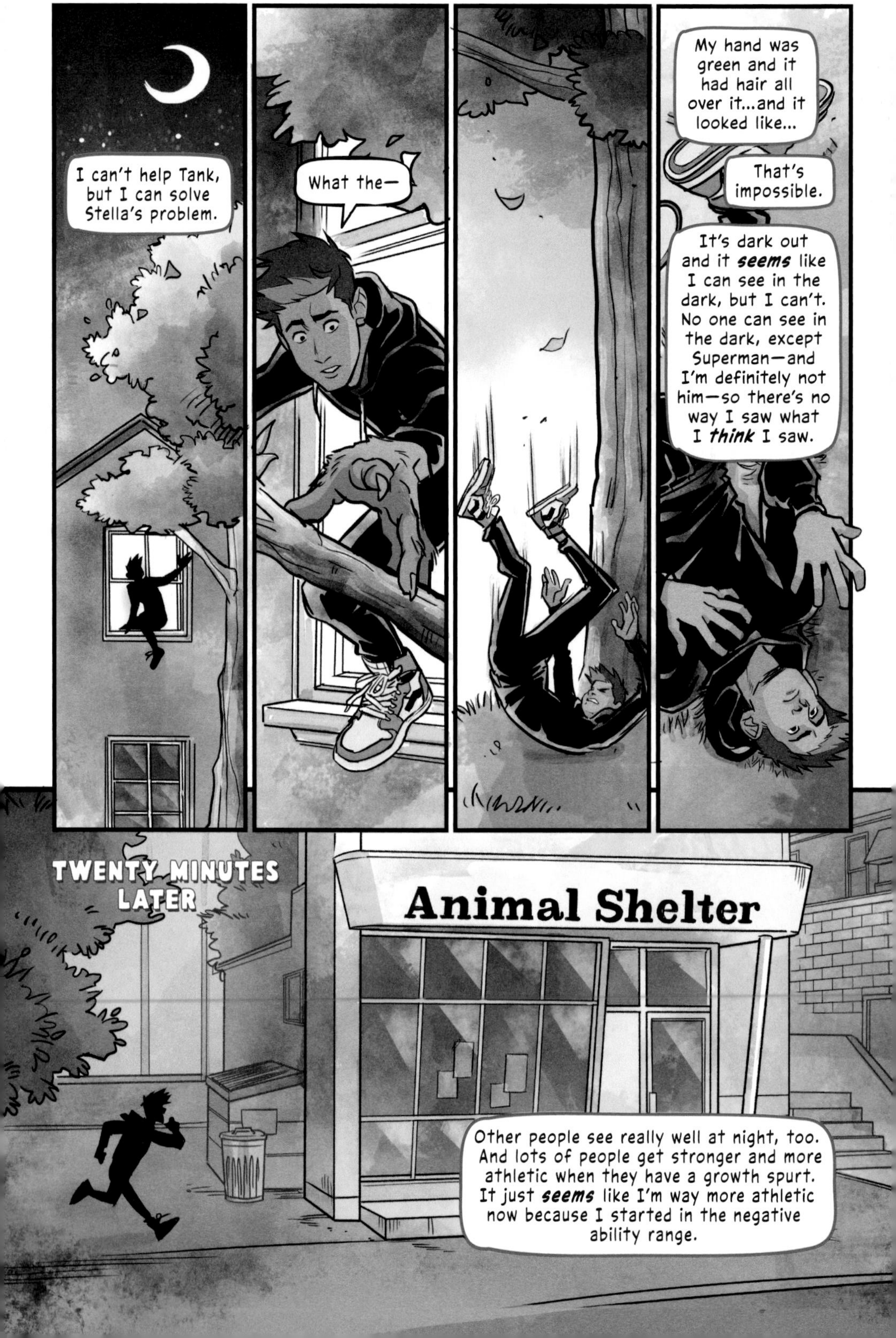

I can't help Tank, but I can solve Stella's problem.
What the—
My hand was green and it had hair all over it...and it looked like...
That's impossible.
It's dark out and it *seems* like I can see in the dark, but I can't. No one can see in the dark, except Superman—and I'm definitely not him—so there's no way I saw what I *think* I saw.
TWENTY MINUTES LATER
Animal Shelter
Other people see really well at night, too. And lots of people get stronger and more athletic when they have a growth spurt. It just *seems* like I'm way more athletic now because I started in the negative ability range.

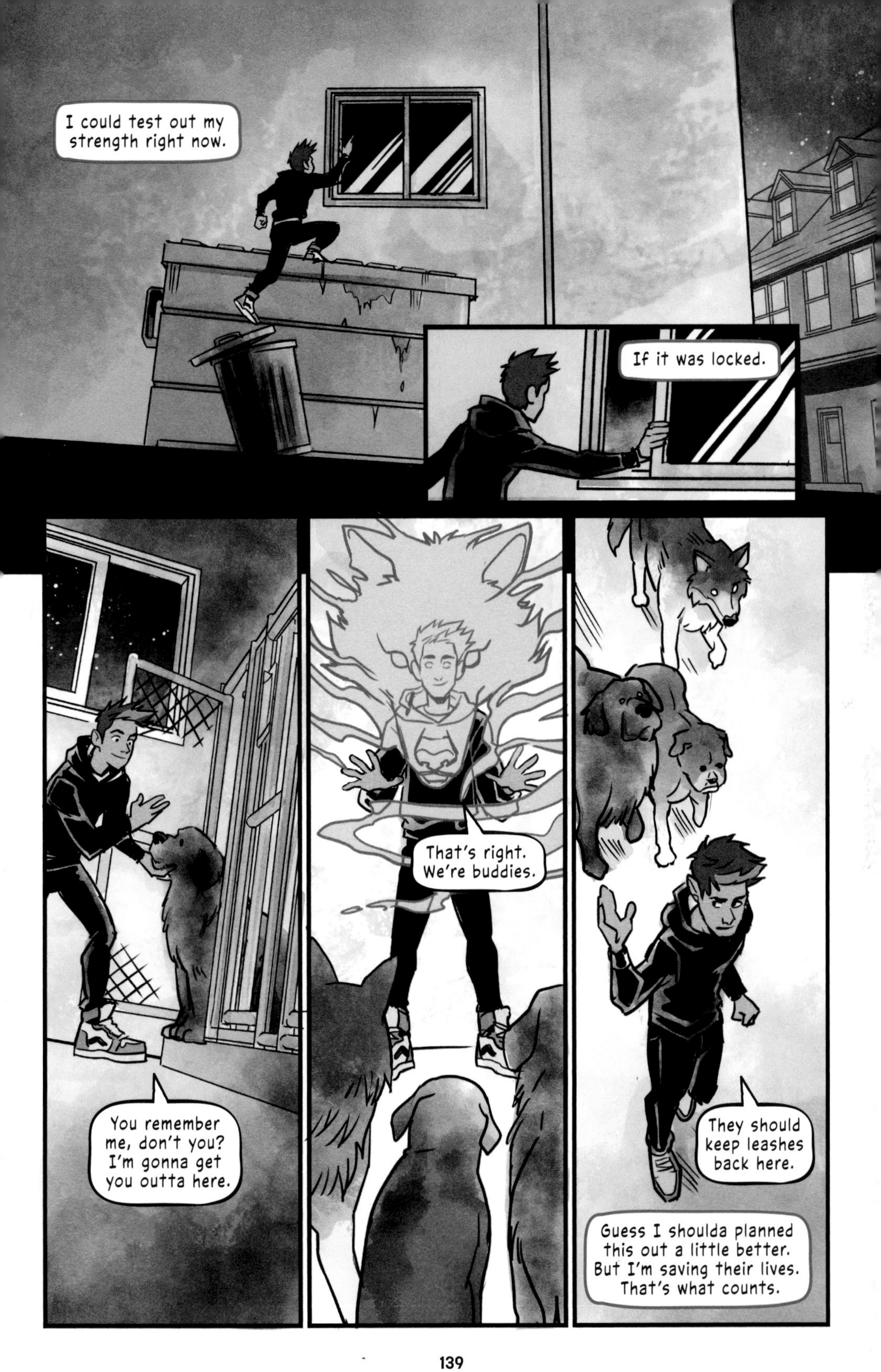
I could test out my strength right now.
If it was locked.
You remember me, don't you? I'm gonna get you outta here.
That's right. We're buddies.
They should keep leashes back here.
Guess I shoulda planned this out a little better. But I'm saving their lives. That's what counts.

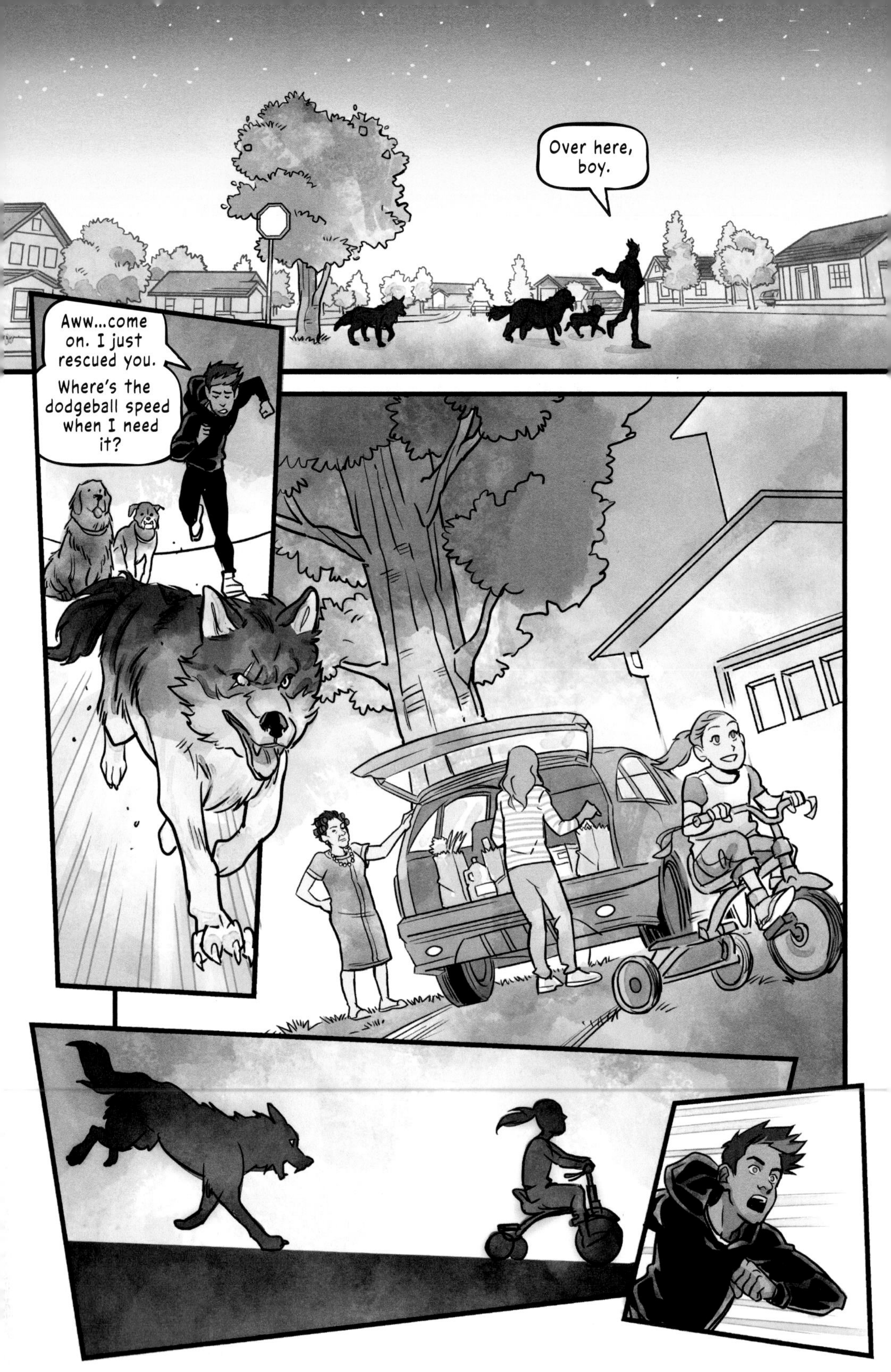
Over here, boy.
Aww...come on. I just rescued you.
Where's the dodgeball speed when I need it?

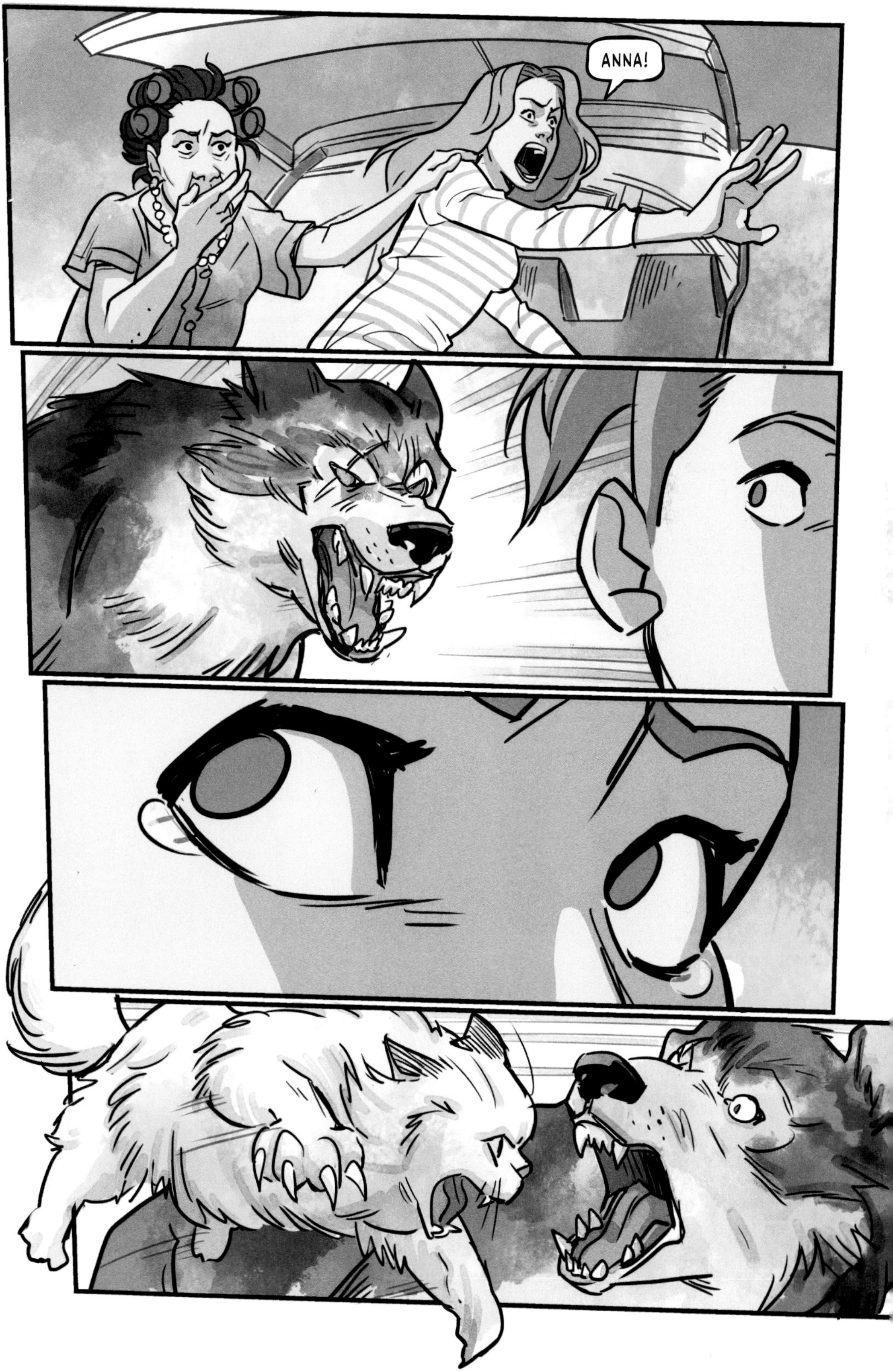
ANNA!

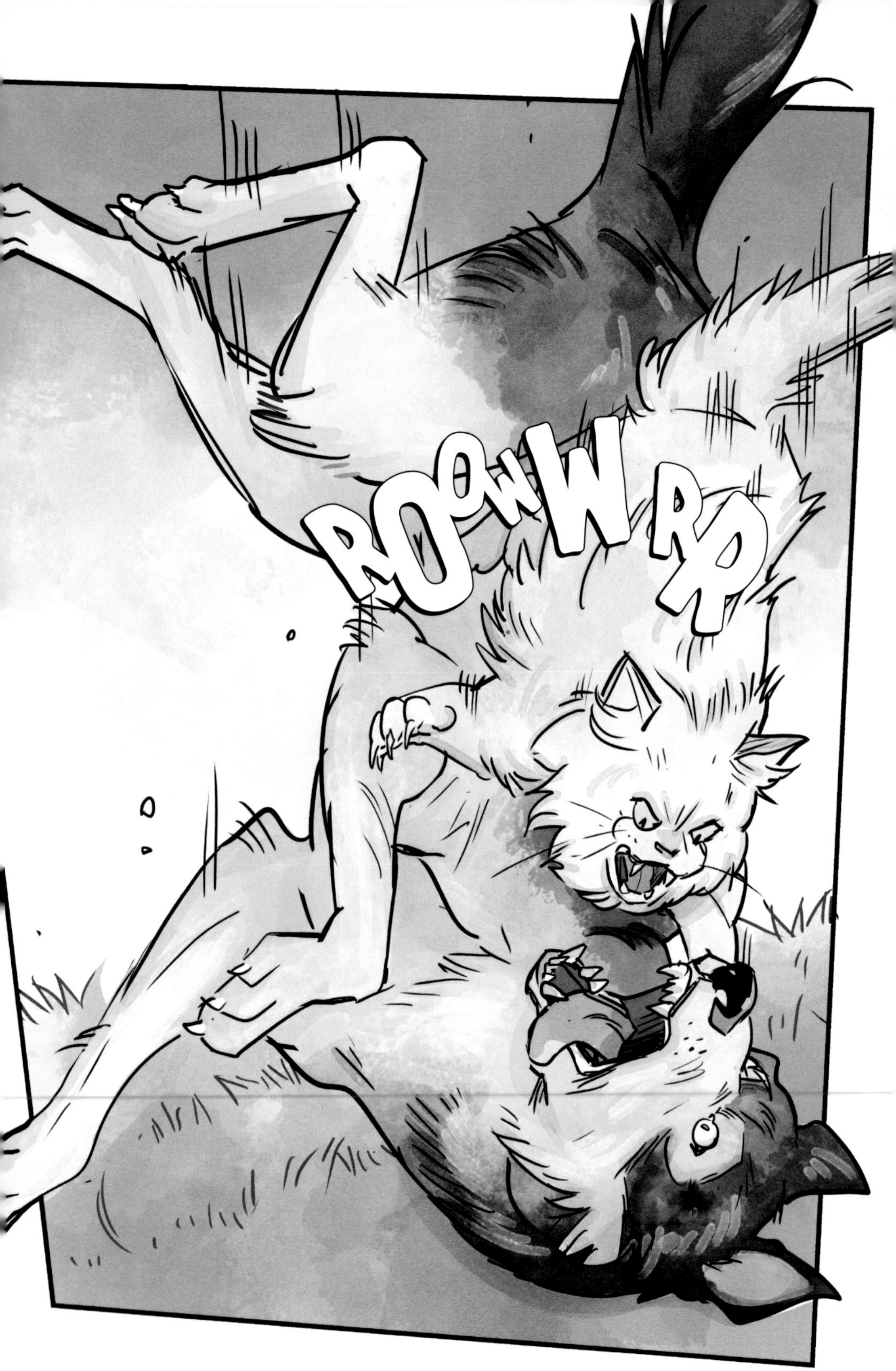
ROOWWRR

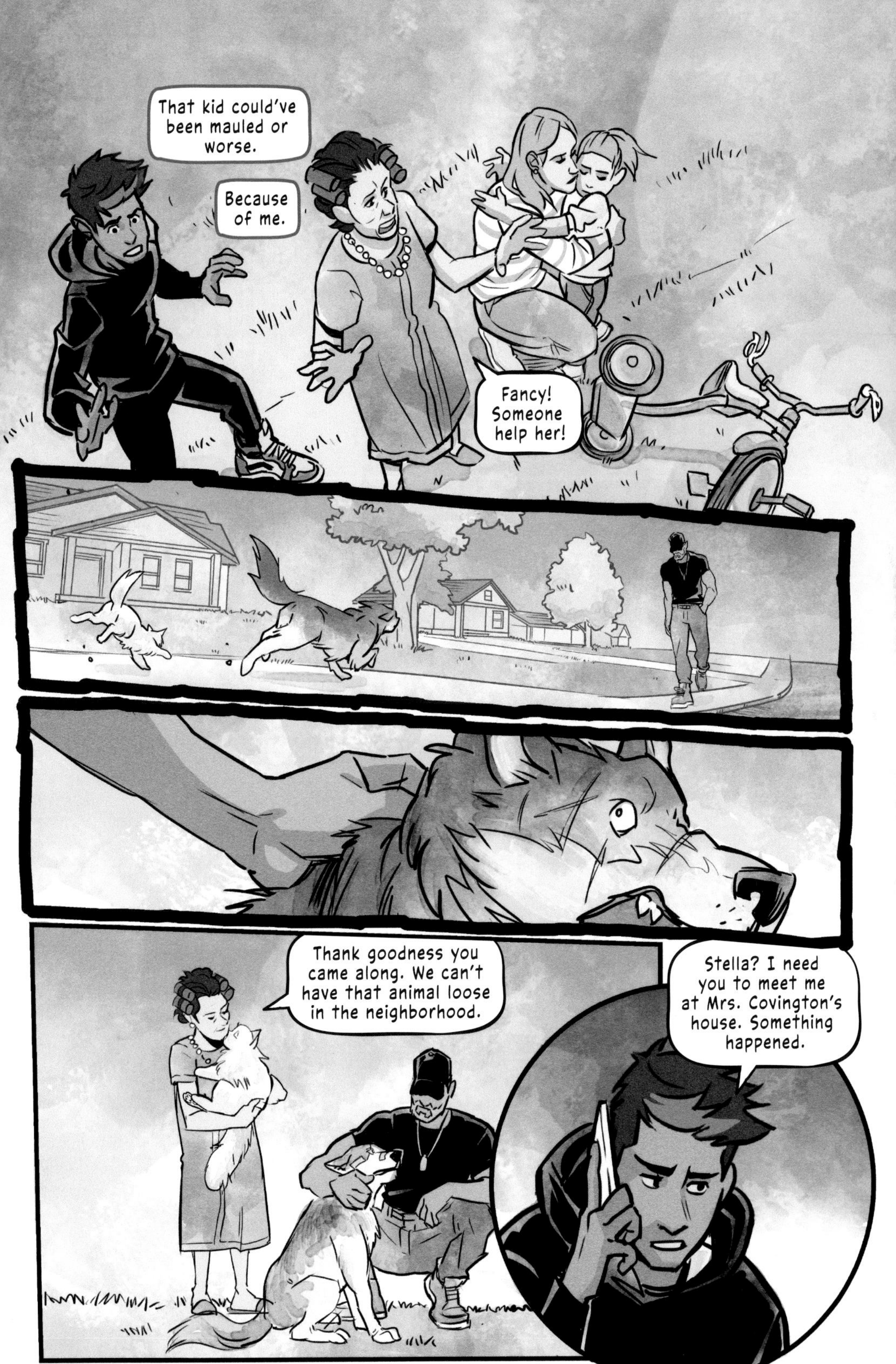
That kid could've been mauled or worse.
Because of me.
Fancy! Someone help her!
Thank goodness you came along. We can't have that animal loose in the neighborhood.
Stella? I need you to meet me at Mrs. Covington's house. Something happened.

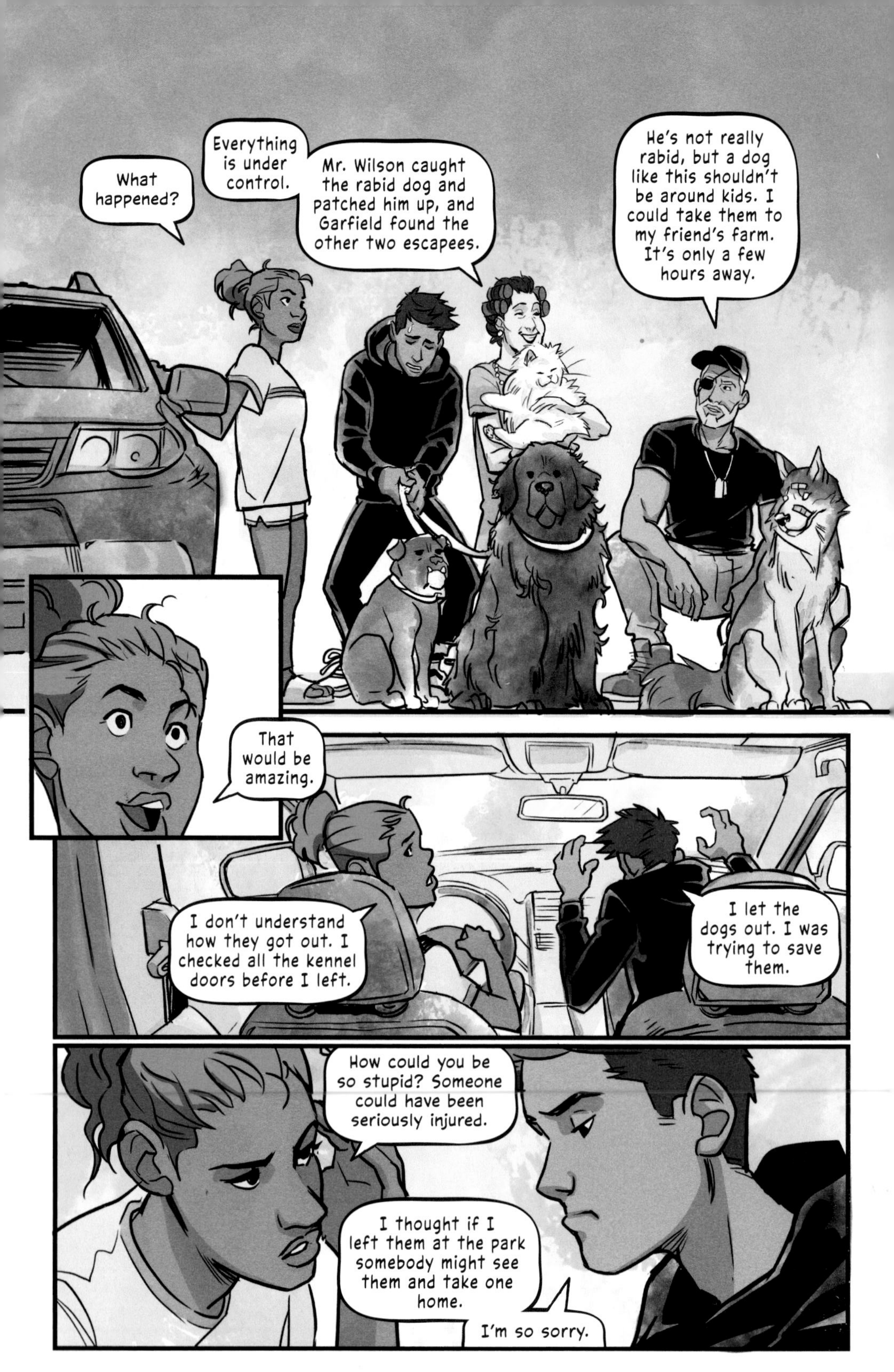
What happened?
Everything is under control.
Mr. Wilson caught the rabid dog and patched him up, and Garfield found the other two escapees.
He's not really rabid, but a dog like this shouldn't be around kids. I could take them to my friend's farm. It's only a few hours away.
That would be amazing.
I don't understand how they got out. I checked all the kennel doors before I left.
I let the dogs out. I was trying to save them.
How could you be so stupid? Someone could have been seriously injured.
I thought if I left them at the park somebody might see them and take one home.
I'm so sorry.

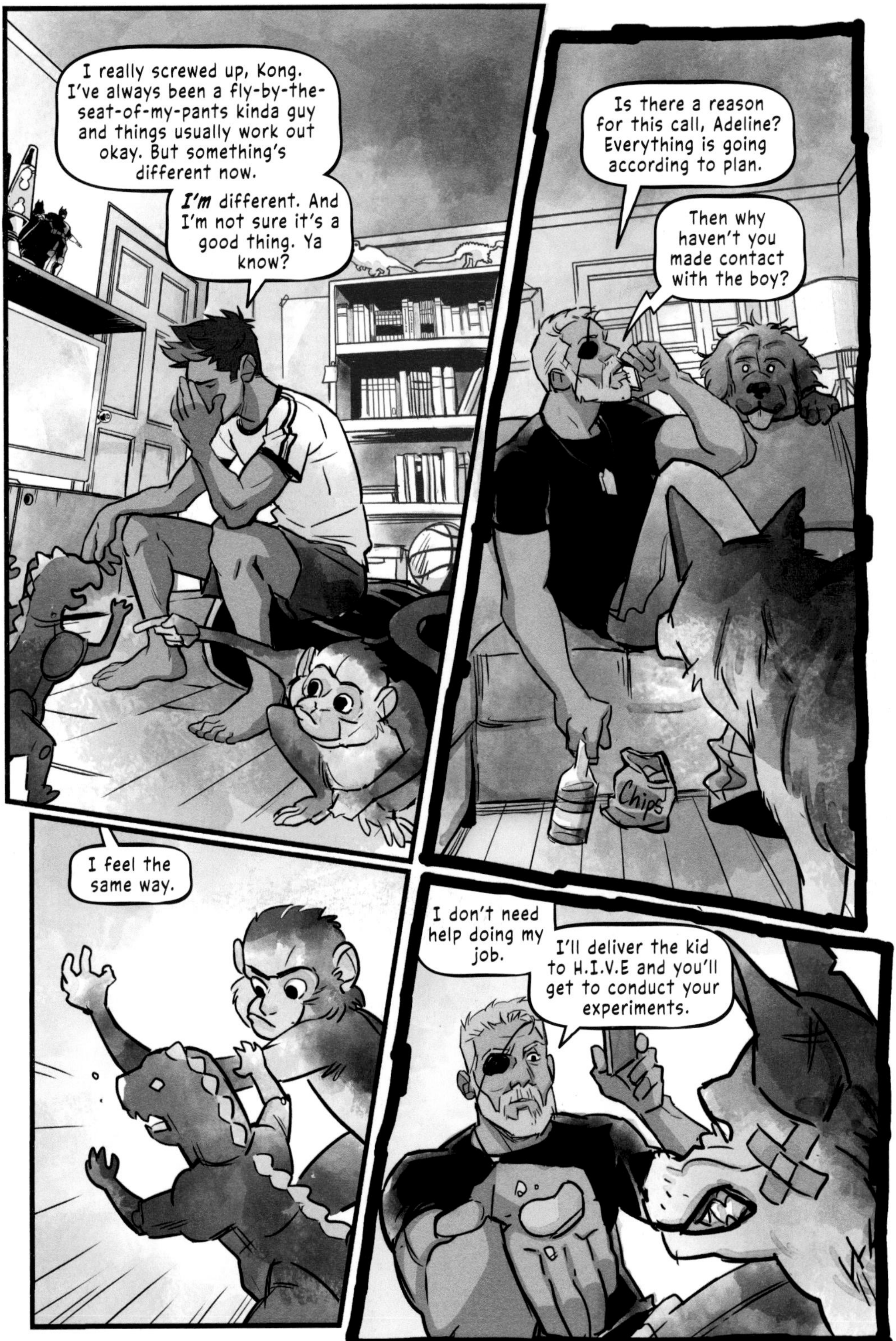

I really screwed up, Kong. I've always been a fly-by-the-seat-of-my-pants kinda guy and things usually work out okay. But something's different now.
I'm different. And I'm not sure it's a good thing. Ya know?
Is there a reason for this call, Adeline? Everything is going according to plan.
Then why haven't you made contact with the boy?
Chips
I feel the same way.
I don't need help doing my job.
I'll deliver the kid to H.I.V.E and you'll get to conduct your experiments.

CHAPTER 14: TRUTH AND TRANSFORMATION

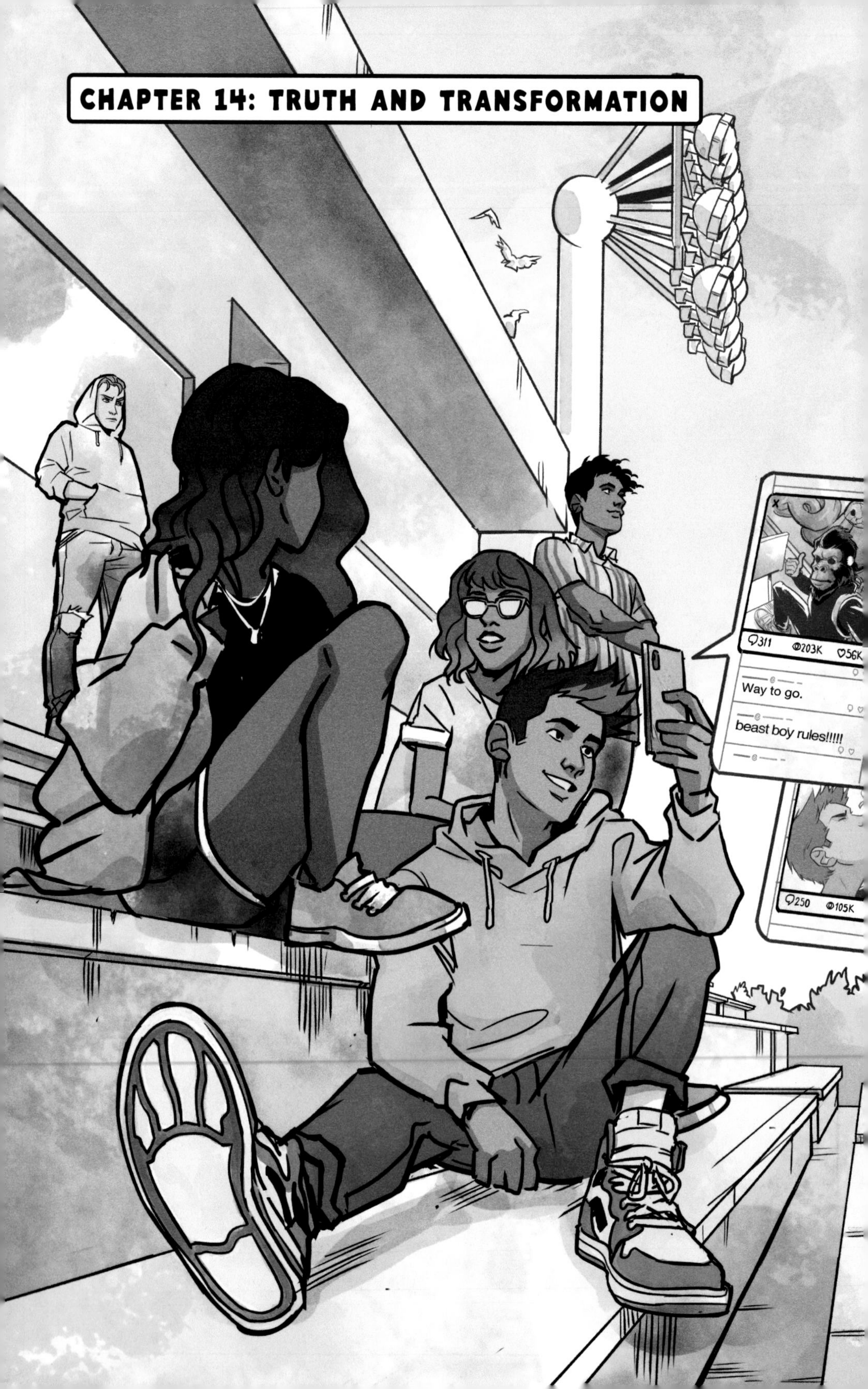
311
203K
56K
Way to go.
beast boy rules!!!!!
250
105K

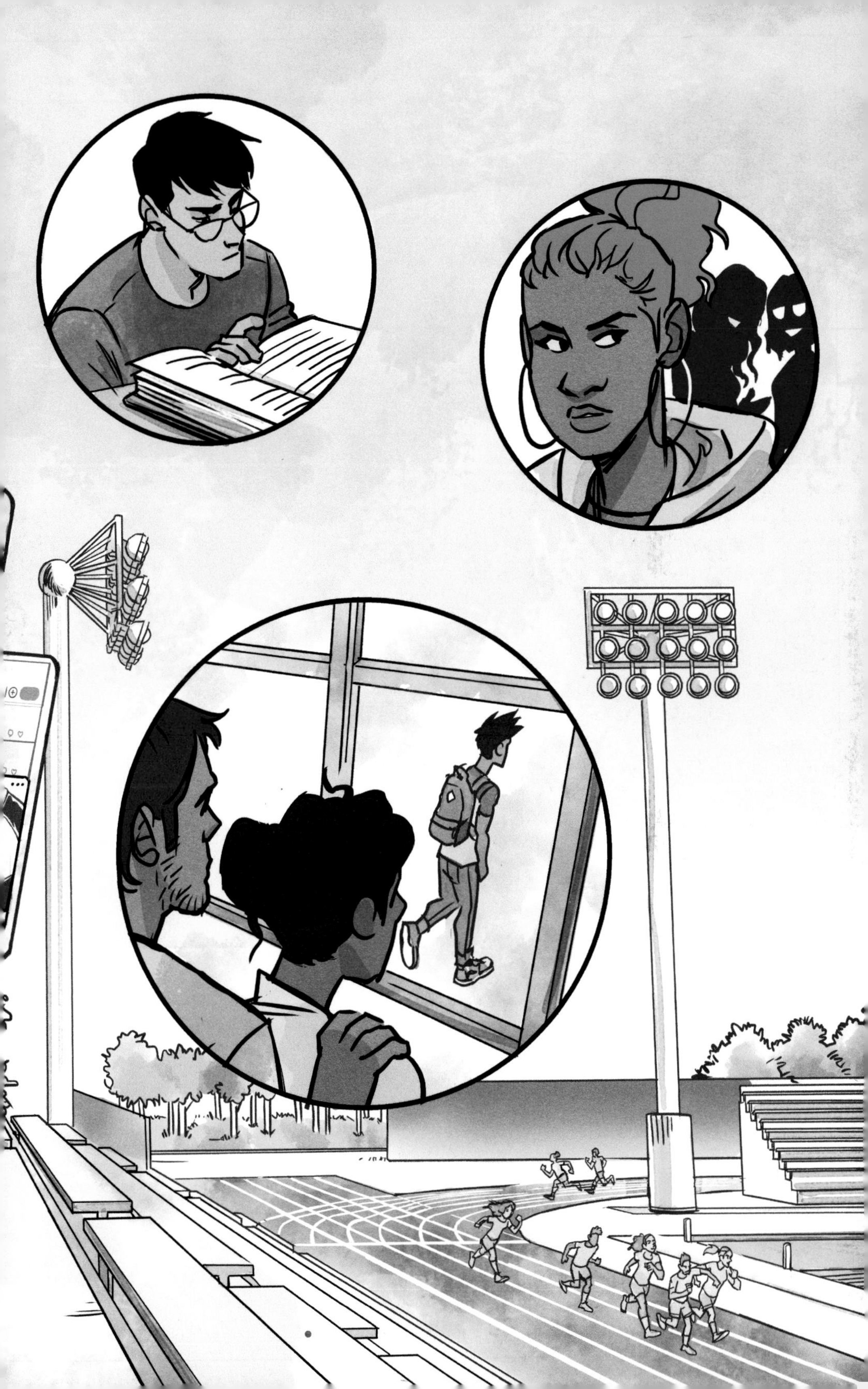

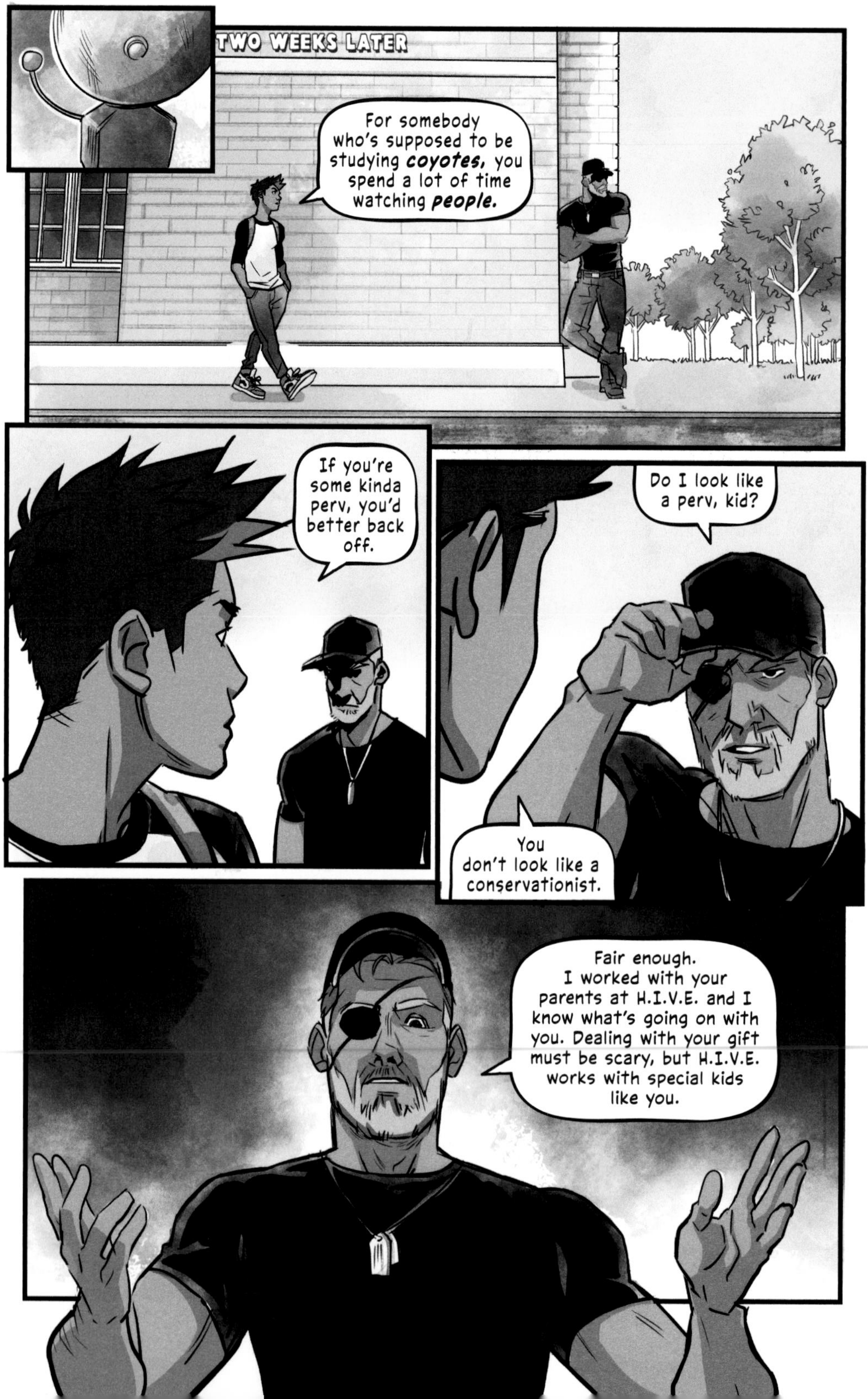
TWO WEEKS LATER
For somebody who's supposed to be studying *coyotes,* you spend a lot of time watching *people.*
If you're some kinda perv, you'd better back off.
Do I look like a perv, kid?
You don't look like a conservationist.
Fair enough. I worked with your parents at H.I.V.E. and I know what's going on with you. Dealing with your gift must be scary, but H.I.V.E. works with special kids like you.

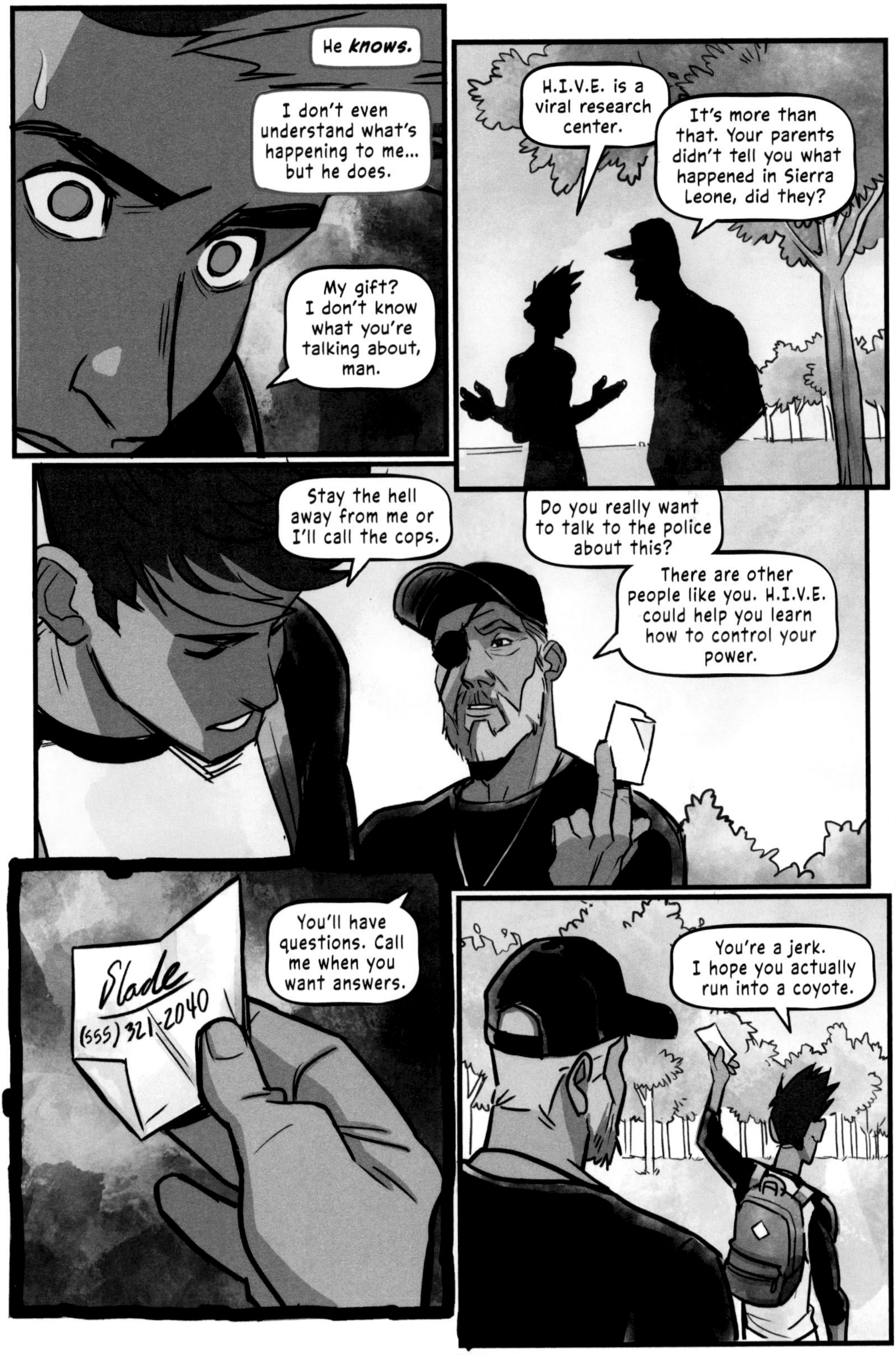
He *knows.*
I don't even understand what's happening to me... but he does.
My gift? I don't know what you're talking about, man.
H.I.V.E. is a viral research center.
It's more than that. Your parents didn't tell you what happened in Sierra Leone, did they?
Stay the hell away from me or I'll call the cops.
Do you really want to talk to the police about this?
There are other people like you. H.I.V.E. could help you learn how to control your power.
Slade
(555) 321-2040
You'll have questions. Call me when you want answers.
You're a jerk. I hope you actually run into a coyote.

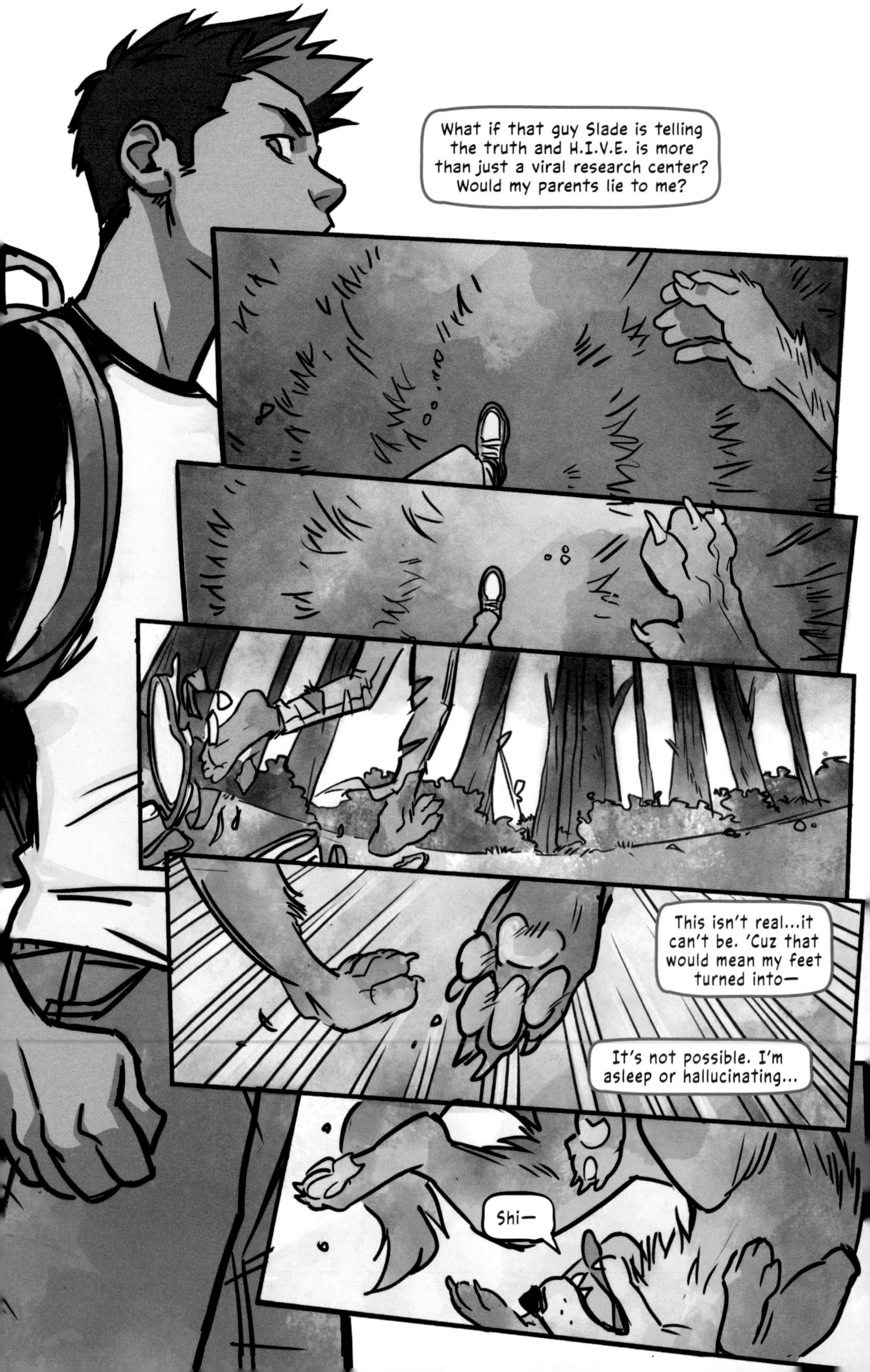
What if that guy Slade is telling the truth and H.I.V.E. is more than just a viral research center? Would my parents lie to me?
This isn't real...it can't be. 'Cuz that would mean my feet turned into—
It's not possible. I'm asleep or hallucinating...
Shi—

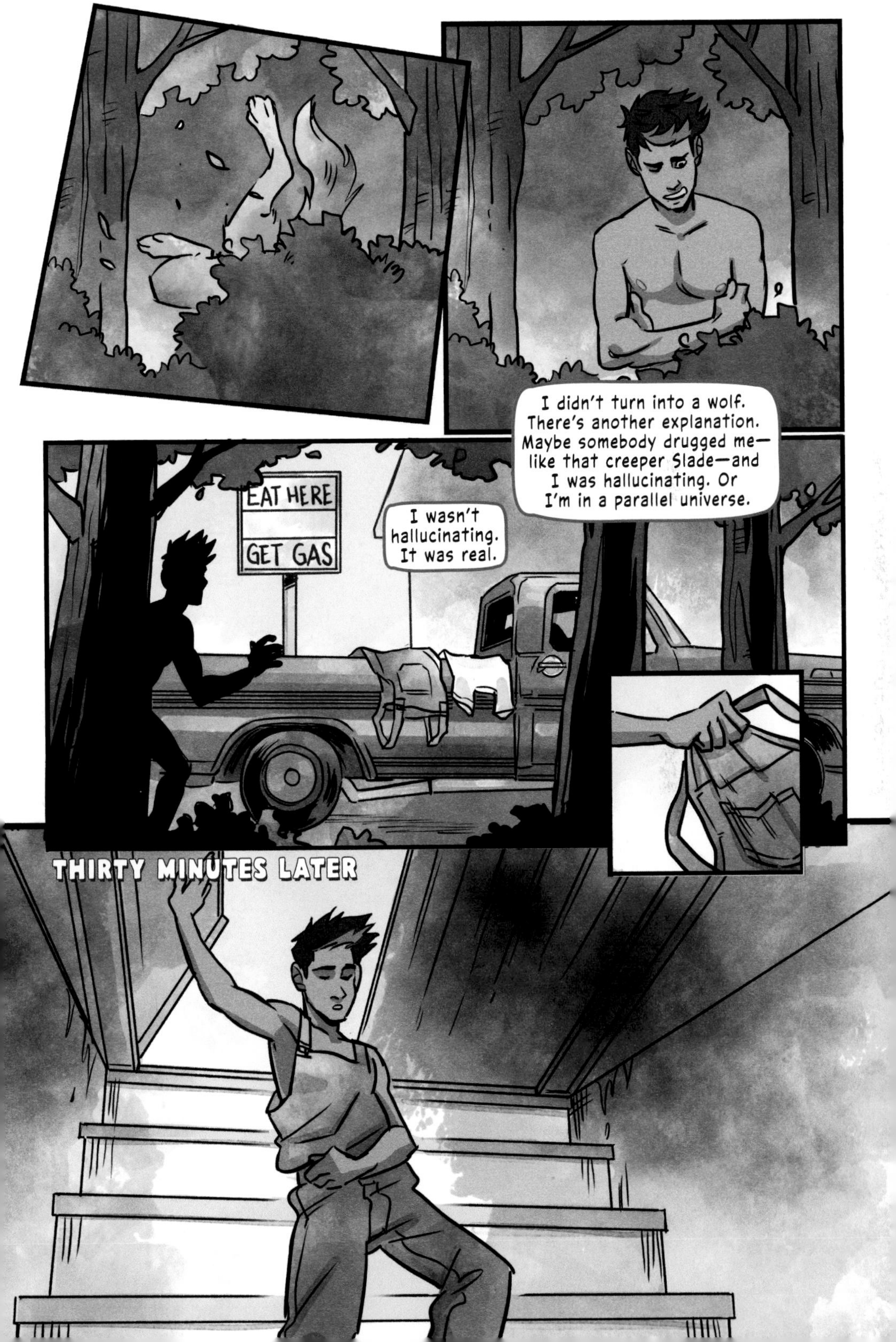
I didn't turn into a wolf. There's another explanation. Maybe somebody drugged me—like that creeper Slade—and I was hallucinating. Or I'm in a parallel universe.
EAT HERE
GET GAS
I wasn't hallucinating. It was real.
THIRTY MINUTES LATER

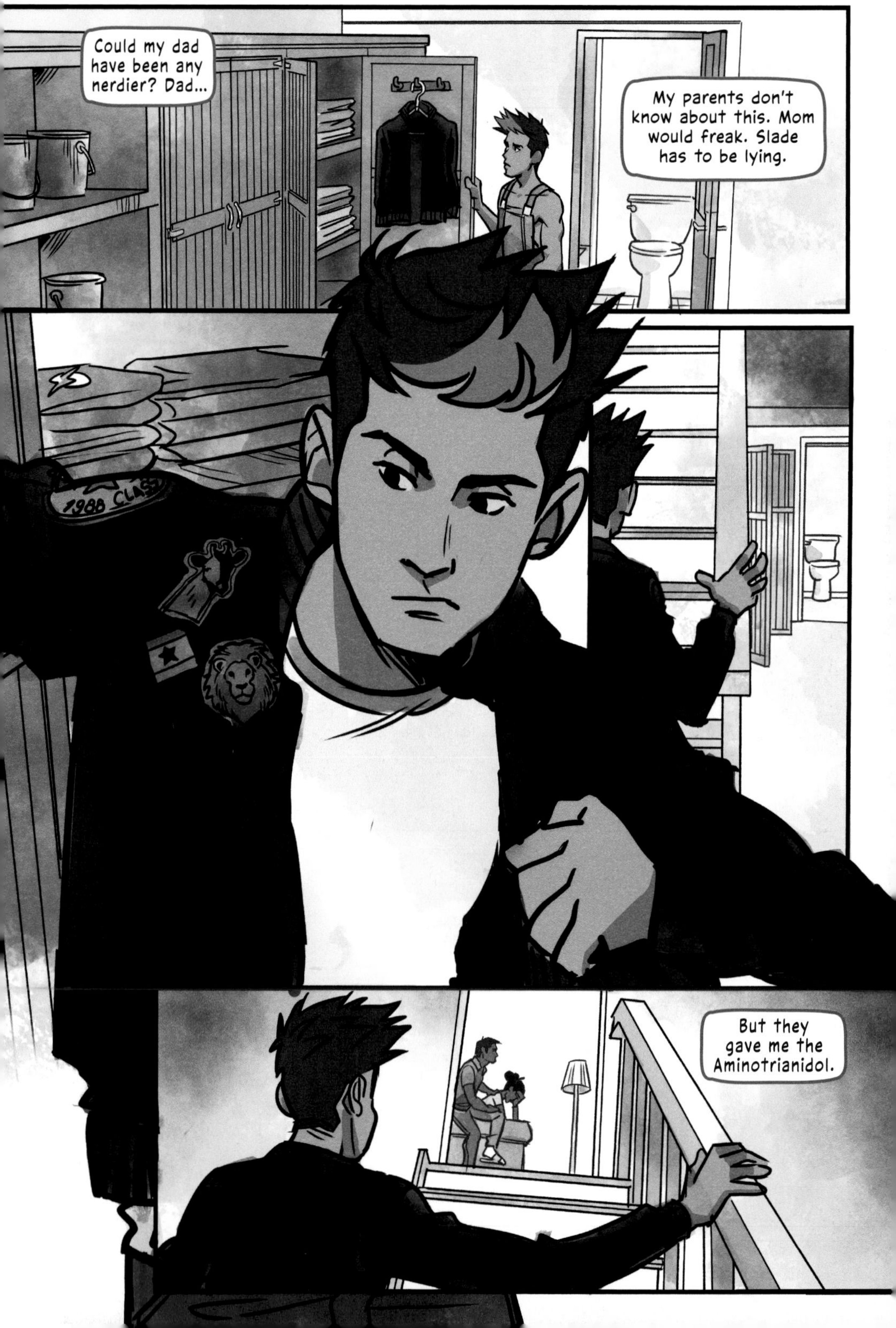
Could my dad have been any nerdier? Dad...
My parents don't know about this. Mom would freak. Slade has to be lying.
1988 CLASS
But they gave me the Aminotrianidol.

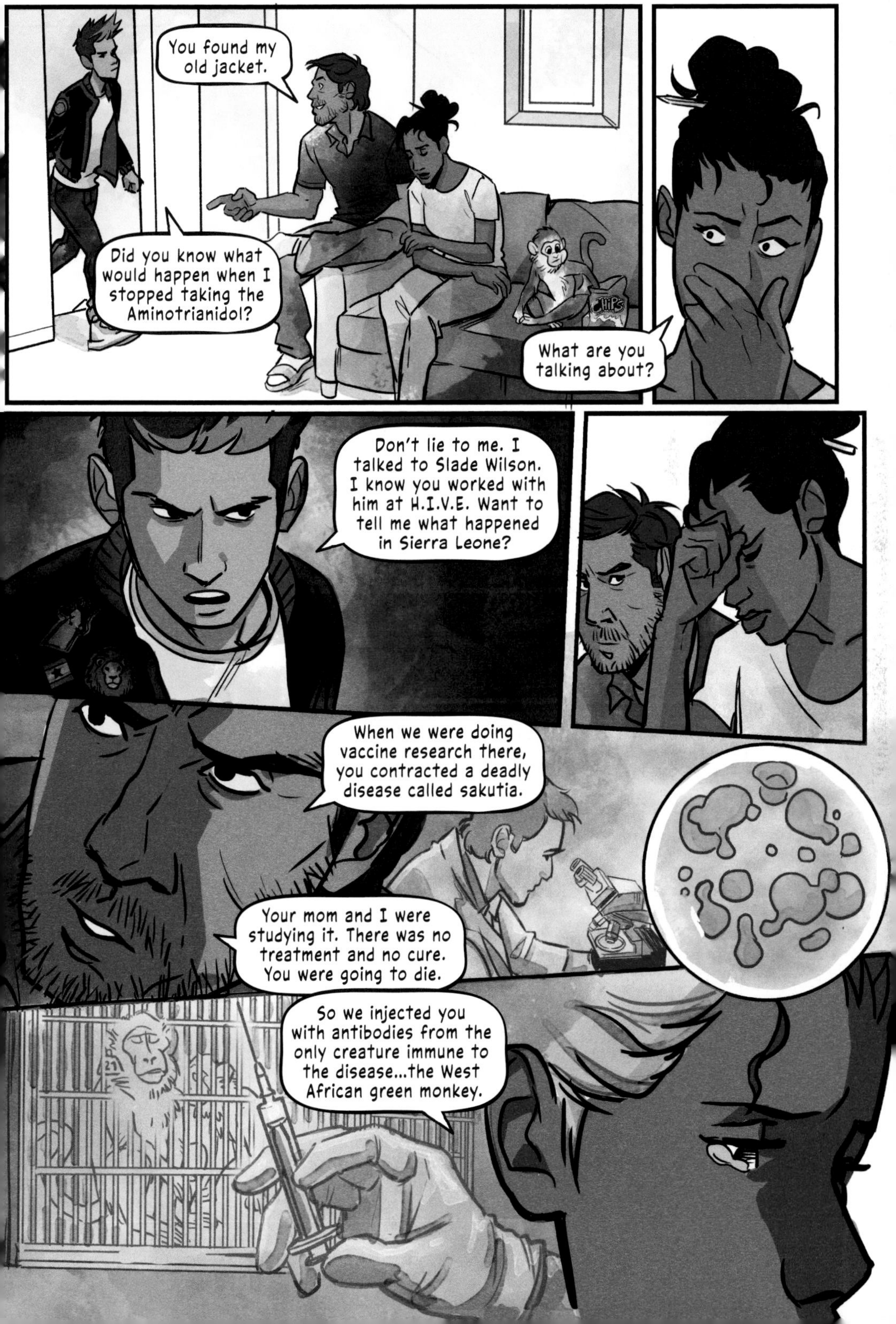
You found my old jacket.
Did you know what would happen when I stopped taking the Aminotrianidol?
What are you talking about?
Don't lie to me. I talked to Slade Wilson. I know you worked with him at H.I.V.E. Want to tell me what happened in Sierra Leone?
When we were doing vaccine research there, you contracted a deadly disease called sakutia.
Your mom and I were studying it. There was no treatment and no cure. You were going to die.
So we injected you with antibodies from the only creature immune to the disease...the West African green monkey.

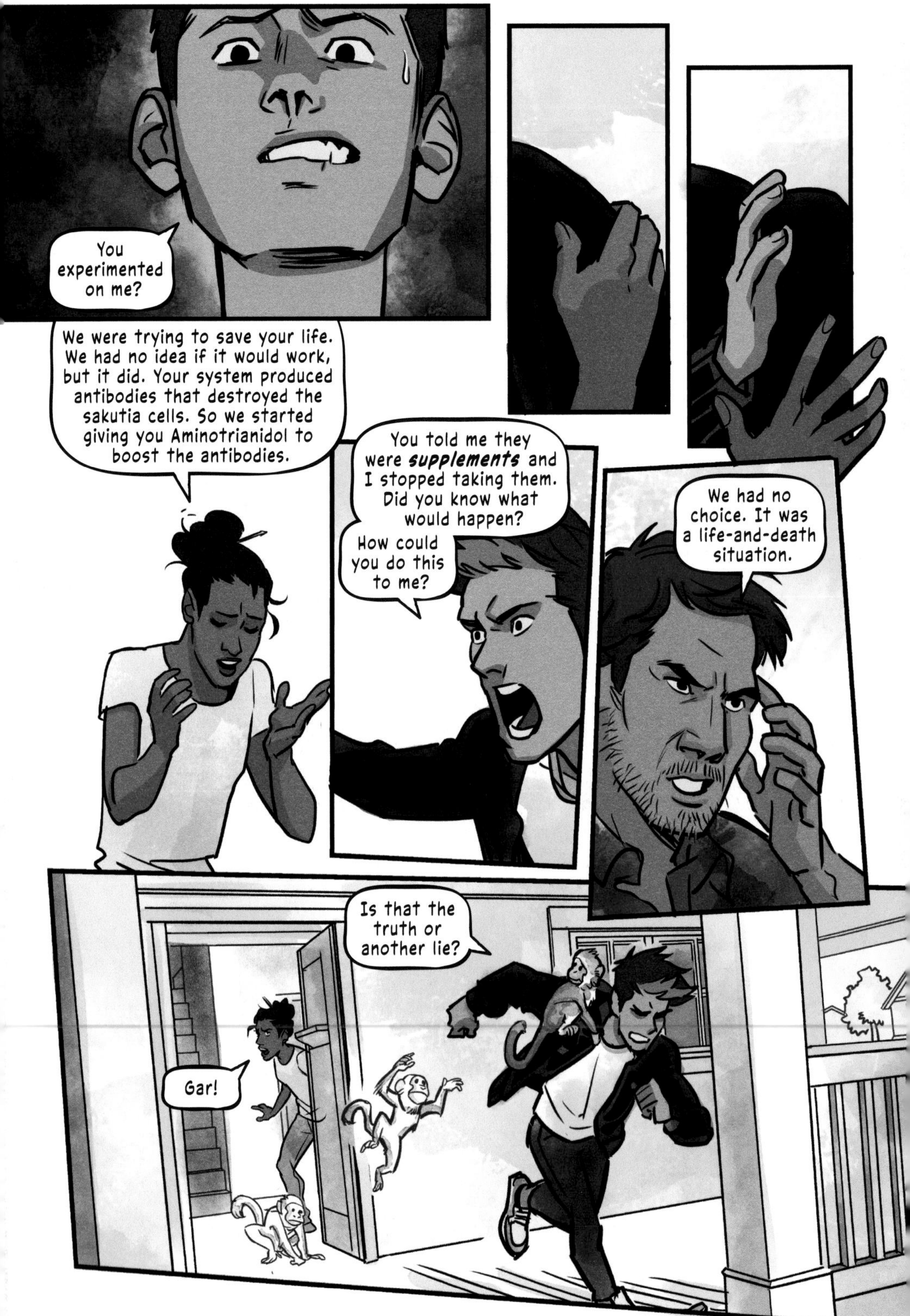
You experimented on me?
We were trying to save your life. We had no idea if it would work, but it did. Your system produced antibodies that destroyed the sakutia cells. So we started giving you Aminotrianidol to boost the antibodies.
You told me they were *supplements* and I stopped taking them. Did you know what would happen?
How could you do this to me?
We had no choice. It was a life-and-death situation.
Is that the truth or another lie?
Gar!

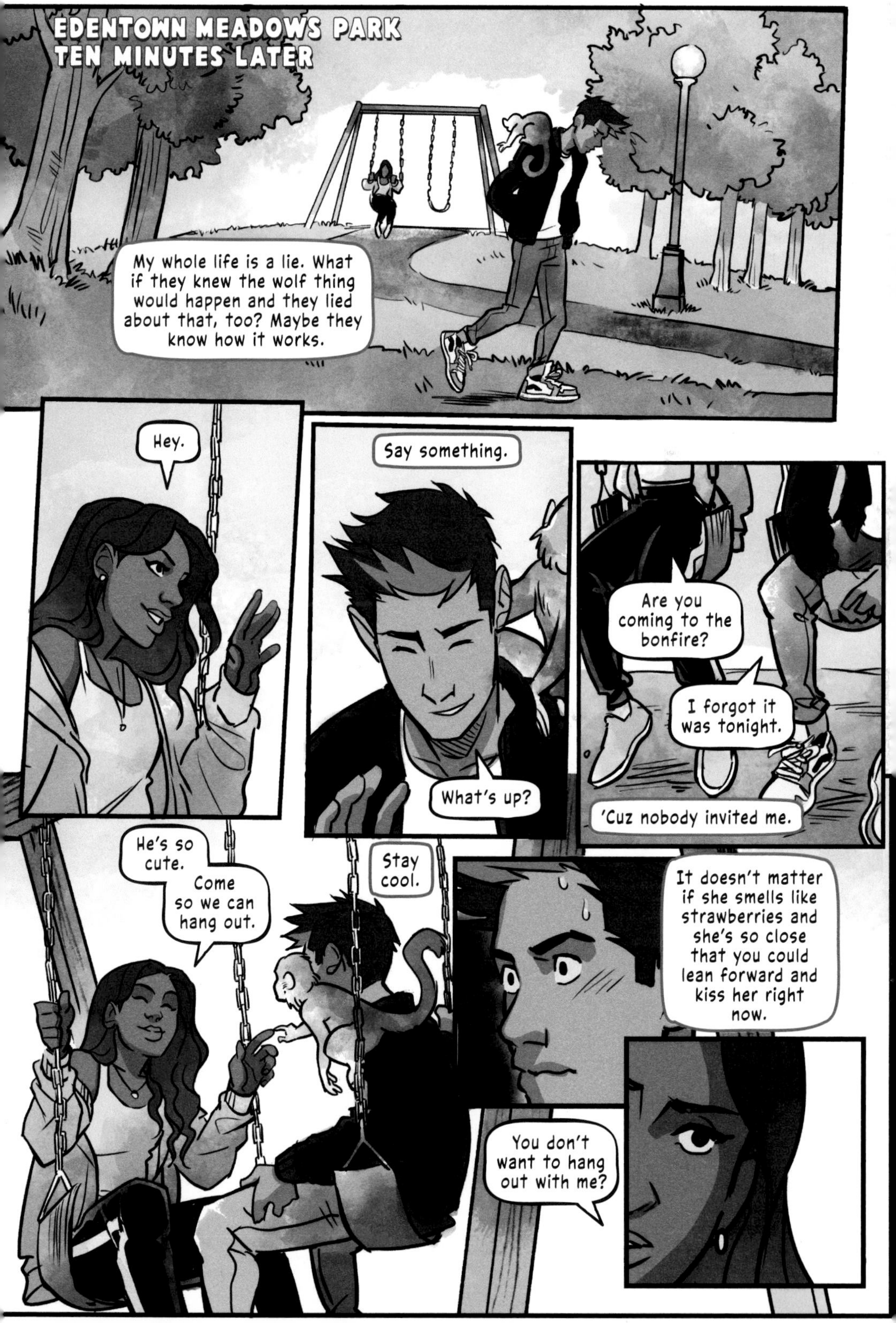
EDENTOWN MEADOWS PARK
TEN MINUTES LATER
My whole life is a lie. What if they knew the wolf thing would happen and they lied about that, too? Maybe they know how it works.
Hey.
Say something.
What's up?
Are you coming to the bonfire?
I forgot it was tonight.
'Cuz nobody invited me.
He's so cute.
Come so we can hang out.
Stay cool.
It doesn't matter if she smells like strawberries and she's so close that you could lean forward and kiss her right now.
You don't want to hang out with me?

CHAPTER 15: BUCKET LIST

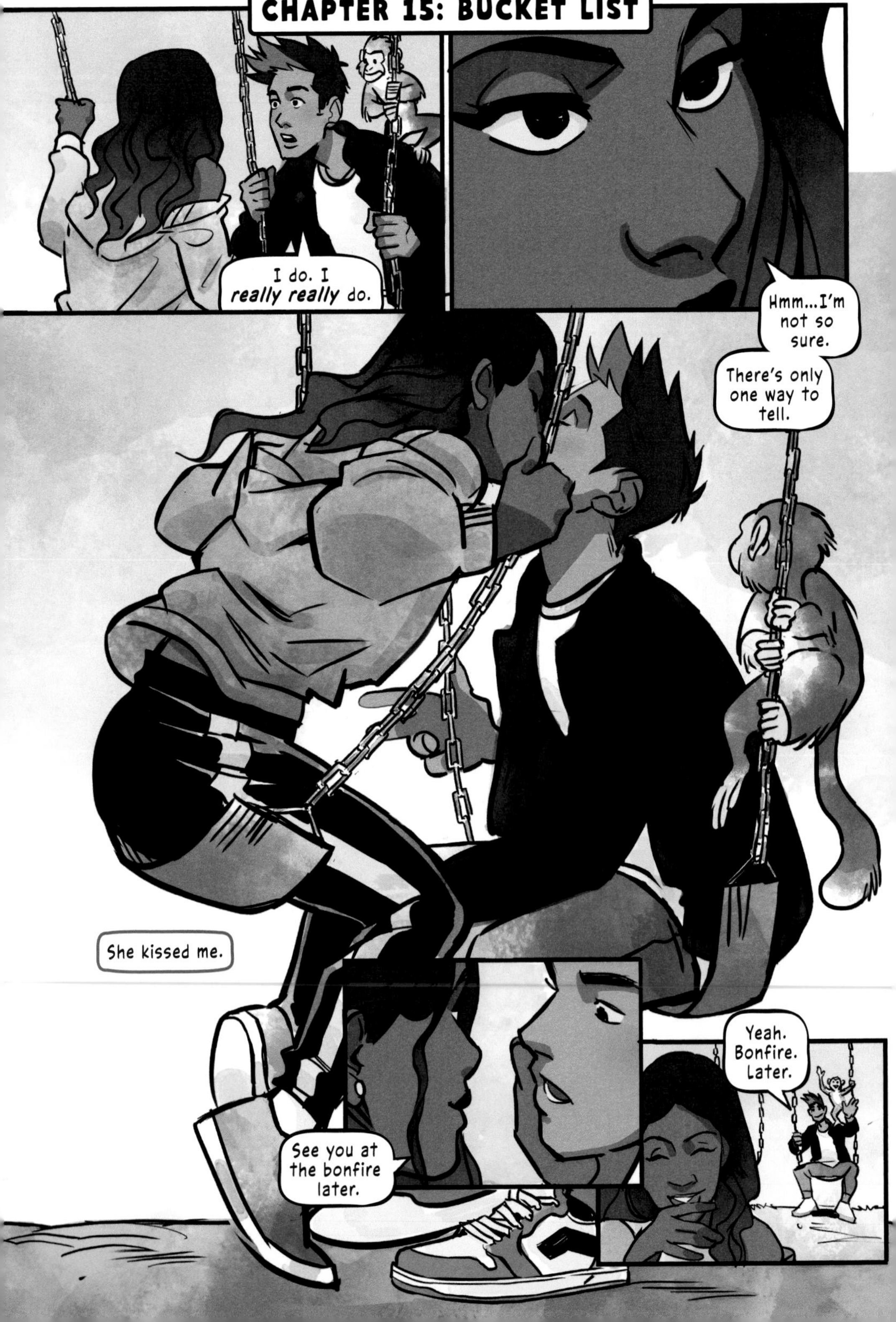

I do. I *really really* do.
Hmm...I'm not so sure.
There's only one way to tell.
She kissed me.
See you at the bonfire later.
Yeah. Bonfire. Later.

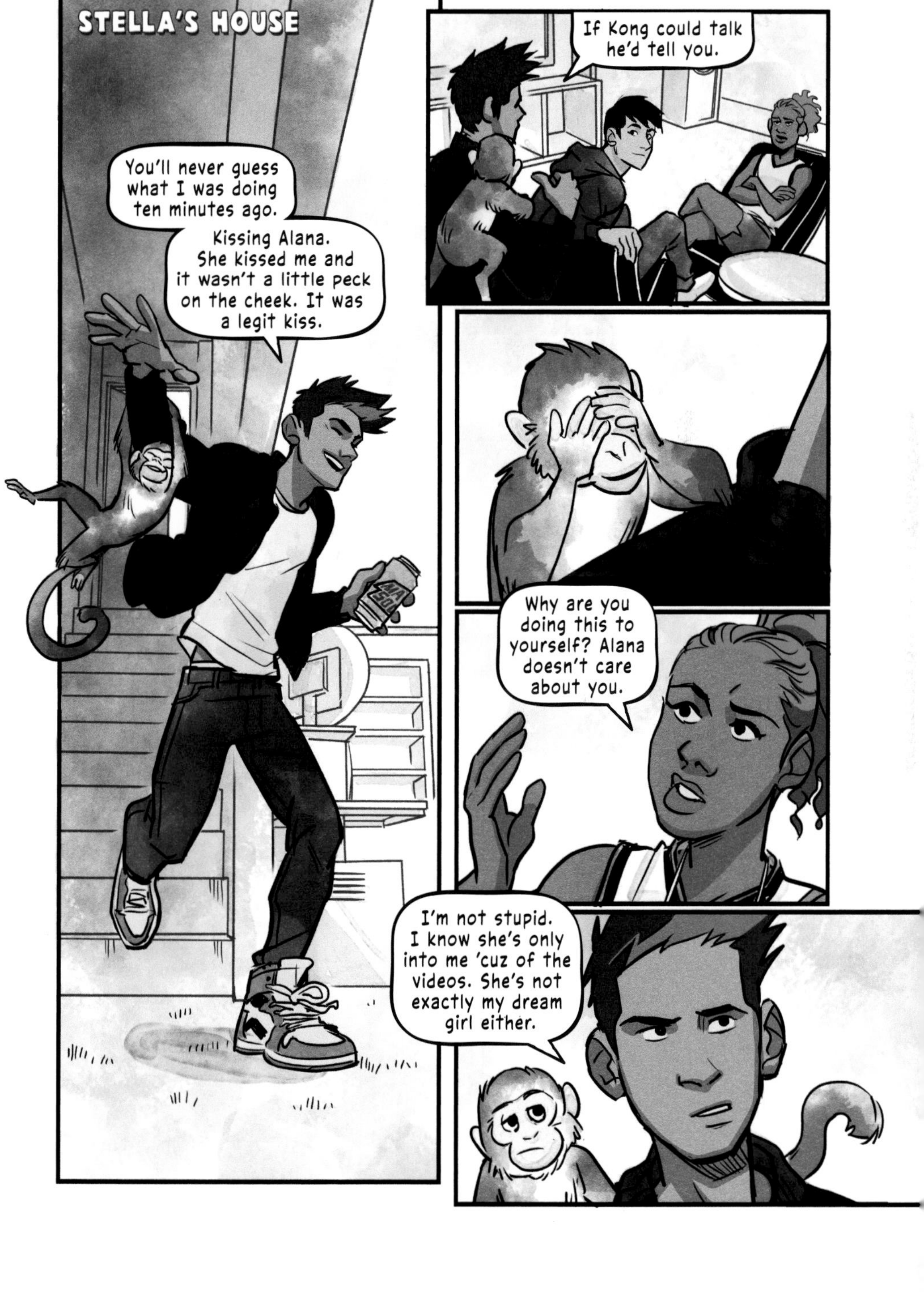
STELLA'S HOUSE
You'll never guess what I was doing ten minutes ago.
Kissing Alana. She kissed me and it wasn't a little peck on the cheek. It was a legit kiss.
If Kong could talk he'd tell you.
Why are you doing this to yourself? Alana doesn't care about you.
I'm not stupid. I know she's only into me 'cuz of the videos. She's not exactly my dream girl either.

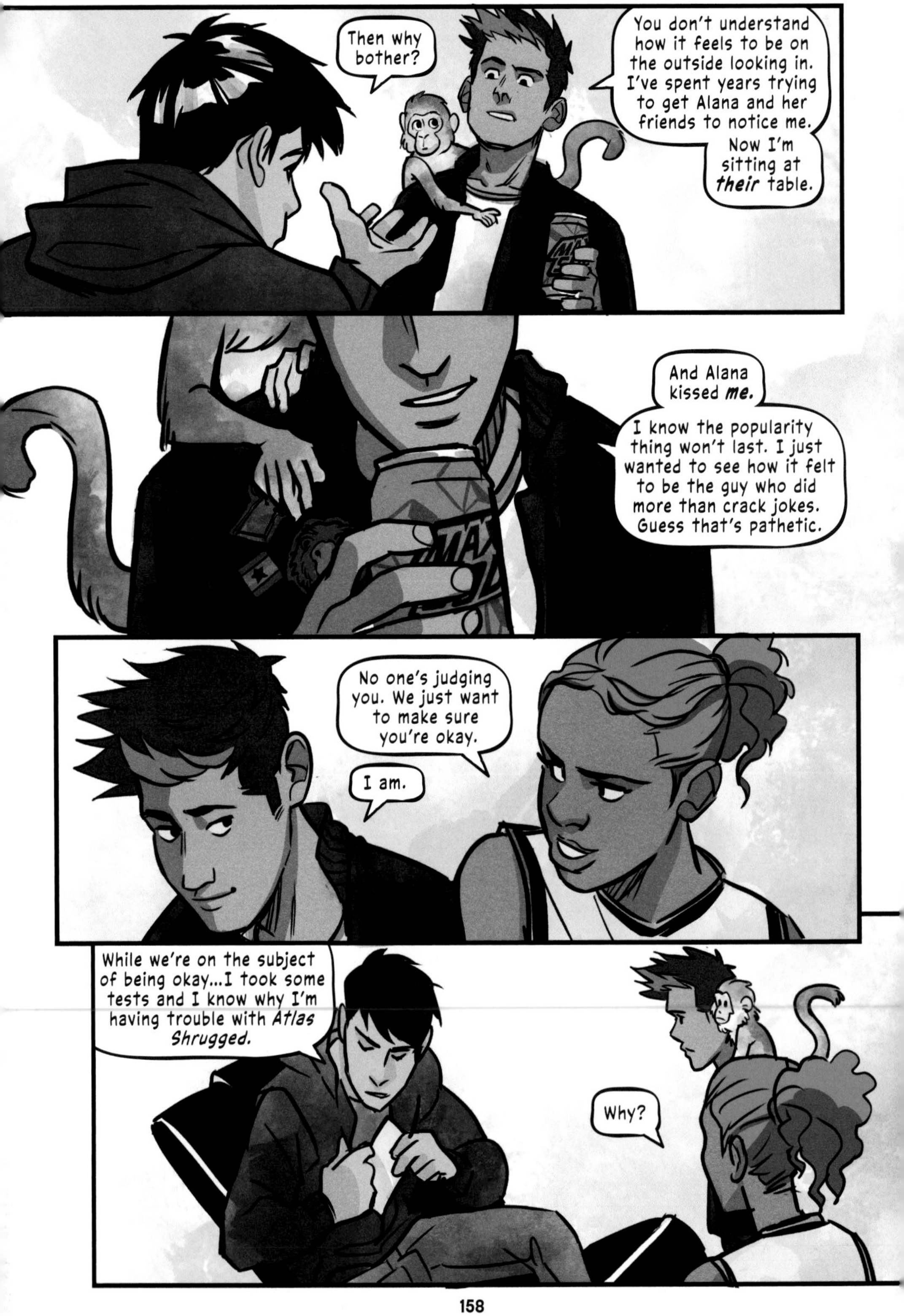

Then why bother?
You don't understand how it feels to be on the outside looking in. I've spent years trying to get Alana and her friends to notice me.
Now I'm sitting at *their* table.
And Alana kissed ***me.***
I know the popularity thing won't last. I just wanted to see how it felt to be the guy who did more than crack jokes. Guess that's pathetic.
No one's judging you. We just want to make sure you're okay.
I am.
While we're on the subject of being okay...I took some tests and I know why I'm having trouble with *Atlas Shrugged.*
Why?

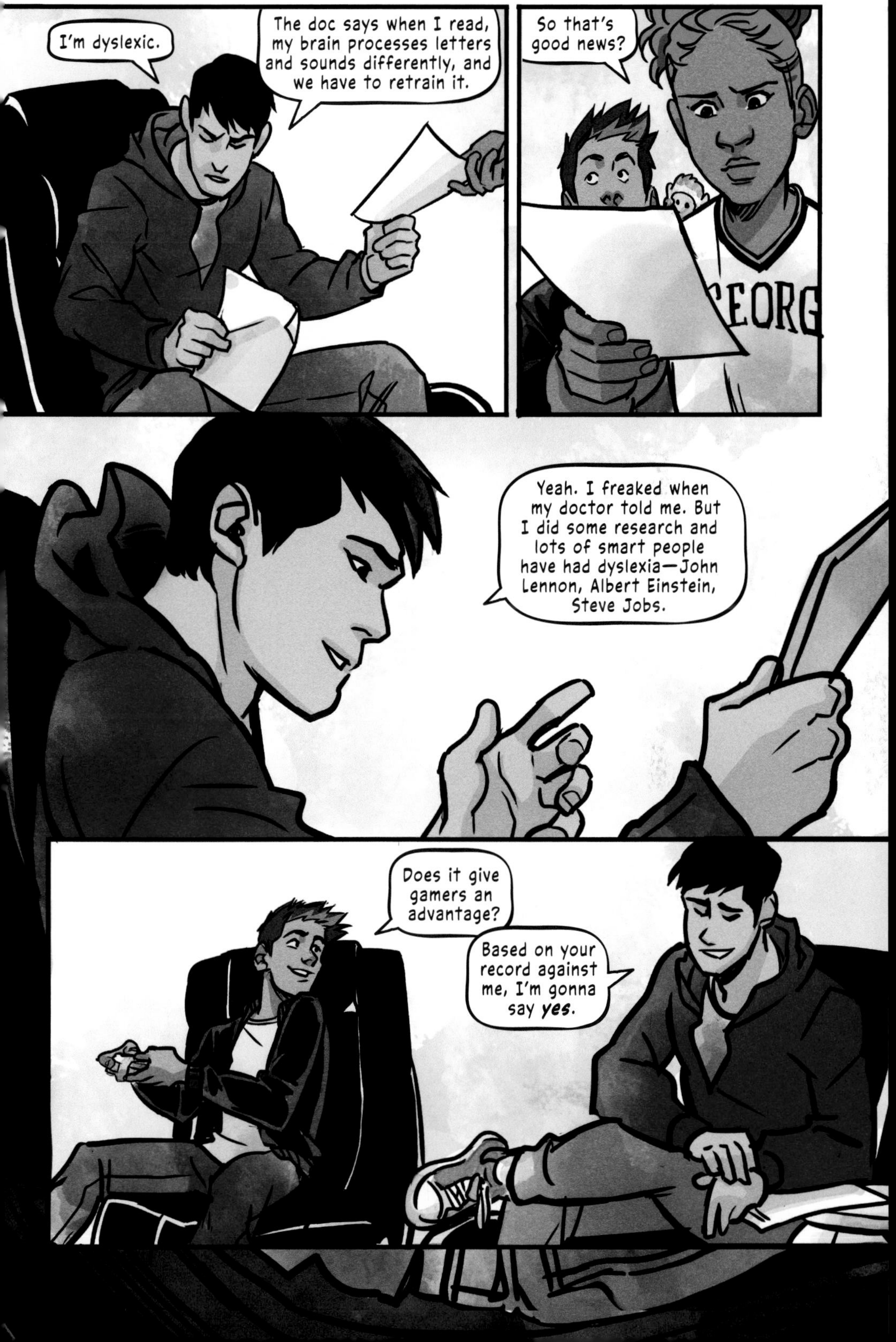
I'm dyslexic.
The doc says when I read, my brain processes letters and sounds differently, and we have to retrain it.
So that's good news?
CEORG
Yeah. I freaked when my doctor told me. But I did some research and lots of smart people have had dyslexia—John Lennon, Albert Einstein, Steve Jobs.
Does it give gamers an advantage?
Based on your record against me, I'm gonna say *yes*.

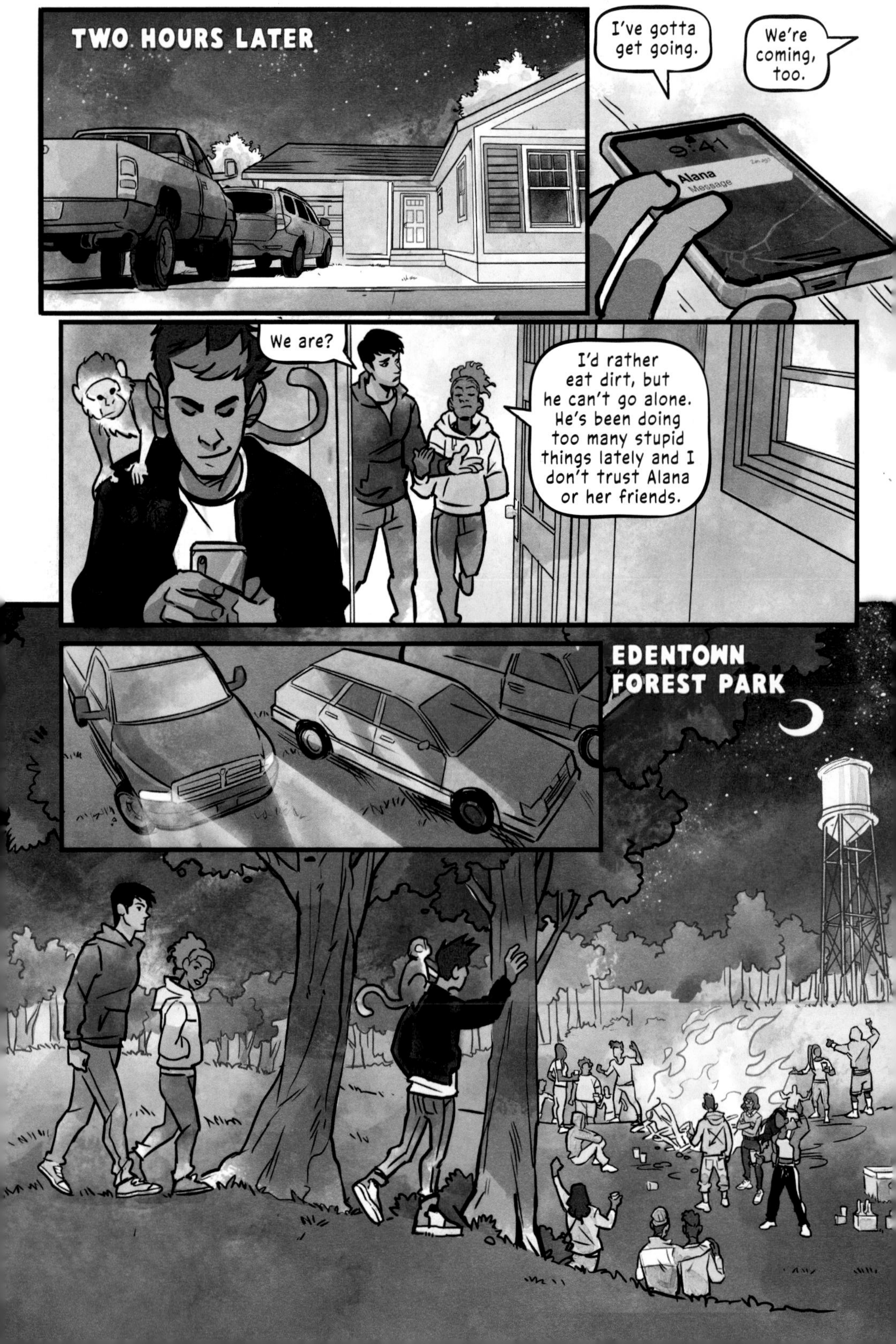
TWO HOURS LATER
I've gotta get going.
We're coming, too.
9:41
Alana
Message
We are?
I'd rather eat dirt, but he can't go alone. He's been doing too many stupid things lately and I don't trust Alana or her friends.
EDENTOWN FOREST PARK

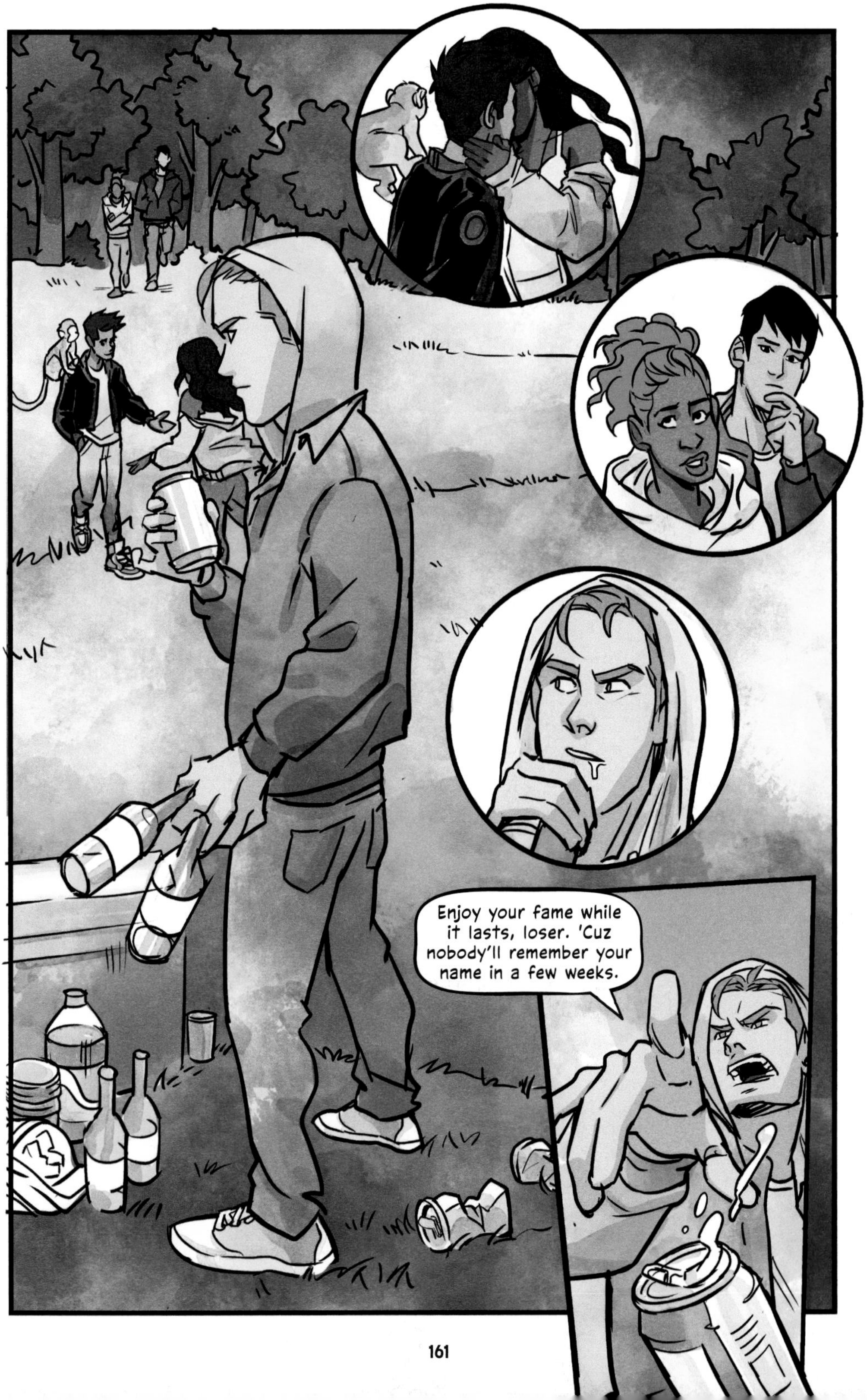
Enjoy your fame while it lasts, loser. 'Cuz nobody'll remember your name in a few weeks.

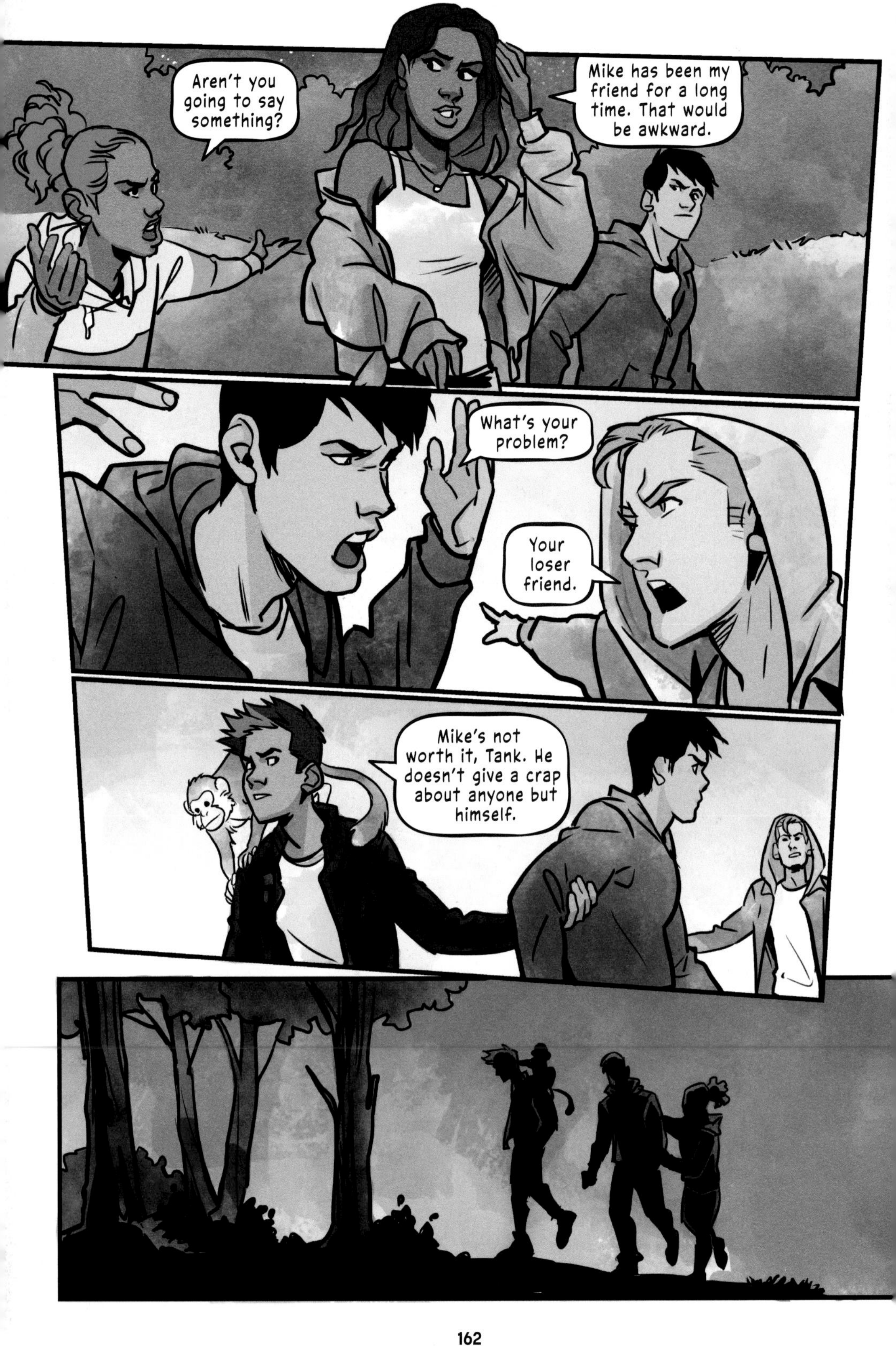
Aren't you going to say something?
Mike has been my friend for a long time. That would be awkward.
What's your problem?
Your loser friend.
Mike's not worth it, Tank. He doesn't give a crap about anyone but himself.

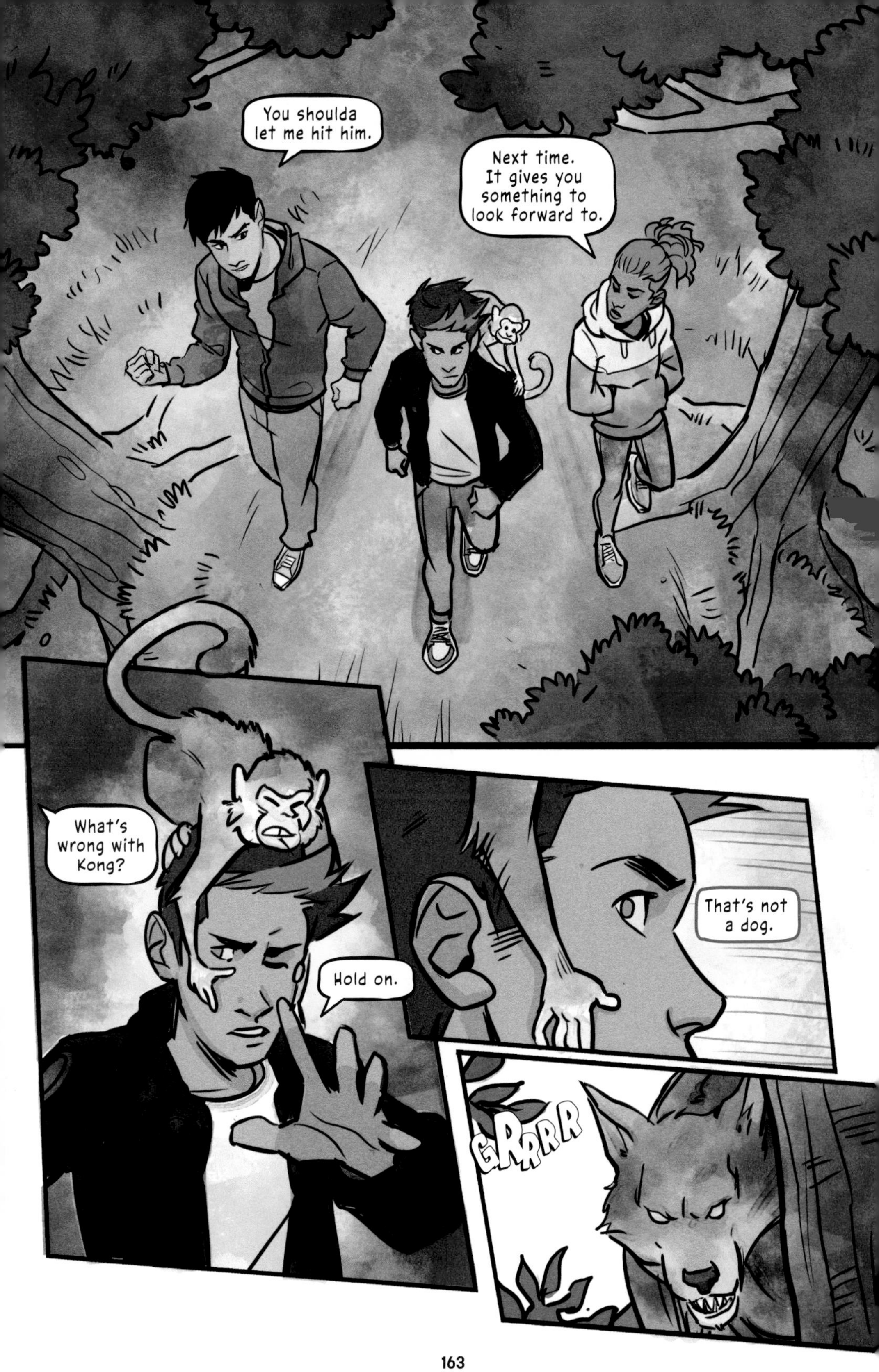
You shoulda let me hit him.
Next time. It gives you something to look forward to.
What's wrong with Kong?
Hold on.
That's not a dog.
GRRRR

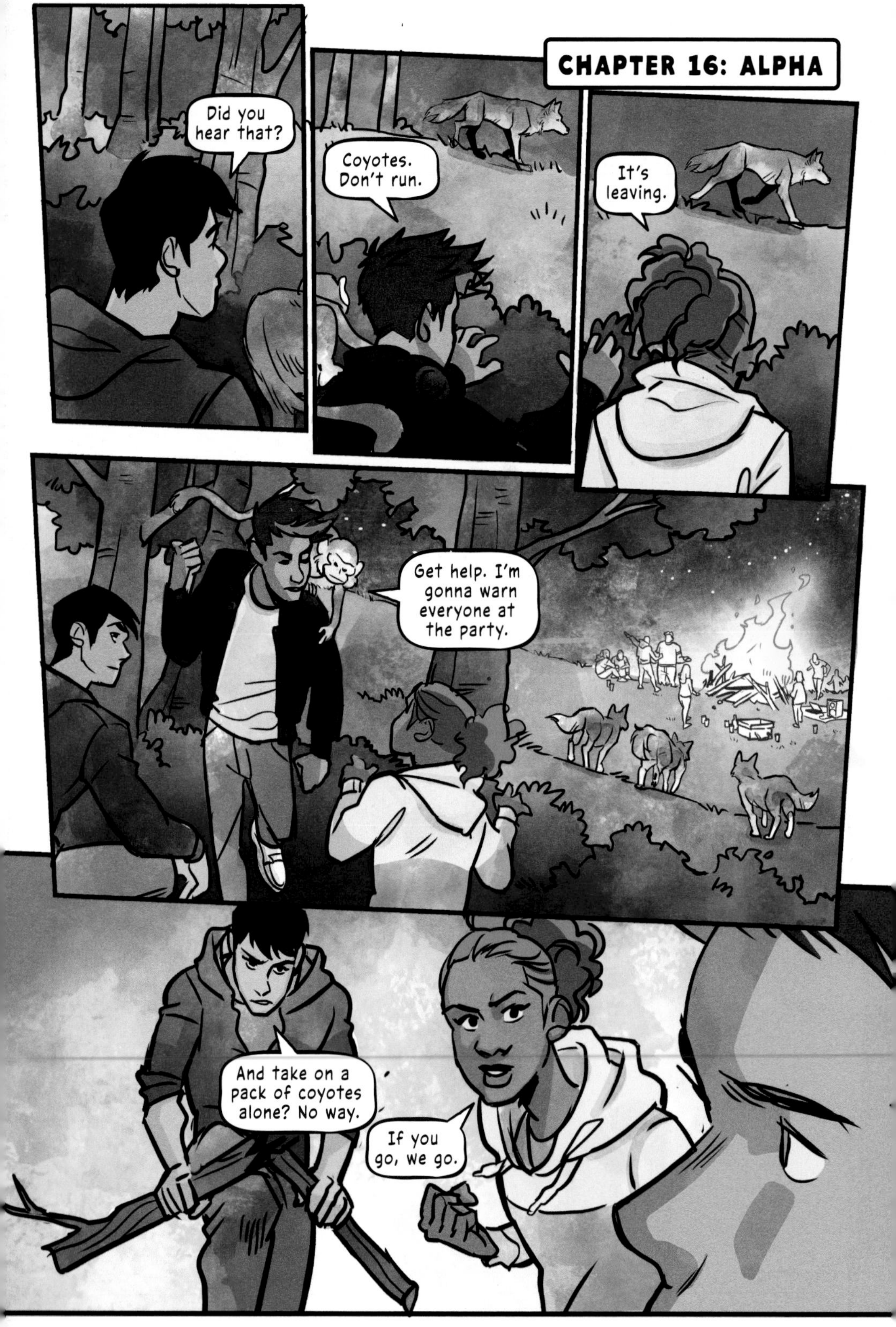
CHAPTER 16: ALPHA
Did you hear that?
Coyotes. Don't run.
It's leaving.
Get help. I'm gonna warn everyone at the party.
And take on a pack of coyotes alone? No way.
If you go, we go.

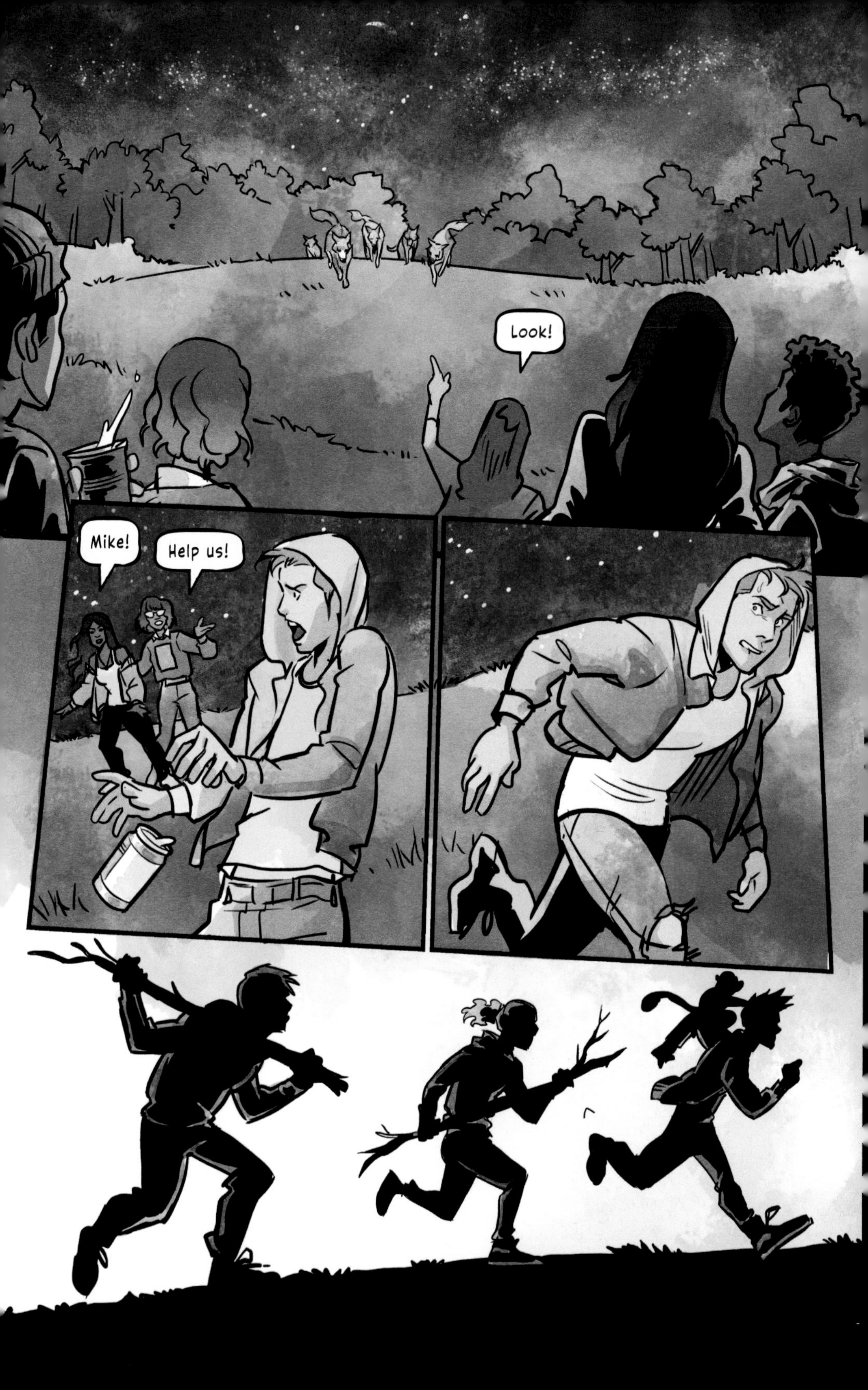
Look!
Mike!
Help us!

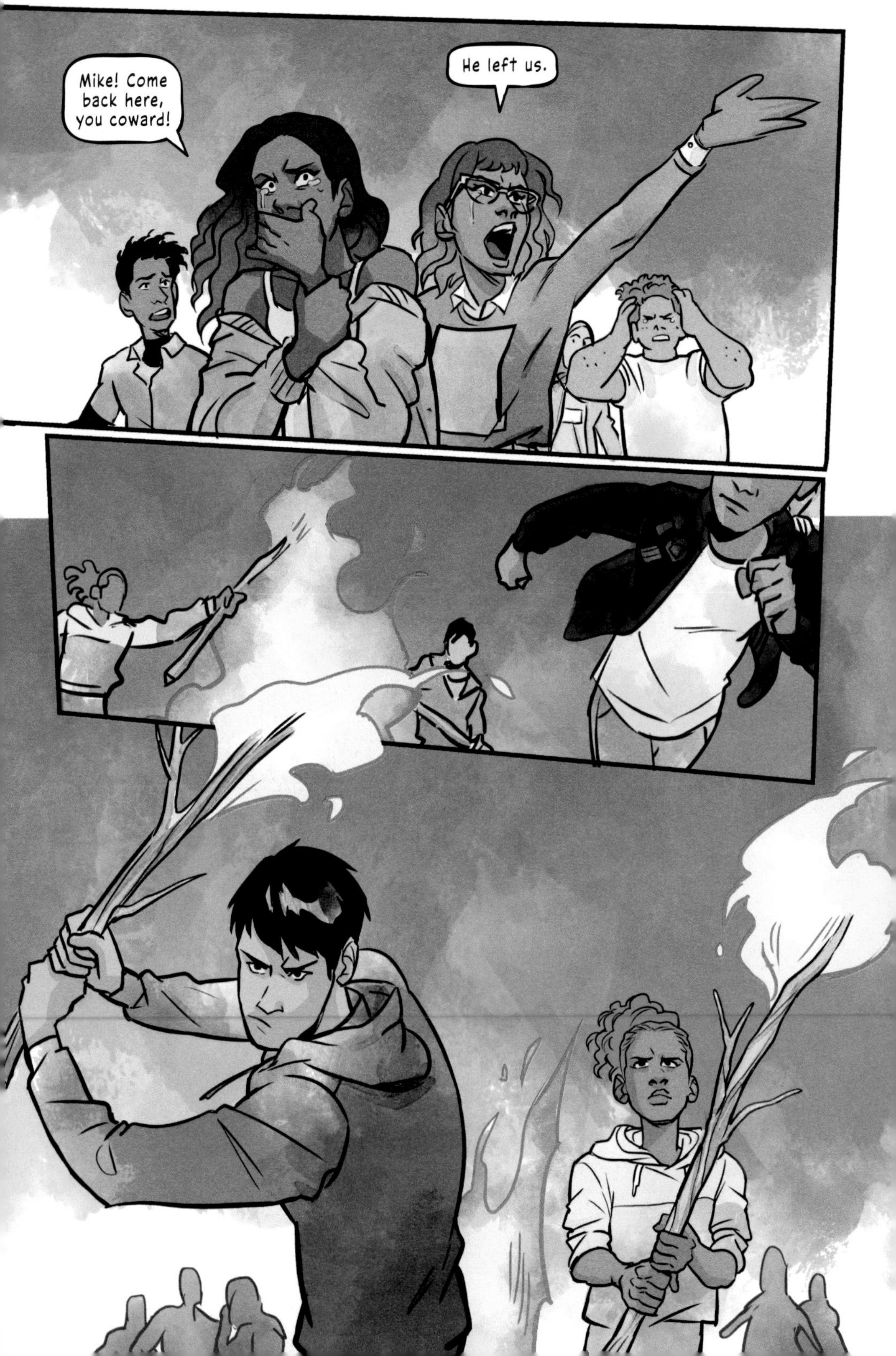
Mike! Come back here, you coward!
He left us.

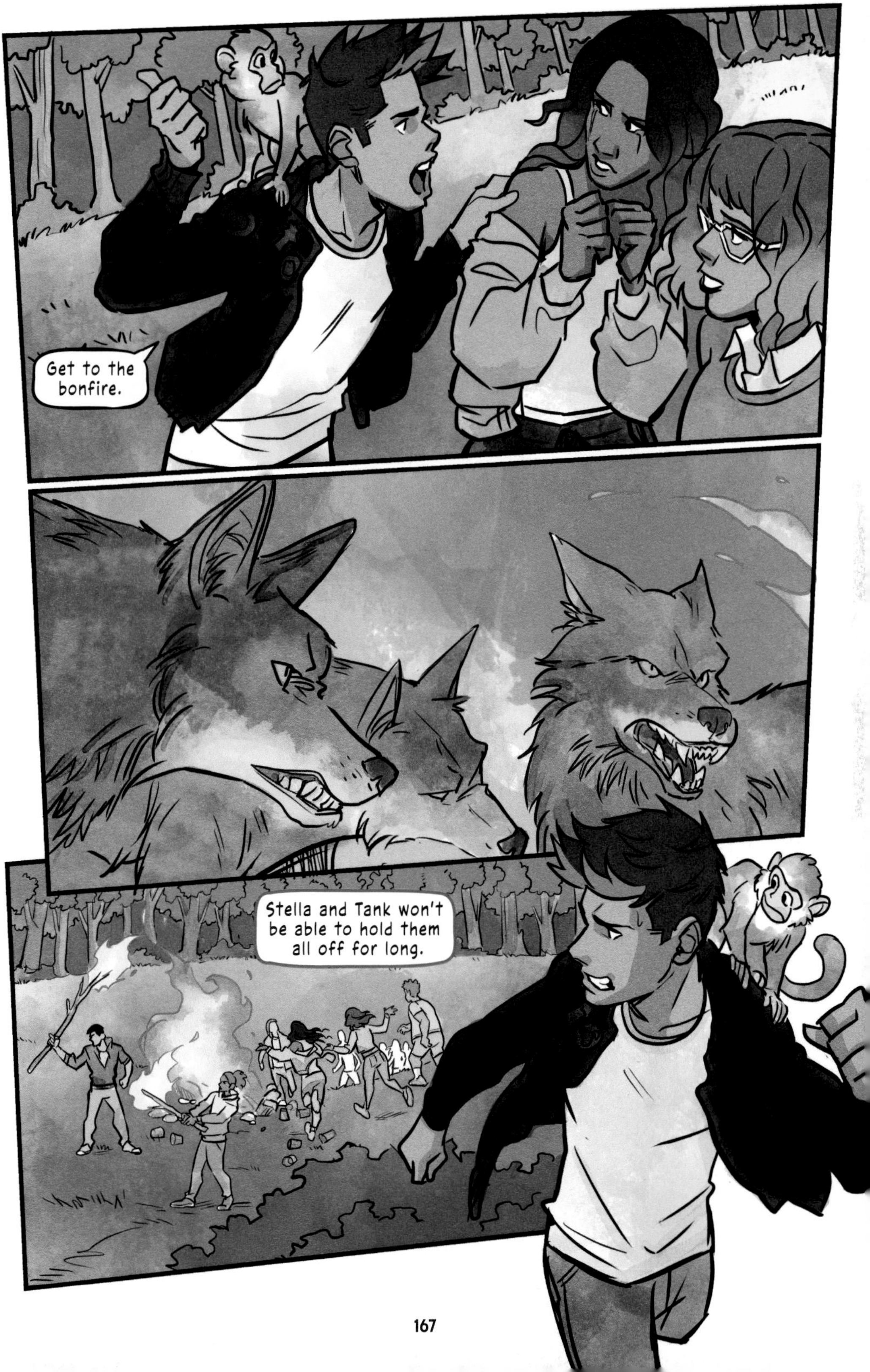
Get to the bonfire.
Stella and Tank won't be able to hold them all off for long.

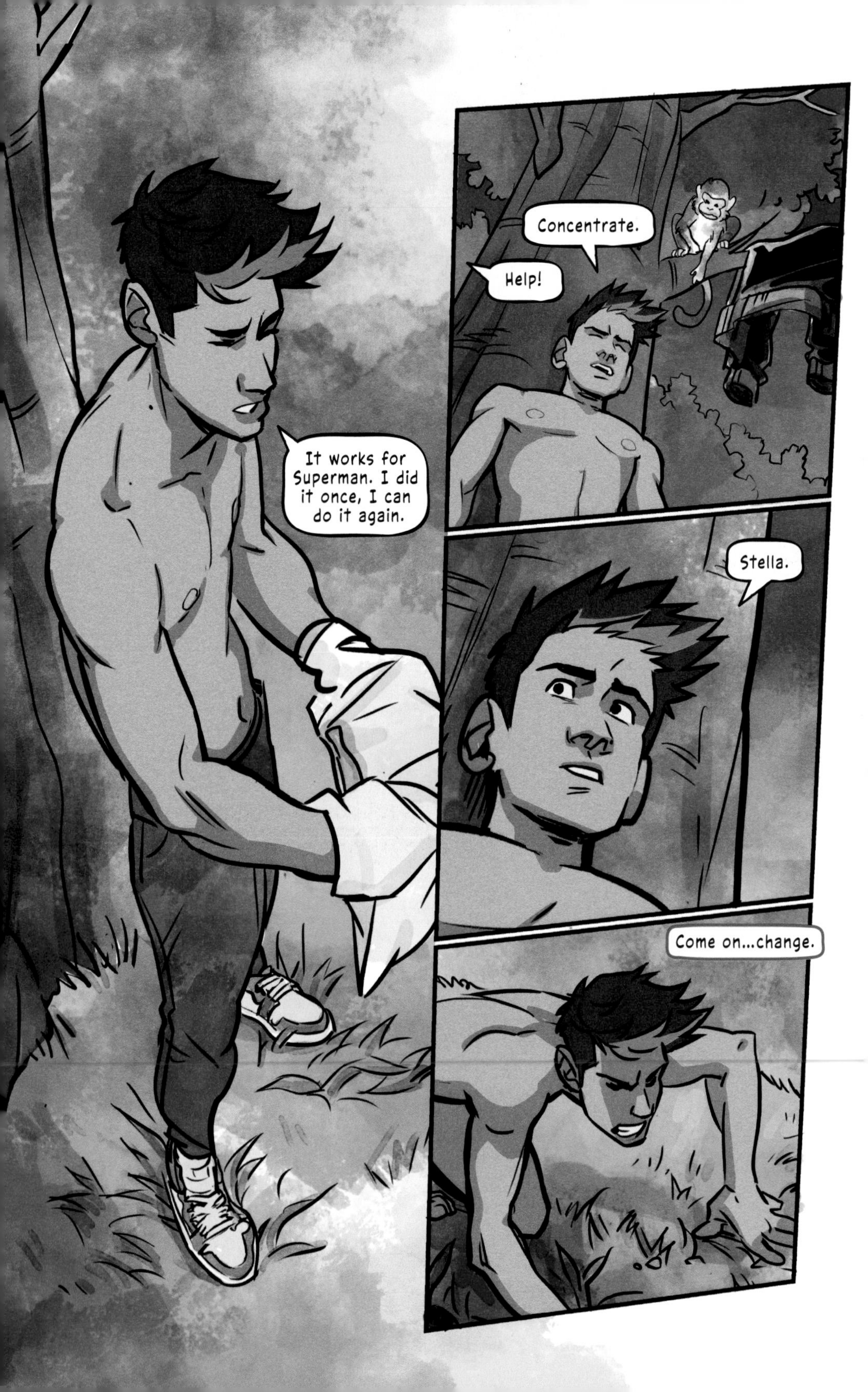
It works for Superman. I did it once, I can do it again.
Concentrate.
Help!
Stella.
Come on...change.

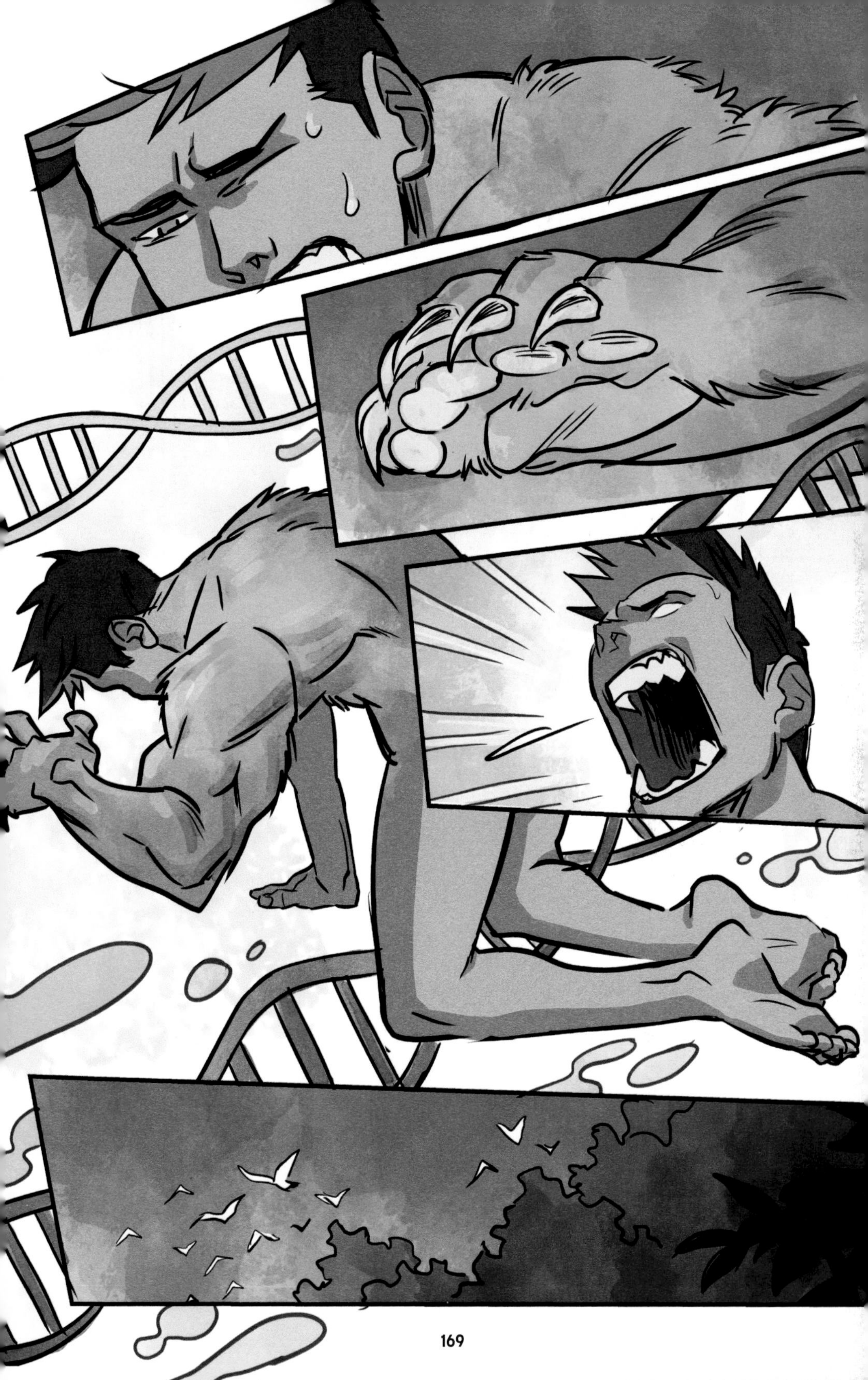

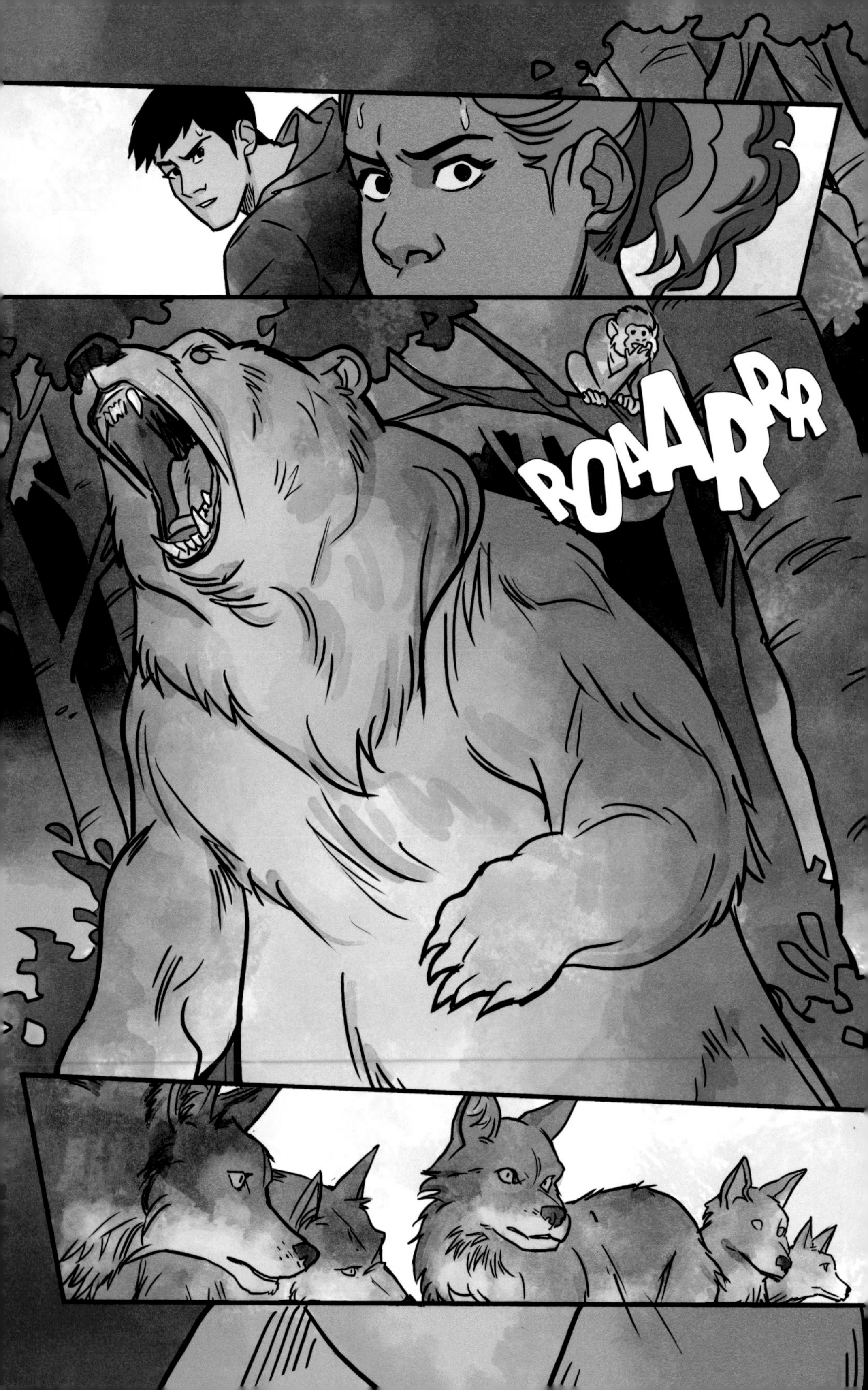
ROAARRR

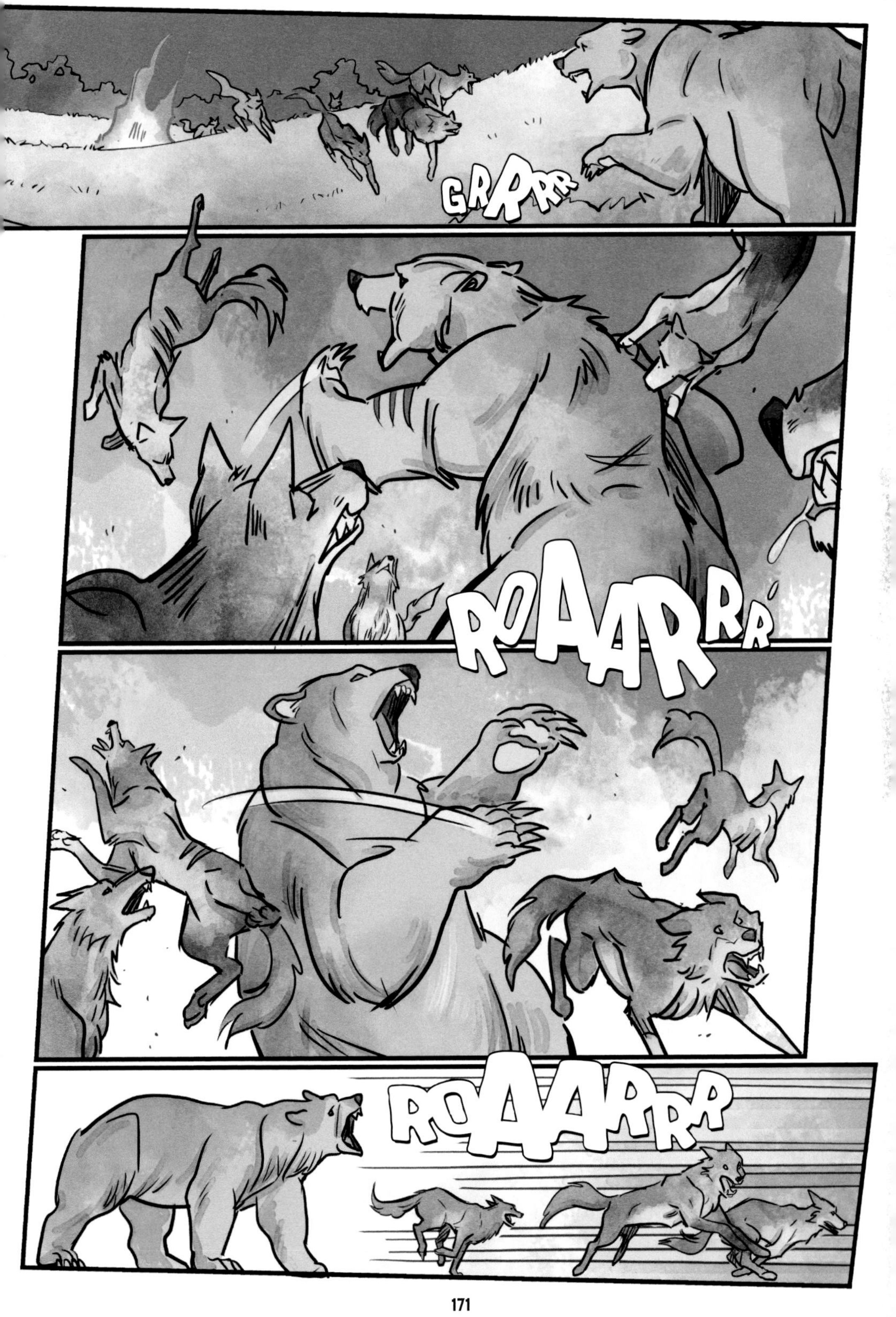
GRRRR
ROAARRR
ROAAARRR

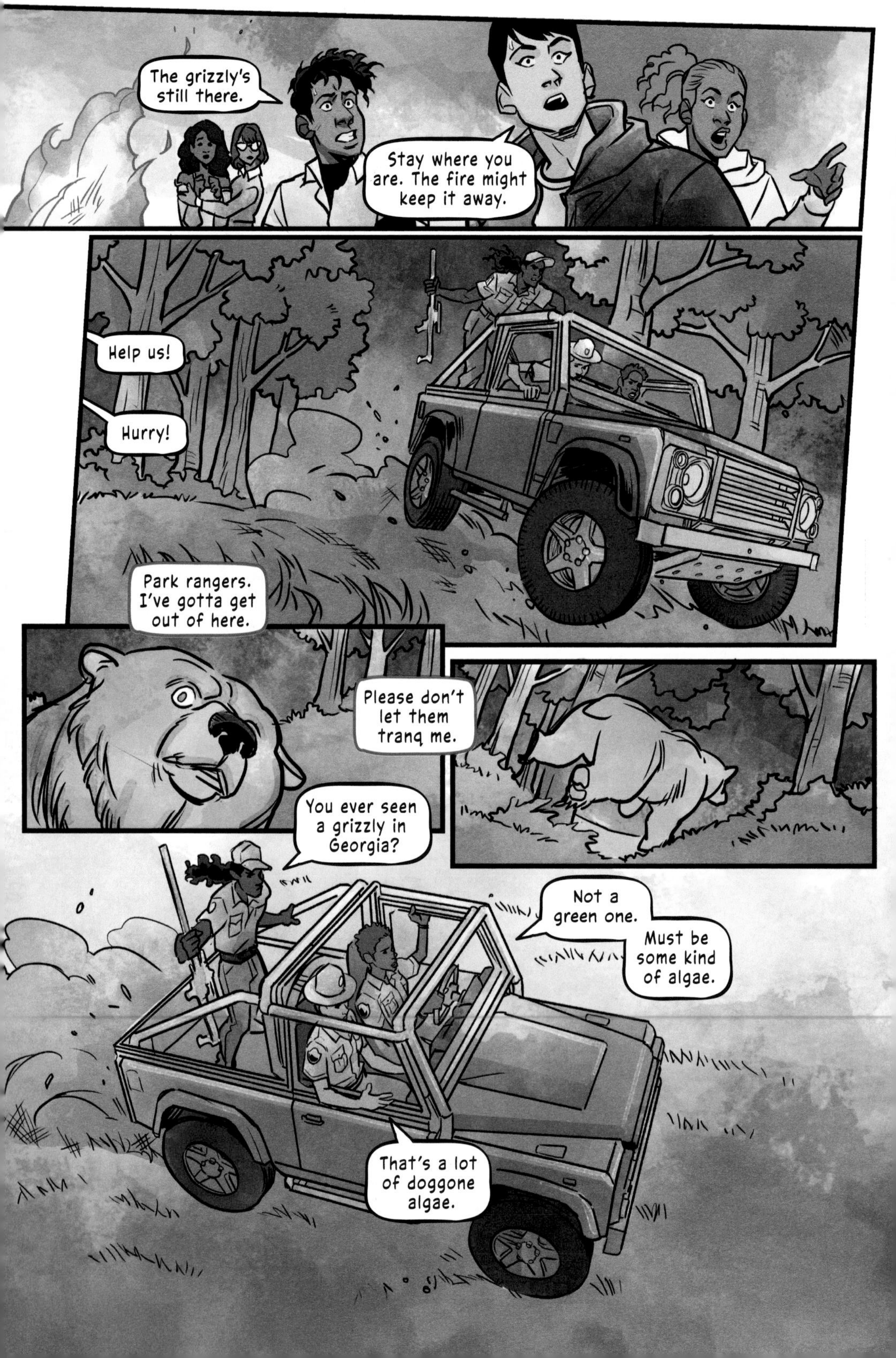
The grizzly's still there.
Stay where you are. The fire might keep it away.
Help us!
Hurry!
Park rangers. I've gotta get out of here.
Please don't let them tranq me.
You ever seen a grizzly in Georgia?
Not a green one.
Must be some kind of algae.
That's a lot of doggone algae.

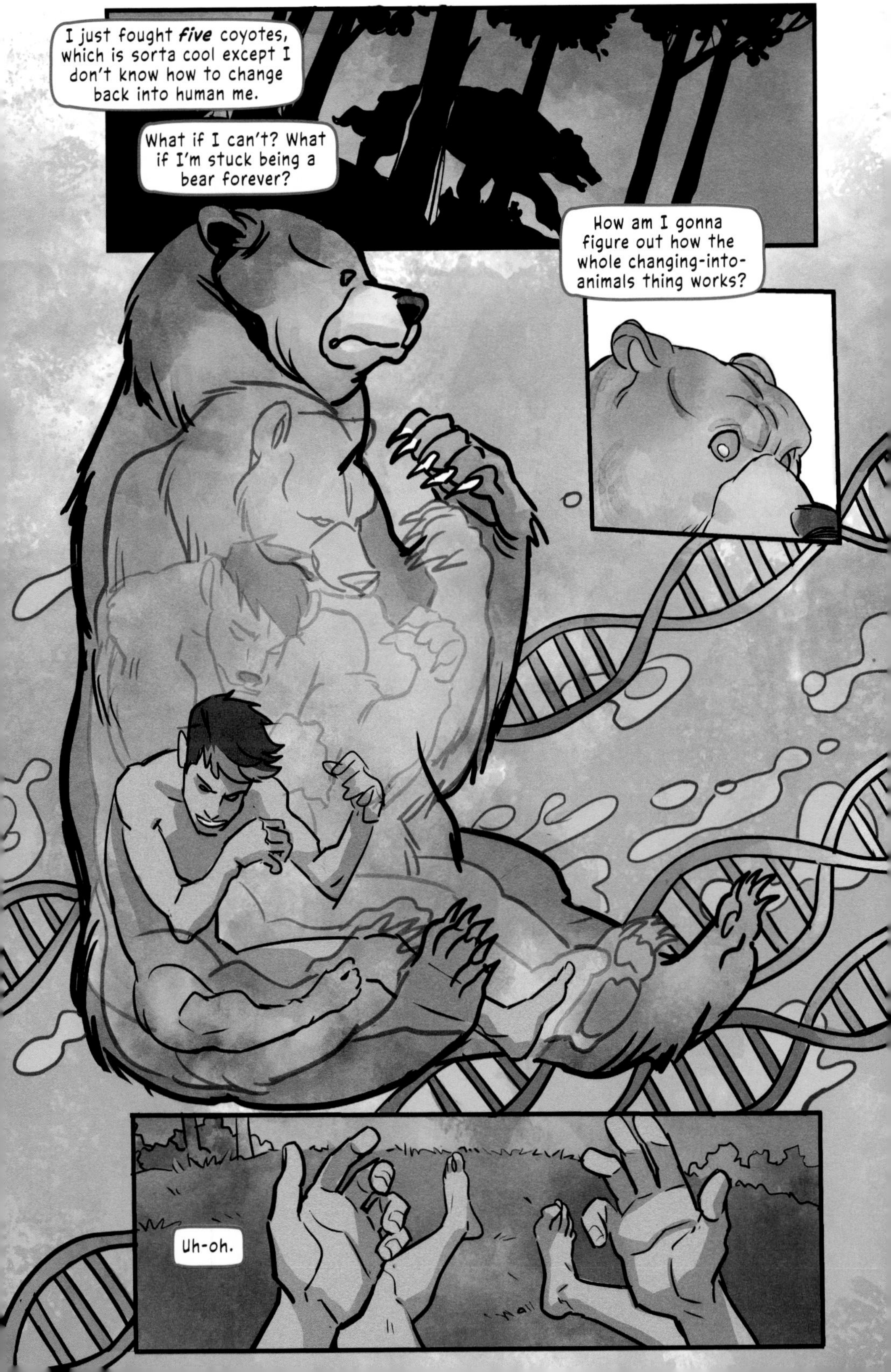
I just fought *five* coyotes, which is sorta cool except I don't know how to change back into human me.
What if I can't? What if I'm stuck being a bear forever?
How am I gonna figure out how the whole changing-into-animals thing works?
Uh-oh.

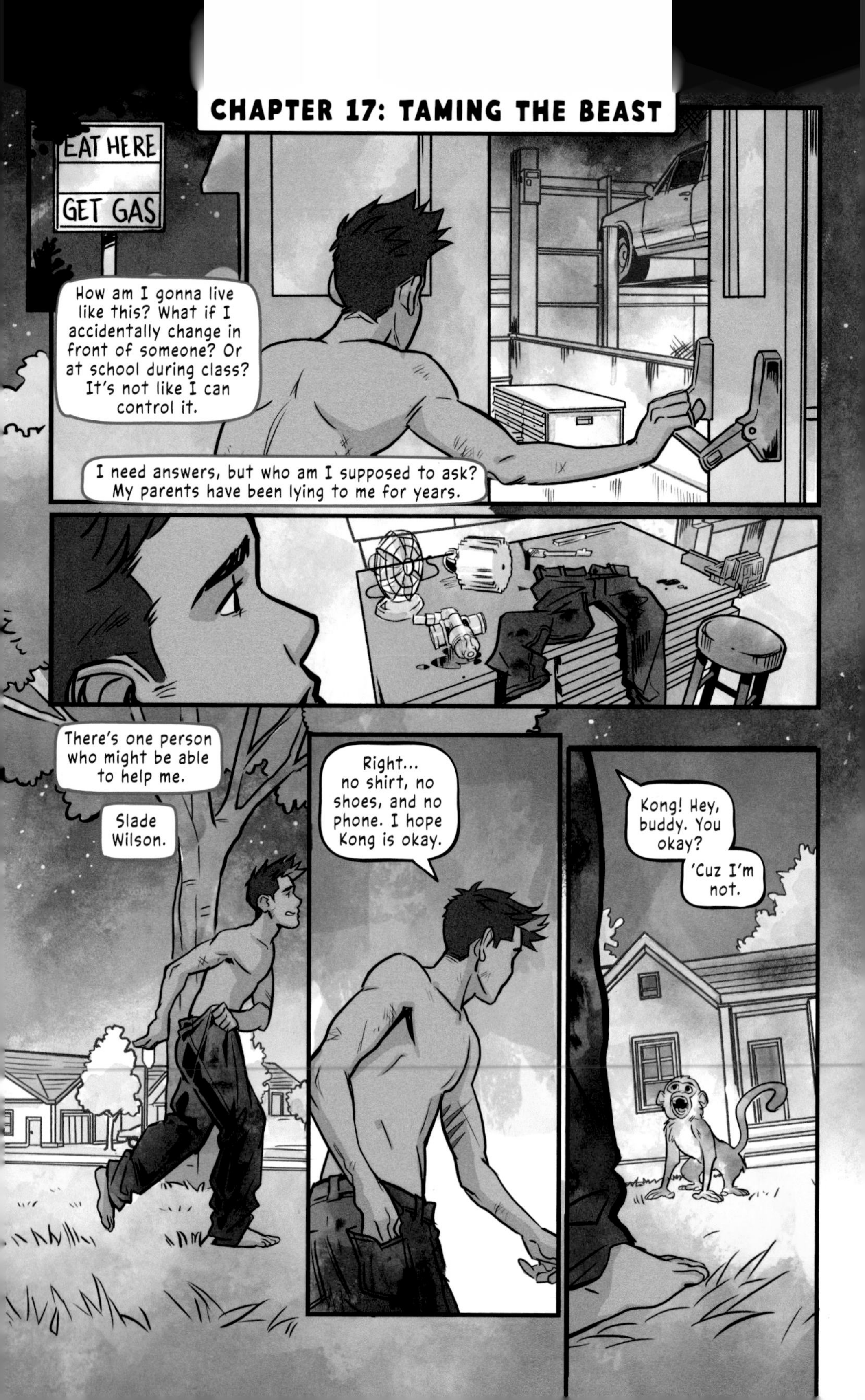
CHAPTER 17: TAMING THE BEAST
EAT HERE
GET GAS
How am I gonna live like this? What if I accidentally change in front of someone? Or at school during class? It's not like I can control it.
I need answers, but who am I supposed to ask? My parents have been lying to me for years.
There's one person who might be able to help me.
Slade Wilson.
Right... no shirt, no shoes, and no phone. I hope Kong is okay.
Kong! Hey, buddy. You okay?
'Cuz I'm not.

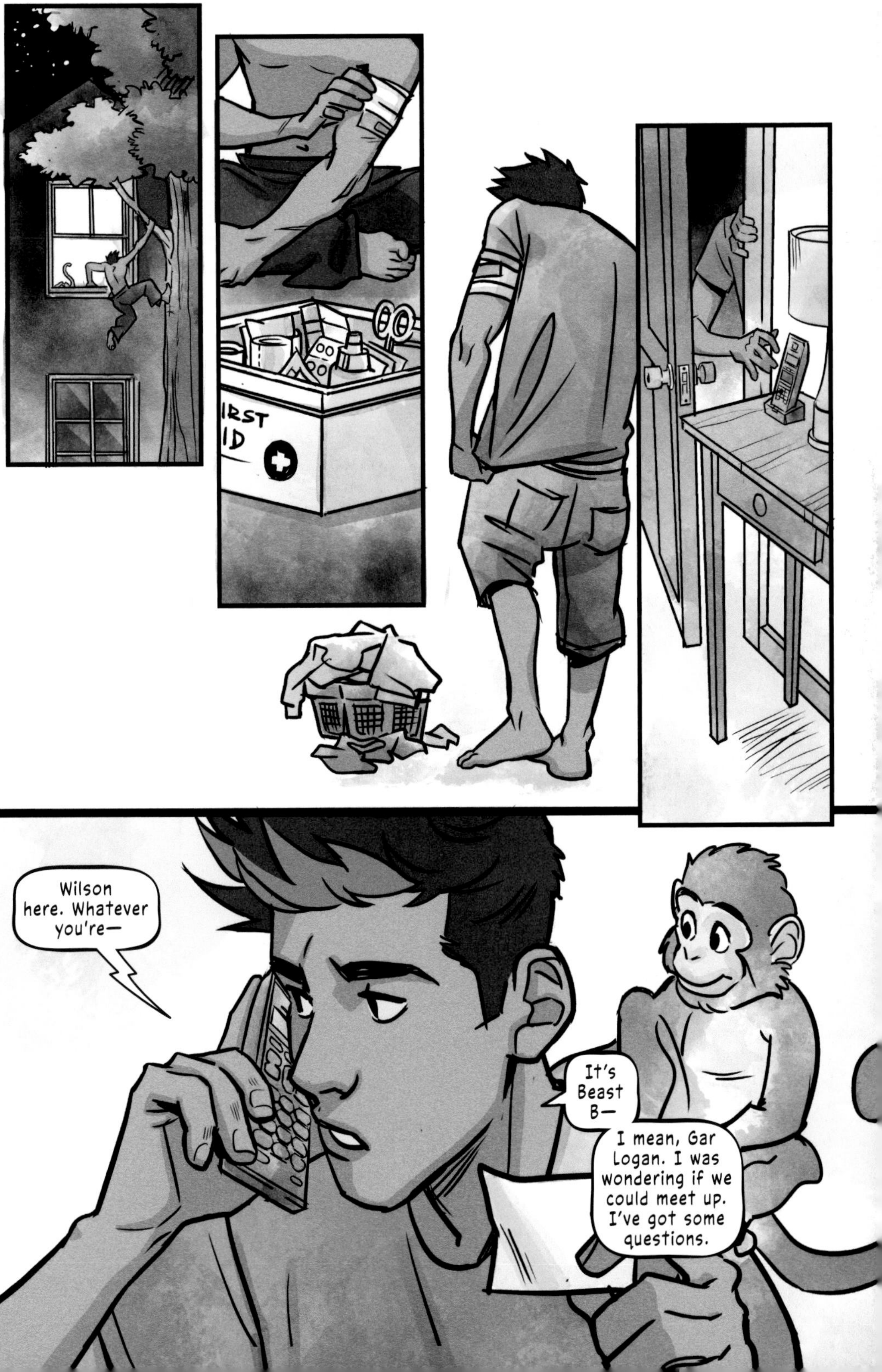

IRST
ID
Wilson here. Whatever you're—
It's Beast B—
I mean, Gar Logan. I was wondering if we could meet up. I've got some questions.

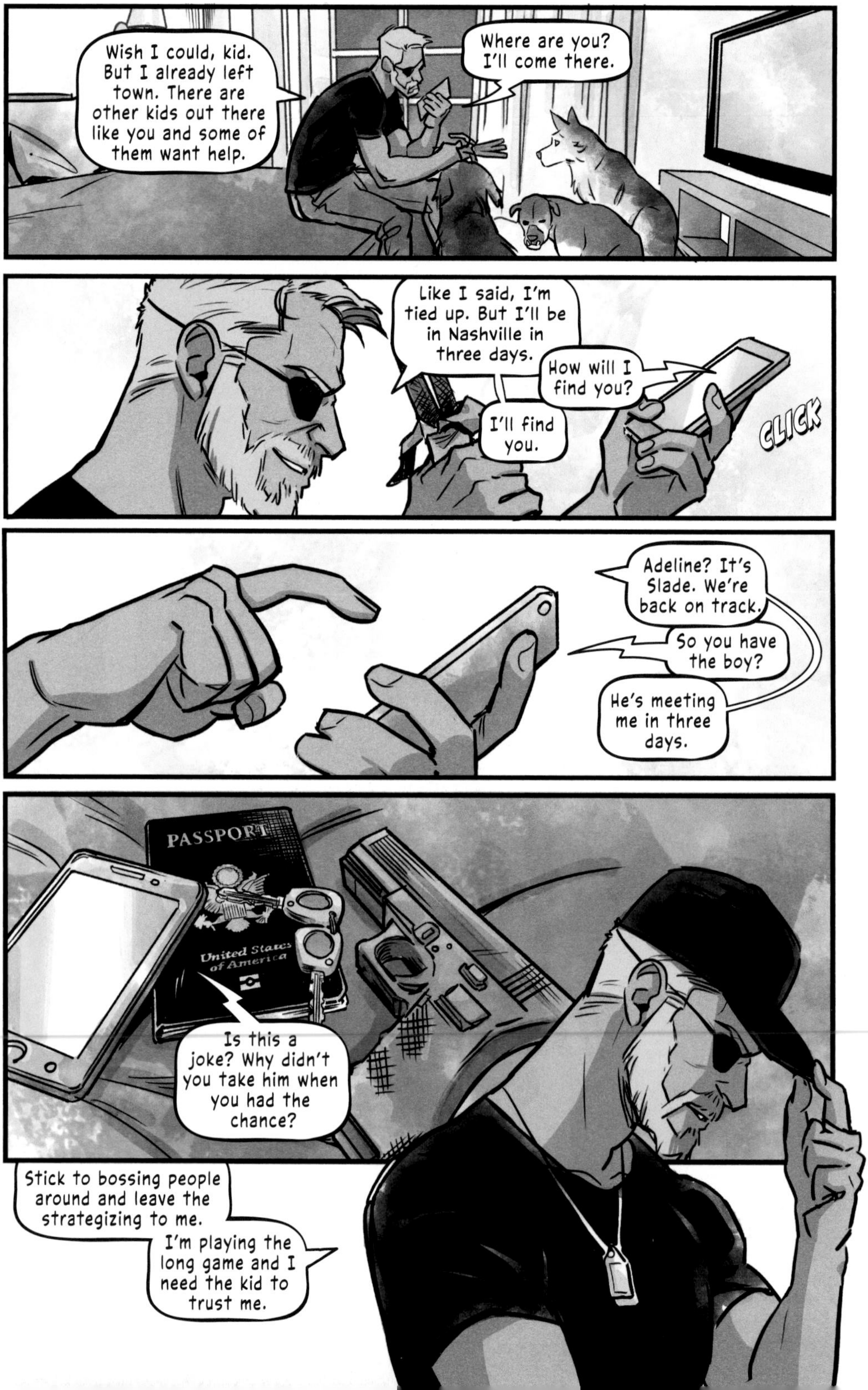
Wish I could, kid. But I already left town. There are other kids out there like you and some of them want help.
Where are you? I'll come there.
Like I said, I'm tied up. But I'll be in Nashville in three days.
How will I find you?
I'll find you.
CLICK
Adeline? It's Slade. We're back on track.
So you have the boy?
He's meeting me in three days.
PASSPORT
United States of America
Is this a joke? Why didn't you take him when you had the chance?
Stick to bossing people around and leave the strategizing to me.
I'm playing the long game and I need the kid to trust me.

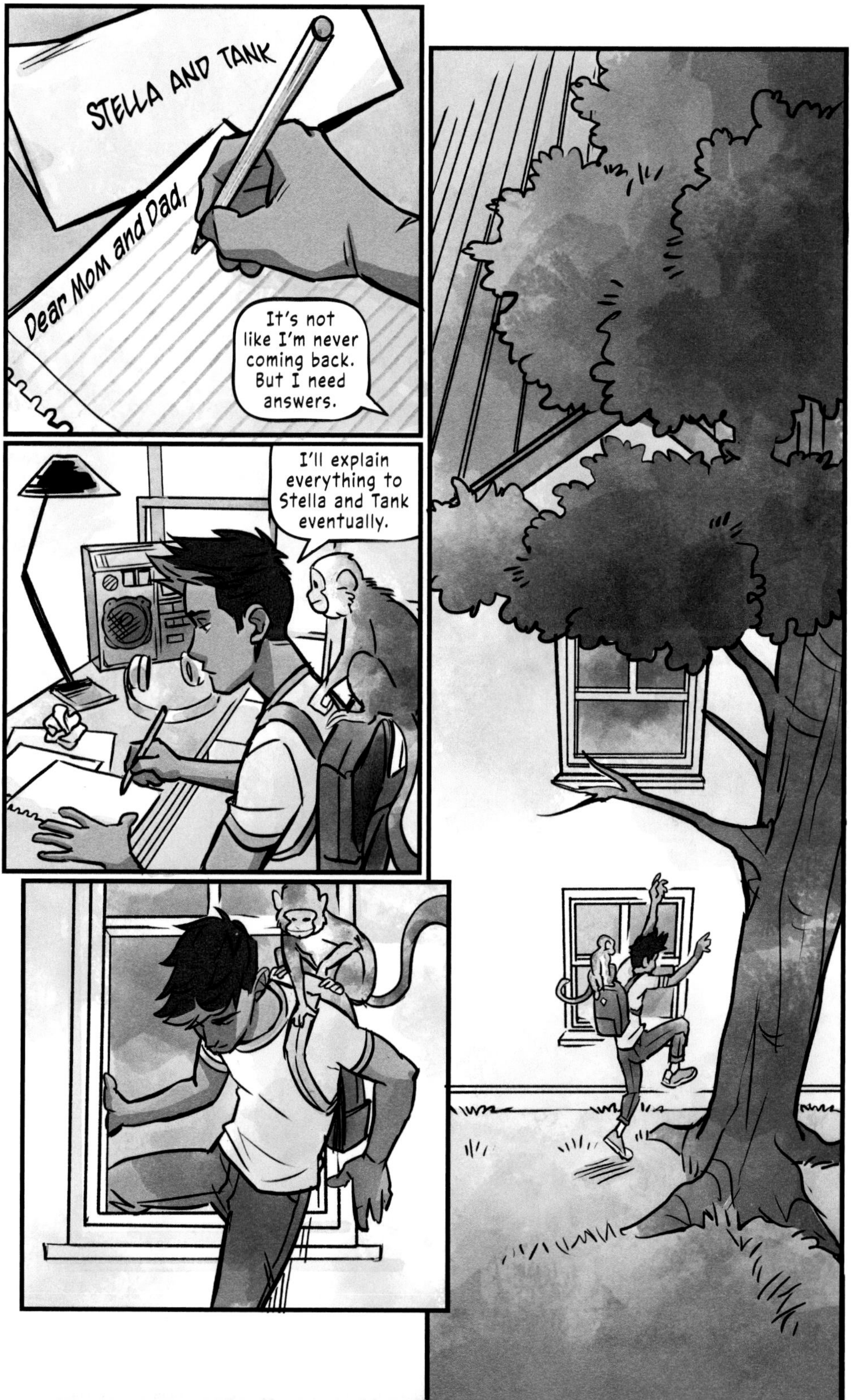
STELLA AND TANK
Dear Mom and Dad,
It's not like I'm never coming back. But I need answers.
I'll explain everything to Stella and Tank eventually.

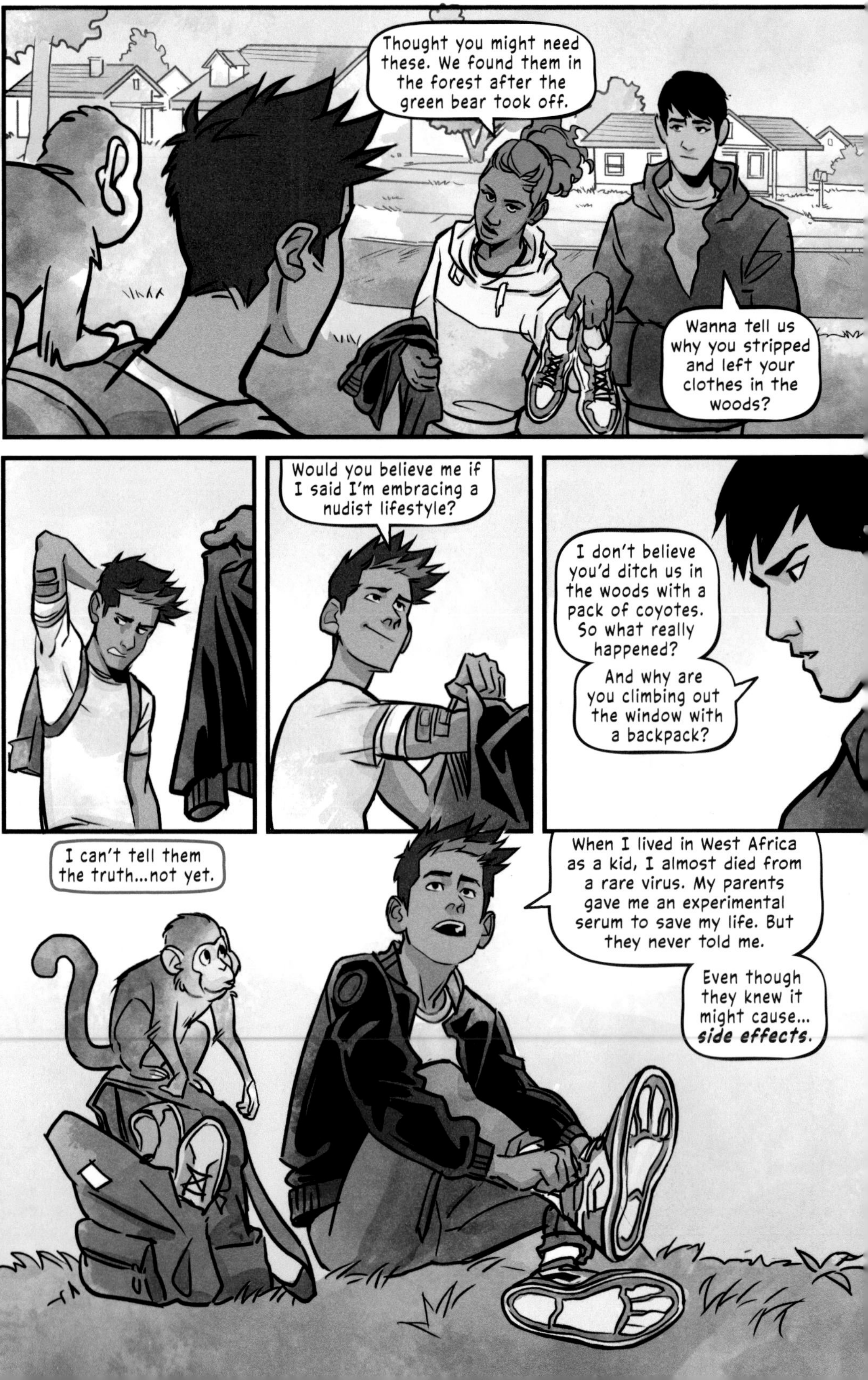
Thought you might need these. We found them in the forest after the green bear took off.
Wanna tell us why you stripped and left your clothes in the woods?
Would you believe me if I said I'm embracing a nudist lifestyle?
I don't believe you'd ditch us in the woods with a pack of coyotes. So what really happened?
And why are you climbing out the window with a backpack?
I can't tell them the truth...not yet.
When I lived in West Africa as a kid, I almost died from a rare virus. My parents gave me an experimental serum to save my life. But they never told me.
Even though they knew it might cause... *side effects*.

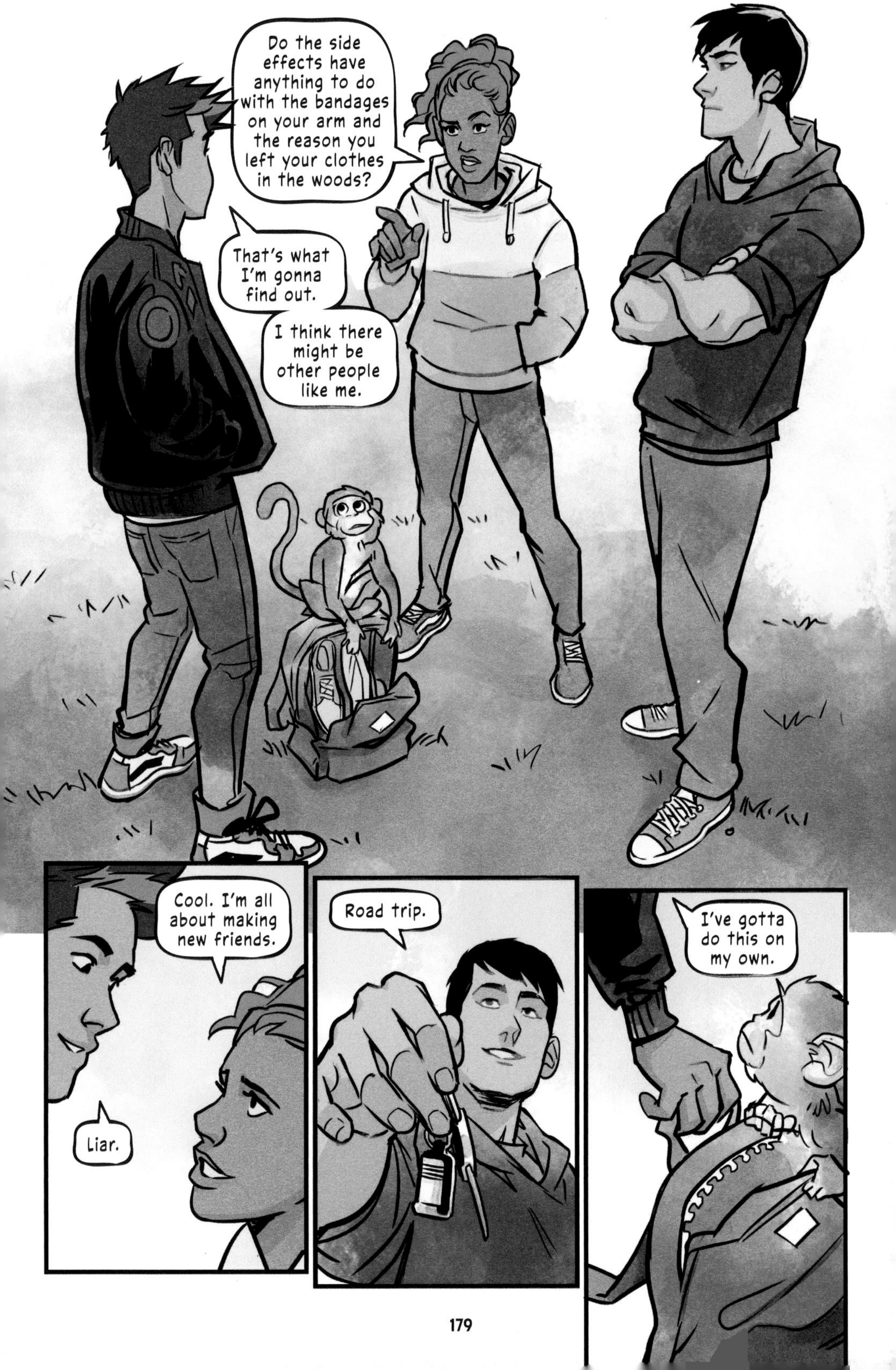
Do the side effects have anything to do with the bandages on your arm and the reason you left your clothes in the woods?
That's what I'm gonna find out.
I think there might be other people like me.
Cool. I'm all about making new friends.
Liar.
Road trip.
I've gotta do this on my own.

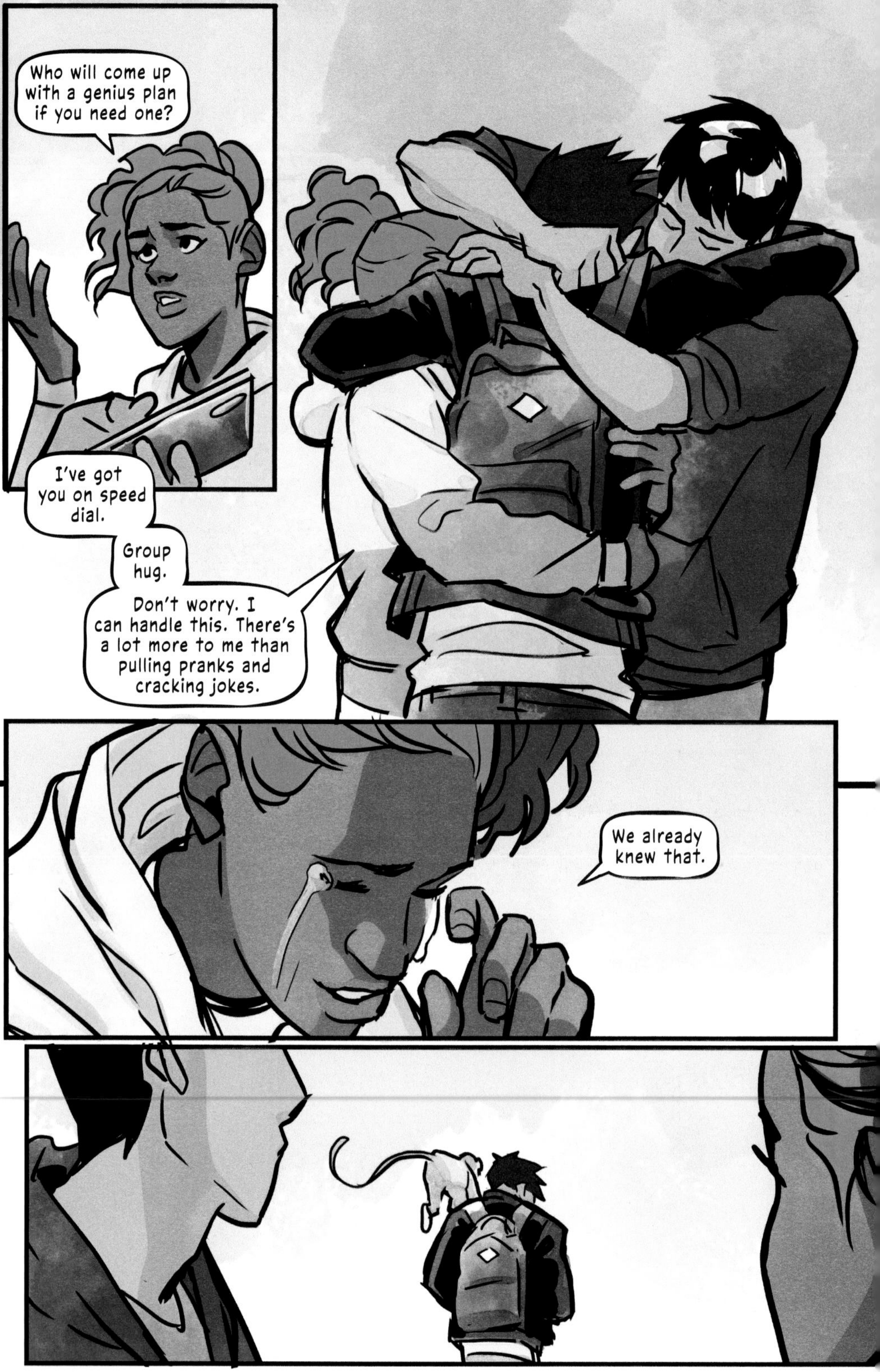
Who will come up with a genius plan if you need one?
I've got you on speed dial.
Group hug.
Don't worry. I can handle this. There's a lot more to me than pulling pranks and cracking jokes.
We already knew that.

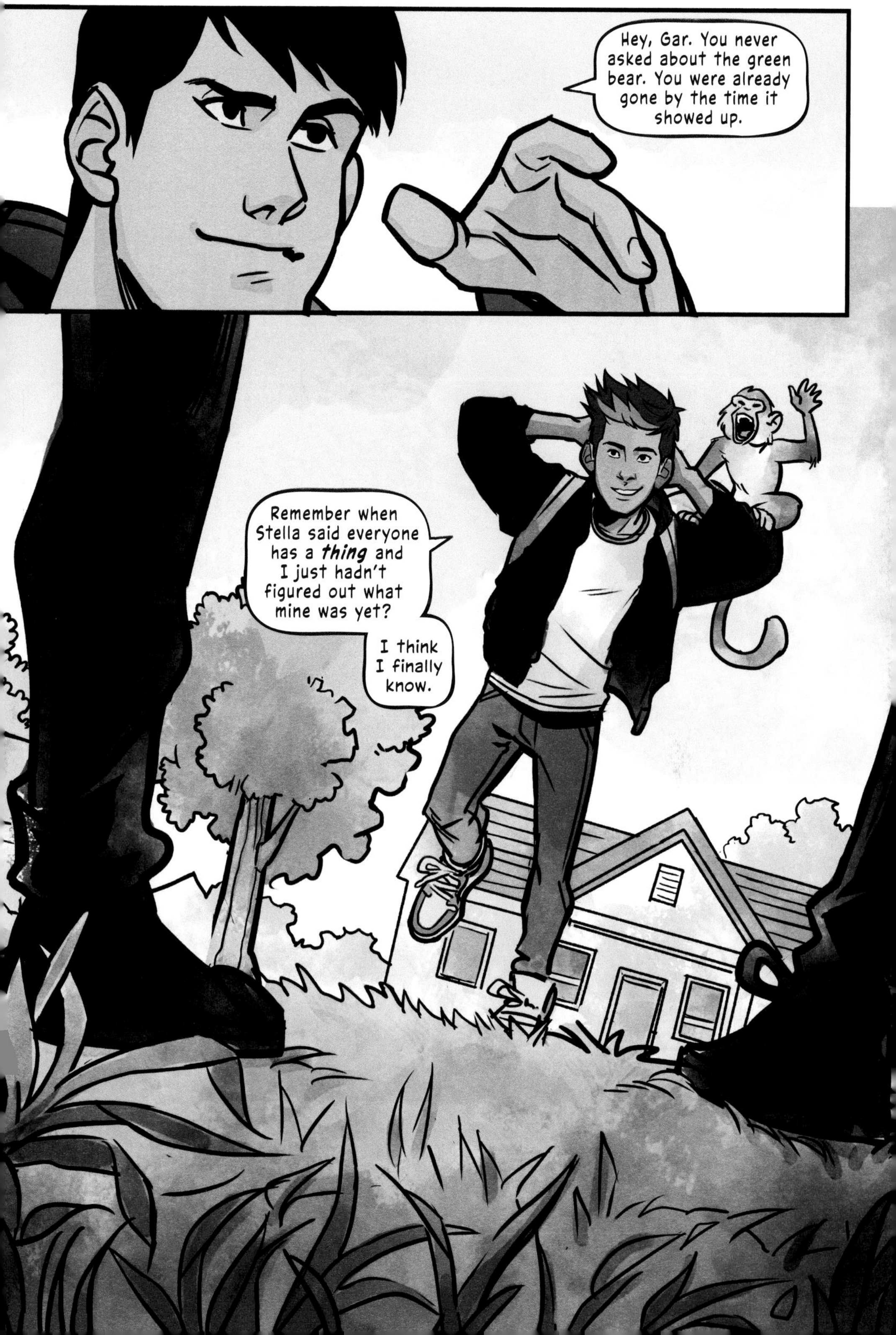
Hey, Gar. You never asked about the green bear. You were already gone by the time it showed up.
Remember when Stella said everyone has a *thing* and I just hadn't figured out what mine was yet?
I think I finally know.

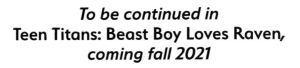

To be continued in
Teen Titans: Beast Boy Loves Raven,
coming fall 2021

KAMI GARCIA
GABRIEL PICOLO
THE *NEW YORK TIMES* BESTSELLING SERIES
TEEN TITANS
BEAST BOY loves RAVEN

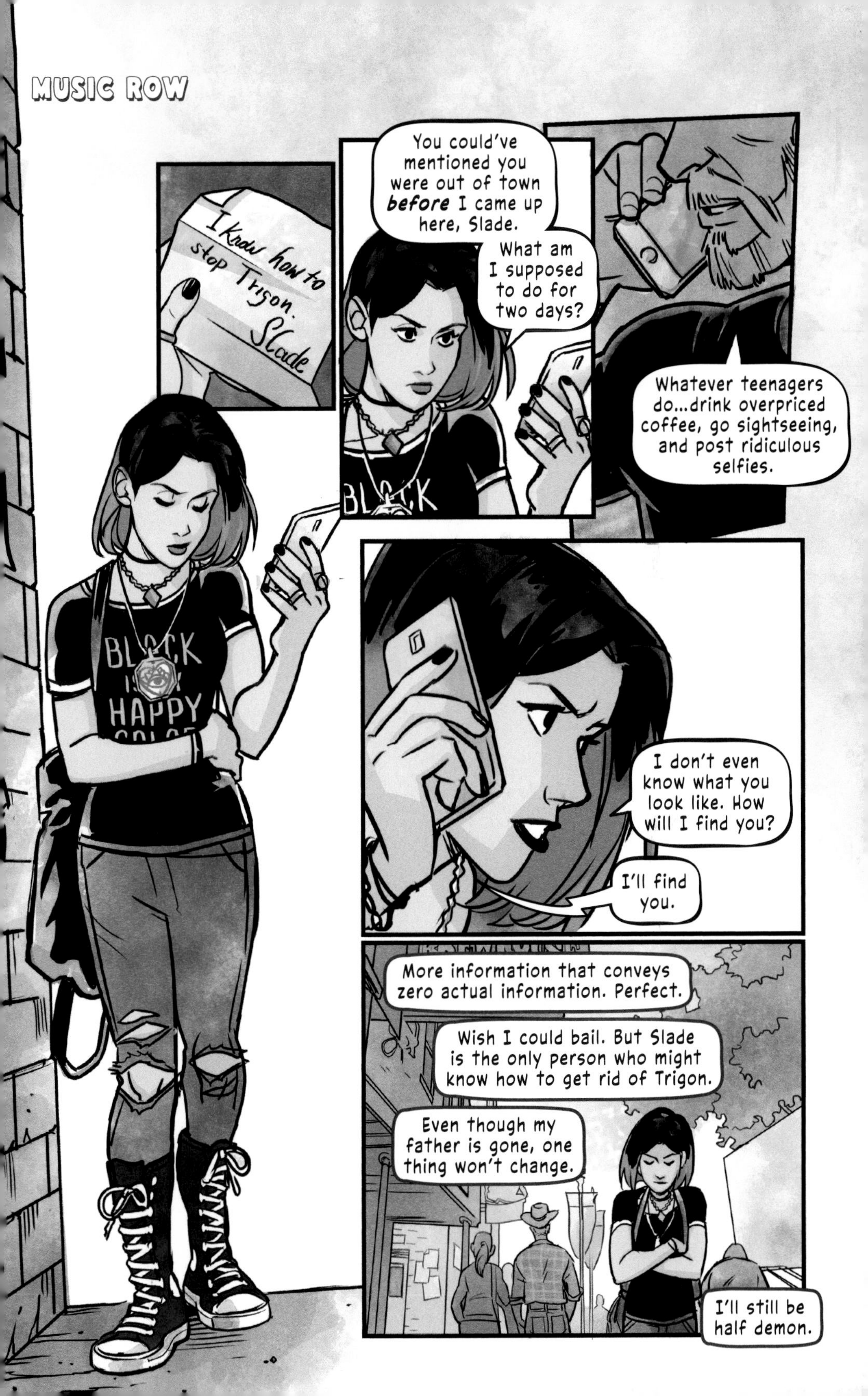
MUSIC ROW
I know how to stop Trigon. Slade
You could've mentioned you were out of town *before* I came up here, Slade.
What am I supposed to do for two days?
Whatever teenagers do...drink overpriced coffee, go sightseeing, and post ridiculous selfies.
I don't even know what you look like. How will I find you?
I'll find you.
More information that conveys zero actual information. Perfect.
Wish I could bail. But Slade is the only person who might know how to get rid of Trigon.
Even though my father is gone, one thing won't change.
I'll still be half demon.

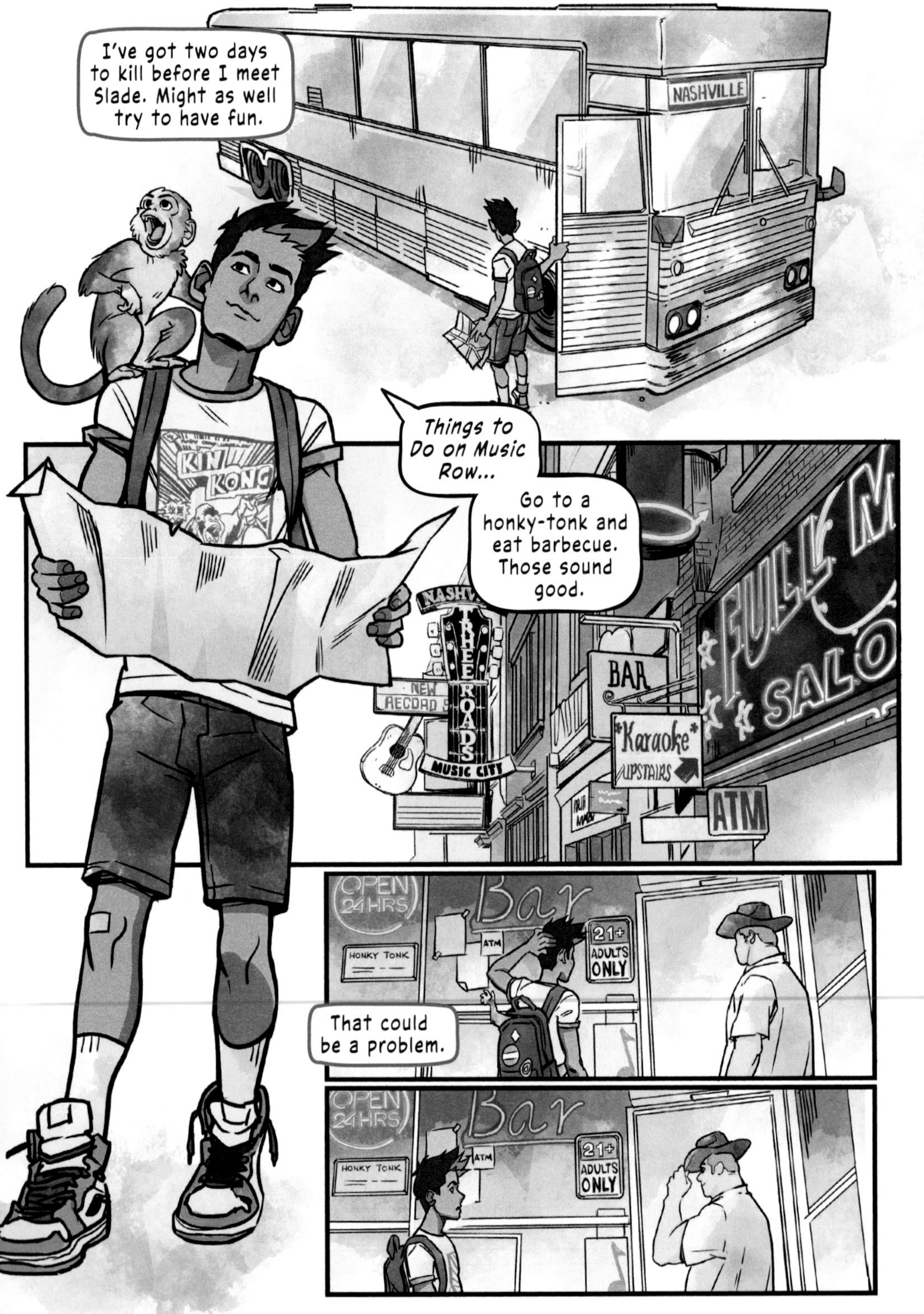
I've got two days to kill before I meet Slade. Might as well try to have fun.
NASHVILLE
Things to Do on Music Row...
Go to a honky-tonk and eat barbecue. Those sound good.
KING KONG
NASHV
THREE ROADS
MUSIC CITY
NEW RECORD S
BAR
Karaoke UPSTAIRS
ATM
SALO
OPEN 24 HRS
Bar
HONKY TONK
ATM
21+ ADULTS ONLY
That could be a problem.
OPEN 24 HRS
Bar
HONKY TONK
ATM
21+ ADULTS ONLY

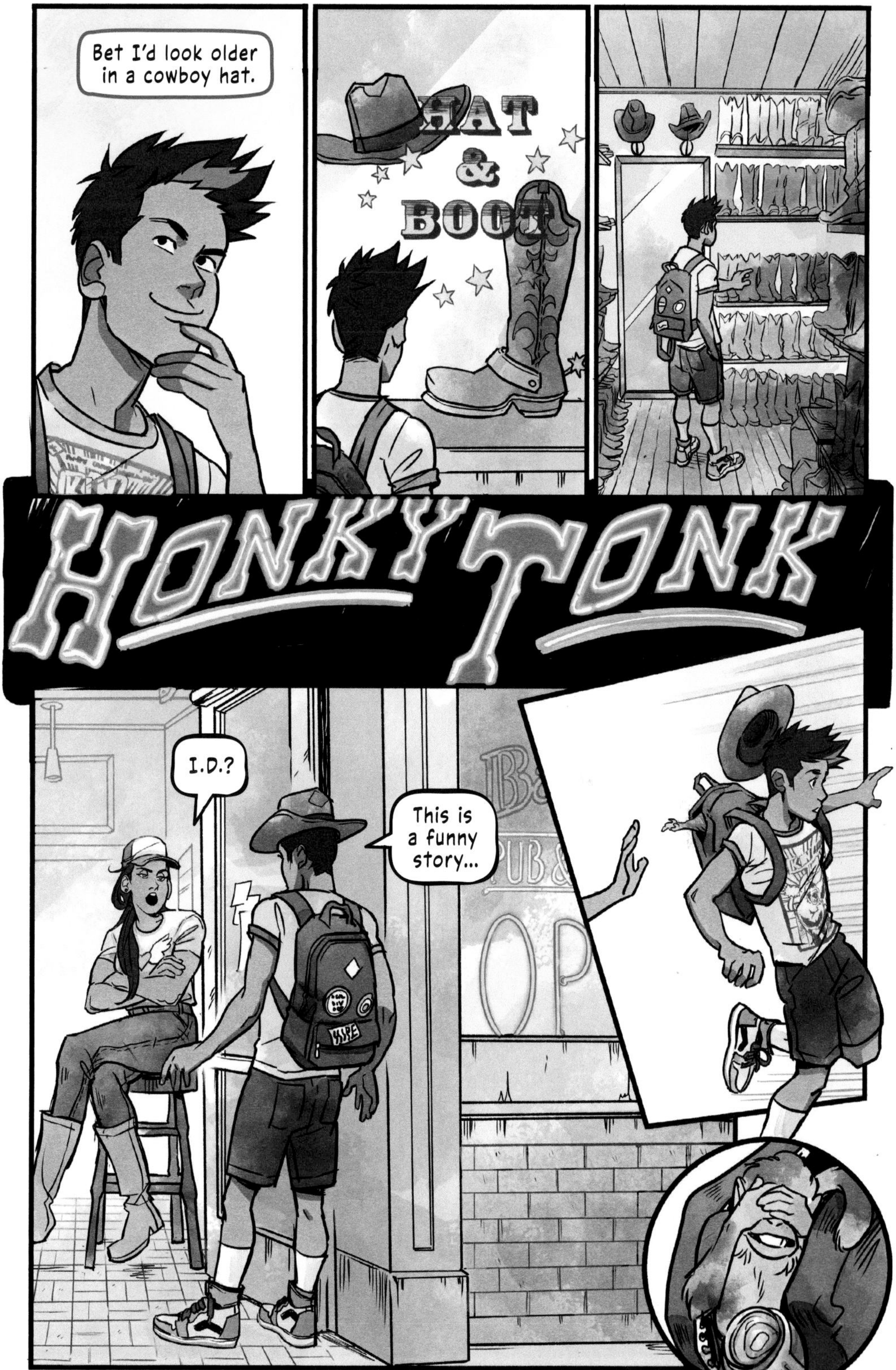
Bet I'd look older in a cowboy hat.
HAT & BOOT
HONKY TONK
I.D.?
This is a funny story...

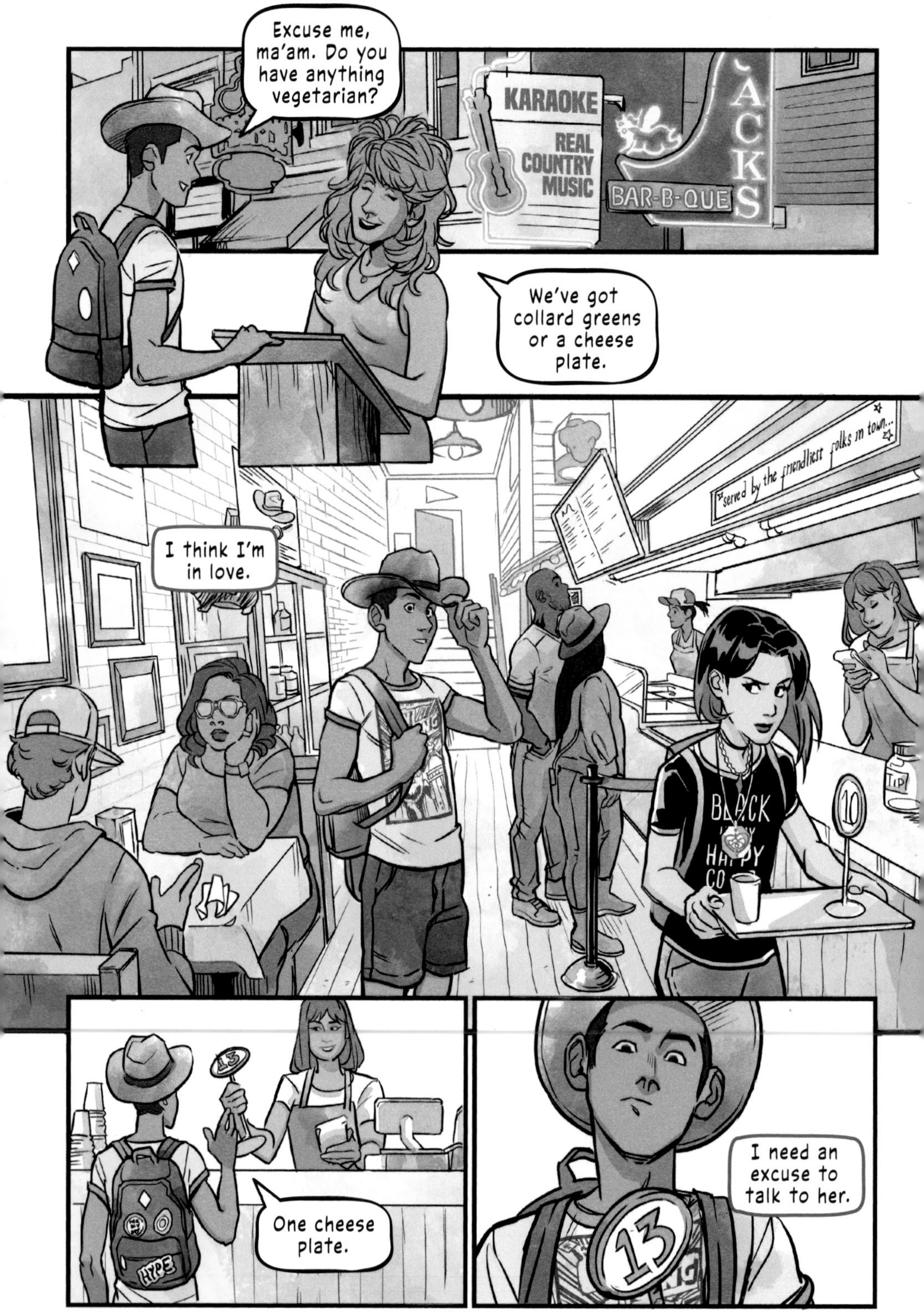
Excuse me, ma'am. Do you have anything vegetarian?
KARAOKE
REAL COUNTRY MUSIC
ACKS
BAR-B-QUE
We've got collard greens or a cheese plate.
served by the friendliest folks in town...
I think I'm in love.
BLACK
HAPPY
TIP
10
One cheese plate.
HYPE
13
I need an excuse to talk to her.

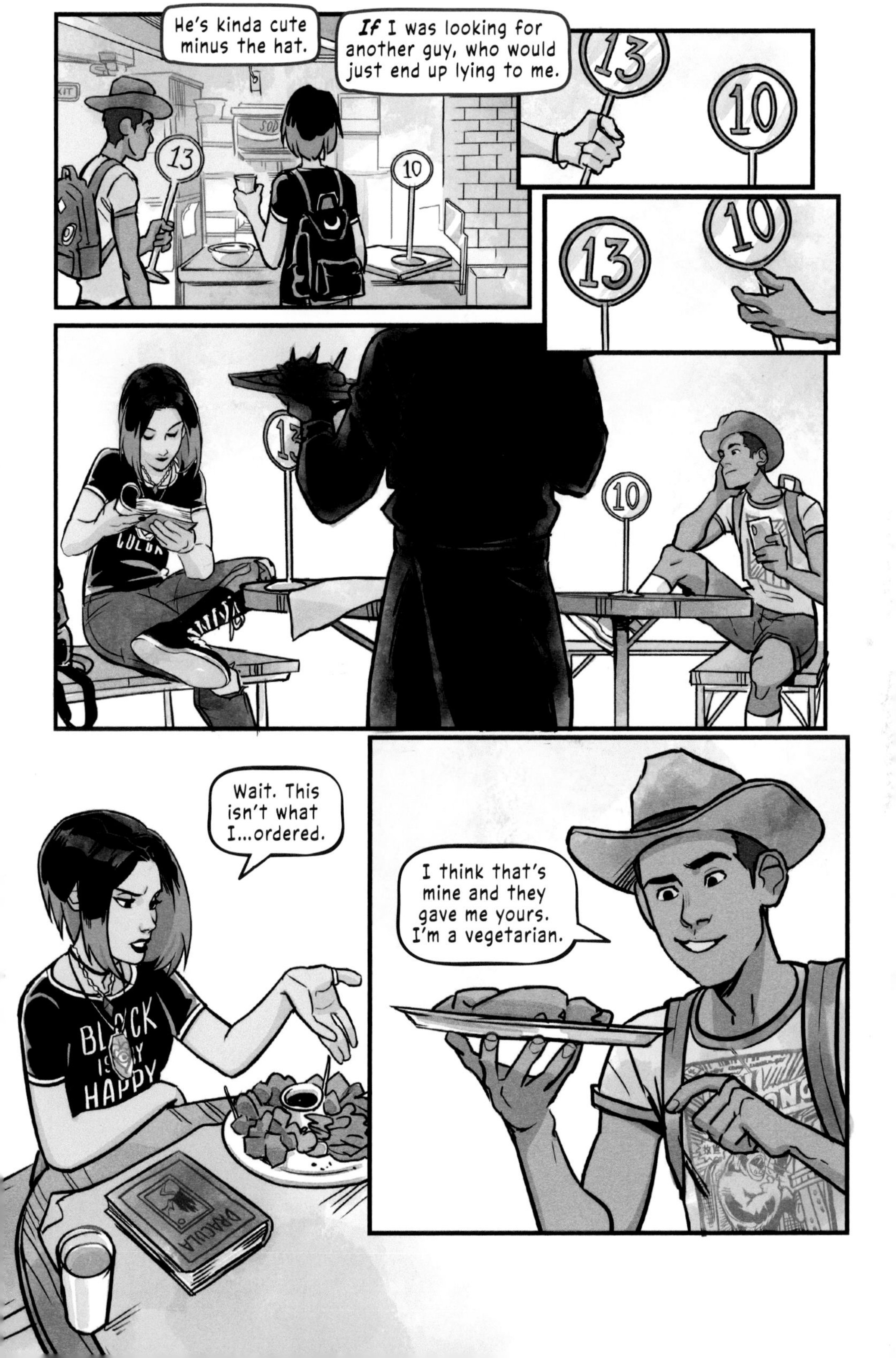
He's kinda cute minus the hat.
If I was looking for another guy, who would just end up lying to me.
13
10
13
10
10
Wait. This isn't what I...ordered.
I think that's mine and they gave me yours. I'm a vegetarian.
BLACK IS MY HAPPY
DRACULA

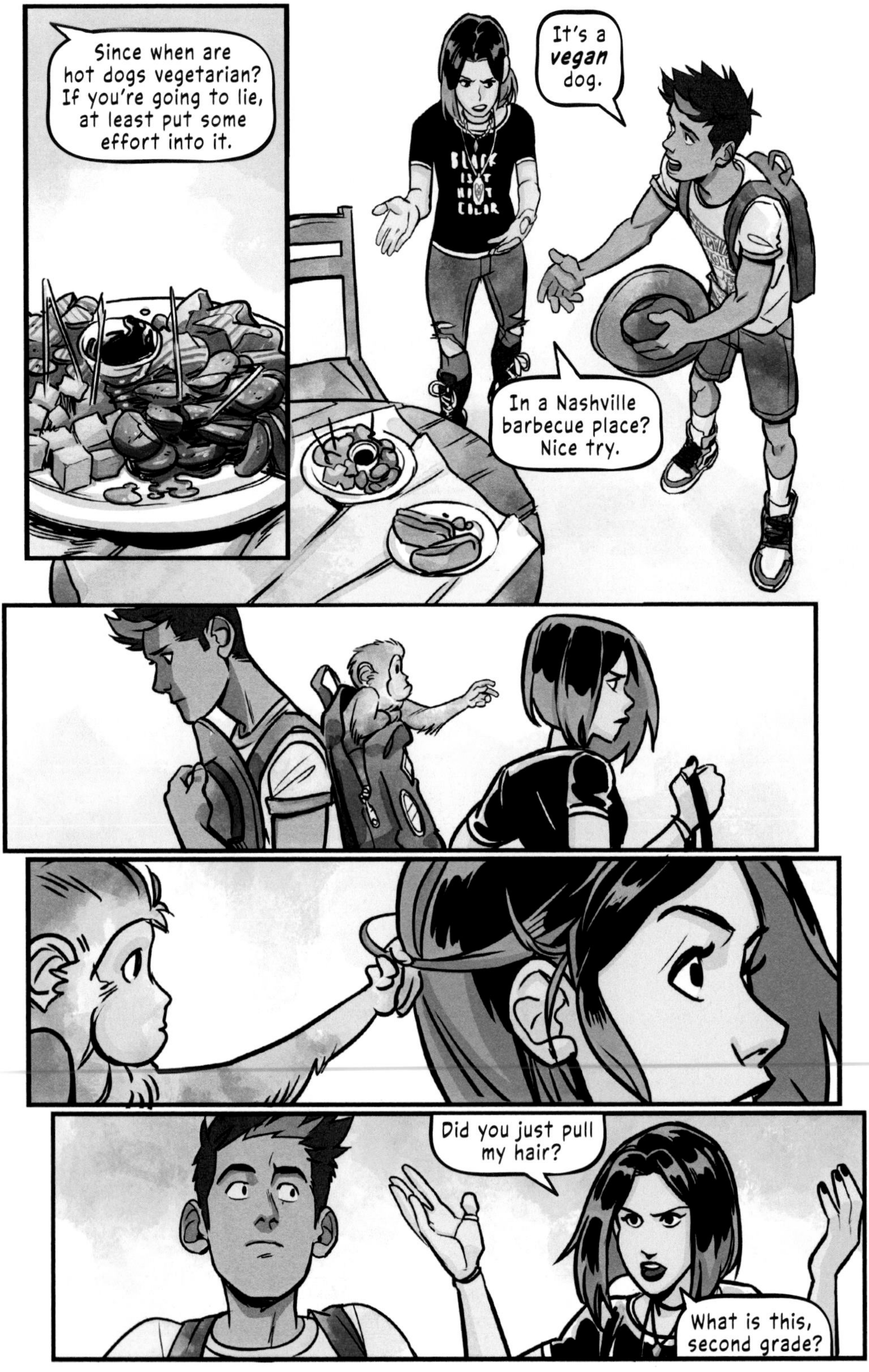
It's a *vegan* dog.
Since when are hot dogs vegetarian? If you're going to lie, at least put some effort into it.
In a Nashville barbecue place? Nice try.
Did you just pull my hair?
What is this, second grade?

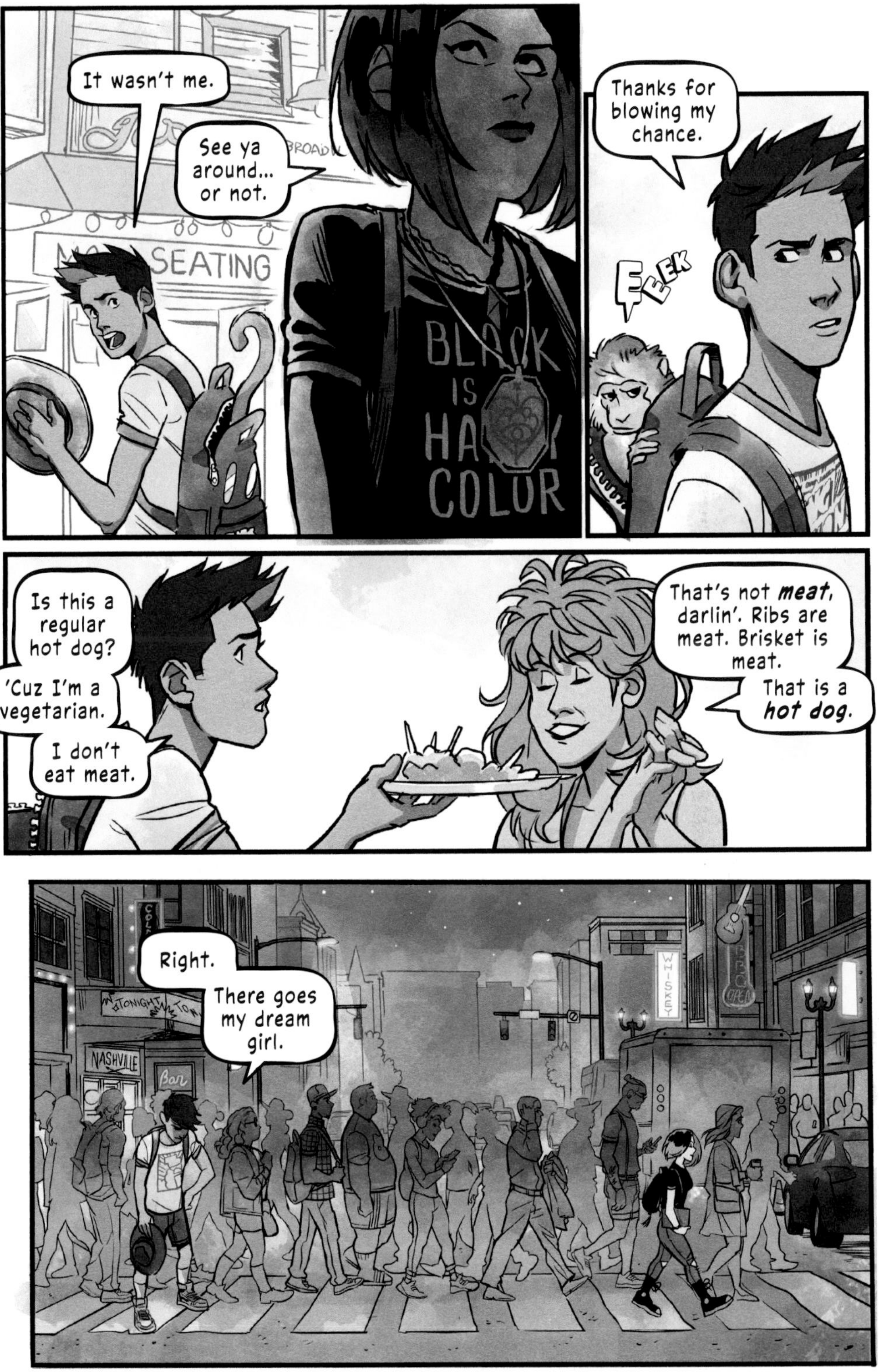

It wasn't me.
See ya around... or not.
BROADW
SEATING
BLACK IS HA COLOR
Thanks for blowing my chance.
EEEK
Is this a regular hot dog?
'Cuz I'm a vegetarian.
I don't eat meat.
That's not ***meat***, darlin'. Ribs are meat. Brisket is meat.
That is a ***hot dog***.
Right.
There goes my dream girl.
TONIGHT
NASHVILLE
Bar
WHISKEY
BBQ
OPEN

kami garcia

is the #1 *New York Times, USA Today,* and international bestselling
co-author of the *Beautiful Creatures* and *Dangerous Creatures* novels.
Beautiful Creatures has been published in 50 countries
and translated into 39 languages.
Kami's solo series, The Legion, includes *Unbreakable,* an instant *New York
Times* bestseller, and its sequel, *Unmarked,* both of which were nominated
for Bram Stoker Awards. Her other works include *The X-Files Origins:
Agent of Chaos* and the YA contemporary novels *The Lovely Reckless*
and *Broken Beautiful Hearts.* Kami was a teacher for 17 years
before co-authoring her first novel on a dare from seven of her students.
She is a cofounder of YALLFest, the biggest teen book festival in the country.
She lives in Maryland with her family.

gabriel picolo

is a Brazilian comics artist and illustrator based in São Paulo.
His work has become known for its strong storytelling and atmospheric colors.
Picolo has developed projects for clients such as Blizzard,
BOOM! Studios, HarperCollins, and DeviantArt.
His first graphic novel, *Teen Titans: Raven,* was a *New York Times* bestseller.

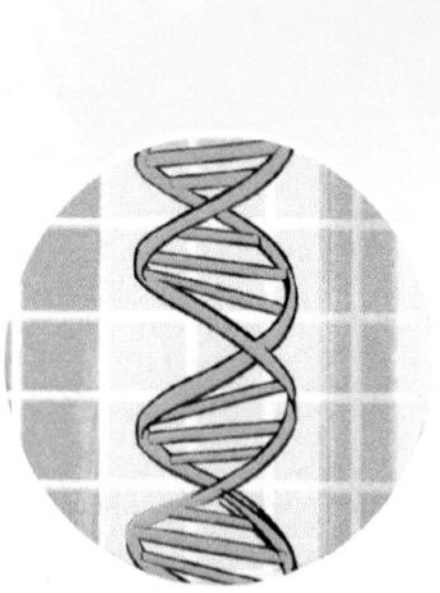